we are all *birds.*

a novel by
Geoff Gray

Copyright © 2012 by Cassowary Press.
All rights reserved

Published by Cassowary Press

No part of this publication may be reproduced
in whole or in part, blah, blah, or stored in a retrieval system,
or transmitted in any form or by any means, blah,
blah, electronic, mechanical, photocopying, recording,
or otherwise, without written permission of the
publisher. For information regarding permission,
write to Cassowary Press.

All characters in this publication are fictitious
and any resemblance to real persons, living or dead,
is purely coincidental.

We Are All Birds / Geoff Gray
First Edition Paperback: March 2013
ISBN 978-0-9849644-2-0

Published by Cassowary Press

Printed in the USA

I approach a newsstand and struggle with which magazine I should purchase, overwhelmed by the options. There is *Men's Health.* There is *Wound.* There is *Black Belt.* There is *Life.* There is *Photoshop Monthly.* There is *Extreme Muscle.* There is *Flex.* There is *Reader's Digest.* There is *Out!* There is *Shout!* There is *Slurp.* There is *Style.* There is *InStyle.* There is *Zoe.* There is *Vogue India.* There is *Vogue Russia.* There is *Vogue Thailand.* There is *HotShoe.* There is *Vogue Paris.* There is *Vogue Poland.* There is *Vogue Norway.* There is *Vogue.* There is *Inc.* There is *Grinder.* There is *Self.* There is *Sposa.* There is *Another.* There is *Lucky.* There is *Purple Fashion.* There is *Heavy Metal.*
I stand there. I stand there for at least forty minutes, paralyzed. There is *Vogue Azerbaijan.* There is *Tiger.* Oh, the options! There is *Teen People.* There is *Vogue Bambini.* Oh the press! Oh the birds!

Acknowledgment:

Scottie Pippin.
Who knew we'd rise to such great heights –

WHEREAS, WE RECOGNIZE THAT THIS SPACE IS USUALLY RESERVED FOR ERRATA OR FRONT MATTER HAVING NOTHING TO DO WITH FISH AND BEING LARGELY COSMETIC OR CONVENTIONAL IN NATURE, WE WOULD LIKE TO RENDER HEREWITH THE FOLLOWING RESEARCH CONCERNING *O. SAVAYENSIS*, WHICH MAY PERTAIN TO THE ACTUAL STORY FOR ONCE:

The Samoan cardinalfish, or *Ostorhinchus savayensis*, is a small, brightly-colored fish from the family *Apogonidae*, no bigger than a wallet. It generally congregates in small groups of fish of similar sizes, and feeds on invertebrates, plankton, and smaller fish. Most species are active at night, keeping to caves or branching coral during the day, usually at depths of only five to ten feet.

O. savayensis, along with several other species of cardinalfish, has a homing ability, wherein it is able to locate its resting sites from up to two kilometers away. Because the fish have no prior knowledge of the area and most other species stay within a few meters of their resting sites, scientists have hypothesized that the cardinalfish uses some kind of navigational cue for homing, such as sound, chemical cues, or the detection of the Earth's magnetic field.

Scientists have yet to agree on which, if any, of these cues is responsible.

Part I
These
People
Care
Nothing
For
You.

I.
The Hospital
Evanston, IL.

Hour four.

You can hear it from the bathroom.

The windows are thick and small and low, but still you can hear it, the wind. Muzzled now but soon schizophrenic, roiling west from Lake Michigan, dispersing like a breaker against the hospital, a great upset.

I shake at the urinal and run water over my hands. I dry my hands. I walk down the halls of NorthShore Evanston Hospital's Kellogg Cancer Center and return to exam room 3F where Denton Brown, my closest friend, a friend I have known my whole adult life, is dying.

Or not.

We're not sure exactly. The hematologist has disappeared around a corner, leaving me alone with Dent and his mother.

Should I say something? I feel like I should say something. It doesn't look like Dent or his mother is going to say anything, and someone has to speak up. Before I manage to open my mouth, Dent looks up:

"You drizzled."

He is staring at my crotch.

"What? Ah. Great."

"You need another shake."

A dark circle has formed on my jeans. I grab a ball of Kleenex from the counter and wipe my fly. I walk to the window unsteadily, rubbing as I go.

There is too much focus on me, on the drizzle. I am not important. Dent is the sick one here. I steer conversation toward something immediate, something not dying-related—oh yes, the nurse I saw in the hallway, the redhead with good breast awareness.[2] I tell Dent how much I would

---

2. If you do not know what breast awareness is, you should probably have yourself checked for cancerous lumps.

enjoy tickling this nurse's ear with a feather. And I would have made a real effort at tickling this nurse, if it weren't for the sign clearly posted outside the restroom:

The administration would ask that visitors refrain from molesting hospital employees.
Thank you.

No. Not the nurse. The nurse is not a good idea.
I should be uplifting.
I should be inspirational.
"Looks like it lists the symptoms here," I say, examining a pamphlet on the bedside table.
"What's it say?"
Dent is leaning against the exam table. His face is knotted. His shirt says MR. BUBBLES.
"I don't know if it pertains to you. It's all pretty general."
"Well, what's the general stuff say?"
"The general stuff?"
"Yeah."
"Hm."
. . .
"You want the good news?"
"No. I mean yes."
. . .
"Yes."
"Sure?"
"Sure."
"Sure sure?"
"Yes."
"Oh. I mean sure sure."
Something heroic should be said here. Something rescuing the conversation from inanity, puerility, propelling it on course to some greater understanding of things. Something *big*.
"The good news is you might bleed out your anus."
"Shut up."
"Not kidding. It says right here, you might experience rectal bleeding. Out of your anus."

"Goody. What else do I have to look forward to? Other than the bleeding? Out of my anus?"

"Blood transfusions, according to this. But only if anemia is present."

"How likely is that?"

"*I'd put your chances of anemia at about 85%.* Are you serious? How would I know? But it says here most people don't get what you have until they're sixty-five."

"Weee! Anus bleeding!"

Dent shifts. His back looks broken, twisted. He puts a hand on his head.

"Christ."

"Yeah. It also says workers in the petroleum industry seem to get it. Do you work in the petroleum industry?"

"I do not."

"No, you do not. Seems like you got lucky."

"*Sheldon!*" Dent's mother gives me a look. She is trembling.

I am not helping.

I quiet down.

The spot is still there, on my jeans.

I consider taking off my pants.

The one thing we know is that it's not cancer. Dent is dying, or at least that's what we've been led to believe, but it's not cancer, at least not according to the doctors. Neither of us understands what he really has, so we thus default to the laziest explanation available: Cancer. Until we know better, it's cancer.

Oh, we should know better. It has been explained to us, more than once, with color-coded charts, pictorials, test results, smears on microscope slides, plastic representations of Dent's innards, which were strangely reminiscent of something you'd flush down the toilet. Even with these teaching tools, I didn't believe it, having always considered Dent exempt from matters of health.

But the oncologist's sheer conviction about the whole thing left me in no position to gainsay him, to call his expertise into question. We should not think of Dent's condition as cancer, he, the oncologist, told us, but as a precursor to it. Or, more specifically, a precursor to leukemia. It used to be called *preleukemia*, but now it goes by something called myelodysplastic syndrome, or MDS, which the World Health Organization has separated into a number of different classifications. Dent's specific classification has something to do with a deficiency in the myeloblasts found in bone marrow, but by then he had lost me. I didn't let the doctor know I was confused, of course, realizing as I did how it would expose my inadequacies as a man.

I conceal my confusion by exaggerating it:
"So it's not really cancer?"
"No. Not yet at least."
The doctor has the build of a cowboy.
"What he has is a form of precancer? Like a primitive form of it? Or an introduction to it? Like a preview before the real thing, before the cancer movie?"
"That's one way of thinking about it."
I draw my fingers into a steeple.
"I see."
I would be impatient with people like me, questions like these, if I were a doctor. I would hold the asker in contempt, insinuate that I am needed elsewhere. But this doctor is calm, even-keeled. His nametag says PAUL. He is wearing a white coat.
"So how exactly does someone get this. . .this complex-albeit-serious-precursor condition?" I ask. Using the term *albeit* will prove something to Paul, show Paul that I am not just some asshole off the street.
"No one's quite sure," Paul says. "It's not transmitted, it just develops, but how it does this is still not so well understood, though it's more prevalent in males. Exposure to certain carcinogens, presumably. It could just be genetic."
Genetic. I knew Dent's mother was somehow responsible for this. I never understood his mother.
"When's your flight back east?" Dent asks.
"Not sure."
"Okay?"
"Morning."
"Early?"
"Yes, early. Pretty early, I think."
"Okay."
. . .
"Around 6.30, I think. A.M."
"Might want to double-check that."

"Yeah. Yeah, I will."

This is a joke, right?

This near-death experience, this afternoon in a hospital, it's a prank.

I wouldn't put it past Dent. Wouldn't put it past him to fake a disease, to force us to confront the billion expressionless minutes of our own lives, incoherent and ridiculous in the absence of his, by creating a hellish little hoax for friends, neighbors, onlookers, putting the poised despair of all of suburbia at stake . . . yes, it's a joke, this whole thing.

This hospital, a theater. That doctor? Brando.

Dent would do that, you see. Dent would insist we've become closer by his horrifying everyone, proving that our muzzled existences are richer thanks to him, that such adversarial behavior only illuminates what's wrong with our own waylaid hopes. Dent—more than a man, a *force*—is some cosmic redress for suburbanites like us. We're all so . . . *normal*.

It would be just like Dent. Dent would do something like that.

The doctor. Look at how he's folding his hands. Real doctors don't fold their hands like that. He's not real. C'mon. You, over there, with the Time magazine? Reveal yourself: You are Dom DeLuise. You are Ashton Kutcher. I've been Punk'd, caught unawares, red-handed, naked for the country to see. An obvious TV set, this exam room. The same they used for Scrubs, right? You got me. Ha ha. You and your candid cameras. Good one.

Fun's over now.

Let's go home.

Examination Room 3F. Hour Six.

This is sad for Dent, so sad for Dent. It must seem somewhat warped to rank the sadness of one person's death over that of another's, but this is in so many ways sadder for Dent, more than it would be for me, or for Joel, or for Dent's bitchy mother. It has more to do with Dent's body than anything else. His body is the only thing he ever respected, ever really honored. If he were to come down with some mental condition instead, like amnesia or some similar cognitive debility, it wouldn't be as tragic. Not nearly.

It's not that Dent's not smart. He is. Outlandishly smart. Like an able-bodied Stephen Hawking. Scholarships should be named after him. Presidents should hire him. Dent could change the world if he applied himself.

"Didn't get a pee bag," he tells me. "I wanted one of those old-lady pee bags for my penis, but they wouldn't give me one. They refused to give me a pee bag. For my penis."

He does not apply himself. He hated "thinking like an economist," as he put it. He always wanted to think like a person who had lived life before, a person who knew how to take full advantage of the body he was given because, at the end of the day, his dick would be as shriveled as any other man's (his words), so he'd better use it. He did this by ritualistically abusing it (his body, not his dick) at least four times a month, at four o'clock each Sunday, for the Bears games, as all true native Chicagoans do.

I walk over to a black and white poster on the north wall. It is an artist's rendering of fallopian tubes. It says FEMALE REPRODUCTIVE SYSTEM.

"Hooh," I say.

I tap the poster and turn away.

He continued to *honor his body*, as he put it, keeping it in great shape. Phenomenal shape, even when embracing the illogical-ness of Midwestern fan-dom. Even after those years of misapplying it at Bears games, gorging it with brats and Pabst Blue Ribbon, or getting it into fights in the Soldier's Field parking lot. Smashed to the pavement sometimes, he would still party like a legend, engaged in some lunatic dance, singing and drinking his eyes out—a blind prophet of sorts. Some people, some less enlightened people, would call it self-destructive, but oh no—it was anything but.

And now that Dent has realized that something is wrong with him, that he would have to go to the hospital and have tests done, be made to feel cold and uncomfortable for an unknown number of hours, this is when he makes me promise never to let him become an agoraphobe. Make sure that if he dies, he does it outside, doddering along a beach in Spain somewhere, suddenly clutching his heart and keeling over. Or in bed, with Laura Linney.

This is why I can't really talk about it, why I have to ask something like, *Isn't that embarrassing?* And then he'll have to say, *What?* And I'll tell him, *To be taken down by something that isn't even cancer? Isn't it disappointing?* And then he'll catch on, and begin to riff, because he was ever the better riffer:

I know. Jesus, I don't even need to shave my head. I mean with this thing, you get your antivirals or whatever the hell they give you, and you're on your merry way. Maybe the doctor gives you a lollipop. But blood transfusions wouldn't work with cancer. With cancer, you've got to get chemo. You've got to burn it out of you."

Not even cancer, I'll say. <u>Precancer</u>. You're not even man enough to get a real disease.

I walk to the window, where frost has formed a porthole-sized circle on the glass, giving the room a nautical look.

The window creaks. I press my thumb against it and feel the cold. A tree has the look of seagrass, bending under the weather. The wind must be really bad now.

"God," I say. "I'm glad I'm not outside."

Dent's mother has disengaged.

She has cornered herself in a chair of ersatz blue silk and is holding a book too close to her face. She puts the book down, flips a page, picks it up, flips a page, puts it down. I think it's *Gone with the Wind*. Or is it *The Wind in the Willows*? I don't know. Something with *Wind*.

Ordinarily, Dent's mom is a beleaguered woman, unmistakably Scottish. Temperamental, hassled, miraculously adept at somehow clawing your eyes out while simultaneously nailing herself to a cross.

But now, nothing.

She does not look at me. She picks it up, the book. She flips a page. Why Dent's dad isn't here, I don't know. She puts the book down. Her lips move, whispering indistinctly, as if learning by rote. She picks the book up. She flips a page. Matte laminate finish, worn by age. She puts it down.

She is no help now. She has checked out.

I look at Dent, sitting there. He has removed a hospital blanket from the exam table and draped it over his head, burying himself like an ostrich.

"Fuck," he says.

"This isn't so bad." I say. I start drumming my stomach. "We're good, we're good," I say in rhythm. Dent doesn't look up.

"Fuck," he says again. His voice is muffled.

Dent's mom has left the room. I can talk to him again. He has made the corner exam table into a bed, pulling a blanket up to his neck and lying face down.

"Know how I know you're going to make it?" I ask. I walk to the sink and run the water. "Know how I know you're going to beat this?"

"Humth?" I think he means *How?* He is talking into the vinyl.

"Because I know you. I know what you've got. Do you know what you've got?"

"What have I got, Shel?"

I pause as a junkie on a gurney wheels by the doorway. His shirt says EQUALITY. He is frothing.

I continue: "Heart. You've got heart."

"Do I?"

"And drive."

"That so?" He turns over.

"It is. And you know, with just a little luck," I put a caesura here, for effect, "you're going to *be something*. You're going to make something of yourself, champ."

"I'm a champ now?"

"Oh, you'll hear people say, *No, he's too small, he'll never make it in the big leagues*, or *He'd be promising, if it weren't for that bum leg of his*—"

"Very nice."

"... *and his asthma* ..."

"Okay ..."

"... *not to mention that rectal bleeding business. Out of his anus. No, he'll never make it.* But then, years later, when you prove them wrong, they'll all be like, *I always knew that kid had it in him. I always knew he'd be a Hall-of-Famer, make MVP.* That's what they'll say."

"How hypocritical of them."

I glance at a muted TV in the corner. Bob Barker is being interviewed about animal rights.

I continue, "But not me. I will have stuck with you always. Because I know you. Sheldon Wirth *knows* you. You, my friend, are a scrapper. A fighter. You, Denton Brown, have the greatest gift of all, the gift of never-say-die."

Shel! Dent's mom has returned. There is murder in her eyes.

She is a sneaky woman, Dent's mom, noiselessly moving between rooms as she does. Other than her well-known intestinal problems, Mrs. Brown was something of a mystery in Northbrook, Illinois. There are theories, of course. My favorite is that she is a frustrated homosexual, stuck in a traditional marriage. This would account for why she is so uppity, and it would explain her stomach problems, which are psychosomatic more than anything else, at least according to rumors.

But the lesbian has a point. *Never-say-die* was the wrong thing to say.

"And don't say *shit*," she says. "You look like an idiot when you say *shit*."

She approaches Dent's bedside and sits down, her back to me, talking in a voice that can only be described as menopausal. She needs some alone-time with him now.

On TV, Bob Barker has become passionate about something.

I leave without notice and explore the hospital.

The hospital is more fun than I expected. It turns out to be more than just a place for the terminally ill, more than a holding pen for people who sit around hemorrhaging, messing themselves, lolling about in their own feces, heavy on the call button for attention or cleanup. I half expected to stumble through a door marked PROCEDURE ROOM to find dark rituals, illicit testing taking place, an alternate universe where decent people are held in cannulated limbo for months.

But no, it is much more enjoyable. Why? Because there is so much to do! On the surface, perhaps, these patients seem despondent. But they shouldn't be. Who will cheer them up? I shall cheer them up. See? There are gadgets to touch, Q-tips to stick into my ears, and—Ooh!—tongue depressors to depress tongues with. The nurses have come, but they are not amused by my invisible POPSICLE, an old sight gag, so I leave them. I venture into other rooms and pretend I'm board certified, telling people I need to swab their arms, clean their ears, cup their privates and make them cough, until someone calls me out, accusing me of inexperience, of not being a doctor. My T-shirt gives me away. It says SEÑOR FROG'S.

I press on. I venture down the hall, pausing to console the men in line for mammograms, suddenly craving the peace of mind of one myself. I make my way into the children's ward, a bonanza of Jell-0 and TECHNI-COLOR playthings. My sheer presence entertains the kiddies. They have never seen anything like me, hulking and awkward. They point at me and shout. They grab onto the pockets of my Levi's, something they shouldn't be touching, since a combination of tobacco and ranch dressing has been ground into them over the years, but I allow it.

I have in hand a stolen stethoscope.

I place the earpieces closer to my temples than my ears and pretend to shout into it, deafening myself. This is the funniest thing the kids have ever seen, apparently. I awe them. I delight them. This may be awful to think, but delighting sick kids doesn't seem all that difficult.

A lab assistant catches me playing with the stethoscope and gives me the managed-care stare down, as though he expects me to apologize, or feel shame for my behavior. I try to redeem myself. I try to engage in intelligent-sounding chitchat, asking him if these medical devices meet ISO-13845 management system standards for hospital equipment.

"I'm sure they do." He confiscates my stethoscope.

I leave this pediatric neverland, away from this—oh no, not doctor—goddamn *lab assistant* (Am I being too hard on this lab assistant? Maybe I am too hard on him.) and move on to adult patients. Oh yes. These people need cheering up.

"I need to touch your feet," I tell one of them, a lady. She laughs. Good. I raise my voice and announce to the room that I must touch their feet, have been sent to examine their feet. Most of them get the joke, so I continue, explaining that I need to hold them, those beautiful extremities. That it's a new kind of therapy. I need to turn them over in my hands, rub them, maybe lick them. In the name of medicine, of course. I get enthusiastic about it, wring my hands. See that Johnson & Johnson bottle over there? Do you know what I am going to do with that bottle? That's right. I am going to squeeze a dab of the lotion into my palm and rub it on your feet. Really knead those mothers.

I then excuse myself, telling the patients I am too excited to stay. The people who get the joke—Methodists, probably—love it. They love it, and they applaud.

I walk back to Dent's room to find Bob Barker still on but in a chic new tie, flashier than the last one.

"Where's your mom?" I ask.

"Bathroom."

I announce there's a pervert loose in the hospital, one of those foot sickos. Dent laughs and tells me I'm an asshole for messing with sick people. We're not quite sure what to say after that, so we avoid meaningful conversation—

"Anything you'd like to accomplish before you bite it?" I ask.

"This is sort of embarrassing, but I've always had this thing . . . I've always wanted to molest a leper. Really invade his space. Is that wrong?"

"I know the feeling. I'll contact Make-A-Wish."
—by making fun of a disease much less palatable than precancer. It's not as satisfying with his mom not there. Her disapproval gave it meaning.

Our conversation is encouraging, because he hasn't changed. We can still be assholes together:
"Shel?"
"Yeah?"
"When I'm gone—"
"Yeah?"
"Well, you didn't know this, but I have a son."
"Oh?"
I spot an open wheelchair. I sit in it.
"Yes, a little, illegitimate bundle of joy. And I need someone to take care of him. Will you take care of him when I'm gone?"
"Of course I will."
"Thanks."
I wheel over to a magazine rack and pick up an issue of GQ, flip to an article about a Nazi propaganda exhibit at the Guggenheim. It is too long. I put it down.
"So what's his name?"
"Whose name?"
"Your son's."
"Right. Javier. His name is Javier."
Hispanic jokes. Good.
"Javier will need all your love and support because he's originally from Guadalajara. He'll be a stranger in a strange land. In all likelihood, he'll imprint on you from a young age."
"Sure, I'll take care of Javier. I'll give Javier all the care and attention you would have given him."
"Thanks."
See? We are bad people, people who make jokes like this, people who jettison discretion in the face of . . . well, pretty much everything.
"I'll tell him that if his father were still with us, he'd be disappointed."
"That's nice."
"And that Javier is a bastard, really."
"That his mother was a trick you picked up in Tijuana. Until she met you, she was nothing but a lifty-shoed floozie."
"It's comforting to know you'll be there for Javier. Please remember one

thing: Be sure to smack Javier for me. Not as a punishment. Randomly. To keep Javier on his toes. And if Javier cries, just hold him under the faucet. Bastard-kids like Javier need discipline like that."

"They crave it."

"That's right. Crave it."

There was much hoopla surrounding the hospital visit—concerned voicemails, preemptive Hallmark wishes—but it really went as well as it could have gone. I grab his ankle and shake it, the way my father—I usually called him *DAD*, but he liked the way *FATHER*, sounded: formal, distant yet looming—used to grab mine before I went to bed, but as soon as I do, I realize it is a mistake. It is too close, too much touching for guys. I withdraw.

"I don't think I can take this." Dent says. "I don't think I can take being an anus bleeder."

God, Dent.

I lean against the wall. They are really white, these walls. They are too white. I don't like these walls.

We sit together in the room for another fifteen minutes. I should tell Dent that he has been a hero to me, to all of us. I should tell him that he—leader, legend, madman—is that controversial figure that every neighborhood, every nation, needs. I should tell him about the coiled rage we all feel (at what, exactly? God? The universe?) at the possibility of his being taken from us, should tell him that—

"Javier. Jaaavier. Haaavier. Hgggggaaavier. Hggggavierrr," he repeats, rolling the *r*. "My bones are falling apart, Hggggavierr."

—he is the ablest terrestrial creature I have ever met. Instead, I say, "You're much more interesting when you're sick, ass man."

This is the one of the last times I see Dent. A month or two later, he has an urge, a very *Dentian* urge: He decides he needs to travel while he still can, needs to, as he puts it, *honor his body* (that Laird Hamilton body, that body that looks like it belongs in a HANES ad) a bit by sending it to the farthest corners—or *deepest reaches*, his words—of the earth, some godforsaken continent on the cusp of civilization. Damn the men with PhDs and clipboards—he's *going to live*. Denton Brown—Midwest visionary, champion. Rule breaker, death defier. Not long after the diagnosis, he buys a ticket, and that's it. He doesn't tell me about his departure, about his travel plans, before I return to Boston. He leaves me, the one person who knows him better than anyone else, who loves him like a brother, but he says nothing.

I get lost on my way out of the hospital. I wander NorthShore Evanston Cancer Center's south wing, roaming past the puzzled residents of Room 909S at least five times before a receptionist with gold acrylic fingernails catches me and points me to the way out.

I wake up at 4:24 the next morning. I arrive at O'Hare airport at 5:35 AM. I board American Airlines Flight 983 at 6:24 AM. It departs for Boston Logan at 6:40 AM. I have a window seat.

Boston, Two years later.
The Office, AM

My work is interrupted by a call from Joel. I answer—
"Hello?"
"Sheldon P. Wirth! What's up?"
"Hey. Joel?"
"Yeah. What's new?"
"Not much. At work."
"Living the dream?"
"Guess so."
"Anything to report?"
"Nope."
"Nothing?"
"Nada."
"Hm."
"Yep. Hm. Nada. Nada nada."
—and speak longer than I intend to.
"Heard from Dafna lately?"
Dafna is my ex-girlfriend. Even worse than talking to Joel is talking to Joel about Dafna. I do not talk about Dafna. Talking about Dafna gives me hives. It makes my nose run. It gives me dry scalp.
"Nope."
"Dent?"
"Nuh uh."
"And we're not just being elliptical again?"
"Nope."
I cross my legs, wondering if I should change my *Men's Health* subscription to *Men's Fitness*.
. . .

"So."

"So."

I uncross my legs, determining that I enjoy *Men's Health*. *Men's Health* does just fine.

"Sooooo . . . I called because I just heard that—"

"Hey, haven't I asked you not to call me here?"

I have asked him not to call me here. I ask him not to call me here every day, disliking the way my iPhone amplifies certain sounds. Wet, private sounds, like breathing and tongue busy-ness. This is too close for me. It is too close to Joel.

"I know. I just called about Dent."

Joel still calls me. Joel never listens.

"Oh? What about him?"

"He's coming back home."

"Back to Boston?"

"To the States. He'll be in Seattle, crashing at my place."

I lean against the conference table. It does not look like your standard cherry wood conference table. It looks ominous. Foreboding. Something important men gather around just before declaring war.

"Hey, can we talk later? Really under the gun tod—"

"You've got to look at this website," Joel says, interrupting.

"I don't want to know."

Joel can access pornography from work. He can watch other people's girlfriends undress. He likes to tell me about it.

"I'm on this website, and there's this girl. You should see this girl. What a smokeshow."

"Great. Fantastic."

"Really. You should see her. Total smokeshow. She's <u>objectively</u> hot. Believe me, I'd touch every important part of her body if I had the chance. Amazing buttocks."

"I don't need to hear about her, um..."

"You would if you saw her. Beautiful."

"Not now, hombre." I say.

"It's the kind of butt that's too nice to touch with your hands. The kind you just want to gently rest your balls on."

I convulse.

"That's weird, Joel. That you think those kinds of things. It's creepy."

But I listen to Joel when he tells me about these girls, his *finds*, his *smokeshows* as he calls them. As if my mind weren't already a coagulate of irrelevancies, I listen when he speaks. I listen as he becomes a kind of salesman for this girl, as if he were reviewing a prospectus about her, bullet-pointing each item with a pinky finger. When he assures me that I *won't believe what this dude's girlfriend can do with a pomegranate*, I listen. I don't mean to listen—

"Her name is *Tiffani*, spelled with two *i*'s and a heart over the second one. Know what that's called? That's called *metaplasmus*. It's the intentional misspelling of a word for stylistic purposes. They say these buttboobsandsometimesbrain.com guys aren't smart, but this use of the metaplastic figure is really quite ingenious, really *something*."

—but I do. I listen. Intently at first, ruminating on his findings, as if I had some kind of a stake in the whole thing, but then less so.

"Interesting," I say. I am struck with the sudden doubt that Joel has ever played Charades. No person who has engaged in a family game like Charades (or *Sorry!*, or pick-up sticks) would talk like this. This man lacks wholesomeness. If he didn't consider censorship the highest of praise, I'd say something.

"Very interesting," I say again, now not at all so.

"Here. I'll send it to you."

"Please don't."

He sends it to me.

I open the email to find Tiffani-with-two-*i*'s. She is wearing only glasses. A copy of *Watership Down* is on her lap. Or maybe it's *Blackhawk Down*. It's hard to say. Something with *Down*. It soon occurs to me that Joel should not be so caught up with her name. She, Tiffani, does not seem to be 100 percent female. Yes. I do believe that woman is a man.

We are hardly a year out of college—or at least I am, Joel having dropped out during junior spring to do a semester at DeVry and then work for his uncle—and already there are distractions. Women. Online women. Joel has been obsessive, indiscriminate in his affection for them. It has been the same with him ever since sophomore year at New Trier, when he lined his locker with *Sports Illustrated* or *Victoria's Secret* clippings, his facile sense of romance governing most of his decisions—which classes to take, which clubs to join, which seats to occupy. I wasn't much better, of course. Even when I took the SATs, concentrating was difficult:

> 12. Linda is twice as old as Tom. Tom is half as old as
>   Gina. If Gina and Linda fondle each other, will Tom
>   get to watch?

But I've learned since then. I am mature. I am adult.

Joel continues, listening more to himself than to me. "Definitely one of the better girls I've seen lately. Seriously. Big time smokeshow. *Seriously* seriously. Total—wait a sec. That's weird. It looks like—what's wrong with her arms? It looks like one is longer than the other. Is one longer than the other? Man, this is gonna bother me."

I cradle the phone between my shoulder and ear and step out of the conference room, into a mess. The office is a mess. I survey the 101 State Street SpectaCop Security, LLC workplace with disgust. Unhung pictures on the tables; wires everywhere. A Coke Zero, empty, next to the wastebasket. An inexplicable *Terminator 2* poster on the wall. A gumbo of paramilitary blouses have spilled out of the uniform closet. The only brightness to the area is a fluorescent notepad on my desk. *Write On*, it says.

It is dark down the hall. I flick the first of five switches. Nothing happens. Stupid light. I hit the other four switches one by one. The bay lighting system springs to life, giving the hallway a mottled, vaguely whorish tint, calling to mind images of slot machines and showgirls. Vegas. A bulb must be out.

"Did you see the thing from Dent?" Joel suddenly says. Good. He has forgotten about the website for a moment.

"What?"

"Dent's email—did you see it?"

I know I should change the bulb. I should be concerned that it's out. I should make progress toward the utility cupboard, find a 60-watt, and fix the problem—this all should be ingrained, Standard Operating Procedure—but I don't.

"Yes or no—there's no wrong answer here, remember," Joel says.

I know. I will make my coworker change the bulb.

I find him, my coworker, asleep in the adjoining office. His shirt says FCUK. He is upright in his chair, still erect—a scarecrow—his head nodding just so much. An issue of *The Amazing Spider-Man* is draped over a knee.

Nod, goes the head. It has the nose of Meryl Streep.

"Hey there, dreamer."

Nod, it goes again.

It mumbles something with little affinity to modern English.

I position a pen between his lips in a way that gives him the appearance of a woman in labor, biting down.

Nod. The pen falls out.

Shit. I tick my nails on the door frame.

"Um. No, not yet. I mean I haven't seen Dent's email yet," I say to Joel, wandering back into the hallway, miffed at my own inattentiveness, my half-heartedness—for failing to change the bulb, for failing to follow through on the pencil-mouth project. There is a faint smell of cinnamon here, the result of a Glade plug-in that I bought to cover the room's original smell, the smell that was here when I arrived, of Taco Bell tacos. But the tacos are strong. The tacos are dominant.

"No, haven't seen his email yet," I repeat.

Then it strikes me. The Glade plug-in, it is nearly the size of my coworker's mouth? Will it fit? There is only one way to find out. Sneaky, sneaky back to the office.

"Well," Joel says, "look at it, and tell me you don't want to visit after reading it."

"I told you I didn't have time to—"

"Just check out Dent's note. And get some rest. You don't sound so great. Chin up, man. Chin up."

Chin up?

That night, I drag Joel's lifeless body from the trunk of my car, pushing it over the Tobin Bridge to the river below.

Ha, ha. This is a joke. I do not really mean what I say. Joel is alive, and healthy. Happy. There is no way I could have done those things to him. He lives in Seattle. I would have to fly to Seattle, kill Joel, then fly back with his body in tow, drive all the way to the river and dump it in. There is no way I could have done all this. It does not make sense, logistically. Also, it is not ethical. I am still in my office, and Joel is still in his office. He is fine. He is not expendable.

Yes, there it is. Dent's email. I am staring at the subject line but have not opened the email. *Serge*, it says. Do I know a *Serge*? No. I do not.

I pretend that I haven't been waiting for this, that I don't look forward to Dent's notes, to finding out who *Serge* is, what relationship Dent has with *Serge*, and possibly *Serge*'s height, weight, surname and work history. I pretend that I would rather be here, in my office, my craigslisted, rent-stabilized apartment—re-reading Dent's email, unpacking his language, combing his sentences for *something*, some hint to his whereabouts, to why he left.

We all had our own theories about this, about his reasons for leaving. Dafna thought it was because he didn't want his friends to see him suffer. She discarded the idea when she realized how uncharacteristically considerate that would be of him. Joel thought—

"I bet Dent's getting one of those massages where tiny tea ladies walk on your back. Man, that's what I need to do before I die. Have a friendly Tea Lady walk on my back."

—it was for other purposes. My theory, strangely, was the most controversial.

He left because of me. It was my fault.

I posited this 'Reason for Dent Departing,' in an email to Dafna one day. It was about as popular with her as I expected it to be.

I'm not even going to begin to go into the arrogance of that statement, she wrote. That afternoon, I called her up to disagree. I conferenced in Joel, to adjudicate:

"Am I wrong?"

"Give me a break," Dafna said.

Joel kind of liked it.

"Think about it," he said, his voice a flatline of earnestness. "Just before Dent decided to leave, he went a little batshit on us. He was all —"

"That's just like you two," Dafna said, interrupting, "to make everything about yourselves."

"How would you know what it was about? You weren't there."

There was on the wraparound porch at Joel's house, over Homer's Burgers sliders and iced tea. *There* happened—

"I *was* there. Remember? I was the one that stopped your bleeding, Joel."

—only a few days before Dent decided to leave Northbrook, Illinois.

"Oh. Yeah. The bleeding. I guess you were there."

There hadn't been discussed for months afterwards, because *There* wasn't something they were eager to remember.

There didn't go well.

THERE: Three days before Dent's Departure, 11 January, Afternoon.

A living room. Joel and I are playing a football game that uses the voice and likeness of John Madden for commercial purposes while listening to Billy Idol's "White Wedding" on 100.7 WZLX, Boston's classic rock. Dafna is on the sofa. She is reading.

Dent enters, wearing a Chicago Bears hoodie and holding a sheet of notebook paper.

"So, you guys ready?" he says.

"For what?" I say, taking the final bites of a Oaxaca Hut burrito. Oaxaca Hut burritos always leave me hungry. I buy their burritos only so I can see the old Chilean lady at the counter. She flirts and calls me *Papi*.

"Ready for what?" I say again.

"He said he had a secret for us," Joel says to me, then turns to Dent. "You said you had a secret for us. What's the secret?"

"Well, I was thinking of some last words for when the, you know, the, *you know*, finally happens. And I wanted your advice."

"Oh, that's so sweet," Dafna says. She puts down her book. It looks like it's *A Raisin in the Sun*. Or *The Sun Also Rises*. It's hard to see. Something with *Sun*. "Let's hear them."

"Wait, that's your secret? That's not a secret. That's just information."

"Yeah, it's just information," I say, distracted by John Madden, who is giving us some pointers. Useless, all of them, though Joel gives an appreciative look. *Thanks, Mr. Madden!* he seems to say. *You're a real friend!*

"But it's secret information."

He unzips his hoodie. I think it is an intentional unzip. His shirt says MEXICO.

"Oh, I was just—"

"Just *what?*" Dent says, clearly upset that his MEXICO shirt isn't getting the kind of attention it deserves.

"Yeah, just what?" Dafna repeats.

"I dunno. Just hoping for something a little more exciting."

"You're more than welcome to leave. No one's stopping you from leaving."

He gestures.

"No, no. I'll stay."

"You sure?"

"Yeah. Sure."

"Good."

He clears his throat. "So I've put together a list of the topics I'd like to touch on in my last words. In no particular order, they are: Courage, Cycles, Futility, Manhood as a correlative to Courage, Homecomings, Mortality, Overconsumption, The '85 Chicago Bears, The Chicago Bears, all other years, Living Freely and Without Inhibition, Being Honest to Oneself, to Others, Why Small Things Matter, Urban Living, Suburban Living, and as a subcategory, Weird Suburban Rituals, e.g., community theater, pot luck dinners, The Summer of '89, Why Fred Willard Is a Force for Good in This World, Hopefulness and Why It Is Important to Distinguish It From Mere *Hope*, Money: The Hard Truth. And Youth, and Sadness, and Stubbornness—another correlative to Courage—and What Now?

"Now, I don't have to cover all of these. I'm just putting ideas out there right now. I'm *giving energy*, as my weird pastor used to say. Trying to get those gears moving. I really don't care what these words are. Their order and style don't really matter. I just want them to, um, you know . . . mean something. They should be pertinent if not stand-up-and-cheer brilliant."

"I think they're won-der-ful, Dent," Dafna says. "I just love them."

"They're gay," Joel says. He pauses the game mid-snap.

Dafna winces. "Don't use that word."

Dafna knows as well as the rest of us that Joel is one of the only people we know who can get away with using that word. Who can get away with speaking in ignorant terms without coming off as ignorant himself.

"Besides," she says. "It's not helpful."

Joel ignores her. "How about: *I've lived*," he says. "Something short, bold. I know you need to cover a lot, but brevity is key here."

"Yes! Totally! Brevity!," I say, trying to sound enthusiastic, overdoing it a little, spending most of my energy thinking that an adequate description of Joel's appearance might be, *not at all like Willem Dafoe*. "Memorability is clutch."

"I don't care so much about memorability," Dent says. "I care more about pertinence, as I said. I was thinking about also discussing Relevance, because it dovetails nicely with—"

"I know, but you're going to want memorable," Joel says.

"Yeah. You'll want memorable," I repeat. It's not my intention to be glib. But glibness has been the tone the whole afternoon. Acting any other way—forlorn or something—would sound wrong right now. So I say, "How about *I Wish I Had Climbed More Trees*? Or *Tell Corina I Love Her*, and you'll have everyone guessing who Corina is? Or go cautionary: *Don't Drink and Drive*, and you'll get people thinking that's how you died. A good learning lesson."

"Or *Take Time, Make Time*?" Joel says. "Repetition works, and it's sorta catchy, not too specific. You should stay away from specifics."

"Stop, guys," Dafna says, "This is serious."

"Yeah. No specifics. As much as you'd like to, *do not* mention the Pueblo Indian People of the Rio Grande. They've had their time."

I nod in agreement.

Dent sits on the couch. Joel continues:

"How about *This is the End*, and you start dying on 'end,' dragging it out, so it's like *ennnnnnd?* That would be perfect."

"Yeah," Dent says distantly. "I'll keep thinking."

The discussion is interrupted by a very catchy WZLX ad informing us that even though the weather outside is becoming *frightful*, shopping at Costco is absolutely *delightful*. We give the assertion a minute's consideration, discuss, and then concur. Then we flip to a mildly offensive cartoon—an old *Popeye*—featuring one of those over-the-top Japanese caricatures, a brown man with buck teeth and improperly pronounced alveolar consonants. Joel is inspired. He runs out for sushi. He returns an hour later, plopping a Homer's Burgers bag on the table.

"Sushi place was closed."

We move outside to the wraparound porch, settling into four weatherproof patio chairs surrounding a wicker table. Joel distributes the burgers, throwing them like cards across the table, then slides a pilsner to each of us. Dafna brings out a pitcher of iced tea. Dent eats in silence, an anomaly. Why is Dent so quiet? Dent is never this quiet. I ask him why he is so quiet—

"Why are you so quiet?"

"Mmmm," he says, munching.

—but he resists.

"Cat got your—?"

"Mmmm mmmm," he says.

"Is it about your last words? Were we not helpful enough when—?"

"DEEEEEE JAAAAAY!" Dent yells, his mouth full.

Oh no. This is not the first time Dent has pretended to be a DJ. He pretends to be a DJ about once per week. He is goading again.

"What are you going to know me as?" he says, holding his fingers out like a Glock.

Joel gives him the assist: "DJ Denton B."

"Say again?"

"DEE JAY DENTON BEE!"

DJ Denton B, one of Dent's many alter egos, is from De-troit. Not 'Detroit.' De-troit. Dee. Troit.

"That's right. Dee-dee-dee-dee-dee-Jay. De Jay from De-troit." He starts scratching an invisible turntable.

"DJs don't sound like that," I say.

"You shouldn't have to identify yourself as a DJ," Joel says without looking up, his energies concentrated on applying squeezable ketchup to his bun in the shape of a well-hung stick figure. "You couldn't sound more white."

"DEEEE JAY!" Dent repeats. He opens his pilsner. "Denton B, The Dee Jay from De-troit!"

This name, Denton B, is an awful name for a disc jockey. Dent is well aware that it is an awful name for a disc jockey, is proud of the horrid-ness of the name, wanting ever so much to invoke and embrace the culture of transiently popular late-80s disc jockeys.

"Dee Jay Denton Bee," he says again, louder, pouring a little beer onto the ground, throwing up what I assume is meant to be a gang sign but looks more like an 'A-Okay' gesture, ever-proud of his willingness to embarrass himself in front of his friends. He does a little jig.

"You wish you were thug. Ha, the only way you're—" I start to say but trail off, depositing whatever it was into my subliminal cauldron of Things Best Left Unsaid.

"What was that?" Dent says. "Did you have something to say?"

"Nothing, nothing. Never mind."

"You were saying something. Tell me. Tell me what you were saying."

"It's nothing. Really. I was being stupid."

Dent folds his arms.

"We deserve to know what you were saying."

"I was going to make a joke. A stupid joke."

"So what was the joke?"

"Nothing. There was no joke."

Oh no. We are going to have The Conversation.

"You just said there was a joke. I'm asking what the joke is."

We have had The Conversation before. It is agony, torture, extraordinary renditions, this Conversation. But it is unavoidable. I relent.

"The joke was—it's stupid. I was going to say that the only way you are *thug* is that you've had family in jail. At least—"

"Shel," Joel says, stepping in. "Not today."

"At least *what*?"

"At least nothing," Joel says. He looks to Dafna for help.

"Ver-bot-en," she whispers with the fullness of her body, her back turned to Dent, face agitated at the fact that I shouldn't need reminding about this.

"*At least,*" I continue, encouraged more than anything by Dafna's annoyance and noting never to use the word *verboten* myself, "*at least* until your dad struck a deal with the DA," I say. If Dent wants to cross-examine me, fine. Fuck him. "How'd that go, by the way?" I say. "The deal, I mean."

"Jesus, Shel." Dafna touches her lip with a finger. Dafna was probably the only one sensitive to the fact that Dent's appreciation of a good personal attack did not at all translate to insults about his dad, Mr. Brown.

"As I recall, it didn't go so well," I say, a thrill of fear running through me at the likelihood that Dent, who was always looking for an excuse to cross the line, would.

Dent gives a vacant laugh and wipes his mouth. It has been half a decade since the trial ended, and with it, apparently, his shame about the whole scandal. Dent's tension ended, his justifications and evasions ended.

"Are you *trying to* start something?" Joel asks.

"No, let him finish," Dent says. He pulls a pack of MARLBOROS out of his pocket and sucks out a cigarette.

Dent was as familiar with my own disgraces as I was with the Brown family's. Even so . . . today, I just don't seem to care.

"Most guys don't let the past get to them," he begins, cigarette still dangling from his lip, but more snidely now, as if facing an ill-trained firing squad. "Most guys sacrifice for their families. Because most guys are sure of themselves. They don't have doubts. Most guys are—here's a surprise—men."

"Whass that thupposed to mean?" I say. My mouth is full.

"Cool it," Joel says, again the mediator. He is wearing a FIGHTING IRISH jersey. There was something Catholic about Joel's family, even though they weren't overtly religious. If there were any other group they admired as much, it might have been the Amish ("great work ethic"). They really liked their "look," the Amish.

"Just ignore him," Joel says. "He's baiting you."

"I'm not baiting him. A man's just a woman with a penis, when you think about it."

Dent was never afraid to issue trite, sometimes ridiculous statements for the sake of making a point.

"I'm leaving." Dafna gets up and goes inside.

"I'm simply pointing out. You can't spell Shel without s-h-e."

"So, Dent," Joel says, almost shouting, "how's the treatment going? Still have the pussy cancer?"

It would be an effective change of subject, if not the most subtle. Joel invented the name *pussy cancer* in reaction to Dent's decision, when he was first diagnosed, not to discuss the MDS. He, Dent, did not have the energy to put up with sympathy from Joel, an awkward handler of compassion. And I promised Dent I wouldn't get specific about the disease, which was easy to do. I still didn't quite understand what was wrong with him in the first place, recalling only that it had something to do with myeloblasts and bone marrow. After that, memory failed.

The only drawback to Dent's obliqueness was that it was left up to Joel's power of invention to find the most indelicate way of discussing it. It was either this, the pussy cancer, or an indiscriminate line about mercy killing.

Dent seemed fine with it. I knew that the last thing Dent wanted was for his pussy cancer, to interfere with drinking nights. Death, if anything, was a topic that could dampen a good time. We could picture it: He, Joel, Dafna and I would be drinking, doing shots of JAGER, or playing Asshole, when it would come up, the question would be posed: *Are you sure? Are you sure this is good for your [cancer/leukemia/liver failure/diabetes/head wound/SARS/swine flu/sickle cell anemia/all of the above/none of the above/MCD/OCD/lupus/Worse Than We Could Have Ever Imagined, God Help Us All/Other]?*

This did not fully work, as Joel, inventor that he is, made up the nickname as a way to whitewash the tragedy most people associate with death by turning it into stand-up material, however lowbrow. *You sure this is good for the pussy cancer? You sure you can have that drink?* Dent, you see, once a paragon of health, was now a pussy for having whatever it was he had. Dent always seemed to have a sense of humor about it, so Joel remained faithful to this nickname until the day Dent devised a crisp, penetrating response:

"Still inexorably killing me."

It always seemed to shut him up pretty good.

Tonight, Dent doesn't answer. He doesn't smile. He usually smiled at the joke. He slumps, as if comatose. Joel looks to me in confusion. Then, Dent laughs. It is sharp, a bark. He laughs again, louder this time. He stares at the wall, laughing. It isn't until Dent starts holding his stomach that I realize he's faking it. It becomes crazed, the laughter. He rises. He is agitated. He is babbling. He jerks and lurches, as if dragged by a kite, in a twisting wind.

Dent stumbles toward Joel, putting a hand on his chest for support. Joel slaps his hand away. At this, the swatting of the hand, all of Dent's boxed up and stowed away furies are recalled. There are one or two *cocksuckers*, numberless *motherfuckers*. He pushes Joel to the wall, a hand on his chest, shouting with the ferocity of someone berating an umpire. He pulls Joel toward him by the collar, then pushes him away, throwing him out the screen door.

"What the hell are you—" I start to say, but before I can finish, Dent has followed Joel out the door. The laughing has stopped.

I run out, the door still swinging behind Dent. I jump down the steps. Dent and Joel are at the end of the driveway. How did they get all the way over there? Dent has grabbed Joel's shirt and made like he is going to tear out his stomach. He throws him to the ground. Joel's face hits the concrete. Dent bends over him. He looks brutish, like a mad orangutan, something loosed from the zoo. He starts kicking him. *Poor piece of shit. White trash*. He stops laughing. Dent is now singing, singing and spitting and kicking Joel in the gut:

GUM-MI BEARS / BOUNCING HERE AND THERE AND EVERY-WHERE /

HIGH ADVENTURE—

His kicks have become syncopated. He is winding up.

THAT'S BEYOND COM-PARE. THEY ARE THE GUM-MI—

On *bears*, he pounds Joel with his heel, as if stomping out a fire. His ribcage. He drills his heel down, again the ribs. He punts him in the stomach. Joel curls up.

It's bullshit, he says. *Bullshit*.

I am on Dent, hooking him under the armpits. I pull him away. Dent is kicking the air.

There is a shriek. Dafna has heard the screaming and stands outside the screen door. She runs to Joel's side and cradles his head. She bunches her blouse and presses it against his knees, stoppering the blood. *I'm okay*, Joel mumbles. *I'm okay*. She helps him to his feet. Joel leans against her shoulder, devastated, crouching like a squaw, his face scratched, legs lacerated. He is holding his side. Dafna presses a hand against his cheek and helps him inside.

"Peed blood that night," Joel reports later. "Got me in the kidney."

@ggray: So that's when Dent started elbowing you?

@shelgames: Yes. I was holding Dent's collar, and he started jabbing me in the chest. Not the response I was hoping to elicit.

@ggray: What happened when Dent started elbowing you?
@shelgames: He started calling me names. Cocksucker. Piece of shit.

@ggray: Yes, but what did you do? When he started attacking you – did you fight back?

@shelgames: No. I just repeated Calm Down Calm Down Calm Down. I didn't understand why he was attacking Joel. I mean I . . . I was the one who insulted his dad, I was the one who was . . . anyway, Dent kept elbowing me. He told me I wasn't smart enough to understand. He kept saying bullshit bullshit bullshit and told me I was clueless, stupid. He said I'd never know what he knew. He said I'd never be as smart as he was. Whatever that means.

@ggray: Then what?
@shelgames: Then I bloodied his nose. It wasn't very smart of him to make me bloody his nose.

Dent is now bent, his head in his hands, a quarterback taking a knee. I am standing over him. I lean down and grab Dent, guiding him up by his bicep. He has a bruised look on his face. He is sweating, drooling. There is blood. Too much blood. He throws an arm around me. He pulls me to his chest. *Please don't*—Dent says. His chest is strong against my face. *Please don't forget me, Shel. Please don't forget me.*

This is my chance. It's my chance to tell him that I'll never forget him, that no one who has ever met Dent could forget him. It's my chance to tell him that if he ever leaves me, if he ever slips away, I--

I --

I will be losing more than a friend when he goes. I will be losing a brother. For the first in a very long time, I will be alone.

I don't tell him this. I don't say a word. I rest there, face against his chest, breathing.

Please don't forget me. Even hours after the fight, it's all I hear from him. *Please don't forget me, Shel. Please don't forget me.* His words give way to murmurs, then sighs, then sleep.

Half a week later, Dent catches a taxi to O'Hare and is gone.

INTERLUDE: DAFNA.

I do not talk about Dafna. Talking about Dafna makes my tongue go dry. It makes my cuticles crack. It makes my nipples shrink.

Dafna was soft. She would lie on top of me, knees touching mine, an ear to my chest. I would breathe, and her head would go up. I would put my fingers on her hair, lightly, and she would make a purring sound. We'd then play the forever-ever game. It was strange, this forever-ever game.

Will you stay with me? she would ask.
Sure, I would answer.
I mean, forever.
Yeah, forever whatever.
(And I'd usually say sure, because I said yes to her
   a lot, because have you ever tried saying no to Dafna?).
I mean in my senility. My sterility? My do-tage?
Her face has taken a dramatic turn.
Yeah. Your dotage.

Dafna knew this wasn't a real conversation, it was more of a performance, a *pas de deux*, or a competition—Wimbledon?—but for me it felt like an interrogation. Dafna was verbally frisking me, snapping the figurative latex onto her hands in preparation for a thoroughly humiliating exam. Sometimes I'd resist, I'd improvise and say, "Hell no – *you ugly.*"

Dafna would then act hurt (Oh! *Ooooh!*) and move to a different room, expecting me to follow. I would follow. I would follow and tell her I was kidding, sorry, foolish, wrong, stupid, oh, so *stupid*. I really cannot stress enough how stupid I was. I would tell her I'm kidding again, and her response would be a finger, the finger, an obscene puppet tootled into the doorframe. I would move to the room and say tender things, inexcusably tender things that I had no place saying to her, using words like *sweet, together, promise, you, me, dear, true*. She would ask again, a hand in her hair, as if she were pulling out a pin:

So?
I will stay with you.

I would put my arms around her and feel her back and her beautiful hair and there is nothing but protecting her and being protected by her. I could fall asleep in her hair, to die in it.

In your do-tage.

This should be enough, but she is insatiable, ravenous.

No matter what?
No matter what?

We are in a room with blue curtains, a console table. Potted bamboo in a jade resin container. There is something uterine about the carpeting here. I try to steer the conversation to a different topic, something sports related, like the Ice Capades. She is determined:

No mat-ter what?
No mat-ter what?

This woman is tireless. She is Shackleton.

No matter <u>what?</u>

Unforgiveable Dafna.
"You have to let them soak," she'd say whenever I tried to help her with the dishes. "You're not letting them *soak.*"

FACT: One out of every four Jews I know is named Dafna.

I do not talk about Dafna. Talking about Dafna makes my eyelids twitch. It makes my buttocks spasm.

Dafna was a crazy girl. In the middle of reading quietly, a cover story about *Octuplets* or *The Hamptons* or *Gay Pride* or *Climate Change*, after hours of noiselessness and studiousness and concentration, she'd look up,

Bop she wanna wanna!, she'd burst, and make movements.

I would ignore her. I would continue watching Ren and Stimpy, waiting for the inexorable point in every Ren and Stimpy episode that Ren begins slapping Stimpy, to great comic effect. But she, Dafna, would not laugh at Ren slapping Stimpy. She would not have the patience to learn that Ren, although he looks like a cat, is a dog. And Stimpy, dog-looking, is really a cat. Instead, she would dance. I don't know why she'd do this. She's a crazy girl, as I said.

Unyielding, unforgiveable Dafna. Dafna, woman of appetites.

"I'm a bird!" she'd cry, stretching her arms. "I'm a bird!"

I'd watch her dance.

I do not talk about Dafna. Dafna does not believe in weddings.

There was nothing wrong with Dafna. Dafna, and that hair of hers, her perfect hair, her clean dirty-blond sun-smelling hair. Dafna was beautiful, smart, strong. Dafna was Helen of Troy.

"How are you today," she'd ask. "Are you splen-did?" That way of speaking, it would always get me.

"I hope you're splen-did."

"Come read with me," she'd say. "Come here and read."

Dafna does not understand that because she is a Woman, she is good at Language and Books. And I am a Man and therefore good at Math and Everything Else.

FACT: Dafna has a good womb. She has a very fertile womb.

SURPRISE BONUS FACT: I respect Dafna for her mind as well as her body.

THE OFFICE.

Yes, there it is. The email. Dent's note.

He, Dent, is infinitely better at obeying my email-only rule than Joel. I like to think I have something to do with Dent's abstracted phone manner, the way he interrupts, drifts off, behaves like a general space cadet when I am talking to him. The way he changes subjects abruptly. His emailing, however, is more likely a product of his not being in the fifty contiguous states at the moment, and, even if he were, being the non-confrontational type.

```
From: Dentseven@Dentlives.com (3)
To: Dentseven@Dentlives.com
Subject: Serge
```

Hey friends and people lucky enough to hear from me,

How's not being here? Probably not as cool as being here, dudes. Lil sun, lil surf, lil booze. Rays waves babes brew, man. BABES and BREWS, man! Bail out now, companeros.

But Seriously, all is fantastic out here. The experiment is going well but slow. It took a lot more prep work than I thought but now that is over and I only have about 2 hrs in the field each morning to collect data. Also this 6'7" guy named Serge joined me on the project so it is a lot more managable. Right now my days consist of finding and reading new papers that I can reference as well as helping other groups with there projects. Its fun.

Because of the current phase of the moon we are not getting too many recruits (damselfish don't settle on corals during new or full moons). We are getting a few random recruits though including a surgeonfish, scorpionfish, wrasse, blenny and two sweet little tiny trumpetfish. So far we have not had any recruits of any kind on corals with visible hawkfish nearby....that could be really cool if it stays that way. So that's what its like here...pretty cool eh? I have not gotten the packages yet, but i'm sure they'll make it
 soon. Thanks for sending me stuff it will be very helpful considering the absolutely rediculous prices here. Speaking of which...Friends of mine: send money if this email has moved you. I think my checking has only $50 or so in it now. That would be sweet.

> And mom, how's Griffy? Is he minding better when you walk him?
>
> That's all I got now. Tell everyone I forgot to put on this list I say hi. I've been able to check email every week or so here so keep 'em coming. I should be hitting the states soon, so for anyone out west, stay tuned. I have something to tell you. Details to follow.
>
> That's pretty sweet about Joel, huh?
>
> OK, i'm out. Thug life,
> DENT!
> P.S. Attached herewith a picture of someone's nipple. Not mine. Someone's.

I read the email slowly. It sounds like, even with everything that has happened to him recently, even with the medical bills and his dad's own problems (the heart thing, that systolic murmur of his) and the naysayers—yes, naysayers, who told him *not to take the trip, it's a bad idea to take the trip, why would anyone in your state, your infirm condition, do such a thing?*—it sounds like DENT's doing great. These letters, slapdash affairs typed in a mildly illiterate hand, a sub-fluent dialect, prove this, and so do the pictures. Oh God, the pictures. He routinely posts online images of himself—tanned, hair kinking out, face solar, and in a medley of wealthy situations and poses, most of which occur on boats that do not belong to him—that prove he's doing great. The message is clear: *My name is Denton Brown, and I am doing great. Just look at how great I'm doing! Pretty great!*

This is terrible news.

"Are you done?"

I do not want my friends to be doing so great, living the *National Geographic* life, when I am not doing so great.

"Are you done?" Joel repeats. "Have you read it?"

I thought I had hung up with Joel. This man is Houdini.

"Yeah."

"So?"

"So what?"

I know: I'll REPLY ALL to Dent's email. And, in the body of that email, I will make fun of Dent. I will call Dent a name.

"Dent has something he needs to tell us," Joel says. "And there's no mention of the fight."

"I'm sure it's nothing. He's bluffing."

"No, he's not this time. It's more than that. He called me about it. Dent says he has something to tell you. A secret."

"A secret?"

"A *top* secret."

My toe itches. I scratch.

"Is it about his last words again?" Joel says. "Those were so gay. Don't you think they were gay? Why doesn't he email?"

"And have it forwarded to his friends and family, current and former lovers?"

"You know Dent's bluffing. You told him I wasn't going to visit him, and he's bluffing. Why doesn't he just tell us over the phone?"

"He says it's complicated."

I stop scratching.

"He says it's a big deal, but whatever." Joel continues. "It's a *top* secret."

"Yeah, top. I heard that part," I say. "Dent's bluffing. He doesn't have a secret. Does he?"

"Not now, Joel."

"And that's why we need you to come visit with us. To take this vacation. We think your job's devouring your soul."

"Who's *we?*"

"Dent and me."

Shit, Joel.

"Dent thinks everything devours your soul. He thinks standing in line devours your soul. Remember that time when we went to see *Back to the Future II* at the Skokie Loews? Those were his exact words."

I've been on the phone too much today. I need to end this conversation. "Anyway, I can't talk for much longer—"

"He mentioned me," Joel adds.

"What?"

"Why do you think Dent mentioned me, in that last part? What's that last part at the end supposed to mean?"

"Oh yeah. Sure did."

"And?"

"It's nothing. Dent's just being an idiot. You know how he likes to start rumors. He's just trying to get to you."

"That's not even a rumor."

"See? He's gotten to you."

"But it's not even a rumor."

I tap my thigh with my phone-less hand. It pisses us off, Dent's departure. We knew he would leave this town, eventually. But not now, not like this. It was seen by so many of us as abandonment, betrayal, and it enrages all his friends, or at least two of them, us. It infuriates us to know that this disease, or malady, or whatever it is, has given Dent, the fulcrum of our friend group, the liberty to do what we all should be doing. What we would be doing if we were dying—living outside, throwing Nerf balls, throwing parties, finding women (total smokeshows, Joel says, *total smokeshows*) and gently making love to them. Or not gently at all.

"Did you say you were getting Boar's Head?" I ask.

"No, I said it looks like Dent's *getting bored*. I can tell from his emails."

"Oh, I thought we were talking deli," I say, suddenly hungry.

Inventing, drinking, cavorting, sweating. Recklessly ordering copies of Billy Blanks' T3 Tae Bo videos from Amazon. Doing, freely and without warning, cartwheels. There is no space in this office to do cartwheels. Taking some screwball job for the U.S. Fish and Wildlife Service, hanging out with dockworkers—no, *longshoremen*—and out-drinking them. Because no, Dent is not obligated to justify his life to us—

"Exactly *what*," Joel says, irritated now, "is 'pretty sweet' about me? It just doesn't make sense. Do you really think it's a rumor? Isn't a rumor supposed to have, you know, more *to* it? Some scandal? *Joel doesn't know how to use a napkin*—that's a rumor. Or *Joel's sperm is slower than a normal person's*. Does he really understand the proper use of that word?"

—but it'd be nice, and possibly helpful. Because we don't know what he's thinking, we don't know what it's like to be dying, unless you subscribe to that notion of life as one prolonged march-to-the-grave, one long decay: our skin flaking off, innards deliquescing, bags under our eyes drooping to the floor, chin swinging in a slight breeze. And we, working all day to buy makeup and clothes to cover the mess underneath, to hide our shame that we are melting. That we, embarrassingly enough, are mortal. Because we don't have the balls to get out of the office, into the wild and kill ourselves some dinner. Dine on fresh meat. Kill meat and dine on it. Not because it keeps us alive. Because we love the taste of blood.

But who has that view? It's absurd to have that view.

"*Weeego, weeego*," Joel has started muttering, watching Viggo Mortensen on YouTube again, pronouncing it "Weego," and referring to the site as "The YouTubes."

This is when I hang up.

FACT: Joel thinks he is tough. Joel is not that tough. Joel throws like a girl.

Joel.

Joseph J. Jones grew up in Birmingham, Alabama—city of, in my mind, gunfire and hootenannies—and has always insisted that *Forrest Gump* was a true story about a guy from his area. Joel lived the life of a Military Brat even though his family had no affiliation with the armed services. His family moved from Louisiana, to Georgia, and finally, Alabama, after his dad quit his job at an insurance underwriting company that was going under due to management problems: Rumor had it that the CEO lost composure after reading about trouble with the financial markets and burst from his office yelling, *All is lost! Abandon ship! All is lost!*

The Jones family arrived in Northbrook, IL just as Joel was entering high school, where, after an initial period of culture shock (which included bewilderment at this magical thing called *snow*), they met our family, the Wirths.

"May I introduce you to the Wirth family? They're part Jewish, you know."

"Part Jewish? Oh. How embarrassing."

Our town didn't frown on part-Judaism as much as it did on the flaunting of our part-Judaism. This most flagrantly occurred when I was failing at baseball. Or when I was condemned to **The Elkridge Camp for Poorly Dressed Families** for the summers, where they'd attempt to teach us about the wonders of geodes. The kids in the rich camp were boated out to Lake Michigan for waterskiing classes.

For the past two and a half years, Joel has been working for his uncle, and during those two and a half years, he has spent most of his time on the phone with me. I am not quite sure what Joel does for his uncle. I do know from the annual flu shot weeks at Emerson that he does not like needles, is terrified of them, in fact. I don't imagine him handling them much.

As far as I can tell, he is responsible for ensuring that when the hypodermics are shipped, they go to specialists at hospitals and med schools, and certified non-specialists—like people with diabetes—and no one else. This doesn't seem all that difficult to do, but what do I know? I am not in the needle-distribution industry. Joel says his job is more about developing a rapport with people, ensuring that they use only his uncle's hypodermics and no others. This entails, Joel says, expensing meals and getting his client's jokes. *Ooh-wee, that's funny!* I'm sure he says. *You're a funny guy! Look at this funny guy here! Ooh-wee!*

Working for his uncle wasn't Joel's Plan A. Joel, good spirit that he is, wanted to teach. He spent one year as a Seattle Educational Associate—a teacher, in other words—after which he couldn't look at those advertisements in the subway anymore, which should have read:

What do you call a room full of chemists, engineers and artists? Your first period class.

But after a year at a PS school in the Bronx, started looking like:

What do you call a room full of conmen, thieves and rapists? Your first period class.

He then tried to get a job at my company, SpectaCop, LLC, as a security manager, but didn't qualify. His problem wasn't a lack of intelligence—

"No go, Shel. Failed the pee test."

—but rather a lack of discipline. He couldn't keep clean long enough to pass the drug screening, couldn't go *two weeks* without getting high. So, after unsuccessful interviews at AGCO Corp and Georgia-Pacific, he took a job with his uncle, who, an early victim of the savings and loans crisis of the 80s, now runs the manufacturing arm of Marx Industries, a company that distributes branded medical supplies, including syringes (20-250 ccs) and hypodermic needles (short, med., and long bevel). And, if success is measured by the brightness of one's Enzo, does a very good job of it. Until I met Joel's uncle, I didn't realize Seattle was a Ferrari-owning type of city.

Joel's uncle, Mr. Enzo Driving Man, also—and this astounds me—has an elevator in his house. He no longer has to deal with stairs.

"You should come to Seattle, try out my elevator, huh," his uncle tells me, urging me to be impressed, ending nearly every sentence with *huh*. "It's ThyssenKrupp. *Cutting* edge of vertical transportation. Just like the one at the Ritz, huh."

"Huge a-hole, my uncle," Joel says of the man. "You should meet him one of these days. You two would get along."

"My elevator? It's just like this one. *Just* like it," he says when we step into the elevator at the Ritz.

"*Just* like it," he repeats, staring.

The Shit.

"I'm not so sure about your uncle," I say. "There's something . . . something *I-don't-know* about him."

"He's a little eccentric. He's a good guy."

Joel's uncle acts like The Shit. But he is not The Shit.

"Still, I can't take him. I'm not sure what it is, but he—"

"Whatever, Mr. Makes-Snap-Judgments."

Joel's uncle is not so smart. He refers to himself as "Chuckles," but in earnest. And to women as "cheeky broads," in earnest. His instinctive reaction upon seeing me is to give me a titty-twister—

"Tiiiiiiittytwisteeeeeerrrrrrrr!" he yells, lunging at me.

—despite the innumerable times I have made it clear that I do not like titty-twisters, that I would not wish the unwanted twisting of titty upon anyone.

"Now this guy, this guy *loves* tittytwisters, don't you . . . what's your name again?"

But he is not the type of guy who listens to someone like me. He is more preoccupied with talking about his protein diet, or his "hammies." He is a man who likes to make it known that he can dead lift 400 pounds. A man who uses words like higgledy-piggledy only because he can dead lift 400 pounds.

"Know what my secret is, huh?" he says as if enlightening me. "Two words: muscle confusion."

It would be nice to put him in his place, to cause him mild discomfort, like talk to him at a louder than necessary volume.

You a homo, huh? he says when I don't talk about cheeky broads with him. *You can tell me if you're a homo.*

I am in the middle of a *Sci-Fi* show, a program very much *like* the *X-Files*, noticeably influenced by the *X-Files*, but decidedly not the *X-Files*, and he wants to know if—

"When are you going to introduce me to Mr. Wirth, huh? When are you going to introduce me to your *husband*?"

Joel's uncle is sub-normal.

He seems like a guy who has trouble conjugating his verbs. Who has trouble with square roots. Who does not appreciate the musical mastery of the Boston Pops. Who eats sandwiches on the toilet. Big sandwiches, dropping pieces into the water as he munches.

I cannot over-emphasize how unpleasant I find Joel's uncle. I have picked more charismatic things out of my stool.

"Now this guy, *this* guy," he says, pointing to *that* guy, presumably a friend of his, "*this* guy likes poooontang!"

I want to tell him that no, I am not gay, that I have a beautiful, sensual girlfriend, and that his homophobia tends to be, well, revealing. He might do well to talk to someone about this obsession with others' sexuality. You know, get help.

"Man, you're swishier than the Vienna Boys Choir, aren't you, Shel?" he asks.

Nah. Fuck him. He looks like a guy who finds no joy in Cirque du Soleil. Who buys into the NordicTrack extended warranty agreement. Who misuses action verbs. Who thinks the answer to every math question is pi.

"What's 2 plus 2?"

"Pi."

"How about 2 plus 3?"

"Pi."

"2 plus 5?"

"Pi?"

Who overuses words like dillydally. Who does not fully appreciate the beauty of palindromes. Who corrects people on *Star Wars* pronunciations. Who fails at sex.

This is a man who strikes his wife.

"I don't understand why you don't like my uncle," Joel says. "You're both sorta assholes."

Asshole, for Joel, is another word for *sellout*, and Joel suffers from the wrongly held belief that this is what the two of us are. But I am nothing like Joel's uncle. I do not own or lease a 12-cylinder mid-engine sports car. I do not strike people with an abrupt desire for mouthwash on sight. And I am not a sellout. Using inert terms like *sellout*, Joel must know, is itself a form of selling out, at least in a lexical way. I suppose this is why he always says *asshole*.

It baffles, this charge of selling out. I never claimed to buy into anything to begin with. Oh, I rebelled, sure, but in a very conformist manner, doing things like drinking too much, or mouthing off, or engaging in subprime lending to people who couldn't possibly afford it. I work for a security company, managing rent-a-cops, joining the firm because I thought it would be like *Cops*. It is not like *Cops*. This is not selling out. It is Joel, if anyone, who has sold out. He works in, here it comes:

An office park.

Joel needs to reevaluate. When your work address is 506 Research Drive, just off Technology Way, you seriously need to reevaluate.

Trumpetfish: *n*) <u>Tropical</u> <u>fish</u> with a <u>long</u> <u>snout</u>. Native to Atlantic and Pacific waters. <u>Aulostomus maculatus</u>, Aulostomus chinensis.

It does exist. The trumpetfish does exist. I had thought that perhaps Dent was making it up—it sounds made up—so, as soon as I can, I look it up online. There it is, dictionary-defined.

Trumpet.

Fish.

Two sweet little tiny trumpetfish.

I cannot concentrate on anything but this, the line, the worst line in the email. The unnecessary editorializing on trumpetfish strikes me as boastful.

Joel knows. I'm sure of it. He knows that this Dent death scenario isn't something I haven't considered before, isn't anything I haven't turned about in my head I-don't-know-how-many times.

I close the browser, trying to recall the last time I *actually hoped* Dent would die. Years ago, by now. I used to remind myself to wish Dent dead at least once a day.

Dent, as smart as he was, never could get past his *honor thy body* credo. He did stupid stuff to it, stuff he saw on WWF and skateboarding shows, like constructing go-carts out of lawnmower engines. Or parachuting off his parents' garage with only a bike helmet and blanket.

Or setting his arm on fire. This was clever, I admit: He'd rub himself with Sterno, the stuff you light to keep fondue cheese warm. He'd put that on his arms and run around, yelling, *We're exploding! We're burning! We're exploding!* He'd do this on Halloween. I was a Teenage Mutant Ninja Turtle, the orange one; he, Strawberry Shortcake; and Joel—though this confounded most people he came across—was The *April Fool. Of April Fool's Day* fame, he explained. Soaked with shaving cream and pumpkin guts, he would go to school the next day with a hairless arm and still-visible TMNT makeup.

Or he would vocally complain during the *Pride and Prejudice* unit junior year that mandatory class discussions were "forced intercourse" and unlawful. Or turn the winter recital into the *Arsenio Hall Show* after his sister's (absolutely in*cande*scent) piano rendition of *Dance of the Sugarplum Fairy*. Or become more physical than necessary when playing backyard games like smear the queer, (which we could have just as easily called maul-ball if the name were nearly as detestable). Or employing only waders and a jumprope to kneeboard Lake Michigan (and wearing, incongruously, a goofy, yellow bifurcated snowboarding hat). Or openly carrying a pack of Marlboros in front of my mom, if only for the shock value:

"Dent, not in the house. My mom's home."
"Where am I supposed to put them?"
"I dunno. In your pocket?"
"Does my butthole count? The butthole's like a pocket, for the body. Ever see *Pulp Fiction?*"

Times like these were when I wished him dead.

I by no means wanted Dent to stay dead. It was simply for educational purposes. Perhaps he could have some painful run-in with an outboard motor, or a school of bloodthirsty trumpetfish, swarming over him pell-mell, leaving an arm or a head hanging by a tendril—but then return immediately, unblemished, to see what he had done, how stupid he was to put his life at risk, to treat his sometime genius-mind and Adonis-body so carelessly.

Oh no, Dent's dead!, I'd say, and until I heard that he actually *was dying*, this was all simply playacting, harmless fantasy. A way of making myself part of Dent's adventure, to experience his thrill, give myself an emotional stake in it—albeit in some smallish, warped way. It was vicarious. It was a tribute.

A tribute didn't seem so bad.

But now it's different. Now that I know about, now that the whole town knows about, the results, his pathology slides, I don't do it, and Joel certainly has no right to do it. Now that that word has made its way down the stark, drab, hallways of New Trier, our alma mater, into its congested lunch room, now that the whole town of Northbrook knows that Dent will end up bedridden, moldering in a hospital bed with little to no bladder control, calling for the nurse to sponge him, to wipe him, I don't do it. I don't have those ghoulish fantasies.

And everything that his dad (with his own problems, his heart issues) and his lesbian, lacking-in-the-way-of-matrimonial-fulfillment mother might have to go through, with the medical bills and the funeral arrangements and the whole grave-selection process—which must be the hardest thing in the world, picking out a plot for your only son, perhaps second only to actually burying him—I don't do it. I don't think of Dent's spending this last part of his life, ahem, "finding himself," shedding his inhibitions, (assuming that's what he's doing) which, sadly, some people still don't understand—

"Finding yourself is so JV."
"All the way. Poor control of the image. It's like that kid from *Into The Wild*. Very JV."

"So That-Kid-From-*Into The Wild* JV. A total Junior Varsity move, finding yourself."
—as weak, or a copout, at least not any more. Oh, and the rumors:
"Did you hear about Dent?"
"Who?"
"Dent. Dent Brown. Guy who dressed up like Strawberry Shortcake for Halloween."
"Uh..."
"Who got that Chicago Bears tattoo last year, the big football fan?"
"Oh! Yeah. That guy. That guy's cool. What about him?"
"Tried to kill himself the other day."
"What?"
"Yeah."
"No."
"Yeah."
"How?"
"Tried to hang himself."
"No."
"Mom found him in his room, ready to string himself up."
"God."
...
"That's pretty JV, man."
"Oh yeah. *Poor* control of the image."
"Jay vee all the way. Total junior varsity move, hanging yourself."
With these rumors, and his dad, I don't do that anymore. Now that all of this has happened, I don't have those fantasies about Dent, I don't think those things.
That would just be sick.

The Hatred.

It is after five PM, and I am still in the office. I am not working, but I am still here. Why am I still here? I do not understand why.

I spend the next two hours in the bathroom.

I sit in the bathroom stall, staring at stall graffiti that poses the question ARE YOU HAPPY. This forces me to wonder if I am happy, which makes me think that I may not be the happiest I can be, leading me to buy books and instructional videos on increasing my gross happiness, compelling me to question the very notion and definition of happiness, realizing that if I don't take some steps toward making my life a happier one I will never be happy as long as I live. Then I empty my bowels.

Then I exit the bathroom. Then I exit the office.

I overhear a child singing *Twinkle, Twinkle Little Star,* a song that I love and admire and have over the years formed an emotional connection to. Still, I can't help but wonder: Is there a techno version?

Then I enter a restaurant.

Then I politely ask the waiter for more of those delicious olive and pesto breadsticks but he says no. So I say again *more bread please,* but he says they have no more bread and I ask *why do you have no more bread.* And he says *because all the flour is gone* at which point I burst out the door and kick over the nearest trashcan I can find. I walk away only after making one hundred percent sure no one is around to see me go.

I return to the office.

I spend the next hour and a half to two hours in a variety of ways. I sort the items in my desk into piles marked "Safe" and "Unsafe," brainstorming ways to somehow alter the "Unsafe" items in ways that would make them otherwise. I make room in the corner of the office to do push-ups to exhaustion, which ends up being eleven and a half. I listen to a radio commercial informing me that I could be making thousands of dollars a week if only I'd harness the power of the internet, making me feel bad about not having harnessed the power of the internet already—I really should—compelling me to put it near the top of my TO DO list, just below UNLEASH THE BEAST and DISCOVER THE MAGIC OF VELCRO. I visit a lecture given by a female doctoral candidate on the topic of populism in mainstream media, which makes me reconsider my previous position on monetary policy in twenty-first century—WOW LOOK AT HER BREASTS! OH HOW THEY JIGGLE SO!—for our already-overburdened state legislatures.

I poke my head out the window and inform a passing pre-teen about sex. When a young boy of 10 or so years passes, I stop him, warn him that come puberty, his body will change in ways he can hardly fathom, watch him flee. Then I have a staring contest with a passing mail carrier and make him my bitch. Then I perform three ten-yard wind sprints with fifty seconds rest in between, after which I am spent. I return to the window and belt *OL' MAN RIVER* at the top of my lungs, even though there is no river in sight, even though I am more of a tenor when the song really should be sung by a bass or at the very least a baritone, even though I begin getting looks from passersby. I send an inquiry to the (*very* historical) Smithsonian, <u>your</u> portal to a universe of education and entertainment, with the intention of buying either Grandmaster Flash's turntable, Bozo the Clown's wig, or the Picasso Kunzite and Pearl Necklace but have second thoughts once I run some numbers and realize that any one of these three is much too much.

Then I give a knife to a baby as a playtoy.

I take a girl to PoundTown. Then I take her to Dumpsville. Then I go to Coolsville.

Someone named Kamal calls, a wrong number, and my immediate assumption is that he's of South Asian origin. Is this wrong? Then I take a moment to decide whether I should dress up for Halloween this year, and if so, if I would be more convincing as *Sexy Aaron Burr* or *Sexy Zach Braff*. And, if I happened to have a pet shar-pei, would I dress him up as Shar-Pei-let Johannsen or Joe Shar-Pei-Borough? I should remind myself NOT to let little Al Shar-pei-ton eat Snickers, as the chocolate could kill him in minutes.

This is how I spend my days.

I occupy the last half hour filing Inspection Reports and recounting the previous Saturday, which was spent watching *Ratatouille* (2007, Dir. Brad Bird) and a newly purchased Blu-Ray version of *Natural Born Killers* (1994, Dir. Oliver Stone). Amid stamping and organizing the papers, I wrangle with the question of whether the films were a good use of my time and finally decide that they were: Both are deeply symbolic cinematic masterpieces involving misunderstood but ultimately validated protagonists. I also consider their disparate depictions of the role of the media and its failings. After further thought on the issue, I conclude that I would definitely have sex with Kylie Minogue if given the opportunity.

Interlude
Somewhere in the South Pacific:
Possibly New Guinea, Probably French Polynesia.

The afternoon was fading and the cream-colored surf had turned blue-green when Denton Brown waded in. He blinked, angled his nose skyward. He inhaled. The air was cooling. He checked his watch, a stainless steel Casio Analog. Half past six.

He trotted farther out, passing two individuals whose genders were open to interpretation. The water was just below his knees now. The way he ran, his breaths measured, his gaze direct, palms flexing as if he were squeezing a plum—he had something in mind. He removed a wrinkled turquoise item from his back and sat, soaking his board shorts, water spilling over his waistline, inducing a shiver. He propped up his legs, using them as a sort of trestle for the item he had just removed from his back—a rucksack. He opened it and produced a few bound papers, the July issue of *Science*, a Turow thriller (bookmarked, miraculously, at the story's mathematical middle), and a postcard. Palm trees, bikinis. The statue of *David* in a thong. *Venus De Milo* in nothing. He reached for his breast pocket and withdrew a pen with a *Semester at Sea* logo, abandoned by some BC or Wesleyan freshman at the hostel's front desk. He placed the postcard on the science journal. He clicked the pen and started writing.

It was natural, of course, for people back home to expect him to communicate, to e-mail occasionally. So he did, though not altogether forthrightly. He tried to be consistent with the fictive Denton Brown—the free spirited, lion-hearted Dent—so many people back home mistook for the real Denton Brown. He could have treated these postcards as a sort of suicide mission, if he chose to—putting down that image some held of him as brave but troubled, clever but misguided. But trying to disillusion the unwilling seemed impractical, so he'd circulate the propaganda, reinforcing that view of him, that popular view. Yes, he was diving every day, partying at night, and getting tan and drunk and laid. And although it would be a mistake to think that tanning and drinking and screwing were all he was doing, that didn't mean he wanted people back home not to make such a mistake. If they believed that the epicurean—or hedonistic—lifestyle served the hungers of someone in his state of life, fine with him.

A distant, swooping bird plucked something out of the water. A red-footed booby, Dent noted. It took off. Dent liked the solitude of this place.

The main purpose of his letters was practical. They indicated (in not so many words) that his travels were safe, the sex was safe, he was safe.

Everything's fine, always will be, was his message. What resulted were foreign dispatches that played into their fantasies of him abroad by animating them with particulars (the hawkfish, the trumpetfish, Serge), and adding a happy ending. They were the Tolkien trilogy. Or was it *The Twilight Zone?* He would never apologize for it, but Denton M. Brown (Ind.) felt at times that he was prevaricating, running for office. Yes, these notes were propaganda.

The line of the pen turned from dark blue to sky blue to achromatic. He licked it, shook it like a cup of dye. The ochre, leaf-shaped pendant around his neck—a parting gift from a part-time girlfriend, a better-than-average Tiffany's knockoff—began to quiver.

Even if they were to end up as emails, he preferred composing his messages this way. Writing by hand, *penning*. It was tactile, real. He could dip a thumb in the water and smear the ink. There was something strangely *progressive* about it, in the archaic sense of the word. His wrist was spry, operational. It was eastbound. Typing, on the other hand—the flailing fingers, captive wrists, masturbatory posture—seemed dishonest. It seemed work-shy.

He scribbled again on the postcard, creating an invisible furrow across the paper that soon filled again with ink. He continued his note.

Dent liked the way the surf encircled his ankles, how it occupied that space between the thighs and torso, creating a little eddy in the center of him. He would compose the postcard here, nearly waist deep in surf—those beads on his back, were they perspiration? The water's spray?—then, later, rewrite it at the computer. Transcribe it to email, in hack job form. Foreseeable adjectives, ramshackle sentence structure, wrong diction. He aimed for lackadaisical, and he presumed his recipients would take a lackadaisical approach. They would skim it, forget it. They would delete it. Yes, they would surely delete it. They would have no idea that he was up to something. Was he up to something? If so, it would be impossible to tell from this undue emphasis on the wrasse, the blenny, the trumpetfish.

Screw the trumpetfish. Really. Who remembers something like that?

The sky had now darkened. Dent fed the papers into his rucksack and zipped it up. He loped back to shore, toward a beachside pub with a sign that said BARRACUDA BAR. He passed silver streamers and sat at the bar, cupping a black and rust-red ashtray labeled THE BUTT HOLE, his head nearly touching one of the lower rafters. The bartender was a bald, birch-skinned man with a *Macy's Thanksgiving Day Parade* tee shirt. He was clearly a dumbshit. The dumbshit bartender recited their drink offerings:

Bud or Bud Light.

"Oktoberfest?"

Fuck you. Bud or Bud Light.

"Hefeweizen?"

His Bud Light came in a mason jar.

Dent sipped the Bud Light. He removed the postcard from the rucksack and held it up to the light. He reread it, memorized it—or the jist of it—then tore it into strips and deposited them in the THE BUTT HOLE. Regardless of whether he was or wasn't experiencing pain, the only thing he never discussed in those notes was whether he was experiencing pain. He didn't *feel* sick. He felt calm but powerful, fighting fit.

Trumpetfish? Screw the trumpetfish.

He swilled the remainder of his Bud Light. He burped and called for another, making cursory inquiry into the going price of boats, something safe and cheap, a pilothouse or skiff, aluminum preferably. Then he swiveled and leaned on the bar with the half-eyes and left behind elbows of a man who had every intention of carrying out nothing that month. The bar was out of clean mason jars. His Bud Light came in a Coca-Cola mug this time.

Dent's Stories—Not Recommended Reading.

We expected certain things from Dent's emails. We expected them to be dirty, gritty. We expected to hear about the bars, the strip clubs, the peep shows, the sex shows, the live sex shows, the red light district, everything. We expected to hear about places with signs like ALL NUDE REVUE and PING PONG SHOW. We expected that one story—of dubious authenticity but still somehow right-sounding, somehow just plausible enough to produce a collective shudder from everyone in the room—about Beddy, the Scottish Protestant from Jacksonville, FL.

Oh, you don't know about Beddy?

So this one guy, Beddy, the 5'6", 260 lb Scottish Protestant from Jacksonville, FL, joined the tour group at the tail end of the trip after challenging us to a game of Hearts at a bar in Tahiti. Throughout the duration of the game Beddy kept insisting that WHEEL OF FORTUNE's Pat Sajak was stalking him, hitting on him, trying to sleep with him, which was strange, but we assumed it was just his deadpan sense of humor.

The next day, Beddy convinced everyone to spring for a $200 hopper flight to Bora Bora, where he became separated from the group, appearing again two hours later insisting that he had just slept with a middle-aged Thai hooker who gave her name as Bye Bye and smelled of Winstons and marmalade. Beddy decided to relate every salacious detail of his rendezvous with Bye Bye, and for weeks afterwards, after everyone had returned to work, in their barren little office cubicles, they chattered about the story over email (using Code words like *Code Red*, in reference to the event, so as not to set off company alarm bells), agreeing that yes, Beddy probably wasn't lying when he said he slept with that girl named Bye Bye; and he probably wasn't lying when he included the detail that Bye Bye was having female issues; and he probably wasn't lying when he included the additional details that Bye Bye had genital lice and that—close your ears, because this is what I mean when I say it gets 'dirty'—he went down on her. Needless to say, Beddy was an off-duty United States Marine Corps Staff Sergeant.

Possibly true, probably untrue story.

It was the kind of story we expected from Dent. Instead, we got the trumpetfish.

III.

@ggray: *So that day, just before he left—do you think he was trying to hurt you guys so you wouldn't forget him?*
@shelgames: Yes. At least that's Joel's theory. I can't be quite sure. Dafna thinks the opposite. She thinks he was trying to hurt us so . . .
@ggray: *So you wouldn't have any desire to remember him?*
@shelgames: Yes, it's an oversimplification, but essentially that's what she thinks. Thinks that by becoming more contemptible as a person he was making his eventual passing less tragic for us.
@ggray: *Do you agree?*
@shelgames: With Dafna or Joel?
@ggray: *Either. Both.*
@shelgames: I guess they're valid ideas.
@ggray: *You have a better one?*
@shelgames: No. No, not really. I tried to call him the day after to talk about it, but his mom picked up. She said he wasn't there. I couldn't tell if she was lying, but she said that he wanted to visit the planetarium before he left. This sounds strange, but you don't know Dent—he loved that nerdy *final frontier* stuff. He'd spend hours in the planetarium. He'd browse the exhibits, he'd get lost in there. There was something about exploration, about discovery—anyway, I haven't really thought about why he flipped out. Why think about it? Why try to remember or forget it? It happened. It's unchangeable. I'm not sure it can be explained, but what's the use of trying? Dent's dying. That's all I need to know.

@ggray: *But you can always change your perspective on it.*
@shelgames: *That's a bullshit argument. You can change your perspective on anything. Why start with this?*
@ggray: *I guess that's one way of looking at it.*
. . .
@ggray: *Spank me.*
@shelgames: *What!?*
@ggray: *Nothing, nothing.*

THE OFFICE, PM

It is just after four o'clock now, and I am troubled. I have just secreted a gelatinous substance and am holding it in my palm. I can't determine which of my orifices it came from. I think *mouth*, because I felt something in there. Though some of it is still hanging from a nostril—did this mystery substance come from there? I poke it inquisitively. It responds by sighing.

This is worrisome, this goo in my palm. I have never seen anything like it.

It moves.

I swear I see it move. It seems to swell in my hand, shapeshift. I wipe it off with a Kleenex, deposit the Kleenex in a Ziploc baggie, drop it in the trash, my paranoia abating.

But still. The thought of it sitting in the trash disturbs me.

I am in need of a banana. I am struck with the feeling that such scrutiny of the glob, this deconstruction, is somewhat silly, like the director of an infomercial demanding more from his actors. Eating something might take my mind off of it. So I grab a banana, always a good distraction, because I have a banana ritual. It proceeds hencely:

1) First, I pretend I am Frank Langella.
2) Second, when the banana is fresh and unpeeled, I break it in two. This demonstrates my strength.
3) Then, I stuff an entire half into my mouth, but I don't chew, believing passive ingestion to be more conducive to nutrient absorption. This demonstrates my wisdom.
4) As it dissolves in my mouth, I think about nothing but the banana.

Cha-qui-ta ba-na-na!, I sing, immediately fearing my coworker might have heard.

Did he hear? No. He is shouting at his computer screen. I think I hear him threaten to sue the internet.

I am mid-banana when the phone rings again. I soon discover—
"Hello?"
"Sheldon Wirth?"
"Yes?"
"This is Coach Peyton Gladdup."
"Coach Gladdup? From New Trier?"
"Yup. I'm calling as part of my –"
"Joel?"—that Joel has no idea how to make a crank call.
"No, this is Gladdup. I'm calling as part of my child abuse rehabilitation program."
"What are you doing, Joel?"
The banana was a bad idea. It has become messy.

Coach Peyton "Gym Shorts" Gladdup was the varsity wrestling coach our Junior year at New Trier, the public high school we attended. Gladdup had a coldly scientific, Lenin-esque stare, and by no means endorsed the *There Are No Stupid Questions* dictum held so dearly by the other teachers. I instantly liked him. Gladdup said what you'd expect from any coach, but briefly, and in the way that made you forget he was just talking about a mat and three two-minute rounds. He would then blow his whistle—it was always that green whistle—and everyone did takedowns for ten minutes. Then—in a grand show of power—Gladdup would flex his gluteals. You could see it through his shorts.

Are we men, men? he'd yell.
We are.
*Are we **men**, men?*
Yes, sir.
Full bore! Gladdup would yell. *Go at him FULL BORE!*

Two years after graduating from New Trier, we learned that Coach Gladdup had been indicted for abuse, for hitting a student.

"No surprise there," Dent had said, but I thought it was my job to defend him. *It was a motivational technique, a **go-get 'em** tap, and the kid was hit, not harmed*—but it was useless. We never read about the outcome of the case but assumed some kind of plea bargain was reached.

Now, on the line with Fake Gladdup/Joel, I'm not sure I have the patience, but Fake Gladdup/Joel continues:

"Step eight of this program is to call my victims, to find out how they're doing and apologize to them."

"That's for alcoholics," I say. "I'm pretty sure child abusers aren't supposed to contact their victims."

"I also have a confession. When you were wrestling, I used to fantasize about you in that tiny singlet you wore. You were so alive, so vibrant. So young. I wasn't able to touch you, so all I did was blow on that whistle of mine. It was the only release for me."

"We're on child fetishization now? Terrific. So classy."

This must be the end point. It's over.

But no. It's not close to over. Nothing for Joel is ever over. Joel never listens to me.

"When I used to coach you, did you see me flexing my butt muscles?"

"Your gluteals?"

"My gluteals. Did you see me flexing them? That was for you, Shel. I did that for you."

"That's nice," I say, busy with a piece of scratch paper on which I have scrawled and Xed out Joel's name five or six times.

"And in case you were worried, I no longer have that whistle. I threw that whistle away. Now, if I may, I have some advice for you."

"Oh good," I say, scratching out *Joel J. Jones* for the eighth time.

"I think you should visit Joel and Dent and in Seattle. You haven't seen Dent in months, and he's not going to be stateside all that often. You should make the trip. I know you've tried, but I need you to redouble your efforts."

Coach Gladdup always liked that phrase "redouble your efforts." He seemed to think it would in some way motivate us.

"Can you do that for me? Can you redouble your efforts?"

He wants to play? Fine.

"I would visit, I was *planning* on visiting, to see Dent, but I hear Joel's going to be there, and I don't know about running into him. Grade-A slapdick, Joel is. A waste of life. Did you know he hasn't had a real job since college? He works for his uncle, putzing around all day, selling catheters or something, and boozing and womanizing at night. You should try calling him. You should—"

"They're not catheters." Gladdup has died. "We sell hypodermics and syringes, not catheters."

"You broke character."

"I know."

"That's pretty unprofessional of you, to break character and all."

"I know."

His accent is back. He sounds like a hick again.

"And you forgot to mention Gladdup's divorce. Remember how he always talked about his ex-wife? How their divorce was tragic, psychologically ruinous for him? You didn't really prepare for the role all that much, did you?"

"I know, shut up. It just seems like, whenever you used to communicate with us, you used to act interested. Engaged. Now, nothing. Is there something wrong? I mean other than—" he says, clearly setting himself up for a joke, swallowing his mirth, "other than your castration nightmares and functional diarrhea?"

Does The Apollo know about Joel? It should.

Joel wants to know if there is something wrong with me. Yes, there is something wrong with me. Very wrong. Ted Bundy-esque, but in an endearing way. Something so wrong that I often think that it, this wrongness, will somehow manifest itself physically. I'll wake up one morning to discover that I have some sort of scar, or spinal disfigurement, or better, a supernumerary nipple. I'll wake up and be radioactive. I'll wake up and be invisible. Or an invertebrate, a bug, transformed to a Kafka-esque state, something too hideous to keep from my parents or neighbors or State Farm guy. An indication, a sign. Joel knows.

"Just tell me what's wrong," Joel says. "I'll understand if you just tell me."

I got a bad haircut once and thought that was it—*This is it!*, I thought, *This is the sign!*—but it grew out.

"Nothing's wrong."

"Promise?"

"Promise."

We pause.

"You on drugs?" he says as if asking whether I've had lunch already.

"I wish. Why do you care so much?"

"You're just so negative all of the time, and that's . . . that's wrong. It's my job to disabuse you of that notion."

"Don't use that language with me."

"*Disabuuuse you,*" he coos.

"I'm serious."

"I mean, don't you remember the good times you had senior year, with Dent? When you'd freak out the cheerleaders?"

Oh, I remember. We, Dent and I, would skulk through the hallways, asking the cheerleaders, whom we could hear from across the hallway (Boys!!!!! Eeeek!!!! Boys!!) if their "chicken" was quote-unquote *funky* (and if so, *how* funky?), and which of the following would best describe their "goose":

a) Loose!

b) Totally loose!!

c) Cooked

d) None of the above

This behavior gave way to other activities as soon as we were old enough for driver's licenses, at which point we amused ourselves by holding Autobahn-inspired drag races on Lake Shore Drive.

Dent was always the initiator. He was always the one who gave voice to every opinion I was too afraid to express myself.

"Yeah," I say, "We got the strangest looks. Pretty funny, all that."

"You can relive that! Don't you want to relive that?"

"*Relive* that?"

"Recapture it. With *him*. Anyway, I'm sure he'd like to see you."

"I know. I'm just not sure I have time."

"I'm sure he'd appreciate it. We don't know how long it will be until he's back here again."

"Let's be rational about . . . this," I say, catching a pencil about to roll off my desk. "Like I told you before, I don't know if I have the—"

"Especially with the cancer, and you being the only close friend he has, the only thing that really keeps him alive, it seems like—"

"*What?* You're making it out like I'm crucifying him, like I'm some kind of Pontius Pilate. I'm the *only thing that's keeping him alive?* Dent doesn't have cancer. He's vacationing."

"It just seems like visiting him is the least you could do."

"Dent *doesn't have cancer.*"

I did not start out this way. I was a good person once, brimming with promise. Only two summers ago, I would volunteer errands for my neighbor, an elderly woman whose unbroken longing for extra liniment and tissue paper at K-Mart I might have classified as neediness if it were any fault of her own. Or spend an afternoon handing fittings to a turpentine-scented plumber, his head under the sink, the exactness of his consonants that of someone delivering a baby.

Joel, too. Joel would quarter up with an old Korea vet for an evening, sorting through his wilted issues of *Waterfowl* magazine, liking the shiver of his voice and slipping a pinch of Vicodin into his drink at his request. We used to be people who volunteered for elder care, helping the lady on Manitowic Ave. file her old 1040s into an accordion folder labeled "DEATH AND" for storage. People who donated our old slate-faced G.I. JOEs to the Christmas Toy Drive.

Now?

"So this girl," Joel says, amazingly transitioning from our Visiting Dent/Having Cancer discussion, "*this girl* is interesting, see, because I <u>do not</u> think she is in the least attractive, but I <u>would</u> like to lick every part of her with my bare tongue. So she's a tricky one. Her name is Karen."

Now we wait, biding our time in our offices, sustaining ourselves with food from the Wen Ho Chow guy with the prohibitive sneer, our sense of purpose stunted, regard for appearance long since atrophied, wearing shirts underneath shirts that say I CAN'T BELIEVE IT'S NOT BUTTER or RED LOBSTER or NIKE, frittering away our days bragging about imaginary sponsorships. Or reminiscing about that one kid in high school who took the ACTs instead of the SATs, wondering what kind of smack he's selling now. Or posting obvious questions on the Jews-for-Jesus message board.

Now we speak gibberish. Now—

"Mine smell like stroganoff."

"Mine have muscle memory."

—we discuss our privates over the phone. Or feuding over which would win in a death match between competing teen summer programs, *Nols* or *Outward Bound*. Or making up new names for Fenway's wall, deciding *The Green Monster* has become tired: *The Jade Dragon. The Jolly Green Giant. The Emerald Gargoyle.*

Have you heard the one about the Seventh Day Adventist and the Jew? No? The Seventh Day Adventist/Jew joke is not a funny joke; in fact, it is a terrible joke. But we have told and retold the SDA/J joke, making the very repetition of the joke into its own little joke, telling every person walking into our office that joke (Sometimes the Jew becomes a rabbi, a distinction which, for the purposes of this joke, does not need to be made), then falling on the floor over ourselves at the telling of the story of our beloved Seventh Day Adventist and Jewish person, delighting in the badness of the joke.

How lucky of Dent to have had such wise and funny mentors. We, Joel and I, are still under the impression that we molded Dent. That we taught him our sense of humor, our way of thinking and acting and being. We, somehow, were responsible for his maturation, his familiarization with and integration into the high school food chain. We helped him navigate the hallways of New Trier, taught him how to cope with the sometimes dense teachers in Cook County's 203 School District, the sometimes surly cops in the 60065 zip code. Told him that Stussy shirts were for posers and Nautica shirts were for homos. Told him which smoking circles to join, which to avoid. Told him whom to approach for answers to his problem set, and who to sit with at lunch, and who to avoid at lunch. We tested him and tempted him. We showed him who should be rewarded, who punished. We taught him how to steal, just for the thrill. How to *quote* take names *unquote* and *quote* kick ass *unquote*:

See that guy? We should make life tough for that guy.

Why? Why would we do that?

Look at him. The one with the Reeboks.

You don't like him because of his Reeboks?

No. See how happy he is?

Yeah. He looks pretty happy. That's nice.

His life is too easy.

How do you know what his - ?

We should make life tough for him.

That's not a good reason.

He doesn't know what we know. He doesn't know that life is unfair. We can help him understand how unfair it is. Steal his Reeboks. Or something.

What are you talking about? You guys are lucky. You have it made. Your life isn't tough.

We're not saying it is.

So then what are you—±

But what if it is? What if our life is tougher than you realize? You don't know what kind of pressure we're under here. You don't know.

Pressure? We're freshmen. You know this is wrong. You know this is treacherous territory.

His life is too easy. Look at him and his Reeboks. I bet he wants us to make life tough for him.

This is absurd. You know how absurd this is, right?

We should at least slash his tires.

Dent would have been helpless without us.

We instructed him, held him under our tutelage, knowing that coaching him on how to run roughshod over the considerations of others would steel him, prime him for future success. But it was just for the time being. It was done knowing he would surpass us. He would take the school by storm. And after the school, the state. And then the nation, and then the world! Everything! He would take everything by storm. All thanks to us. And after this storming of the state, the nation, the world, he would represent us. He would remember us.

This is how we would be immortalized. *We*, Joel and I – we knew how to spot talent. *We* were the ones who found him. We discovered Dent.

Sheldon Wirth and Joel Jones discovered Denton Brown.

"You are being churlish with me," Joel says when I refuse to talk to him. "You are a churlish churl today, Mr. Sheldon Wirth. Chin up, man. *Chin up.*"

I should not be here. I should not be doing this. I hold the phone to my ear regardless, as if there were nothing left of me.

"Churly churl!"

There is an hour left in the day. I have no idea what to do right now.

I know what to do right now.

Right now I am in love with Ruane Manning.

Yes, I adore that man, Ruane Manning. Ruane Manning is my hero, my everything. Ruane Manning came to me in a dream, held my hand, was tender with me, talked to me about the differences between vertical thinking and lateral thinking, carried me when times were rough. I have to ask my coworker about him—

"Hey Gregory, what do you know about Ruane Man—"

"Not now, Shel."

—but my coworker does not know who Ruane Manning is. If you do not know who Ruane Manning is, you should learn who he is. Ruane Manning is a well-known horse painter and positive-psychology guru of sorts. He has the name of a black person, but get this—he is *white*. We used to call this sort of person a wigger, which is a white person who looks or acts like a black person.

"Ruane Manning!" I say.

"Ru-ane! Man-ning!" Joel says, somehow still on the phone.

"*Motherfucking* Ruane Manning," I say again.

Ruane Manning's reverence for the animal form is well known. Do you own Ruane Manning's lovely painted horse clock? Or his decorative hummingbird sandstone coasters? You should.

"If you were stuck on a desert island with Ruane Manning—"

"Oh I would. I so would."

I am not sure if Ruane Manning is still alive. Can I be honest with you? I hope he is. Mr. Manning needs to be researched. I return to my office. I kick off a shoe and open my browser, humming, clicking the mouse in 4/4 time.

There are scores, hundreds, nay, thousands, of websites dedicated to Ruane Manning. Mr. Manning would have appreciated each of them, even the negative ones, as they are all unique in their own way. They highlight his optimism, his welcoming, understanding manner. And although he is an icon of the seventies more than anything else, they point out that he is as relevant today as ever.

Maternal Instincts. Striped Innocence. Love and Devotion. These are some of Ruane Manning's most heartfelt works. Eagles. Wolves. Kittens. I search for more on Ruane, and decide that tomorrow, I am going to wear a hat to work. Tomorrow I'll be a hat person. A bowler. Or a deerstalker. Or I'll take up an interest in wicker. But for now, I spend hours on the web, poring over *I HEART Ruane Manning* literature, until, just before I leave, the phone awakens me from a near-reverie:

"Hello? Joel?"

"Hey, Shel."

But it's not him. For the first time today, it's not Joel, unless he star-six-sevened. But I don't think Joel knows how to star-six-seven. This is momentous, that it's not Joel.

"It's Dafna."

Oh. Shit.

"Dafna who?"

"Asshole."

"Dafna *who?*"

Dafna, the only person outside my nuclear family who causes my usually defective emotional memory to function at normal levels. Dafna, butcher, meat-seller, annihilator of reproductive vitals. Dafna, the woman who doesn't believe in weddings.

"Dafna, the erstwhile love of your life."

"Never heard of her."

There's a soft sigh.

"Dafna-shut-up. I just called to talk, Shel."

"Did Joel tell you to call?"

"What? No."

"Oh. I was just on the phone with him, so I thought—anyway, I'm not home right now. You free to chat later?"

"Of course I'm free, Shel-don. You'll call—What day is it today again? Friday?—you'll call sometime tonight?"

"Sure."

"Ok, I'll talk to you—"

"Wait. One more thing."

"Yes?"

"Whom do you think is the superior painter? The early Ruane Manning or Ruane Manning during his later years, his so-called *blue period?*"

"Who?"

"Never mind."

"Okay," she says, "I'm going to bed at 11:30. Remember to call before then. Bye."

It crosses my mind to tell Dafna that she's mendacious. Two-faced. That she was a false friend, a false girlfriend, a liar. Conniving. That she ruined my life and the lives of those around her. I could tell her all of this, but I won't. I could call her a bitch, a slut—a slutty, slutty, woman-slut. I could call her an ignorant-of-all-things-Ruane-Manning-philistine, or a lifty-shoed floozie, but I won't.

Bye, I forget to say.

I hang up and turn on *Recovery Radio* just as they are breaking for a commercial extolling the virtues of healthy gums. My thoughts quickly turn to the alarming effects of gingivitis, then to possible ways of combating it. Although *Crest Whitening Expressions Cinnamon Rush* has been refreshing as well as effective, I should consider *Colgate Luminous Paradise Freshô* if I really plan on getting the most out of my toothpaste, but before I can form a coherent opinion on the topic, *Recovery Radio* returns just in time to take a call from Christopher—recovering Computer Solitaire and methamphetamine addict—who, now 50 lbs less obese than he was a year ago, has some very positive things to say about second chances.

Chin up.

I was not honest with Dafna. I am not going to call her back.

I was prepared to say things to her. Things like: No Forgive Late Last Down Bitch Never Stop Wrong Not Nope Slut.

Also, ho bag. Ho. Bag.

But I don't. I don't say those things.

You'd have to be a bad person to say words like that to a woman.

I do not talk about Dafna. If I talked about Dafna, I would talk about the time at Walmart, how I remember everything I bought, to the item.

11 February, 2003, Walmart Aisle 2.

I am in Aisle 2 at *WALMART*, carrying Band-Aids and dental floss and Fig Newtons and breath mints and A&W Diet Cream Soda and condoms, balancing them against my chest, ready to pay. As I approach checkout, I spot a Butterfinger at the counter. I grab it.

"Is this on sale?" I ask the check out clerk, holding the edge of the Butterfinger like a dirty Kleenex. The clerk immediately strikes me as someone who cuts corners. One of those people who took a sponge bath when he really should have taken a real shower. His name is GARY.

"Uh . . ." GARY wants me to ask him about their specials on Wet Wipes. I refuse to inquire about such matters.

"Uh, I don't know. Don't think so." I do not like this name, this name of GARY. I am not going to name any of my kids GARY.

"Okay. Thanks."

I wait as GARY checks me out. It takes longer than it should. He doesn't ask for a discount card. I don't have one, but still. He should ask.

"De da doooo," I say, waiting for GARY to finish.

I take the bagged items and leave. I return to the apartment and head into the kitchen. I sit on the counter and begin unpacking my items, sliding the Fig Newtons down the soapstone surface. They fall into the sink. I unwrap the Butterfinger and take a bite.

"Shel. Shel-don."

I glance behind me. Dafna is on the sofa, one leg draped over the arm. I lower myself from the counter.

"Come here," she says.

I walk around the couch. Yes. Oh Yes. She is wearing almost nothing. Save for some very tight short-shorts (they say DUKE) and a few pages of newspaper draped over her body, she is naked. It looks like *The Post*.

"Did you get them?"

She is trimming her cuticles.

"Yeah. Here."

I hold out the condoms. It looks like the newspaper she's wearing is in fact *The Onion*, I can't tell. Are the headlines funny?

"So, are you ready?"

I smile. Ready.

"I've taken off my purity ring." This must be meant as a joke.

Is she's wearing the *Huffington Post*? It's hard to tell. I'm not sure if the HuffPost comes in print format. Some interesting news about De Kalb today, looks like.

There is too much light. I draw the curtains.

"Shel-don. Relax, Shel-don. I'm just being a goad, a *tease*," she says, the *s* in *tease* sibilant. She has been drinking.

She turns over. Her back. Look at it. She always had the sexiest back. Soft like bread. She has no idea how much she arouses me, how her smell, her taste, arouses me. A less diplomatic boyfriend might tell her what he wants to *do* to her. Not me. I am not that type of person. I used to be that type of person. I was the type of man who approached women like a steam engine, treated them like steer. I was Western in my approach. But I have learned from my mistakes. I now view romantic interaction more like a peace concert, a smoke-in. I recognize the importance of patience in intimacy. Abstaining from pleasure, I now know, can be as sensual as engaging in it.

This has prompted me to experiment with deep oil massage and scented candles, has led me to the realization that the nonverbal components of romance are—

"Come here," she says. "Come here *now*."

I obey.

I sit on the couch, brushing aside an old Com Ed bill and a paperback Narnia book. It looks like the *Dawn Treader*.

I press my palms into her shoulder and press down, in a CPR position. Dafna sighs.

"Mmmm," she says.

HEY **BUDDY.** YOUR GIRLFRIEND HAS PRETTY NICE **EYES.**

What was that?

I turn, look at the twenty-one inch Trinitron, which is showing a movie that has been formatted to fit the screen. A group of teenagers is having problems with their virginity.

DID YOU HEAR ME MOTHER**FOOLER?** I SAID YOU GIRL-FRIEND HAS PRETTY NICE **EYES.** I COULD **PARTY WITH** HER ALL NIGHT.

This must be network TV. The dubbing is terrible.

I AM GOING TO **SLAP** YOU IN THE **FACE, STUPID** says someone else, presumably the boyfriend of the girlfriend.
"Now rub my shoulders," says Dafna.

DON'T YOU MOTHER**FOOLING** TALK ABOUT HER LIKE THAT, **STUPID.**

"Lower. Softer. That's perfect. You're perfect, Shel-don."

OH YEAH? I WOULD **PARTY WITH** HER IN THE **GARAGE,** IF I DIDN'T THINK YOUR DIRTY **VOLKSWAGEN** HAD ALREADY BEEN THERE.

We laugh. What might have been a pretty good insult (though it's hard to tell) has been ruined. Or improved on, maybe.

FOOL OFF.
KISS MY **CHEEK.**

We laugh again, fall over each other.
"You're per-fect."
We bump noses, click teeth. She giggles. Sometimes awkwardness improves sex. She digs her nails into my back. Sometimes pain does, too.
I stop massaging her. I smell her. I can't place it exactly, but her scent is that of some sort of spice. Nutmeg? I kiss her shoulder, the same spot I had just been rubbing. It is a tender kiss.
"Mmmmm," she says.
She turns over and grabs my belt with one hand. She runs her finger down her body and **RUBS** her **FEET** with one hand, grabbing my **BELT**

with the other. I take off my shirt, unbutton my pants. I grab her **PURSE** while she **KISSES** my **CHEEK**. Then I tenderly **DRIVE MY VOLKSWAGEN** into **THE WASH** and start **REVVING** her **ENGINE** until she **IS CLEAN**. She has a small tattoo of a starling on her abdomen. I kiss it.

Call me Fraulein Maria, she whispers.

We are tender with each other. We are so gentle.

Oh Korvettenkapitan George Ludwig! she cries. She frequently does this, the minor role-playing, exploring various forms of the master-slave relationship. I wasn't so sure about it at first, but I she has made me come around. There is nothing violent about it. It is transgressive, sure, but isn't that the point? There is nothing degrading about it, not in any real sense, at least. Even when she is **CHANGING** her **OIL**. It is all so careful. It is considerate. It is clear we care. We both care so much. And just as I am about to **HIJACK** her **JETTA,** my phone rings—

"Shel! Hey Shel! Guess what part of my body I'm touching right now. Can you guess? I'll give you a hint: It's not my head and it's not my knees. It's below my nipples."

—and I talk to Joel. I know I shouldn't answer, but I do. Dafna gives me a *What are you doing?* Look. I give her a *sorry!* look. I drop the phone. I resume, slowly **LIQUIDATING** her **INVENTORY,** and grabbing her **PURSE** with my **WALLET**. But something's wrong. I can't concentrate. *Man, I cannot concentrate.* Because now I am thinking about Joel, about what part of his body he was touching. He has planted this seed in my head. It will not—

"Okay, now I'm now pinching it. Guess which part of my body I'm pinching.'"

—let me go. *His ankles? Is he pinching his ankles? His bellybutton?* Even as I am trying to **PRORATE** Dafna's **MORTGAGE**, he is likely not touching any part of the area near his crotch. That would be obvious. On the other hand, Joel is the obvious type, and—

"Have you guessed? Here, I'll hold it up to the phone for you. There. I'm holding it up to the phone. *Can you hear me? Is it making a noise?*"

God. Why is he doing this to me? This call, it was ill-timed, de trop. To say the least. But it is too late. I need to know what part of his body he is touching. It has me hypnotized, dazzled. *Holy fucking shit, I need this information.* I will not be able to go on with my life if I do not obtain this information. I will not last one more minute without knowing what Joel and his *worthless*—

Dafna pushes me away.
"Forget it, Shel," she says.
"What?"
"This isn't working. You're somewhere else."
"No. Stop. Just let me—"
"I said *forget* it."
She grabs her shirt and goes into the bathroom. I am alone.

FOOL *YOU*! says the T.V.
WELL **FOOL** YOU, TOO, **BUDDY**!

I cannot tell you what Dafna did. Dafna did the worst thing. She did the unforgivable thing. Talking about Dafna makes me remember. I do not talk about it, about Dafna.

I do not talk about Dafna. Talking about Dafna makes my toes curl. It makes my gonads shrink.

FACT: Dafna is stronger than she looks.

IV.

Saturday Morning.

No, no. People are trying to hurt me today. It is afternoon on Sunday, and I have made a habit of never going to church (as I've done all my praying for the fiscal year), so I am still in bed, hiding under my Gainsborough bedding, seeing nothing but the slate-gray coloring of filtered light.

I usually spend Sundays parading naked around my apartment, singing Lady Gaga songs, substituting the words "Sadly Chaste" for "Poker Face," and changing the lyrics *"bluffin' with my muffin,"* to *"toggle my hornswoggle."* But today is different. Today, I can't move or speak. I lay awake last night wondering if Simon of *Simon Says* fame has a last name and whether he accepts parcels at his home address. Then I stayed awake considering whether underarm odor and the taking of steps to effectively combat underarm odor is ever a priority for you if you're the type of person who kills prostitutes.

Now, I can't expose myself to the day. Bad things will happen. I know it. Even with the day half spent under covers, wasted, it will not go well. Comets will rain from the heavens. There will be a plague. Sudden impotence will hit. Already I have a cyst on my arm, huge, in the shape of a mini cheese wheel, one of those wax-covered things—and I realize I have caught Dent's disease. Yes, it's contagious. I'm now the first face-melting victim in a sequel to *Outbreak*. I should be hospitalized, hooked to a machine that represents my vitals graphically, aurally—with bolt-shaped lines, high-frequency burps—and now I am a patient in one those medical miracle dramas—one who has just awakened to learn that he was technically dead for two minutes, his heart having stopped in the middle of a procedure with the word *bypass* in it, revived only by God's good grace and the wherewithal of some prodigy summer resident.

So I know the day will not go well. I can sense this. My instincts are to peek out, survey the terrain, take stock of potential dangers, and if anyone tries to approach me, retract into the covers, tell them, "Go away! Shel's not here!" Can't I be a voyeur today? Can't I watch? This bed is in need of a periscope.

Or a catheter. But these kinds of arrangements have not been made, so I get out, pulling the comforter behind me. I wear it like a muumuu and lumber to the bathroom. There is hair in the toilet bowl. Gross.

Then, the phone. This is when my phone rings. Why does my phone harass me so? It is an evil phone, this one. Osama bin Laden must have had a phone like mine.

I pick up. It is worse than I thought.

"Hey. It's me."

"Dafna who?"

"You didn't call me back."

Hooh boy. She is out for blood. She is going to crucify me.

"Sorry I didn't call you back. Really. I was busy. It slipped my mind."

. . .

"Forget about it."

Forgotten. Bloodless.

. . .

"So, what are you up to?" I ask. I step on a scale, still wearing the comforter.

"Nothing. Just trying to find Roquefort right now."

"The place?'

"The cheese. Is there such thing as the place?"

I step off the scale, then on again.

"Yes? I don't know. One would assume."

"One would."

I step off the scale again. The scale sucks. The scale's broken. "That's weird," I say.

"What?"

"You grocery shop. You never used to grocery shop."

"How did I get food if I never used to grocery shop? Everyone grocery shops."

"I mean you never used to make a thing out of grocery shopping."

I shuffle to the sink and draw a glass of water. It is lukewarm.

"How do you know I'm making a thing out of it?"

"You're buying fancy cheeses," I say between gulps.

"Is Roquefort fancy?"

I return to my bed, pull the covers up. My head is going to cave in, explode.

"It has to be. It was named after the place."

"There's a place named Roquefort?"

"Yeah, it's a commune. Remember how we always talked about having a wedding there?

"I thought that was Rochester."

"No, it was Roquefort. Remember how we discussed how tough it would be to convince people to get out there?"

I should not have brought up the wedding. This is bad, that I have made the connection between Roquefort and weddings. Things will be resurrected, memories. Dafna will recall our annual argument, our cheese/wedding argument, a powerful memory, a juggernaut of a memory. It will take the form of a flashback, in the fuzzy sepia of a daguerreotype— oh, and here it goes, she is remembering, sharing:

"Hey, speaking of weddings, remember, remember when . . ."

On the Matter of Weddings.

An apartment kitchen. She is cutting zucchini. I am in the fridge, letting the cold escape.

"Susan. Susan Shifflet. Yeah, that's it. Susie Shifflet."

"What?" I say. This is out of the blue. Sometimes Dafna says things out of the blue. "What?" I say again. "What are you talking about?"

"Oh, nothing. I was just trying to remember the name of one of our classmates back in high school, Susan. Do you remember her? I ran into her the other day. You know the girl in college who refused to go to class because all she wanted to do is act? The one with the supernaturally big boobs, who called education the destroyer of talent?"

"Oh yeah, Shiftie Susie," I shut the fridge. "I remember her. Joel always thought she was a hottie, a major "smokeshow." There was always weirdness between us."

"One guess as to what she's doing now."

"Is she getting roles?" I fumble with a jar of peanut butter.

"For some small productions. But she's on stage alone a lot."

"I bet she loves being alone onstage. *Look at me*, I bet she thinks. *'Fucking look at me, people!!'*"

"She had a strange abdom – a weird torso." Still fumbling with the peanut butter. Lordy. I am all thumbs.

"Yeah. She had a weirdly shaped body. She looked like—like one of those traffic things."

"Conical."

"Yeah. She looked conical."

"Wasn't that a thyroid thing?"

"Not sure."

I grab the remote from the counter and flip it to a music channel where Usher's groin is coming closer to the camera than makes me comfortable. There is heavy jiggling in the background.

"I heard a rumor she had some glandular issues. It made her sluggish or something. She was on medication, for body dysmorphia issues. I know her parents enrolled her in dance therapy, to help her with that. Can you believe it? *Dance therapy.*"

Dance therapy is not a legitimate form of therapy. I have never engaged in dance therapy, but I am pretty sure it is meant to take advantage of people less intelligent than the dance therapist. Dance therapy does not work. I am sure it does not work.

"Yeah, she does rage dances to express . . . whatever, now."

"Strange. Maybe they help. The rage dances."

"Anyway, guess what? She's with child."

"Wait, she's married? I thought she went off to Tibet or something. After the rage dance thing, I thought she started training to become a yogi. Last I heard."

Usher is now pretending to have sex with a Maserati. His jacket says USHER. It is bedazzled. I flip to the Money Channel, where a CEO with a very good eye for suits is stressing the importance of loyalty during this merely cyclical economic downturn. He overuses the word *cognizant*.

"That was two years ago," Dafna says. "Now she's having trouble being cast. And she's all frantic because her husband was just denied a mortgage for some reason."

"I thought she was still dating that MBA guy from INSEAD . . . and why didn't I get an invitation to the wedding? Do you know why I didn't get an invitation? Did you get an invitation?"

Dafna doesn't answer. The CEO has started handing out toddler shirts that say LITTLE LEADERSHIP CONSULTANT. I flip the channel again. Roddick is about to serve. He serves. What a serve. That first serve. Man. Roddick is a stud.

"And when I saw her, it was pretty bad. Really preggers."

Good for her. Good for Shiftie Susie.

"I mean we were close. We were really close. She said she always liked my 'aura.'"

Susan Shifflet was always into natural healing, which leads me to believe she'll request one of those water births. Or take those weird baby portraits, where the whole family's nude, save for some judiciously placed flowers. She's one of those people. Not a hippie. A post-hippie. I hope she at least has enough sense to get an epidural when she goes into labor.

"I mean, very preggers. Her inny's an outty. Wait, I thought you said there was weirdness between the two of you."

She, Susie Shifflet, is likely into that self-teaching Montessori stuff for her kids. Real psycho.

"Not really. I hear she's going to have a really nice wedding, though."

"Why are you so caught up with weddings? They're stupid." Dafna never believed in weddings because she said they, weddings, harken—yes, she used the word *harken*—to a pre-Biblical era where love was a financial negotiation. "It was always just a business deal, when two families celebrated the day one of the fathers finally sold off his daughter as chattel."

"That's just an excuse that women who aren't marriageable use," I say. "It's a nice thing to do, especially for the mothers. It's a union that makes perfect sense."

I prefer not to go into why this is so, while also sensing the impending disemboweling of my theory. Ah, here it goes: She puts the knife down.

This gesture, the putting down of the knife, it means everything. It means she will make her argument undistracted, will be clear and direct, rather than projecting her words into the cutting board, which is what happens when she is not giving them her full consideration. Or, rather, when she is regarding the whole conversation as nothing more than light banter, frivolous.

But Dafna, knifeless now, says: "Not when I'm a mom."

"Then for the guests." By some mystery, I remember throwing a CHEETO into my mouth at that point. "Or the family. It's about introducing two families to each other."

"You know in Central Asia, bride kidnapping is considered less of a sex crime than a legitimate union."

This confused me. "What does Central Asia have to do with us?"

"I'm not talking about us. I'm talking about the male instinct to control. It's universal, but it's more flagrant in some cultures than in others."

"Daf, usually the women are the ones who want the weddings."

I flip the channel again, where a WCVB reporter has grabbed a bearded, overweight person. He is from Emeryville, CA and would like to share his opinion about: **HEALTH CARE**. What appears to be a bra strap is showing.

"It always seems like a desperate act. And dumb women want them, because they love parties. They're princess for a day. It's not because they're in love."

Yes, it looks like a bra strap. You can see his arm fat bunching around it when he motions. Why does this arouse me? This should not arouse me. His shirt says LEGALIZE IT.

"Give me a break. Weren't you the one who said *only virgins fall in love?*"

"Yes. Jokingly."

"Right."

"I don't need a wedding to show the man I'm going to spend the rest of my life with that I'm in love with him."

"Aren't you independent."

"Central Asia was just an example."

A guy wearing a HABITAT FOR HUMANITY shirt and—not a doo-rag, exactly, but perhaps its close cousin—has wandered into the frame of the WCVB reporter.

"Excuse me. *Excuse me,*" The reporter is saying.

"Well, to hell with that," I say. "I'm going to have a huge wedding. Huge and tasteless. And as old-timey as you get. We're going to ride off in horse and buggy. And I'm going to demand a goddamn embarrassing dowry from my father-in-law and make sure it's paid in livestock or acreage. We'll somehow work a corrupt church official into the mix."

Joel had laughed. Joel was there that day.

"And we'll have at least one inbred cousin—as the ring bearer."

Another laugh. Joel is my #1 fan.

Joel and I always thought the act of spending your life with only one partner as nothing less than superhuman. This was why I, from an ostensibly stable family, wanted a part of it, and why Dafna, child of divorce, victim of alimony squabbles, didn't. I continue.

"It'll be retro. We will have been selected for our strengths. Me, for my heroics. You, for your fertile womb."

Dafna hates the word *womb*. I love the word *womb* because she hates it so much.

"Don't say that."

"*Womb. Woo-oomb.*"

"*Don't.*"

"Womb-sounds-like-tomb. It's a kind of tomb for a baby. A pre-life tomb."

"Stop."

"Womb, womb, womb. *Womb.*"

"You're . . . gross."

"I am."

. . .

Dafna clucks.

"Sounds like you're really going to love your wife."

"Why believe in love but not weddings?"

"You shouldn't—"

Joel pipes up.

"You sure you guys aren't confusing your terms? You sure you aren't getting *weddings* and *love* mixed up with *marriage?*"

"Stop, Joel."

"Yeah, Joel. Shut the fuck up."

I can't remember why Joel was there. I remember he was drinking Pepsi.

"One shouldn't need the other to survive," Joel says.

"It's just puppy love. It doesn't last."

I can't believe this woman, this cold woman. I bet she'll refuse to breast-feed her kids, if she has them.

"Sure," I say, "but the puppy love blossoms into different kinds of love. Emotional, or psychological, or intellectual, or—"

"Vaginal! Vaginal love!"

"Didn't we tell you to shut the fuck up, Joel?"

Dafna is on the warpath.

"Yeah, Joel," I say. "Shut the fuck up."

Joel complies.

"If you say so," Dafna says.

"I do say so, mi*lady.*"

"You know you're wrong."

"You know *you're* wrong."

"Good thing I'm going to marry a woman who doesn't have opinions."

Dafna scowled. It wasn't so much that I said it. It was that I said it in front of Joel. It was that improprieties like this were private—a thing between the two of us—and should be kept that way. In fact, she liked it when I was the macho Shel, the asshole who threw fits and made sexist remarks. She liked the chauvinist in me, perhaps even more than the real thing.

I would say to her, for instance, *I've been thinking today*, but not in my normal voice. In *DafnaVoice*.

"Is that right?" Usually, Dafna wouldn't look up. Usually, she'd be in a book. Usually that book would be about Jewish writers writing about Jews.

"And it is awful how women are treated in certain cultures. Just awful."

DafnaVoice is high, wispy, nasal. DafnaVoice sounds different every time, and nothing like Dafna's real voice. Sometimes, when she's trying to be too serious, I make it deep, husky. There is a frightening but real sexlessness to it. It sounds a lot like SmokerVoice, less the laryngitic wheeze.

"But did you know? Did you *know*," I cry in DafnaVoice. "that in some cultures, women are treated as legal tender? You can use them to bar-ter, exchanging them for food or sundries."

Then—Suddenly! Without notice!—DafnaVoice changes.

She is (I am) being nerdy. When Dafna is (I am) being nerdy, the voice called *NerdyVoice* engages. NerdyVoice sounds like the voice of all T.V. robot voices circa 1950 and contains a lot of computer blips and beeps.

"It is your duty as a modern female to address this! This sexism! Chauvinism! To alter this. You must address this, must, must, m-m-m-m-m-MAL-FUNC-TION! MAL-FUNC-TION!"

When I yell, MAL-FUNC-TION! MAL-FUNC-TION!, it means the computer has malfunctioned. NerdyVoice, just like PremenstrualVoice and PostcoitalVoice, falls under the DafnaVoice umbrella, by virtue of the fact that it is agony to listen to.

She gives another soft laugh. "Stop being stu-pid. I'm reading." She swats me away with her book. It looks like *Bleak House*. Or *Little House on the Prairie*. It's hard to tell. Something with *House*.

NerdyVoice is equally as masculine as BankerVoice, which I use when I am valuating Dafna, recommending to an imaginary client if they should go long or short on her. I base this on how happy I am with her at the time.

BankerVoice originated a week after Dafna and I discussed financials—two college students pretending they had real responsibilities—and I thought it would be interesting to integrate this mode of thought into our relationship.

I recall walking to the dry-erase board on the door and making a ticker symbol, DAF. I decided DAF should open at $15. So I wrote $15 on the door and circled it.

"Are you serious? Do you know how offensive that is?"

"Oooh, we're having our doubts about this particular equity. You've suddenly dipped to just below 11."

I cross out the 5 and replace it with a 1.

"You're telling me I'm worth 11 bucks?"

"Of course not. It's merely what the market thinks you're worth. They don't recognize your true potential. Prove them wrong, Daf."

"It's on your door. Everyone can see it."

"Sure, what'd you expect? It's public information. It wouldn't be fair if it weren't available."

I continued on and off with this for a number of days, and Dafna, strangely, became angrier, especially when I told her I'd allow her outlook to become a little more bullish if she'd be a doll and run out to get me a little something to eat. I should not have asked her to get me a little something. And I really shouldn't have called her a doll. It would be funny to me, my friends. It is not funny to most women. I apologized and, just to show that I was sorry, said that first quarter results have come in and made DAF jump five points.

"Quit it, Shel."

"Quit what?"

"This game. It's not funny."

Her mouth has taken the form of a cashew.

"It's funny. Why would I quit an activity that increases my happiness so dramatically?"

She does not understand that I am hilarious, a clown, a *card*. I am Steve Martin.

"Because I'm your girlfriend and I'm asking you to."

"Yeah. That."

That day, henceforth known as black Friday, was the day she took down the dry-erase board.

She gives another soft laugh. "Stop being stu-pid. I'm trying to read. You're being stu-pid."

Not for long. I place my tongue in her ear as a final insult. She pushes me away and then jumps on me. *Gaaaaaaah*, I say, leaving a halo of saliva on her neck.

We could spend hours on the marriage question, but it spurs more memories, and we (or rather Dafna has) have moved on to other reminiscences, just as asinine. Now, on the phone, she feels it necessary to share.

"Remember when I—"

"Remember when Dent—"

This is Dafna. This is what she does with our current relationship, fitting it with components from our past, as if trying to resuscitate an old Studebaker, jamming it with discontinued parts, making it work, *willing* it to work. Willing it, against all laws of mechanics, to run. She continues to tinker:

"Remember when we—"

"Remember when Dent—"

This will be endless. This is the Iditarod. This is Wagner.

I shuffle back to bed and lie there.

"Remember when I helped you shop for shower curtains?" she says. "How we bought a great set, with the *rainy day* clouds on them, but you had trouble installing it, because you refused to read the directions, and got so mad about it? And your face got so red-hot about it? But then I—savior of the afternoon, thank you—patiently snapped the rings together while you were sulking in your bed?"

Yes, I remember the time with the curtains, when she picked out overpowering indigo curtains that I had no choice but to like.

They are overpowering, I told her. She thought they were elegant.

"Yeah. I remember." I pull the comforter over my face. "You were a lifesaver."

Is this it? Is our conversation over? Can I go? I nearly raise my hand: *Pardon me, Ms. Schwartzers, but may I be excused?*

I have now placed the phone on my face, the earpiece sitting atop my forehead, the receiver resting on my mouth. This is a great way to talk on the phone in bed. It is innovative and energy-efficient.

"You sure? You sound like you just woke up."

"Of course. Just a little hoarse."

"It's just that you have so much in that head of yours –"

"You sound like a mom. Not mine. But someone's mom. It's weird."

She continues. "I just don't feel like you're able to get any of it out. You act like you don't have anything going on up there because you say *yeah* and *sure* all the time, but I know that's not true."

"Yeah. Sure."

"That's not funny. You need to communicate."

"I will."

"Not let everything stay stuck inside."

"You're so right."

"And you think we can't tell when you're being sarcastic. I can tell. I can tell when you're being sarcastic."

"Okay."

"So are we going to be better?"

"Yes."

"We're not going to be sarcastic?"

"No."

"Okay. We're going to work on sincerity. Sincerity is a growth area for you."

"Okay?"

"Sure."

"Now. I'm not calling because I need to see you again. I'm calling because I'm worried. All of your friends are worried about you."

"I'm fine," I say. Unless you count the fact that I wasn't invited to Susan Shifflet's wedding. I mean, I exchanged PreCal notes with her. I was her study buddy. Whatever. I bet the ceremony was terrible. I don't care that I wasn't invited," I said, thinking how *Wasn't Invited To The Wedding* would be a great music video subject.

"Will you talk to me?"

"Sure. About how her wedding probably sucked?"

"No."

"Oh." I am crestfallen.

. . .

"About other things."

"Okay. Sure."

"Well, how are you?"

"Not about that."

. . .

"What should we talk about, then?"

"I want to talk about sex, baby."

"Shel –"

"I want to talk about you and me. All the good things."

"This isn't working. And it's *'let's talk about sex.'*"

"All the bad things."

"That may be. But I'm serious. I really do want to talk about—ok, I'm sorry for saying this—us. About why it was so bad at the end. We had so many problems. Why? Why did we have those problems? It's been bugging me. Has it been bugging you?"

"Has what been bugging me?"

"Us."

"WHAT?"

I go deaf. Sometimes I go deaf when I'm on the phone.

"I called to talk about us."

"We've talked about us. What else is there to talk about? We've been over everything."

"We haven't really talked. There's a reason I brought up Susan Shifflet. I want to talk—"

"You mean the Susan Shifflet who didn't invite me to her wedding? That Susan Shifflet?"

"Yes, that Susan Shifflet. We need to talk about the alien."

She's right. We have not talked about the alien, but we do not need to talk about this, about *it*. Because we'd been over it, the blob, the monster, the alien-thing from Planet X. Just when I was almost done forgetting about the episode, forgetting about Dafna, mentally elbowing her below the foundational levels of my awareness, this. I do not like that she calls it *alien*.

"Please let's not call it *alien*, ok? I thought we had discussed this already."

We had already been over our breakup, and Dafna's secret getting pregnant, and Dafna's even secret-er getting un-pregnant (we didn't like to use the A word. *A* was our scarlet letter). The hell we had gone through, not just emotionally, but physically, with Dafna's body not responding to the procedure as expected. The pain, and the heaviness of her breasts long afterwards, their weight reminding her of what she lost. Or disposed of.

We already made promises that we wouldn't tell anybody about our little E.T., a name I still hate, preferring to call it SB, for Surprise Baby! (as in, *What happens when you forget your NuvaRing? Surprise Baby!*). We were both, frightening as it was, adults, so we told ourselves that the procedure (Christ, we made it sound so clinical) would be easy—and that we would die before we told anyone else about it. That except for the doctor and the wonderful people at *Planned Parenthood*, with their advanced android technology and superhuman powers of understanding, no one would know.

Except for Dent.

The only one I told about this episode—no, this *saga*, this *soap opera*, this *made-for-TV-slash-straight-to-DVD-miniseries*—was Dent, because I needed someone to talk to. I needed to *vent*, as they say. And although I know all his top secrets (which I'd never give away, no, no, never-ever give away), I can't help but suspect that Dent, if the right opportunity came along—or just for a laugh—would give away all my top secrets without a second thought. And I'd forgive him for it. This is what kills me. I'd forgive him for everything.

A Quick Word From Denton Brown, Interloper:

> It's not funny.
>
> That's wrong. It is funny. It's so, so funny. It's hilarious.
>
> What happened to Shel. It is so funny. I'm not supposed to tell anyone. I really can't say. I told him I wouldn't say.
>
> It's hilarious. I can't help it.
>
> I really shouldn't repeat this. I really shouldn't say.
>
> Shel Wirth was raped.
>
> Yes. Raped.
>
> And, yes, I told Joel. Why wouldn't I tell him? Joel says it's wrong of me to find it funny. He says it's unfeeling, whatever that means. But it can't be wrong. It's too good to be wrong.
> If it were a figurative rape, like, "oh, the last quarter raped us," or "I just raped that level on my Sony PlayStation," I wouldn't be as worried, and if it were play rape, I wouldn't be worried. But that's because it wouldn't be as funny. The fact that Shel was actually raped by his girlfriend – by Dafna - is funny. It's awful. I'm going to hell for laughing. I know it. But it's Shel. If it were anyone else, I'd be outraged, shocked, nauseated disgusted, et cetera. But it's Shel. Sweet Dafna? I can't believe it.
>
> It's wrong, but it can't be. I mean, Jesus - look at him. The guy's a walking bicep. I don't know how it happened, but can you imagine that scenario: a thick-necked guy like Shel, squealing like a piggy as Dafna—that determined Jewess—holds him

down? I mean, she's an athletic girl, but there's really no competition there.

How is it even possible? I just don't know how a guy of that size could let such a thing happen. The only way I can imagine it happening is if Dafna somehow drugged Shel. I heard—and this is unsubstantiated, I only deal in unsubstantiated stuff—she slipped him some kind of Viagra-roofie cocktail. This makes the whole thing infinitely funnier, of course. You know, he probably drugged himself . . .

I don't think it's possible. Someone must have made it up.
But it has to be true. I know Joel says it's just a rumor, but it's too perfect. It would explain everything. I know it's wrong, but I've really got to get this out of my system:
Imagine his dating profile after this, or his support group. "Hi, I'm Shel Wirth. My hobbies are being pleased with myself and asking pointed questions about luxury cars. And yes, I'm also a victim of forced intercourse."
Or the litigation:
"Will the plaintiff please point to his assailant? Let the record show that the plaintiff pointed to—a woman? The defendant's a woman? Are you sure? I could understand a rather bulky homosexual, but—a woman? Let the record show that the jury is snickering. Let it also show that the plaintiff has no penis."
Or, she should become a spokesperson for the cause. Dafna Schwartzers presents Rape: Why not?
Okay. I'm done.

I'm not done.
This is momentous. This needs to be recorded. There will be entire mythologies constructed around this. I think the whole episode could be best expressed in heroic couplets—a narrative verse about *The Rape of the Shel.* It's only proper that it be recorded. For posterity.
Don't get me wrong. I'm against rape, of any kind, regardless of far fetchedness. And the whole baby part and the abortion part, that's not funny at all. That's tragic. That really is tragic. But

this, there is something special about it. Something too perfect to be criminal.

And now he's working for this SPECTACOP organization, this SECURITY FIRM, managing RENT-A-COPS. That makes everything so much weirder. Is this some kind of twisted penance? Some weird form of self-abasement, to make up for something he didn't even do? That he allowed to be done to him? Is it his way of reclaiming something that was lost that night? How does a guy recover from something like that, anyway?

Have you been raped by a female? If you have, call 1-800-I'M-NOT-REALLY-A-MAN-BUT-SOMETHING-LESSER-LIKE-A-EUNUCH-OR-A-NEUTER.

God, I hope he took a post-Dafna shower, curled up at the end of the tub, weeping, scrubbing the rape off himself, calling himself a dirty nancy.

Now I'm done. It's really not funny.

Guess what his middle name is? His middle name is Percy. His middle name sounds like a woman's handbag. Sheldon P-for-Percy Wirth. I think I'm the only one who knows this.

And this, this, is what got her pregnant. I'm almost positive this is what got her pregnant. I mean, I'm not supposed to know about the baby, but of course I know about the baby. I wish there were something I could say here, but raising a kid's no joke.

Sheldon Percy Wirth. What a pussy.
Oh Rape, there is nothing unfunny about you.

Do we have time for calls? No? No time?

Well, that's it for today on Sixty Seconds From a Guy with It-Might-Be-Cancer. Coming to you from The Darkest Corners of The Earth, I'm Denton Brown, and these are my balls.
Back to you, Shel.
END FEED.

I'm against continuing this conversation, but Dafna insists. She wants to reopen wounds.

"It's just that—" she says, "—it's just that I never told you the real reason we broke up."

I'm not getting into it today. We've been over it.

"We broke up because of the *bzzzzzz*." I say, now standing, shifting from foot to foot. "Remember how we agreed we weren't going to bring up the *bzzzzzz* again?"

Just as we called the baby *the alien* instead of *the baby*, as if it might somehow pop out of her stomach and do battle with Sigourney Weaver, *Bzzzzzz* was the name we gave a subject that we both, as would most people, found unpalatable—Dafna's abortion. Her pregnancy occurred after a strange night with her, and we treated Dafna's abortion—or *bzzzzzzz*—like a procedure that required slicing her stomach open with a buzzsaw. We thought, perhaps mistakenly, that by substituting some levity in our language about it, however inappropriate, we might distract ourselves enough to forget what was happening. *Bzzzzzzzz* wasn't the most accurate placeholder, but it was a placeholder. Anything to avoid actually saying it.

"So you needed time off, which turned into this. Right?

Right?

"Yeah," she says, "but there's more. More of a reason, I mean."

"Don't feel any—what's that word? Obligation or anything."

"I know, I know. It's for me. I never told you that the real reason—God, I can't believe I'm saying this—the only reason I wanted to break up—and that's what it was always supposed to be, a break up, is—"

"Suspense is killing me."

"—is because I couldn't imagine you as a father."

Why is she telling me this? She is an evil woman for telling me this. I turn on the TV to a History Channel retrospective on Punch and Judy, trying to drown her out amid the sounds of domestic violence, but her voice cuts through.

"I couldn't imagine you, this guy who—let's face it—has some self-esteem issues, has some mommy and daddy issues—it's just that—I just couldn't envision you providing for our family. *Protecting* our family. Because that's what I want. I want a family. A real one. I'm tired of your halfheartedness. I mean, it's not only the reason why we took a break. It's why I went to the clinic."

I flip the channel to find Hulk Hogan hitting John Cena with a 2x4, which suggests to me that WrestleMania referees may not be as even-handed in their officiating as I have been led to believe.

"You think I don't have money? I have money. You've seen my Blu-Ray player, my Kenneth Cole watch. And my iPhone? Does my iPhone count for anything? You've seen those things. And I'm thinking about getting a Ducati. I swear. I was looking at the Ducati website the other day. What about Macho Shel? I could be Macho Shel."

"Yeah, that was an act. You work in security. You're not exactly rolling in it."

"Yeah, but you are, so who cares?"

"I care."

"I don't believe you."

I flip the channel to an advertisement. A lizard talks me into buying car insurance in about half a minute.

"I really do. Anyway, those were the reasons. It's why we decided against keeping the – why I Bzzzzzzzz."

She almost slipped. If she had slipped, I would have ripped her apart. I would have slaughtered her. But she didn't slip, so I stay.

"And I know it's weird that I'm telling you this, but it's because I have something more important to tell you, something that—"

"Foreverrrr!" I sing, suddenly remembering the wrong words to my favorite power ballad. "If only foreverr! Riight noooow." I am a self-important baritone, and I sing. I sing a terrible '80s song (Is it *Can't Fight This Feeling* by REO Speedwagon? Or *Come Clarity* by Swedish death metal band In Flames? I'm not quite sure.) making it worse, or, in a parodic way, better.

"Stop."

I do not stop. I sing.

"You only loved me for my voice. I know you only loved me for my voice, Dafna."

This is Ravinia.

"I'm hanging up."

Or Carnegie Hall.

"Okay, that one was a joke."

"You're not funny. I'm trying to talk."

"You're talking. I'm singing. FOREVEERRR!"

Jesus, I'm good. Really good. Move over, Pavarotti. Liberace? Screw yourself, Liberace.

"You're a child. I'm hanging up."

"No, you're not. You're listening to me. You're listening to me and—"

Yes. Dafna hung up. Dafna hung up on me.

"You don't actually hang up," I say to no one. "You say you're going to hang up. You don't actually hang *up*. No one does that. But you did. That's not okay. You're supposed to keep warning that you're going to hang up until I stop misbehaving, which you know will happen—it will happen eventually—but actually hanging up . . . that's not right . . . especially when you're being a *total fucking* . . ."

But I don't finish the thought. I close the phone. I breathe. Okay, she hung up on me. But this is not a problem. Because I am going to hold back, be judicious in my choice of words, holster my vituperation. Because she is gone, she is gone forever, and it is over.

It's not over. I re-open my phone:

"That's fucked up, Dafna. That's really messed. I dare you to do it again. I dare you to hang up on me next time. You think you hurt me? Get over yourself. I don't give a shit about you. I don't give a shit about you in so many ways."

I continue with this for the next minute or so, using the following words: Shit Pretend Again Into Never Wrong Fuck Bitch. I think *Nympho* slips out

I pause, occupied by the irrelevant thought that if I were ever to open a butcher shop, I'd give it some cutesy, cornball name, like *What's Eating Ewe* or *Go Groundchuck Yourself*, and consider retail property somewhere in Boston's North End. Then, as if rebooted, I continue:

"Is that really the best you can do? Hanging up? Really. Really. Oh, am I ruining your day? Well, you ruined mine. So I'm going to ruin yours. Yeah. Pay it forward. *PayPal* it forward, lady. How do you like that, you . . . you . . . ?"

I don't recall exactly what I say, but I believe the following words come out: Slut How Wrong Slobbering No Used Callous Unfair Never. I use the word *criminal*, and not in a figurative way. I sing again, and my head hurts again. It kills. It's my harried conscience. Or rumbling from my head's small god. Or the note I'm about to hit in my power ballad reprise. It kills, whatever it is. My conscience. A memory. A bad memory. A nightmarish remembrance, which I have withheld, denied. No, it's vomit.

I double over, throwing aside my comforter/muumuu contrivance, disrobing in a single *shunt*. A trail of sickness follows me to the bathroom.

"That didn't seem to go well."

An animation is talking to me.

This is another way I know something's wrong with me. I see animations. One of the animations—I'm not sure of his name—is talking to me. The way I know there is something wrong with me is because animations like this one talk to me.

"Clearly not," I tell the animation. I am not going to call Dafna back.

"She hurt you, didn't she?"

He looks and sounds very much like Dennis Kucinich.

"What are you talking about?" I say.

"I can tell she hurt you."

I clutch the toilet.

"You can't let these things get to you. You have to be strong. Think positive. Chin up, man, chin up. And if you ever need anything . . ."

I look up at Dennis Kucinich, grimace.

Usually, animations like this Dennis Kucinich-looking one are of men. Usually these men engage in madcap goings-on, like bumbling, or making life difficult for a joyless partner, or not having class in classy situations. On occasion, they insult me. They tend to speak honestly. They are more often than not perverted about what they do.

"I'm serious," he says. "Just let me know if I can do anything to help. No more of that hangdog look. Chin up."

Chin up.

RETURN OF THE HATRED.

That night, I do the following things in no particular order: Research the exact value of a ha'penny and poll homeless people about whether they are open to receiving one as alms, discovering the answer to be a resounding *yes*. Giggle at the sight of a very short, very fat man passing my apartment window. Giggle again when the very fat, very short man catches sight of me giggling and starts giggling himself. Then I stay up late wondering if it was either ethical or appropriate of me to burn that book of American Flag Stamps when ABC rescinded its offer to let Toby Keith sing on its 2002 Fourth of July special on account of the controversial lyrics of his hit single, *Courtesy of the Red, White and Blue (The Angry American)*.

Then I put on a Hawaiian shirt. Then I stand too close to a teenager with headphones. I am very close to you, teenager. I am too close to you.

Then I compose an elegant Petrarchan sonnet, rhyming eternal with diurnal and best with hest. Then I take off my shirt and fry bacon.

Then I join hands with people of all colors and creeds and nationalities in singing the chorus and first two versus of Michael Jackson and Lionel Richie's WE ARE THE WORLD, swaying and snapping and clapping to the music, keeping an eye on my wallet the entire time, because you never really know with these people.

Then I light a candle. Then I smash a taillight. Then I your mother.

Then I learn that Marshall Field's is now owned by Macy's and become upset that I hadn't heard of it earlier. I then realize that Chipotle is owned by McDonald's and become even angrier. I have been deceived, hoodwinked, lied to. Taken advantage of, used by these faceless corporations, chewed up and spat out like gristle. When I realize that Dasani Water is a Coca-Cola product, I flip. I fantasize about grabbing a man in a suit who I assume to be an executive at some fancy big-time firm and throw him to the ground, telling him to bite the curb, then step on his head. I walk down the street, acting as if this fantasy were real and dusting off my hands like I have accomplished something, passing a sign that says CURB YOUR DOG, smiling perversely at both how appropriate the sign is and how unfair the world can be. I buy a copy of the *Wall Street Journal* and learn that Mars, Inc. just bought William Wrigley Jr. Company for $23.2 billion dollars. That's a reasonable number, right?

Then there is the emptiness.

(I breathe.)

Later that evening, distressed, thoughts of Dafna never farther from my mind, I follow a tradition I started one dull Presidents Day and have repeated on a bi-weekly basis for the past seven years: I set aside a block of two and a half hours to dress in a dark suit and blood red tie, pour myself a stiff Grey Goose martini, and enjoy a solo viewing of the 2000 blockbuster *American Psycho* (Dir. Mary Harron) while both reading *American Psycho* (Brett Easton Ellis), the bestselling and critically-acclaimed book, and caressing an *American Psycho* Patrick Bateman action figure, setting the wallpaper on my Power PC to the *American Psycho* promotional poster ("*Killer Looks*"), all the while listening to *American Psycho: Music from the Controversial Motion Picture* soundtrack, reaching what may be total bliss or temporary blindness for a half a moment. I TiVo *American Idol*.

At roughly 3 AM that morning, I wake up and pace the room. I wash my hands, brush my teeth for the second time that night. Something haunts me. I open my freezer and check the ice. I fill the empty ice trays, refresh the full ones. One can always use more ice. I head back to bed and lie there for another hour but am unable to sleep. I go to the 24-hour store and buy three bags of ice. I put them in the freezer and lie down for another hour and a half before I finally go to sleep again. An hour later, I wake up in a panic, fearing that three bags may not be enough, but fall asleep again only minutes later after convincing myself that I'll be fine.

You can never have too much ice.

I sleep fitfully for roughly three hours.

I wake up two more times with the concern that this newly purchased ice may not be separated into easily retrievable cubes, that it may be clumpy. I attack the bags with an ice pick, stabbing at them mechanically, determinedly, thrusting through each one until I am satisfied that all clumps have been eliminated. Just to be sure, I drop each bag of ice on the floor and jump on it. I return the bags to the freezer. I wake up only three or four more times that night, just to ensure I didn't lose any ice when I dropped it on the floor.

There is nothing worse than clumpy ice.

Somewhere in The South Pacific.

Dent throws his duffel into the skiff. He steadies the boats as the crew climbs aboard and follows them, pushing The Sea Note IV away with his feet. He walks fore and looks over the bow, leaning on his toes. No hazards are visible. He can't see the bottom.

Dent had been out there for a long time, relatively speaking, and had long ago begun a kind of physiological memorization of the place. The tonic of the air, the swag (that's what they called it, *swag*) of the boat in his knees, the morning stimulants—microscopic jellyfish stings, the water's chill—on his skin, an invigorator superior to espresso. And the counting. The counting while diving. The counting while in the air and the swagging boat. The counting while on shore. His job description was *research director*. His actual job was fish-counter, or at least that's how the joke went. It was much more involved, but try explaining that to anyone else. Try mentioning the words *Ostorhinchus savayensis* to anyone back home. *Patronizing* would best describe the tone of voice they adopted.

Sometimes, when he was diving, he would reach out for the fish. He would almost touch them, cup them in his hands like rare metal, or a magical orb, before they swam away. He once touched one of the more lenient fish—a humphead wrasse—gently. It was soft, like the endocarp of a peach, but it swam away.

This was the *why*. Why he had left his town, state, country and continent. To be underwater, in a completely new dimension. To be in a place where the only thing you could hear was the sound of your own breathing. A place where, if you were careful, if you were patient and motionless and lucky, you could, almost, touch the fish. There were only a few places back home where Dent felt—well, at home like this. One of them was called the Village Green, and it was where some of the town's most violent behavior took place.

The Village Green.

The Village Green was the only reasonable place for Dent. It was the only place without conflict—or at least real conflict—simply because conflict was the whole point. It was there that games of pickup football materialized. Tackle, no pads. Dent usually organized, and Joel brought the mouth guards and jock straps—

"Anyone need a penis cup? Got a few extra penis cups here. For your penis."

—clearing the green of any younger players who might have interfered. Everyone referred to each other by their last names. They didn't need to, because none of them shared a first name, but they had to, because.

> *Great, an injury. Mitnick, why are you always the injured one?*
> *Yes, Davis, that's a football. You've seen a football before, right?*
> *Jesus, Gruenbaum, why do you have to be so fucking unathletic?*

First names would be too familiar—too gay?—so they say their last names. They kept it formal. They kept it military.

Fuck it, Crach. I called a goddamn audible. Or do you not know what an audible is? Prick.

Baker, you're being a pussy. Stop being such a pussy.

Baker was a pussy. His dad made a killing building and selling DynamaFlex Laboratories—contract manufacturer of private label monolayer and co-extruded polyethylene film—and Baker was a rich pussy.

Are you kidding me, Brown? Are you KIDDING ME?

It was on that green, before that Last Supper of sliders and iced tea, that Dent confided something to Shel that he had only recently found the courage to say.

"Sometimes I feel sorry for Dafna."

He always had strong opinions about Dafna, even when she and Shel stopped going out.

"Because of me?"

"It has nothing to do with you. She's rich, and she doesn't believe in marriage. She has nothing to look forward to. Not making money. Not falling in love."

"She can have love."

"Sure, but not *sanctioned* love. Success, sure, but she never came across as one of those ambitious types. She has always been at odds with her family in some subtly rebellious way."

"She has a life. She's not a typical girl. She seems happy to me."

"I know she seems happy. She always *seems* happy."

"She doesn't let her money depress her. It's easy to let money depress you—ISN'T THAT RIGHT BAKER, YOU RICH PUSSY?!—or at least that's what I heard. Or that's what Dafna told me, which I believed. I couldn't imagine that person whose parents hoard money for themselves, who would walk over anyone for a profit, could raise a daughter who was so giving of herself, so sensitive. Who in a second—and I'm as certain of this as anything—would give her an inheritance to assure that eventually she would find something that made her happy."

"It's just strange."

Brown, Wirth, you guys done making out over there?

"Stop feeling sorry for that woman. She isn't as sweet as you think."

Did you know Emory doesn't have a football team? Dent yells, loud enough for everyone to hear. *A Southern School <u>without a football team</u>!*

Yes, there were no first names. First names were out of the question.

INTERLUDE: THE CLINIC.
Winter

I am at the clinic. I am bored. I used to be panicked, concerned. But not any more. Right now I am just bored. On my way here, I passed a man who overused the word *hellfire* but I am no longer concerned with him.

I glance over at the side table and pick up an issue of *Wired*. This issue is about: Computers.

"Pfffffffffft" I say. I put it down.

I look at the side table again. I pick up a book this time. It is one of those DISCOVER YOUR BODY books, filled with a few too many photos of prepubescent girls. This leads me to assume that its authors are more than a little pervy. Then I pick up *Good Housekeeping* and immediately put it down.

"Pfffffffffft" I say again.

One of the doctors comes in. For reasons beyond me, I stand at attention. The doctor tells me to relax. He is a black man from Forest Hill, New Jersey. His name is Mark, he has been doing this for ten years, and he is gay. He doesn't mention that last part out loud. You can't always tell, but with Mark, you can tell.

I assume he's here to give me something along the lines of a lecture, but no. He asks where I live. When I tell him, he says he'd love to introduce me to a friend of his, a painter from that area. This always happens when I meet gay men. They like introducing me to people. They love introductions.

But the doctor, Mark, I like him. He is not in-your-face with his sexuality. He is not all like, "Hi, I'm Mark, and I'm GAAAA-AAAAAAY HO HO HORRAY!"

Mark's a professional. I trust him. I bet he had a rough life, being black and gay. I bet it wasn't always easy for him. He reminds me a bit of Theo Huxtable. Is it wrong to think this?

Mark leaves.

An hour passes.

Mark returns. He says not to worry, everything is going to be fine. He has heavy eyes and soft cheeks. We are very brave. That's what Mark tells me. I have a black, gay man telling me we're brave. Then he leaves again.

I go to McDonald's two days later. My McFlurry has an aftertaste of breast milk.

V.

Morale has plummeted. As one half of the *SpectaCop* management team, if I become upset, morale plummets. Ever since the conversation with Dafna, I have taken a dramatic turn for the worse, as they say.

I can't take my coworker much longer. I'm getting fired soon.

I have just come to this decision, trying to get fired. Exactly how this fantasy started is a long story.

I'll make it quick.

It—this fantasy—began one Tuesday when I was bored. Very, very bored. Atheistically bored. "I'm bored," I said to my coworker.

"Oh?" he replied.

"Yeah. I need a hobby."

"You're at work."

"I think I'll take up the pipe."

"Woodwind?"

"No. Corncob."

"That's silly. You don't just 'take up' pipe smoking."

"Why not?"

"It's not like it's a piano."

"How else do people start?"

"It's against best practices."

"Wrong. The SpectaCop manual says nothing about pipes."

"Really?"

"Not really."

"My therapist will hear about this," he says, storming out as if issuing some kind of threat.

I have no idea if SpectaCop employment literature covers pipes. So today, I'm researching. I dig through my desk to find the SpectaCop manual, which has convinced me that getting fired is the solution. You can get paid for getting fired. You can get something called Unemployment. You can also get something called severance. I don't need a job. I will get fired, live life on the road as a free spirit, find my inner Jack Kerouac. I'll travel, interview, research. *I'll write*. Oh yes, this is good.

A *blog*. This is even better. I'll start a blog. That's what I'll do. Not just a blog. A critique. Of SpectaCop. Of what SpectaCop represents. Of organized labor, national security, capitalist mores. A voice in the wilderness. Devastating social commentary. It's going to be talked about. People are going to forward it to each other.

"People are going to forward it to each other," I say, pleased with myself.

I will use my blog to write compelling pretend arguments against my boss, things like, *this man is a retard*, and *this man has no balls*. My boss, Duane Mull, loves the term *hand to God*. I will make fun of his love of the term *hand to God*. I will make fun of the fact that he misuses the term *hand to God*.

"Hand to god, don't you think it's hot today?" my boss will ask, and I will record it on my blog. I will also critique his tie decisions.

See that man, making a commotion, breaking office equipment, saying the wrong thing to an employee? That is my boss. Ha—he has just fumbled a key meeting with a client. In the future, this will all be on-record, this will be reported by my blog. His mediocre attempts to motivate me, and his awkwardness—my blog will cover these things. SPECTACOP SECURITY MANAGER IN CHARGE is what his shirt says. YOU HAVE LIKELY REALIZED BY NOW THAT I AM UNEQUIPPED TO DEAL WITH THE ISSUES OF THE DAY is *what his shirt should say*. That's a joke I am going to make on my blog. As soon as my site is up and running, I will make jokes like this. I will tell the world how he calls me and puts me on, of all things, speakerphone:

"Let me put you on—" he'll start to say.

"No!" I'll cry.

"—speakerphone," he'll continue. "I need the use of my hands."

He will not really need the use of his hands. Who needs the use of their hands? *For a conference call?* I will characterize him as a one-man band of mismanagement, stomping around the office, bowlegged, as if cymbals were tied to his knees, bellowing and snorting, as if honking a trumpet, swaying to and fro, as though some giant drum, or a gong—*yes, a gong*—were hanging stone-like from his neck. He will not realize that he looks like an asshole.

This man looks like an asshole, I will write on my blog.

Not a blog. This is too technical. It will take too much time. I may have to hire programmers, designers. It is too costly. It may take programming knowledge. C++. Or that other one. Java? A blog is not feasible.

I will send a letter. Yes: A missive from a marooned middle-American office worker. It will be poignant. And I will walk to the post office for a stamp. I will even stand in line—

"One stamp, please."

"One stamp?"

"That's right. I have an important mailing."

"You wouldn't like a booklet? We sell them in ten or twenty."

"No. One."

"People who have been waiting in line for fifteen minutes usually buy more than one stamp."

"I have one letter. I'd like one stamp."

"This is a post office. You have to buy more."

"I don't believe you."

—for a lengthier than reasonable amount of time. I'll use a FOREVER STAMP. A FOREVER STAMP never expires.

This is what the letter will say:

> Duane Mull
> SpectaCop Boston Branch Manager
> SpectaCop Security, LLC
> 101 State St.
> Boston, MA 02139
>
> Dear Duane Mull,
>
> I am sending this letter for no other reason than to waste your time. I tell you this up front because, despite this information I have provided for you, I believe you will keep reading. This is how little I respect your judgment. You may think there is a surprise, or vital information, at the end. There is not. You may wonder why I sent a letter rather than electronic mail. It is because opening an envelope and unfolding

the letter takes more time. You may also wonder why the letter was sealed with duct tape. This should be clear now.

Here's the second paragraph. This is by far the longest sentence in the paragraph, perhaps the whole letter. This, the shortest. Have you seen the new Angelina Jolie movie? It's really good, if you ignore her skinny arms. Those weird, skinny arms.

See? I told you. I estimate that I will have wasted about five minutes of your time, all told. How does that feel? Probably pretty bad.

Regards,
Sheldon Wirth
Manager
SpectaCop Security, LLC

P.S. I'm getting to you. I know it.

P.P.S. Have you heard the one about the Seventh Day Adventist and the Jew?

P.P.P.S. Fuck, fuck you, bugaboo.

But I will never send the letter. I know I will never send the letter. I will instead stow it in the bottom of my desk, right next to my sidearm, which I have—

"Is that a gun?" My coworker asks when I bring it in.
"It's a .22 caliber, double action."
"Why do you have a gun?"
"In case I need to blow you away."
"Seriously. Why do you need it here?"
"We're a security company."
"Sure—*un*armed security."
"Whatever."
"Is that even legal?"

—in case I need to blow my coworker away. Also, we're a *security company*. It wouldn't seem right not to have some sort of projectile weaponry. (Not necessarily for attacks on the premises. For pistol-whipping. What's the point of working security if there's no pistol-whipping?) In the meantime, I will place the letter, sealed and addressed, next to the .22, in that bottom drawer. It will, in all likelihood, go untouched, month after month, while I sit here, just inches away from it—a mere arm's length, *not even* an arm's length—in a stew of unrequited contemptuousness, simmering.

I am sure I will never touch it.

Look at my gun.

Look at it and tell me I am not dangerous.

I see my reflection in that window, looking at myself with the gun. I do a little showdown gun-and-holster move, a quickdraw. Shoot it, spin it, sheath it. I am Sheriff.

A bad protector? Not a provider? Is she kidding me? Is that woman fucking kidding me? I have a gun.

A fucking *piece*. A Walther P22 with extra front sight and grip, hardened steel slide, ambidextrous thumb safety, 3-dot sight, and two 10-round mags. And I have used the f-word at least twice in the last minute. No one will mess with me while I have this piece, when I hold it like this, aim it at the wall gangsta-style, make unrepentant use of profanity. I am protector, defender. I am the one who calls the shots (Ooh, a pun! No—I don't give a shit about puns. They are small, stupid things, whereas I am a bigger-picture kind of guy). Not a provider? Not a *provider*? I went to Southie for this piece, went into Boston's ghetto. I scored some heat, scored some pot. I will no longer ponder the smaller things in life, the inessentials, like whether Scotchguard™ is really a brand you can trust (it is). Or if using the word *coaxial* will make me sound smart or just desperate; or if cohabitating Texans are capable of going more than a month without speaking positively about Tommy Lee Jones; or whether, if I were ever to compose a hit R&B single, I would be okay with white people listening to it.

I will not do this. Sheldon Wirth will not do this, because:

Sheldon Wirth is one badass mother*fucker*.

I am hard. Tell me I am not hard ... bitch. And strong. And *potent*. I make virgins blush. I bend metal. I am strong, watch: I run to the gym and do a thousand and four push-ups, holding the thousand-fourth one. I do one hundred eighty-yard wind sprints with five seconds rest in between. I expand my limited understanding of Forex markets by doing an hour's worth of online research. I confuse a stranger by saying "So we meet again" when in fact we haven't met at all. I join a game of wheelchair basketball and take a shot at an honest game for about a minute before standing up and mocking the short wheely people.

Then I smoke a Cuban.

Then I belittle an intern.

Then I shake a baby.

Then I throw a pregnant woman down the stairs.

Then I punch a sign. The sign says STOP. I do not stop. No, I do not stop.

I join in on a worldwide chorus of people of every sexual orientation, preference and proclivity in an uplifting rendition of "Rainbow Connection," singing at the top of my lungs, singing my *heart* out, uplifting every downtrodden soul ever to have walked this great green earth, keeping well away from that one floofy guy who is most definitely giving me the eye, because I'd like to avoid, you know . . . catching something.

Then I punch a puppy in the balls.

Then I cheat death.

If the sound a cow makes in French is *Meuh Meuh*, I'd guess a pig says *Ogi Ogi*, which may or may not be accurate but is a good guess. I call Indians *redskins*. I call old people *old people*. I assault a woman from behind. I take a kid out at the knees. I order three Vegas hookers and a Diet Coke. I single-handedly drive up the price of ceramics in the Czech Republic. I snap the neck of a harmless animal and mix a small portion of its blood into my drink. I garner two Emmys, a Tony, and a Kid's Choice award at the most recent red-carpet event even though my latest film was stuck with an NC-17 rating by the MPAA.

I piss everywhere.

Sheldon Wirth is hard.

Sheldon Wirth no longer cries during *The Sound of Music*. Sheldon Wirth uses two sprays of Binaca when one would have done just fine.

I should have bought bullets. It would have been a good idea, getting some rounds to go along with my .22, but I always figured that if anything were to happen, which isn't at all likely, I could just flash some heat—that's what they do in Spike Lee joints, right? They *flash some heat?*—and that's it, problem solved.

I should head back there, and get bullets and more pot. A dime bag. That'll make me dangerous, scoring some more weed, some ganja. Oh no, sir, I am not joking. I am not joking about the weed and the bullets and the return to Southie. I will go twice in one week. Because Sheldon Wirth is one badass motherfucker. I will return to Southie.

But wait—my coworker is at his desk, working on, or forging, Inspection Reports. Forging was never officially sanctioned, of course. It was simply one of the smaller evils SpectaCop employees nationwide had to commit in order for their branches to run smoothly—*ubiquitous but rarely discussed,* he liked to say, *like sex at a retirement home.* And as I see my coworker, bent over the desk in thought, I know that before anything, there is something I must do.

See this couch here, next to my coworker? Can you guess what I am going to do with it? Can you guess what I am going to do with this blue Freya Microfiber couch? That's right. I am going to pretend there are stairs behind this couch. I am acting like I am walking down to the basement or the pantry to fetch something, waving goodbye as I begin my descent to the underworld, the under-couch.

But there are no stairs here. Nor is there an escalator. No, this is simply a trick. An *illusion*, a joke. Pantomime. Family friendly. I have seen people do this on sitcoms like *Family Matters* or *Full House*, and I am replicating it. I could have told a penis joke, but potty humor is not for everyone. Especially people like my coworker. He fails to appreciate how long it took me to perfect this trick, how much skill and coordination is involved. He does not seem amused. This trick, it is much more difficult than I make it seem, but my coworker fails to appreciate the mastery of it. Does he realize I have a gun?

I will get his attention another way. I sneak up behind my coworker and train the gun on the back of his head. I poke the barrel into him.

"Don't," he says. He swats away my gun.

I do not listen. I poke.

"Stop it."

I do not stop, and I poke.

"I said stop."

"What?"

"Stop!"

"*Hammertime!*"

And this is when I dance.

Exile from my coworker's office has placed me in the reception area, lowered my confidence again. My coworker, after refusing to encourage me—

"Do you think I'm getting fat? How much do you think I weigh? Ballpark guess."

"I'm working."

"Thumb war?"

"*I'm working.*"

—has sent me to this place (sofa, potted jade, in a faux-terra cotta planter) with a makeshift look to it, the look of something not entirely legitimate, like a chop shop. I am to fix an askew **SpectaCop** promotional poster, where a mustachioed *Renta* has zeroed his attention on a visitor, snatching his fist with *both* hands—a phalangeal bear hug—flashing a smile that is more than a little perverted.

This man should be in an Abercrombie & Fitch ad. He is young, handsome. He should be outside with the other immortal models, frolicking and having fun (Look at how freewheeling we are! Look at how rarely we wear shirts! Look, I'm going to throw a football now! Look, I just got tackled! By a blond!). But he, upstanding individual that he is, feels dutybound. He instead stands sentry. There is hardness beneath this man's brow. He considers me soft, a candy-ass. I can tell. Because of simple things: I don't like going out umbrella-less in the rain, simply because I have an admittedly silly fear of most forms of falling water, and of the dancing Six Flags guy, bald and scary. This man does not let his girlfriend take advantage of him.

I straighten the poster.

I return to my desk and step over the only irony to the area, a *High Times* magazine that has made a place for itself on the carpeting after—I believe this was months ago—one of our Security Officers abandoned it in a precarious spot on the end table.

High Times has inspired me.

Because now I will smoke pot in the office.

That's right—I *am holding*. Here I go, lighting up, smoking the pot—this *monkey skunk*, the dealer, a smart dealer, called it, showing off his bud knowledge by noting that because marijuana is a relatively inelastic good, demand for it and therefore its price stays more or less constant, even during a recession. See? Pot dealers can be smart. People think these guys aren't smart. But my dealer, he was, in a kind of stereotypical way. He had dreadlocks and spoke with a Jamaican accent (for business purposes), telling me that newly implemented Massachusetts Bay port restrictions were driving him coco-nuts. Not 'coconuts.' Coco-nuts. Coco. Nuts. His shirt said WORLD PEACE.

I blow smoke out of a crack in the window and can't avoid talking to myself when a squad car passes—

"Whoa, 5-0 guys, cops. Be cool, guys. You guys cool? Be cool, be cool. Fiiiive-O."

—even though there are no other guys with me, even though everyone else on the street *is* cool, even though this crime series-inflected paranoia makes me appear more suspicious than otherwise. If I were outside. Which I am not.

I watch people, small people, scuttling by, windbreakers zipped to their noses on this cold, wet day. I stare at these people in their windbreakers, their cute little winter outfits, mucking about in their galoshes and warming themselves from the inside with their ten-dollar-a-day habit. Anything to keep their little bodies moving, minds ticking, hands industrious. I take another puff. A fifties-era cop would be none too happy with me right now.

This is how captains of industry must feel, surveying the city's hoi polloi. *Yes, suck down that nicotine, my duteous workers.* And, just for a moment, I lean back in my plush rotating desk chair and pretend to have untold industrial riches by muttering a few things about poor people as a class. I pop my lips as I do this.

Pop.

Pop.

I must contemplate the reefer.

The *bird*, the joint. I must look at it, monitor how evenly it burns.

Now these people, these workers, they are gathering below the window, gathering below *me*, awaiting my arrival—expectant, worshipful—as if I were about to address them, emerge atop a balcony and share some thoughts. There is the barking of dogs and the squealing of children, who have been given permission to miss school for a glimpse of me, scrambling up their parents for a shoulder-view. What should I do? This is so . . . so *sudden*. I am not sure how to react.

I wait.

I do not give the people what they want. They must be patient.

There is restlessness.

The crowd begins to question their presence here, their devotion to me, and, as soon as I receive word of these initial murmurings of discontent, I emerge.

And they cheer. They cheer and cheer.

I reveal my common touch, giving the *Rock On* horns, thrumming along on an invisible Stratocaster.

Jubilation is widespread.

They love me, despite my lifestyle, despite my eccentricities, my tendency to lunch at Capitol Grille, summer at the Cape, calling on Timothy (do *not* call him Tim, or worse, Timmy) for Crystal Light. Despite my penchant for Kiehl's bubblebaths and salt rubs. For, on Sundays, treating myself to an OpusX cigar at a speakeasy-themed restaurant in Tribeca (flying to NYC on the Delta Shuttle that weekend, if only because soaring gas prices have temporarily grounded my private jet) that goes by the name of *Nameless*, sitting on a calfskin sofa, alternating between *Victoria's Secret* and *The Wall Street Journal*, exuding prosperity with my Zegna double-breasted Prince of Wales suit, French Cuffs, Half Windsor, discussing—

"At least pretend to be getting some work done, will you?"

My coworker is standing in the doorway, a FedEx pack in his hand. *Can he see it? Does he see the joint? No. Merciful Almighty.* He plops the FedEx pack on my desk. He leaves.

—discussing whom I'll hit on at my 10th Exeter reunion with Wade Washington, my Fourth Form Squash partner and fellow member of the exclusive *Maidstone* golf and tennis club, as well as *Chalice-bearer* in the *Knights of the Broken Raquet Society* (an organization that has yet to admit its first Persian-American, which speaks to its exclusivity). My tendency to call up Hugh Downs on my Blackberry and complain about how everything—food, sleep, sex—has become so very dull. My impatience with the people at *Cigar Aficionado*, always hounding me for an interview. My peculiarity of doing cardio at *Equinox*, weights at *The Sports Club/LA*; and, on Mondays and Wednesdays, Pilates with Franklin (do *not* call him Frank, or worse, Frankie), who, by the way, *is wonderful*. My habit of requesting that Benjamin (oh, he's my assistant—do *not* call him Ben) e-fax my therapist a PowerPoint of this week's issues; expecting a response within the hour.

My immoderate love of lavender.

I enjoy a small pied-à-terre in Beverly Hills, which is both tasteful and tax deductible. It is there that I enjoy the company of hookers. I have villas in Tampa and Baja, where I watch my favorite football team, the

Chicago-based Bears franchise. But it is a bad year for them, the Bears. I am considering selling them.

The people below, they know about these things, they know I have resources to spare, but still they adore me. They know I deserve it, this lifestyle.

Pop.

Pop.

Pop.

Man. I thought *skunk* pot was supposed to be junk weed, but this *Monkey Skunk*, it's very, very . . . this is some good herb.

I poke my head out the window and compliment a street vendor on his smile.

Yes, yes. I am ready. I am officially *hard*. Yes, I have acted illegally in the office, smoked *reefer*, and have procured a .22 without undergoing the mandatory waiting period. Now I will get bullets for my .22. I will be loaded, weapons-ready, so to speak.

Not a protector? Ha. Ha ha. This joke, I find it funny, and your ignorance—that I find even funnier. Ha ha ha. And again: Ha.

You, Dafna.

You thought I was soft. You didn't know me. After I buy bullets, after I travel to Southie and procure ammunition for my gun—then I will find Dent. I will conduct a search, pick up his scent on that island, wherever he is, that exotic place. I will bring him home. Because he belongs here, with us. He will join us again soon. I will find him and bring him home. Because—raise again the bold refrain—Sheldon Wirth is one badass motherfucker.

Secret Redneck Trucker Clan. (MOTTO: *They double-crossed us, man! They kicked us in the balls!*)

That's not the real Denton Brown. The Denton Brown I saw in the hospital, the bedridden-acting, sickly-seeming Denton Brown—that's not really Dent.

The real Denton Brown never shut up. The real Denton Brown was the bartender's best friend. He would talk to him, hit him up for free highballs of Grey Goose, pity drinks, by discussing his sickness, not mentioning it outright, because that would be obvious (let alone tasteless), but alluding to it, starting out innocuously enough by complaining about prices at the local ExxonMobil station, then dropping a few vague phrases like . . . *but that's nothing compared to my medication, which is the only thing that keeps my symptoms down.* Or *Don't get a chance to sit and talk much these days, ever since treatment started. Just so nice to sit here and talk.* I guessed the bartenders—conscience-stricken, hostage to this man who, if he really did have all these problems, shouldn't be at a bar—were likely irked by these discussions. And although I, too, would like nothing more than to talk to bartenders, to tell them a funny story about string beans—about how, at home, there is an itinerant can of string beans, how I have been meaning to eat these string beans for years but have never gotten around to it (shuffling them around the cupboard like chess pieces, boxing them up when I moved apartments), I don't do it. I fight the desire to tell them the age of these string beans, which is between three and ten years—an estimate, because the born-on date has either faded over the years or hadn't been invented at the time of manufacture. I do not know where my urge to share this information comes from, but no, I won't do it. Talking to the bartender is Dent's thing. It usually occurred some point just after he, Dafna and Joel turned into truckers, holding their fists to their mouths like CBs. There were very few nights this didn't happen:

Ssshhht Forty-Seven, Joel would begin. *This is twenty-two on the beast. We got a baby bear on our trail. What's your twenty? Ssshhht*

Ssshhht This is One Four Zero in the beaver trap, shaking the bushes. Ssshhht

Ssshhht We got a brown paper bag up at marker six-one. Ssshhht

"This is stupid," I would say, leaning back in my chair, away from this nonsense, pressing my knees against the bottom of the table to keep from falling. Nothing good ever came from Dent and Joel starting like this.

Ssshhht Smile and comb your hair, boys. Ssshhht
Ssshhht Coming in a short-short. Ssshhht

"It's not all lingo," I said, nearly falling again. "Sometimes they communicate like normal people. In English."

Ssshhht Hang it on your ear. Ssshhht
Ssshhht Think we got an LID on our tails. Ssshhht

Dafna wanted in.

"That's a four," she said.

I would give her an *Are you serious?* look, and immediately decide that I did not like my friends.

Ssshhht That's 10-34. Sshhht. Sshhht And remember to Ssshhht, Ssshhht.

Ssshhht I'm heading into a hole. Ssshhht

Ssshhht On my magic mile. Seventy-thirds. Ssshhht

Ssshhht "We're clear." *Ssshhht.* Dafna again, remembering her *Ssshhht.*

Ssshhht . . .

I hate my friends a little bit.

Ssshhht . . .

Oh yes, I do.

"My friends are losers. Every one of them."

The sole purpose of my going to Margarita Mondays with these people was to get loose and confident enough to talk to women—or if not talk to, at least stage whisper at them, a technique I have found privately gratifying but lacking effectiveness—while simultaneously appearing laid back but not too laid back, while simultaneously looking prosperous, while simultaneously looking—

There's one, at the bar. Should I sit next to her? Yes, I should. How's my collar? Good, I think it looks good. I should stop staring at her breasts.

—not too prosperous, not arrogantly prosperous, while simultaneously looking as though it doesn't matter if I am prosperous, because I am simultaneously appearing like I have (when I don't have—no no no, I don't have) something more to offer them. That I have the means to marry by 30, retire by 60, die by 85, which is exactly what catches the attention of Female 1 and Female 2, who have gone to Ladies Night at a popular Boston nightspot like *Vox Populi*, and whose conversation we are now encroaching upon, catching Female 1 in the middle of a thought:

```
                     Female 1
    " . . . keep telling you that we should have gone
Clery's. This place is dead. Clery's is never dead. Hey,
check out that guy. Well-groomed. Scotch and soda. Or is
that Maker's Mark? Good earning potential, either way."
                     Female 2:
    "Not so fast. See the chin? Weak chin. Signals a lack
of ambition." Not so fast. See the chin? Weak chin.
Signals a lack of ambition."
```

I didn't expect to attract many women, but it didn't help that Joel was there, and it didn't help that Joel, mincing toward a circle of bachelorette partiers to the beat of How Can We Be Lovers?, couldn't help but comment on at least one of the three following topics: 1) Smokeshows 2) Total Smokeshows 3) Boobies. Nor did it help that, about halfway through the conversation, Joel would tilt his head back and start gurgling.

"My Dos Equis tastes funny."

"It's probably in your head. Give it to me."

I take, drink.

"Hm. Did not expect that to be salty."

This wasn't the worst part of the night.

The worst part came with Dent's inevitable decision that the waiters would like nothing more than to engage him in conversation.

"Please don't talk to the waiters tonight."

"I have to."

"You don't have to."

He was almost as bad with waiters as he was with cabbies, whom he always advised to "make it snappy," thinking they would find it funny. Sometimes, for an altogether new brand of terribleness, he said *chop chop!*

"I do have to," he would say, referring to the waiters. "I need to show them I'm not some rich asshole."

"You're not rich," Joel would say, upset that Dent treated servers so well, proudly displaying an orange shirt. It said HOOTERS.

"They don't know that. What if my regal bearing makes me come across as wealthy? Then I'll look like a complete ass."

I didn't like the way he used that word *rich*, especially when talking about people we knew. The communities with which we were familiar were *nice* or *good* or, at the very most, *affluent*. Home to orthodontists and university professors. People who could afford summertime Winnebagos but not the gas to go anywhere. Who, if they were one of the lucky families, had cable TV. (The Wirth family, of course, went without.) They weren't *rich*. *Rich* people wore bowties and used words like *do tell* and *ahem*. *Rich* was a four-letter word.

"They don't care that much about you," Joel says, referring to the waiters.

"They're human, too."

"*What?* I don't think they'd like you saying that about—"

"Look, near the coat check," Joel would interrupt. "Total smokeshow. Look at her. *Look* at her."

"Let me ask one of them, then."

"That's the last thing they'd want you to do."

It didn't matter. Dent always talked to the waiters. He usually started off by baring his soul about the traffic on Storrow Drive that night, following it up with a not-even-close-to-off-the-cuff remark about the hot bartender—*total smokeshow*, Joel would add—specifically regarding her ability to shake up a good whiskey sour—

"Oooh! Want to order sexually suggestive drinks from the hot bartender?"

"Like *Sex On The Beach?*"

"Yeah, or an Orgasm. I'm going to order an Orgasm."

—usually finishing with a good throwaway line about his desire to give the bartender a whisky sour of his own, *if you know what I mean, and I think you do. Oh yeah, you do, cause you're a dude.*

Sometimes he lightly touched their arm. I cringed when he touched their arm.

"Hey, did we find out our waiter's name? Does anyone know?"

Oh no. He is going to do the name asking. And after the name asking, he is going to use their name as an excuse to integrate them, include them in our conversation, as an excuse to—

Our waiter's name is Mike.

"Mike? Like Mike Tyson? Is it short for Michael? Like Michael . . . Jordan?"

How crude it is for him to make such references, to act like he won't really grasp the name until he celebrates its relevance by invoking a congruently named celebrity-athlete. But Mike is a good sport. Mike laughs.

"I should tell Mike that I only eat food that's been pre-fondled," Dent says when he leaves. "Don't you think he'd find that funny?"

So he does, and yes, Mike finds it funny, or at least pretends to.

"Is this rare enough?" Dent says when his steak comes, pressing down on it like a doorbell.

"Oh, yes. Perfect. Per-fect."

Again, Mike laughs. Mike seems to find everything Dent says funny, even if it's not a joke. That liar. That *actor*. His shirt says **UNICEF**.

"Is this guy always like this?" Mike says, in stitches. "Is he always on?"

"Why, all these compliments *complement* you well, Mr. Mike."

Again, mirth.

Will those guys *quit it*?

"Quit it, guys. Seriously, you sound like a couple of homos," Joel says. I do not condone the way he handles it, but still. Thank God.

These days, bars aren't so fun. There is no silliness, and there is no need for me to run interference for anyone. There is no Dent to talk to the waiters, no Joel to spill on himself, to encourage Dafna's teasing of me, no Dafna to do the teasing of me, and no nearby women to make implausible advances on. The Secret Redneck Trucker Clan (MOTTO: *It's not safe here, man! It's not fucking safe anymore!*) has disbanded, for now.

Yes, I will get bullets. Because Dent would do that sort of thing. I will get these *slugs*, they call them, oh yes, I will. And, while I'm at it, perhaps I will pick up an extra light bulb for the office. But I really shouldn't go on an empty stomach, so first, lunch. I'm going to make tuna salad.

Before I go, I tuck the .22 into my pants.

The air outside, it's refreshing. It's not the frigid, hunker-down cold that I felt out the window this morning. It's crisp, this afternoon air, perfect for a walk to the subway, and as I walk there, contemplating my tuna salad—Will I put relish in it? Who knows? Will I satisfactorily drain the tuna? It's anyone's guess!—I could not be more energized. Alive. When I insult a bum opening doors at the 7-Eleven, telling him I "don't speak homeless," (because I am the new Shel Wirth, the *tough* Shel Wirth), I am strong. And even when passing another panhandler, this one dressed as the Lincoln Memorial, I resist hissing and withdrawing, giving in to my innate distrust of human statues (as well as other forms of street theater) and I stride past, unfazed. In fine fettle. *Fine* fettle. Why? Because I have set goals (to reach the subway station; to do so in a timely manner; to do so without excessive crosswalk delays), and setting goals is what *men* do. Also, I have taken the necessary steps to reach those goals, (moving attentively, swiftly, a thousand furies at my back) and—what do you know?—I have accomplished these goals! I am here! At the subway station! The T station! It's so clean! I adore the Massachusetts Bay Transportation Authority, and I adore the T! Even if it's slow! Even if it's lacking a serviceable men's room! Even if, upon boarding, appendages assault me from all angles! Because Ruane Manning would love this subway! He would paint a picture of it (though he does not customarily render cityscapes), a watercolor. He would portray the rush-hour standstill luminously, in earth tones, showing the subway as it is: limbs dangling from cars—doors almost shutting, then not, then shutting again. He would use his drybrush technique to create the illusion of movement, capturing a moment in time and tying it to an emotional state, showing it for what it is: a ritual, a daily competition to be the First Delayed, which for the moment, is delayed. Beautiful. Or, as Dafna, Beau-ti-ful.

I sit on a bench and feel the arm. It is covered with a viscid substance, something the consistency of ejaculate. I stand up.

You know, this is such a beautiful subway. I need to discuss this subway with someone.

I am usually not a person who approaches strangers on the MBTA, but I am out of the office, done for the day, and I need to talk to someone. So:

"This is a really clean car."

"Excuse me?" The man next to me looks up from his book, a James Patterson production.

"This subway car. It's really clean. Have you ever seen a car this clean?"

"I guess not?"

His shirt says TEAM EDWARD.

"It's amazing. I can't speak to the other subways, but when it comes to this particular car, the city has really done its job. Don't you think it's done its job? Whoever is in charge here has done a wonderful job. Score one for Government Center."

Should I high five him? I fight the urge.

"I guess so," the man mutters, twisting his face into something resembling that of a wronged snowman. I take it as a sign and move away.

I try another person, a woman, a nasty aggregation of carmine hair and noisy head ornamentation, holding an infant. Because of this infant, I assume she is the type of person who is approachable, open to talking to strangers on the subway.

"Cute kid," I say.

"Pervert," she scowls. The kid starts to *goo*. His onesie says BLUES CLUES. A tush button comes undone.

Oh dear. She has mistaken me for one of those perverts on the subway—*sick fucks* my dad used to call them, the ones wearing loose-fitting sweatpants, who touch women and children first. This is not me. I am a good person. I pray she doesn't have a cell phone camera, snapping my picture. She looks like the type of person who would readily submit my picture to law enforcement.

In my mind, I have made an enemy of this lady.

You, lady. You, of carmine hair and dangle earrings. I bet you don't understand the lessons of Deuteronomy. I bet you find it difficult saying something nice about the Field Museum's King Tut exhibit. I bet you don't appreciate our military. I bet you're an unresponsive lover. I bet you have neither heard of nor appreciate Chicago Blackhawks defenseman Chris Chelios. You don't look like you're good at being wealthy. You know how some people are good at being wealthy? Are tasteful? I bet you're not one of those people.

Yes, I see how your earrings sway, how they jangle. And I am not impressed.

I genuflect ever so slightly and remove myself from her presence.

This lady, she will not dampen my spirits. I move down the subway platform. As I reach the end, I see a man in a John Deere hat.

He is staring at me. At my gun? Does he see my gun? No, I have hidden the gun under my shirt, and it is undetectable, invisible. He is staring at the broken Detex system I am holding, wondering why I am holding it, which is exactly what I am wondering, except for a different reason. I don't quite know why I'm bringing it home. I am not going to leave it at home. I won't be able to fix it there. I am not handy enough. Never was. But I don't have anything else to carry with me (least of all paperwork or a briefcase) and I should bring *something* home, if only to act like I have a real job. A job with responsibilities and consequences. This man, the staring man, is not doing it in a rude way. He looks interested, earnest. I assume he is looking at the DTX system because he does not know what it is.

"That a patrol system?" he asks, knowing full well what it is.

"Yeah."

I step up to the platform, trying to politely deny this man further conversation. I concentrate on acting as unarmed as possible.

"What kind?"

"DTEX escort. Top of the line."

I say 'top of the line' because I assume it is mandatory for all men to say *top of the line* whenever any sort of driven or handheld equipment is under discussion. Even if it is not really top of the line, and even if you are not fully confident that a line of such items exists in the first place, you should say "top of the line."

"Oh, sure," the man says. He is shaped like a mailbox. "Looks like a newer model. But I'm familiar with the system."

This places him among the elite and lucky few who have ever used DTEX tour verification system, an escort "watch tour" kit, which was designed to monitor the guards, verify that they are really doing their rounds.

"Yeah. Worked with those things after I got out of the service."

The man also has a graying Marine haircut, a high-and-tight, so I believe him. This man has wrinkly knees. I know that most people have wrinkly knees, but his are exceptional. Very wrinkly. I attempt to curry favor:

"So, were you one of the guys giving it to those purple-pissing Japs at Guadalcanal?"

He ignores me.

I should stop trying to impress people. He continues:

"Worked at an unloading dock for UPS. But I was the only one who used those things. Always broken."

This isn't surprising. The DTEX system consists of a set of computerized tags and a wand the security officers carry to electronically mark their route. It proves a valuable, effective device for about two weeks, at which point it breaks.

"Can't do rounds. System's down."

It breaks all the time. A tag is off kilter. Or the wand's batteries are dead. The guards soon learn that it is easiest to break the DTEX wand right off the bat—

"Can't do rounds. Wand's broken."

—by accidentally rolling over it in a chair. Or carrying up to a high place, like the roof, then accidentally jettisoning it. Or accidentally making it into a Louisville Slugger, swinging it against the wall.

"Can't do rounds. Tony lost the wand," is the way the security officers went about losing the wand when the manufacturers came out with an upgrade, making it more durable and nearly impossible to break.

"Everyone look at Tony," I would say, trying to embarrass him, and everyone would look at Tony. He would mutter something, usually an undercooked excuse. Then he would give a look. That my-silence-says-more-than-words-ever-could look. *I know it was wrong,* the look/his silence would say, *but it's okay, because see how apologetic I am about it? See? I'm so sorry, so it's okay.* And it is okay. Because I won't do anything. I won't fire him. I tried it once, and he gave me an *Are you serious?* look. Because no, I wasn't serious, because, yes, I needed him. The site would fall apart without him. Then his coworker, Ivan (or was it Freddy?), would give me *another* look, the gaffe-off look, like he had lost all respect for me:

"Hey, Ivan (Freddy?)." I would say.

"Yo." If not his name, I remember he said *yo*.
"Don't give me that look, man."
"What look?"
"You know."
"Whatever you say, Bubba." I also remember he called me *Bubba*. "Whatever you say."

Tony, even if I had fired him, would have considered it a vacation. These were men who, if ever responsible for handling money, were forced to count it in full view of the security camera. These were men who wore clip-ons to work—

> "Brrrreaktime," they'd say, pulling them off with a communal *snap*, a line of tripping mousetraps.

—who had very little to lose. These were men who knew the true meaning of *foreclosure*.

"I assume you're in a similar line of work? Security or loss prevention, or whatever they call it these days?"

"Yes, yes—" but I stop, nearly discrediting myself by saying *indeedy*.

"—I am," I finish. "But really, I guess you could say I'm in the field of Putting-a-Stop-to-Parking-Lot-Blowjobs. I see your look, but it's true. You wouldn't believe the number of parking lot blowjobs that go undetected every day. They're among the many evils tearing this community apart. It's terrifying. It's a good thing I have this DTEX system, because who knows what kind of terror we'd see without them."

"Long day?" The man seems amused, but I am only half-joking. It must be stopped, this giving/getting of head in parking lots.

"Yessir."

There is something incongruous about this man. Something vegan.

"Yeah, thought the way you were standing, you were packing heat or something. You'd be well advised to change that posture of yours."

"Yessir."

You do not cross a United States Marine.

The subway car stops, and the man, Mr. High-and-Tight, gets off at Downtown Crossing. He smiles and tells me I have *good energy*. Weird.

I step off the Red Line and head down Dorchester Avenue to a short gray-green building with bars on the windows. *Frederick House*, a sign outside says. This is the one, where I bought the .22, which is an apartment complex but looks strangely like an old barn. I take the stairs and am about to knock on 4A, but I hear talking down the hall. Then I see them. They are large. Bigger than me.

Two guys, one white, one Latino. They are talking. They are using language I have never heard before, language belonging to people from a different way of life, perhaps even a different tax bracket. The white guy has a tattoo of a—shit, I bet he has tattoos of Swastikas and Confederate Flags and skeletonized horses with naked women on them. Why is he, this man with a Swastika, hanging out with a Latino? Aren't those guys supposed to be intol—oh, it's actually a rose. That's nice. But there's a dagger through it, blood dripping from the tip. Not as nice. It looked like a Swastika from a distance.

I am stupid sometimes.

I am very stupid now, because I continue toward them. The white one gives a strange smile, a snaggle-toothed kind of grin.

"Nice suit, White Boy."

This man is also white, so I do not understand. Now is not the time to question him. He is wearing a russet colored wife beater by JC Penney and blue jeans by Levi's, c/o Goodwill. His shoes are by Payless. He has dark circles around his eyes and an out-of-shape nose. There is no clear logic to his tattoos.

He gives an asymmetrical look.

"Hey, I'm talking to you, white boy. Don't you know it's rude not to answer when someone's talking to you?"

"Answer him, motherfucker."

His partner, the Latino, steps forward. Long arms, shaky hands. On his face, a mustache looks like the effort of some prepubescent boy.

"Thanks?" I say. "Yeah, thanks."

Snaggletooth approaches. He is sallow, sweaty.

"Where'd you get it?"

"It was a gift."

They look at each other.

"We didn't get no gift. You going to give us a gift, Governor?"

Now I'm governor. What happened to White Boy?

"You deaf? I said give us a *gift*."

Should I pull the gun? This is a bad idea.

"He don't wanna give us no gift. What do we do?"

"We *take* the gift."

Snaggletooth gives a yellow smile.

"You see, down the hall, apartment 5A? I want you in there in ten seconds. Ten seconds, or you die."

He doesn't have a gun, but he makes one with his hand. He gives me a *bang-you're-dead* gesture. I obey.

What would Dent do if he were here? Would he pull his gun? No, just do what the ugly man says.

I move to 5A. I open the door, and a hand on my back pushes me in. I hear footsteps behind me as the men follow me in and lock the door.

"Sit down."

I sit.

"Wallet."

"I—"

"Fuck you. Wallet."

I reach into my coat and throw it to them.

The Latino takes out the cash and my ATM card. It says BANK OF AMERICA.

"PIN number."

I give it to him.

"Idiot." Snaggletooth turns to me and tells me to get on the floor, addressing me as *Asshole* this time. I slip off the chair, to the floor. A poster on the opposite wall says LOLLAPALOOZA. They move into an adjoining room to investigate the contents of my wallet.

"You talk, you die. You get up, you die."

I lie prostrate in the middle of an empty room, staring at the foot of a coffee table—no, a *lopsided* coffee table. It looks like one of its legs is longer than the others.

Is one leg longer?

This is going to bother me.

Somewhere in the South Pacific: Possibly New Guinea, Probably French Polynesia.

Denton Brown wakes up and slowly apprehends, his eyes clearing, that he must have stumbled onto the foredeck last night because he is there now. It's sunny. He opens a Coors, turns starboard and looks over the approaching skiff to shore. Can he swim it? Just dive in and go for it?

Dent can't remember the specific day he left Illinois for this warm, lazy place where marine research sometimes took place. It must have been almost two years since he first set foot in the South Pacific, since he began his island-to-island fish tally. *Just got tired of the scene back home, no real rea-*

son, was Dent's reason for going to the opposite end of the earth. Everyone back in Illinois, he knew, had their own theory about why he left.

Dafna thought Dent's real reason for abandoning his town, state, country, and continent had less to do with any particular "scene" than one or two specific individuals who were cast in it. *Dent's decision was practical: He knows how these neighborhood watch communities work,* she told Joel over the phone one night. Dent had to escape a town where his own mom could use her own religiously-inflected—and wrong in so many ways—kind of morality to bully her way onto the chair of the PTA, and then once there, bully the PTA members themselves. This kind of thing wasn't unusual. Dent's neighborhood was a place where very few people had faith in innate human kindnesses like empathy and forgiveness. They therefore felt obliged to impose it on their friends, neighbors, children. Dafna always knew how much Dent despised the way Mrs. Brown, his mother, relied on the politeness of others to act the schoolmarm, her way of using morality as an excuse for most of her mistakes.

It had been displayed most vibrantly the year Mrs. Wirth, Shel's mom, became PTA secretary. Mrs. Brown and Mrs. Wirth were all but outright rivals. Their PTA infighting was all but public knowledge, the stuff of legend.

Late for the meeting?

Sorry, Mrs. Brown would say, *I was making sure my son said his prayers before bed. Some people in this town,* she continued, all too obviously not looking at Mrs. Wirth, *run the risk of letting their sons tear through the neighborhood on booze-filled rampages, with no concern for decorum. I'm not saying we should mollycoddle them, but . . .*

But isn't 7 PM a little early to put your son to bed?

We needed our prayers. Prayers are a particularly helpful tool to discourage all the language in the schoolyard, never mind the fighting.

Another direct look away from Shel's mom.

Our children aren't old enough to be sailors.

Dent steps starboard as the skiff hovers nearby. The man at the engine throws him a line. They pull the two boats together.

"Hey."

"Hey there."

"Give me a second."

He reaches for a small, watertight duffel, bending down as if bowing to a greater power. He unzips it, throws his body rag inside, rezips it. He tosses it onto the skiff.

His problem with Dafna, his only problem with Dafna, was that she mistakenly thought she knew him so well. She knew him through Shel, and Dent was never really himself when he was with Shel, never entirely open. Shel was his excuse to be crueler than he really was. To be an aggressor:

"Are you looking for a face transplant? I will strike you down, tough guy," he would say to any guy who looked at Dafna for a second too long. "It's too bad you can't control your own woman. Don't go after mine."

Dent felt it his place to wait until the bulk of the conflict was over, then to take a parting shot—

"You got a girlfriend, buddy? No? Really? Now why do you think that is? Your poverty? Your general unseemliness?"

—despite Dafna's objections, despite her contention that it encouraged Shel.

When speaking in threats, Dent ensured always to us the verb *got* over the verb *have*. It was ruled much more intimidating to say *got*.

If Dent were to make the same superficial judgments about Dafna that she made about him, he would say that she wrongly fostered the outdated belief that morality was for two types of people: 1) the middle classes, and 2) people in the moneyed crowd who needed something to be fanatical about. Dent's mother fit both classifications nicely—her money problems only becoming problems after her husband's indictment. The light disapproval she would on occasion display could become rolling pin-wagging sanctimoniousness if the mood struck. The *mood*, naturally, tended to strike when she was most squarely in the wrong.

Does my tardiness upset you? Need I remind you that Sub-Saharan African children don't have anything to be tardy to? Perhaps we should get our priorities straight.

Yes, part of the problem had to do with Mrs. Brown's oblique statements about right and wrong, and the effect it had on her children, and the effect it had on her neighbors, and the effect the runoff from the affected neighbors could have on her children. Dafna had it right, partly.

The Midwest Guarantee.

Dent's intentions for leaving had been honest all along. *Just got tired of the scene back home, no real reason.* It wasn't just about one woman. It really *was* the scene, in its most literal sense: the trees, the houses, the people—even the mute ones behind everything—in the background at the grocery store, or lingering by the tea and doughnuts spread at the USPS office—

who you see and hear about and know about but never talk to. It was anything that contributed to the averageness of an average town.

It was a town in which existed a strange atmosphere of disapproval, a town in which anyone trying to do something exceptional, or difficult, was made to feel guilty. *Those people*, the exceptional ones, were insecure showboaters (or foreigners, or homosexuals), the citizens said. Rare was it that anybody, exceptional or otherwise, had the balls to let their neighbors feel guilty about the way life was draining away in this little town.

When our neighbors thus began to abandon Dent, began to shun and evade him, when they began dissociating themselves from this neighborhood kid with the erratic sense of style, the simultaneously strange and remarkable sense of purpose (behaving like an eighty-year-old and an eight-year-old, often simultaneously) that's when I knew Dent was onto something. Our neighbors were right. Dent didn't belong there. He belonged somewhere much more open, much freer. Somewhere that welcomed him, that allowed him full use of his mental and physical faculties. Dent belonged under water. You learn how to fly when submerged, he once told me. You learn how to pitch and yaw like aircraft.

So, when people began closing themselves to Dent and treating him like an outsider—that's when I knew I must not lose this person as my friend.

Dent sensed this *unbelonging* as much as anyone, growing up in the suburbs, the *scene*. Although he never viewed himself as actually *existing in it*. He tried hovering around it, beside it, allowing various plots, storylines, dramas to develop (sometimes ones of his own making, where he turned into "Man Who Wears Oakleys and Cheers for the Celtics," or "Lady Who Lingers in Aisle Three of Kmart for an Inappropriate Amount of Time," two of his many bravura performances throughout the years), occasionally stepping in himself to wreak havoc. Just for fun.

He wasn't ostracized. He ostracized himself.

Escaping the town—to him, a sort of no man's land—was justification enough.

There was a bleak safeness but also an underlying danger to this town, its ethos marked by an undue leniency toward the elderly, a place where no one ever felt possessed to check a fact against the elders, whose rickety walkers and sly, arthritic movements fooled everyone but didn't fool anyone. *See that man? That's Mr. June Bradley, 78 years young. Listen to him. Obey him. He's old. He knows what's going on. But don't check him. The very foundations of the town will crumble if people start circumventing the logic of seniority and begin checking him.* It was tyrannical, in a strange bottom-up sort of way.

Small things were what gave figures like Mr. June Bradley away, like *Scorch* and *Fred*, Mr. Bradley's two freaky calicos, eyes like lamplights in the dark. Looking and smelling more like petrol-soaked rags than anything else, *Fred* hissed menacingly while *Scorch* stalked and attacked your leg, not in a gentle, playful, manner, but in a *Must-Exact-Vengeance-on-Entire-Human-Race-for-This-Man's-Daily-Neglect-and-Sporadic-Mistreatment-of-Us* kind of way. No genuinely decent human being could own cats who behaved like that.

A great school system, though. You can't argue with the one-of-a-kind school system.

In the city, wealth mattered because the affluent kids went to the private math-and-science-y schools, to Northside College Prep, or the Young Magnet High School. In the bedroom communities on the North Shore, because public schools like Loyola, New Trier, or Evanston High were considered to be among the best in the state, everyone went to the same two or three, regardless of family income. There was no admissions process. Or rather, the graduation process *was the* admissions process, in that if you made it to graduation day without getting expelled, you clearly belonged there.

The situation was far from ideal. The good kids (rich or poor) could be ruined by the bad ones (rich or poor), and often were. There were so many instances where it was unclear whether Shel and Joel and Dent—poorish and poor and less poor but not exactly high society—were the good kids or the bad kids. Sure, they did well in school, excelled in athletics. But they also stole a seemingly impossible load of REBAR from the gymnasium construction site, or distributed new gym shirts with iron-on images of Marilyn Manson, or masterminded the school-wide dissemination of business cards with illustrations of The Dirty Sanchez, The Houdini, The Cleveland Steamer, acts that were sexual—no, *aberrantly* sexual, said the administration—in nature.

This administration was lucky not to have overheard their verbal exploration of autoerotic asphyxiation. In these activities, Dent was both leader and observer. He could play cool, the unflustered onlooker, then turn around and act oppositely: disapproving, judgmental. *Was he mimicking authority? Parodying it?* Either way, he realized it was unapologetically hypocritical. But because he acknowledged he was acting hypocritically, we didn't see it as that bad. *This is a joke, right?* said his followers, but as soon as the words had formed, Dent's behavior had again shifted. He became dispassionate. His was the role of inventor, pioneer; let the others take the credit. This Dent-Shel-Joel team was a favorite of the younger faculty, the bane of the grey-hairs. The best the administration could do was graduate them as quickly and with as little incident as possible.

Everyone else's eminently safe lives in their neighborhood-watched houses, were in large part spent dealing with an older generation for which—

> Dear?
> Yes?
> I was thinking . . .
> Yes?
> How would you like to try anal tonight?
> Why that sounds first-rate, dear.
> Then it's settled. 10 PM. Anal.
> *I'll be there with bells on*, hands quivering as she stabs the last of her asparagus spears.

—propriety had been so yoked to prosperity that the sexual maelstrom lurking beneath it all was often all-too-apparent.

"Remember, everybody: When introducing a man and woman, you introduce the man *to* the lady, not vice versa."

"Does it really—?"

"Don't ask me why, it's just the way it's done."

"But who cares what order?"

"It's *the way it's done, damn it*," now hissed through the teeth.

This was part of ***The Midwest Guarantee***: Service your car, service your spouse, go to church, and listen to Mr. Bradley (he's a *lamb*), and success is guaranteed. Or, more accurately: Success is guaranteed *if and only if* you service your car, service your spouse, go to church, and listen to Mr. Bradley. If nothing else, tolerate, humor, obey Mr. June Bradley. *Do not risk anything.*

Stay safe.

Mr. June Bradley is everything. He is God here.

They, Midwestern teenagers like the Dent-Joel-Shel team, regardless of affluence, therefore created perilous conditions for themselves—drinking, on drugs, knocked up, killed—that they weren't mature enough to deal with. The stupid summer parties, the stupid risks. The pills, the powder, the speed. The life-shattering overdose or DWI-related vehicular homicide every July, an event whose occurrence became routine enough to force the Northbrook PD to retire the term *manslaughter*, considering it unnecessarily descriptive.

And this predictability of the town, harmful itself, some said—catalyzed these events. Wayward clusters of Evanston or New Trier students spent entire Saturdays loitering at the IHOP or at the Schaumberg Acura dealership, formulating names for those hairy men with the open collars and *gold* chains, fake bling. Obnoxious behavior like this provided a safer but misunderstood—

"Want to go to watch little league and make fun of the kids who weren't as good as we were at their age?"

"Oh yes. Let's. Do you have your roller blades? We should roller blade there."

—way of dealing with those blights of suburbia: predictability, propriety, boredom. It's not that the town was cookie cutter, as cookie cutter suggested a shared sense of purpose, however warped. The feel of this town was much more Darwinian, in its most passive-aggressive form. It was an every-man-for-himself, to-the-victor-goes-the-spoils atmosphere, if you considered *the spoils* to be a form of smugness most aggravating to the neighbors.

The summers. Summers were purgatory. People scattered. Some kids went to Interlochen, the music camp; others, to Math Camp at Illinois Champagne-Urbana. We, on the other hand, stayed local, because we were the unknowns—in twenty years, we would either be crossing guards or traffic cops or The President—so we spent our days roller-blading, or selling CUTCO knives door to door, or shopping for and proudly wearing shirts that say CRAYOLA or TIM HORTON'S or GATORADE, offending parents by becoming anti-fans of the local Little Leagues.

"Shit, these guys are actually good. Were we that good?"

"I muchly doubt it. Let's boo."

It was empty time. Empty time was anathema to North Shore teens. No, it was worse than that. It was dangerous. The city, at least, seemed safe in comparison: it had a relentless stream of pre-packaged perils for them. Or at least a chance at meaningless defiance, for little Rebels Without Causes.

"Hey, Kaufman says there's this new decoy police cruiser on Halstead. Wanna break its taillights?"

"I think I love you."

Kids threw up gang signs, formed arbitrary posses and held initiations, employed Super Soakers in simulated drive-bys. They wore beepers, associating beepers with drug transactions, or at least the buying and selling of contraband. They skateboarded across I-94, or in abandoned Splash 'n Slide park or swimming pools or cement parks or parking garages, breaking ankles, wrists, collarbones. These people came from respectable families but acted like white trash because, well, it was Illinois. What else would you expect? It's amazing what people embrace when there's little hope of escape.

*A **No Skateboarding** sign! But Fuck You—I Am Skateboarding.*

Which explained why, when a woman named Laurie Dann walked into Hubbard Woods Elementary in 1988 and shot a teacher and six students—retreating into a nearby house that soon became surrounded by local police cruisers, the only purpose of which, it seemed, was to keep her at bay until she turned the gun on herself, which she soon did—the event was huge, at least by North Shore standards, but not altogether unexpected. It made news in Champagne, in Joliet, down in Springfield, IL. It may even have made it across state lines. the only bigger story that week was weather. A thunderstorm in Iowa, apparently—less tragic but more surprising. It, the shooting, left the parents terrified, the kids fascinated. *So this is what the city is like.* It was tragic, but, to the kids, it was also *cool.* The experts said it ushered in an era of the school shootings across America (This was Pre-Columbine, remember). Or they blamed movies like *To Live and Die in LA* and *A Nightmare on Elm Street*. They blamed it on those shockploitation or vigilante films parents sometimes found under the kid's beds.

The kids, said the experts, were capitalizing on tragedy. Saying certain individuals *identified* with the shooter is going too far, though they certainly didn't identify with the experts, or the cops. They were taught to respect the authorities but couldn't help but be skeptical. It was a skepticism that was reinforced nearly a decade later when they read about Amadou Diallo and the NYPD Street Crimes Unit. But Dent remained dissociated from it all. Or incubated, in a kind of cocoon, a limbo. He didn't take sides yet showed compassion to both. And—could it be?—disdain. It was hard to tell. If any, a fraction of a fraction.

Sure, Mrs. Brown, his mom, was a miserable cow—or, again, perhaps a frustrated rug-muncher—but she gave him everything a son would ever need. She kept him safe.

It took balls to go off like Dent did.

South Boston.

I am still alone in the room. It is dark.

There is nothing to do, so I find something to do. What I do is I invent a rumor about Toni Morrison, then write that rumor on a napkin, then transfer the napkin rumor to the computer. Then I compose a mental journal entry that begins, OMG, I did the most *embarrassing* thing in front of Henry Harriman today. Then I discover something new about myself. Then I kneel, then I will pray, then I swear an oath.

Then I form an opinion on Charlie Sheen.

Then I count my pinkies. There. I counted my pinkies. There are two pinkies.

I am sure there are more but I do not have the time. Who has the time these days? Then a man offering flowers crosses my path and I ask the man offering flowers if he has any of those delightful red, red roses and the man says he has no more red, red roses and I say, "Why do you have no more red roses?" and the man says, "Because the soil is hard." So I take one of the non-roses and break it over my knee, making one hundred percent sure that Mr. Flower Man saw me do so.

Then I smuggle in and set off every type of consumer firework in the states of Illinois, Iowa, Maine, Ohio, Vermont, Arizona, Delaware, Massachusetts, New Jersey, New York, and Rhode Island. Then I carry a concealed switchblade in the states of Alaska, Colorado, Delaware, Hawaii, Illinois, Indiana, Kansas, Louisiana, Maine, Michigan, Minnesota, Missouri, Montana, New Jersey, New Mexico, Pennsylvania, Tennessee, Texas, Vermont, Virginia, Washington, and Wisconsin. Then I sell medical marijuana in every state but the following: Alaska. Arizona. California. Colorado. Hawaii. Maine. Nevada. Oregon. Washington. Maryland. Then I bring the following items through U.S. customs: Alcohol. Automobiles. Biologicals. Ceramic Tableware. Cultural Artifacts. Articles with Military Application. Dog fur. Cat fur. Drug Paraphernalia. Firearms. Fish. Wildlife. Prepared food. Fruits. Vegetables. Hunting trophies. Gold. Meat. Livestock. Poultry. Haitian Animal Hide Drums. Merchandise From Embargoed Countries. Pets. Plants. Seeds. Soil. Textiles. Clothing. Then I smuggle the following things across the Canadian border: Prescription drugs. How? I use my cavities.

Then I—

Then I—

Do these meth heads have ice? What's the ice situation like here?

—award my left nostril the title of "Most Pickable." Then I worry that the song *I'm A Little Teapot* encourages theatricality at too young an age, and wrestle with the appropriate wording for a disclaimer about it.

Then I find Jesus. His shirt says I PUT KETCHUP ON MY KETCHUP.

I have a deathbed conversion.

I do this all as quietly as I have done anything in my life.

I am not thinking about Dafna. I am not thinking about dying.

This is what's known as making the best out of a bad situation.

That woman on the subway, the allegedly offensive dangle-earring-adorned woman—she was not all that bad, not all that out of line. She did not deserve the kind of harshness I directed toward her. She was just a normal, law-abiding woman, a decent citizen who participates in food drives, or her church rummage sale. Who knows? It's possible she's a decent conversationalist. And although it would be wrong to so soon forget my disproportionate acrimony, at least I can laugh at it, considering there are people in this world much less deserving than her.

Snaggletooth and the Latino, who I have just now named Babyface, are in the next room. I look around the apartment, a post-apocalyptic landscape. A La-Z-Boy, not five feet from a TV, a mangled hanger standing in for the antenna. On an old coffee table are signs of catastrophe. A dirty ashtray, dried ketchup, crumbs. Next to it, an upended box stamped *Marx Industries*. Isn't that the company Joel works for? Isn't that his uncle's company? And aren't those his needles? Are they using Joel's needles to shoot up? What are they shooting up?

Or—I look at the ashtray—maybe they're those guys I hear on *Recovery Radio*, the ones I see on that VH1 special about Meth heads. They look just like them, with their sunken eyes, their sweatiness and shaky hands? Their panicked, jerky movements. Are these guys Meth Heads? Tweakers, who can't wait for their next fix, who will do anything to anyone—or *on* anyone—to get it? I should tell them I'm a gangster.

That I was in the Latin Kings back in Chicago. Yes, I was a Latin King. Or a Crip. Would that be any help?

The animation, the Dennis Kucinich-sounding cartoon, is talking to me again.

"A fine mess you've gotten yoursel—"

"Not now. Please."

Why Dennis Kucinich? I do not know. I have no control over this.

"Spank me."

What?

"Call me a whore. Spank me."

Dennis Kucinich wants me to spank him? This is too weird.

"No."

I will not spank Dennis Kucinich.

"Come on . . ."

"*No.*"

"You say something?"

The probable Meth Heads have reentered the room. The Latino, Babyface, has a gun. He looks like one of those guys who takes off his shirt when he goes to the bathroom. Someone who sweats a lot.

"You like this? You like this thing?"

He twirls the gun, points it.

"Your expression leads me to ascertain that you are not a big fan of this thing," he says, tapping it against my neck, clearly pleased with himself for coming very close to using the word *ascertain* correctly in a sentence. His shirt says FORMULA ONE.

I think for a moment that I should just attack, pulling them into a parodical dust cloud of arms and legs, crawling out, unharmed.

Or I could engage them. Yes, talking to them will humanize me, give me the appearance of being an advocate, a friend, and they will take pity.

"Soo . . ." I say, gauging their reception.

Snaggletooth, the white guy, looks up.

"Do you ever have daydreams? I've been having the weirdest daydreams recently."

"Shut up. Wait, what do you mean? Like fantasies?"

"Sure."

"On this stuff? Yeah. What kind? Sexual?"

"Farcical."

"What?"

"Well –"

Snaggletooth: "Dunno. I dream I'm falling. Does that count?"

"No. Everyone has that dream. That's a boring dream."

"Don't call my dreams boring."

"It's nothing to be ashamed of," I say. "Boring people have boring dreams."

Oh no. I am stupid sometimes.

"So I'm boring? Hey, this guy says I'm boring."

He turns to Babyface and thumbs at me. Fuck, God, fuck.

"And you know what he's giving me right now?"

Babyface speaks up.

"What?"

"Guff, man. He's giving me guff."

He pushes the gun into my temple. This feels less than pleasant.

"You sure he's not giving you The Business?"

"Ooh, maybe he is. Maybe he's giving me The Business." He turns to address me.

"That's right. The *Business*. That's what you're giving me, White Boy. I don't think that's very respectful."

He grabs his gun and slams it against my forehead. I hit the floor, hard, face upward. I struggle to stay awake, desperate for light, but it's no use. As I start to lose consciousness, I picture Joel and Dafna and Dent, and as I do, a prickle of regret runs through me as I realize that I've never had the chance to sit them down and look them in the eyes and tell them that they, these three members of the <u>Secret Redneck Trucker Clan </u>(MOTTO: **They got the codes, man! They got Mahoney and they got the fucking codes!**), a group of not overly attractive or intelligent or successful but kind-hearted people, are the closest thing to family I've ever had.

Then, just before darkness overtakes me, another, just as sickening, realization comes to me.

"Why don't we just kill the fucker?"

I am going to die tonight.

Help. I need out of here. Please. Anybody. Help.

My bowels seize up. I start to spasm. My final thought before blacking out is that this room could really use another light bulb.

INTERMISSION.

Please enjoy the next fifteen minutes to use the facilities, discuss the preceding events, or treat yourself to something nice to eat. The author recommends Eggo brand waffles. *They're not just for breakfast anymore.* He thinks, *They're not just for breakfast anymore*, should be the new brand slogan. It has a nice ring to it. For those interested in an outdated valuation report, see below.

VALUATIONS:

In a 2002 Clean Air cost-benefit analysis, the EPA estimated the value of a human life at $3.7 million. For persons over the age of 70, that number dropped significantly, to $2.3 million. The author thinks this is a good start, but much more work is to be done. He has appended his own Blue Book values to human lives, right. As a reminder, the author has also included his thoughts on waffles, above.

U.S. Citizens	$3.7 Million
U.S. Citizens Over 70 Years Of Age	$2.3 Million
U.S. Citizens Who Are Unemployed	$2.22 Million
U.S. Citizens Who Are Currently Hospitalized	$2.1 Million
Allergy Sufferers	$1.1 Million
People Who Work at Blockbuster	$200,000
People Who Give You That Put-Upon Look When You Request Additional Ketchup Packets in Your Super Value Meal	$200,000
Glasscutters	$200,000
People Who Say *I Kid You Not* in Earnest	$50,000
People Who Make Use of Venn Diagrams Beyond the Sixth Grade	$24,000
People Who Don't Run but *Skedaddle*	$22,000
People Who Use the Word *Nifty* in Earnest	$100
People Who Use the Word *Nary* in Earnest	$101
People Who Use the Word *Darling* in Earnest	$102
Those Who Would Seek Attention Through Sartorial One-upmanship	$104
Men Who Wink	$105
People Trying to Be Something They're Not	$40,000
Dwarves in Sombreros	$1.05 Million
Hatless Dwarves	$1.0 Million
Fans of the Turtleneck	$400,000
Mexicans (the tall ones)	$400,000
Verizon Kiosk Guys	$399,000
People Who Say "Believe You Me"	$200,000
People Who Say "None Too Happy"	$150,000
People Who Say "What the hey?" instead of "What the hell?"	$150,000
Guys Named Hector (Any nationality)	$150,000
Mexicans (the short ones)	$100,000
Chinamen (Living in U.S.)	$400,000
Chinamen (Living in China)	$ 8,485
Chinamen (Living in China, riding a train)	$ 4,848
Finger People	$99,000
Ralph Nader	$50,000
The Six Flags Dancing Bald Guy	$25,000
The Pigeon-Toed	$20,000
Awkwards	$3.59
DMV workers	$1.17
Puppies	Market Price
Babies	Market Price

VI.

I like this videotape.

It is a videotape I revisit once in a while, popping it in my old VCR on a Saturday morning like a sideways toaster pastry, remembering Dent, evaluating how it used to be with us, when we were still in high school, when the most that was asked of us was that we take off our hats when we were in the classroom and not get anyone pregnant when we weren't. The videotape reminds me how it used to be with Denton Brown, before I started bloodying his nose.

My friendship with Denton Brown was inaugurated with the more Freudian than funny soap-operatic hypothetical that the two of us were switched at birth.

"I hate my mom," Dent told me one day, looking into his locker as if he had lost something.

I understood what he was talking about when I went to their house for video nights. Spending time with Dent's mom was like spending time in the room in your house that went unused, the one with old family photographs that was always colder than the others, that you could only be in for a matter of minutes before you were overwhelmed with the urge to leave (and that you would have sworn was haunted, had you believed in that sort of thing.) You could only spend a few minutes in that room at a time. So it was with Mrs. Brown.

My theory, of course, was that Dent's mom was a lesbian who, never permitted to pursue any success professionally due to the gender restrictions imposed on all Midwestern women, therefore refused to allow her kids the same satisfaction. She was very good at crushing the dreams of little kids.

"I'm going to be a hunter when I grow up, or a ninja." Dent's little brother, Lucas, told her.

"Not so fast. Those are exactly the types of people who beat their spouses," she said. "Particularly ninjas."

"Then an undercover cop."

"As bad as the criminals they lock away."

It was standard practice in the Brown household to make eye contact with the children only rarely, believing it a tacky habit practiced only by new money—although I didn't consider their family possessed any kind of wealth, regardless of seniority—and for children to observe a seen/not heard mandate. Mrs. Brown, nearly unable to bear the physical strain of having kids, seemed unwilling to undergo the emotional strain of raising them. She treated them not unlike police dogs. No kindness, petting, contact. How for heaven's sake were they expected to perform—in school, athletics, extracurriculars—if they were regarded with too much generosity?

"How about a publisher? Can I be a publisher?"

I don't remember much about Lucas Brown, other than that he was with us at our fifth or sixth viewing of the movie *Clerks*. He was too young for it then, but we were convinced he was ready.

"A publisher? Of course not. Bad hair. Horrendous people."

Dent in turn started ignoring her, writing her off as unqualified to govern the family, using as his excuse the fact that she *married up*.

"I trust you did well on your recent exams . . . " Mrs. Brown would begin.

"Fucking fantastic, trophy-wife mother!" he would say, just to get to her. Whether it was true or not didn't matter.

But Dent didn't care, or seemed not to care. Some people read his behavior as revenge against parents who insisted on being both reverent and not at all so—

> "Let us thank the Lord for this bountiful feast and pray that He kills The Red Menace before it blows us all to smithereens. Amen. Now, Lucas, put your napkin on your lap before I tan your hide."

—in their words and deeds. Dent mockingly relayed this attitude into the hallways of New Trier, where he would mimic the Brown family's *Puritanical Victorianism* by harassing the well-adjusted girls in the hallway.

"Hey Jenny," he'd say. "I like your earrings. They're shiny and nice-looking."

"Thanks, they're just the studs that came with the piercing. They were free."

"You mean those aren't clip-ons? Your ears are *pierced?*"

"Yeah, of course they're pierced."

...

"Whore."

He reveled in this antiquated approach to sexuality, recalling a not-altogether-bygone time in the Midwest when shame fueled social interaction. He liked to parody this ethos by policing the Spring Semi-Formal with a wooden yardstick, chastising any couple whose slow dancing appeared overly intimate.

"Leave room for the Holy Spirit, now," he'd cluck, bringing the yardstick down on any hand daring to venture below the beltline.

"Back, **DEMON**!" he'd shriek, going for blood.

When he wasn't Schoolmarm Brown, or telling lies about his hardscrabble childhood, or running headlong into water fountains, or approaching the school's Double Dutch team with suggestions for rope-skipping songs that most likely had not been approved by the IDDF[3]—

> *Mailman, mailman do your duty.*
> *Here comes a lady with an African booty.*
> *She can do the pom-poms, she can do the splits, I bet you $5 she can't do this: [Do a jump rope trick].*

> *Ching Ching China*
> *Went to Carolina,*
> *Tried to make a dollar*
> *Out of 15 cents.*
> *She missed, she missed,*
> *She missed doing this: [Do a jump rope trick].*

—or being generally disruptive when getting stuck with some insulting craft project aimed at less capable kids, like candle-making with strings and wax, or dressing up like the Prairie Indians and beating on the tom-tom, Dent's frequent attempts to escape his household chores resulted in his relocating to my place most weekdays.

"Do you chores before you go, Denton," his mom would remind him.

"Whatever you say, arm-candy mammy!"

For Dent's mom—and for many other families in her zip code—

---

3. International Double Dutch Federation.

keeping up appearances was like a twisted game of chicken between two families: How close to perfect could each appear before one kills itself, tears itself apart from the inside? Although Dent's free-spirited behavior at school was popular with everyone, even the faculty and school board, Mrs. Brown considered it a sign of weakness, as if his actions betrayed the family's most sacred embarrassments, as if they were wearing these embarrassments on their lapels:

> **HELLO, I'm Trish Brown and I'm:**
> <u>Insecure.</u>

> **HELLO, I'm Denton Brown, and I'm:**
> <u>Unable to control my alcohol intake.</u>

> **HELLO, I'm Lucas Brown, and I'm:**
> <u>What is traditionally known as a 'cutter.'</u>

It was a strange culture in the House of Brown, almost oriental, where Dent may have found himself less incentivized to embarrass his family if not for their acute fear of losing face.

Even so, the Brown family was at once ridiculed, respected, feared. It was unpredictable, and it was rich. Should it be pitied? Envied? There was confusion surrounding this. All that was known—or at least heavily postulated—was that there were dark secrets behind that family's success. I knew Dent's dad was a powerful man, or at least well respected in the insurance world, but I didn't know what kind of trouble he got himself into. I just knew he got himself into trouble.

> **HELLO, I'm Henry Brown, and I:**
> <u>Would ask that you ignore the dead bodies in my basement.</u>

"How about an orthodontist? I like helping people, and isn't that an orthodontist's main job?"

"I wouldn't let those people wipe my nose."

Lucas Brown, for the record, scuttled his plans to become a local DA and is currently studying podiatry in Wentham, MA.

Football, Wisconsin, Buns of Steel.

Worsening relations with his mom made eating at the Brown household a trial. Dent and I passed most of the time in the empty hallways of

New Trier in search of petty, inane things to fight about, like razors. We fought about the invention of the indicator strip on razors.

"What's it indicating?" he asked. "I don't understand what it's indicating."

"It's indicating when it's ready to be thrown away."

"It's done when it's in the trash. The company doesn't trust us to make our own judgments on matters of grooming?" He stuffed something in his locker. It was always badly in need of organization.

"That doesn't matter," I replied. "It's great marketing. That man's a genius, wherever he is," referring to the inventor of razors. "He must be a mazillionaire somewhere."

"Or yet trapped in a company that pillages the genius of their workers. Or laid off," is how Dent saw it, exemplifying an archetypal teenage conflict between us, painting greedy multinationals as greedy, baiting me to rail, tangentially, against the bloodsucking lawyers, who sucked the lifeblood from the only manufacturer of progress and good in this country, the conglomerate.

Somewhere in the ShaveSoft™ corporate offices, I argued, a quiet, virtuous marketing manager hit on an idea for indicator strips—bringing excitingly vital information to millions of men like himself (who would otherwise have no idea what kind of shave they were getting from their possibly-too-old Gillette)—and, in all likelihood, toting home a well-earned Christmas bonus for his family.

"The man who invented those pockets is just another working schmo," Dent said. "He fails to realize his company doesn't really exist. It's just some walls, a few computers and letterhead. It's"—and he said this as if arriving at some cosmic understanding—"*imaginary*."

"Bite me," I countered. "Besides, you're proving my point. These companies are just Potemkin villages. That guy's under no obligation to stay there. He is free to leave whenever he wants."

"Where'd you learn the word *Potemkin*?"

"That's beside the point."

"No, it isn't," Dent said. "You used the word *Potemkin*. I'm not arguing with someone who uses the word *Potemkin*. You win."

"It's not about winning."

"I know, but if it were, you would have won."

He knew this would piss me off.

"It's about you listening to me."

"Of course. Why wouldn't I, seeing as you're the winner and all, with the capacious, ravenous—is that right?—vocabulary? Oh, how I envy you."

But still I admired him. Because he could get away with arguments like these. Dent was an artist.

"I'm an artist," he said when explaining why, as a heterosexual male, he painted his fingernails black.

"You wear a baseball cap."

"It's not a baseball cap."

"Artists don't do that."

Bullshit said Dent, which was usually as sophisticated as his reasoning ever got.

"I said it's not a baseball cap. It has *The Bears* on it. It's a football hat."

"I'm talking about the hat's style, not its content. It's a baseball hat with the name of a football franchise on it. Anyway, that's not the point. The point is you're wearing a hat with a professional sports team on it."

"But I transcend it."

"Jeez, I'm famished. Wanna go to The Weiner Circle?"

Dent never considered himself one of those *out there* artists, the ones who paint with their feces or do controversial things with images of Jesus Christ. He was an artist only by virtue of his philosophy. Artists, Dent said, *feel no need to appeal to logic, and by nature are not combative* (again, his words), unless they are also Bears fans, in which case they are combative about their lack of a need to appeal to logic (mine). Dent was the worst kind of Bears fan.

The worst.

But I gave him a chance, and we fought. About schoolwork, mostly. We were always in the same class, always chose to be paired together on joint assignments. Our first project was a stop-motion animation exercise that drew inspiration from those early-November Christmas Specials with the particularly abominable-looking abominable snowman and—with little more than marshmallows, Elmer's glue, and human hair—earned us a C plus.

The next assignment didn't go so well. It was an autobiographical video essay—this was around the time Gene Siskel and AIDS were big, remember, just after the *Buns of Steel* phenomenon and the fall of the Berlin Wall—we were supposed to make for our summer school film class. Ms. Braver, an openly sexual woman whose unnecessarily public hang-up on Errol Flynn was made all too evident by her unusual reliance on *The*

Adventures of Don Juan as a teaching tool, didn't really care about the content of the video as long as we used the **The Five C's of Cinematography** (cutting, close-ups, camera angles, composition, continuity). She just wanted us to identify them in the video, using the *scroll* function on our Pinnacle video editing systems, and explain and defend them in the accompanying paper.

Our gimmick was that we would be talking about our current activities like adults, like we were looking back on our lives with world-weary eyes. Essentially, it was a weird offshoot of cinéma vérité, interspliced with our version of B-roll footage—Dent extemporizing for a while, throwing in some *fuck*s, if only for shock value. Dent was inordinately good at this:

CAMERA ANGLES.
[A shot of Dent, wearing a Bears hoodie.]
"We pulled some good ones as kids. We would order a water-balloon launcher—that huge slingshot—and position ourselves in a park next to a stoplight. As soon as it was red and a cab came by, fire away. The noise it would make was unbelievable hitting the door. We learned to make the balloons small. They hit the loudest. Other days, we stood on a local footbridge and would wait for cabs to come by and then drop firecrackers onto their hoods. This was fucking great. There was no reason for any of this beyond escaping what we called the purgatory of Northbrookian adolescence. Fuck. We were reading Dante at the time. We were such badasses. But smart, too, because we read Dante.

CUTTING.
[We cut to Dent, wearing a Mike Singletary #50 tee shirt and white hat, backwards, on a bench outside.]

CLOSE-UPS.
[This is Dent's close-up.]
We weren't entirely sure what that showed them, but fuck, That Showed Them.
There were close calls at times. There were a couple of instances when a cabbie would run up the stairs and chase us. He'd be yelling—exactly what, we could never make out—in a

way that made clear his intent was to tear apart our stomachs and feast on our innards.

CUTTING, CAMERA ANGLES.
[We cut to a shot of Dent walking up one of the Skokie Lagoon trails, the camera trailing him like a tourist, he the guide].
Once when there was a bigger group and everyone there was really drunk, Julie Stern, one of the girls who was always hanging out with the guys, didn't run fast enough (she always took one for the proverbial team by never running fast enough), and the cabbie caught her. Everyone was freaked that the guy was going to drag her back and kill her or call the police. The cabbie was just ripshit. Apoplectic. I've never seen a guy of his poundage run so fast. Joel said he saw murder in his eyes. When the cabbie caught her, know what happened? He didn't know what to do. All he did was shrivel his nose and say, "Why would you do that?" and walk dejectedly back to the taxi. That made us feel extra bad, that we were preying on these innocent drivers. Cab drivers really hated us. The cops loved us. They caught us a couple of times but just laughed and called us little pricks—and warned us we were going to get ourselves killed one day. "We're not going to stick up for you when you get yourselves killed one day," they told us. They were idiots, and they called us idiots, mostly for doing white trashy things like TP-ing that giant honey locust in the Walshes' front yard, then heading to Evanston for a Buff Joe's party platter.

CUTTING. CLOSE-UPS.
[Cut to Dent. Head and neck shot. He has on his molester glasses, aka Aviators. A cigarette, unlit, is between his lips. It is unclear whether he is wearing a shirt.]
We were badasses. That's how it was for us back then. It was living without repercussion.
Me [from behind the camera]: repercussion.
Dent: . . . repercussion. Go Bears.
Yes, go Bears.

We made three videos. All three of them went on like that. We neglected to highlight CONTINUITY and COMPOSITION in two of them, thinking their artfulness and lofty music-video-stylistic aspirations would earn some extra points (and the swearing, and we were sure of this, would earn us points with our peer group). It earned us a C plus. Oh, iniquity!

"C plus?"

"That's right."

"But our paper was laminated."

"Your paragraphs were sloppy. I asked for cogent prose."

"Did you hear that? <u>Laminated</u>."

We should riot. Storm the streets. There should be bloodshed, pedestrian killings. Or, exercising prudence here, litigation. A class action thing, uniting all victims of such unfair grading practices under one mad, merciless umbrella of legal brilliance.

But no. We complained, and she got mad. *Inarticulately* mad, a rare thing. The kind where she just looks. We always considered Ms. Braver reasonable, the only one never to revoke our speaking privileges. She was the cool teacher. Just avoid that Medusa-gaze.

It was the Bears endorsement that did it. I hated the Bears endorsement. I was initially going to cut the Bears endorsement, but Dent has always had strong opinions on the Bears/Packers rivalry, and on the greater Chicago area in general. He does not hesitate to voice these, and, for our project we decided to have Dent soliloquize for a while at the end of the tape; then, during the presentation, I'd forget to stop the VCR and let it roll onto Dent's mad-hatter rant.

It was our attempt to give the class a taste of Dent, uncensored and uncut. *RAW: Dent Unhooked: A Behind-the-Scenes Exclusive: Uncut* was a chance for us to show them what Denton Brown-ness was. It would surely score us more of those ineffably valuable student-points:

"You have to understand two things if you're going to understand the Chicago Tri-state area. First, the whole Illi-Wisconsin rivalry thing. And two, a hotdog stand known as The Weiner Circle. Two things, brought to you by Dee Jay Denton B.

Fact 1. [he holds up one finger on his hand] On certain days, we'd cross the border to Wisconsin. Illinois' Biggest State Park, we called it (and they in turn called us FIBs, for Fucking Illinois Bastards. I mean, how creative is that?). We'd go to a place called Kopp's, which looked more like a Laundromat than a restaurant. Stainless steel everywhere. We'd get these huge burgers and frozen custard at like 20,000 calories per serving and would feel like we gained 20 lbs. This gave us license to act fatter, act like stupid Cheeseheads. We'd bounce around, calling, "Wiscaaahnsin, Packers! Wiscaaahnsin. Packers! Wiscaaahnsin."

We became constipated with brats and beer, then, afterwards, diarrheic with ex-lax, pouring it into our drinks, because we were bored, because it was the Midwest, because we were in touch with our own bodies. Our bodies were a source of continuous fascination for us. It was cool to get plastered and break bones, lose teeth, scar. It was cool to try new drugs, to blind ourselves with beer, to see how far these bodies could go. Pain was one of the two best ways of fending off boredom. You can guess what number two was. Number two was beer.

There were times we'd get stopped by the police for having an IL license plate. They'd stop us just so they could slowly get out of their cruisers (They were driving Honda Civics at the time, which seemed like a weird shape for a cop car) and slowly walk over to our car and slowly motion us to roll down the car window and slowly tell us how the Packers were the dominant force on the gridiron, much more dominant than Ditka's Bears, who didn't have much of a shot at anything anymore. We kept quiet because, despite our newfound girth and love of all things Kopp's, Cheeseheads (we didn't actually call them this to their face, because they would have liked it) are very very good at smearing queers, FIBs and any other undesirables, or at least look like they are. We'd be polite, remembering our yessirs, even Joel (you guys know Joel, right—the guy who always seemed to end up riding bitch, regardless of how many people were in the car) and then we'd get a ticket for something. Speeding, usually. Save for the Bears comment, the cops would remain ominously quiet the entire time. Their attitude toward us could be best summed up by the term *unalloyed loathing*.

Final three things:

One: Yes, I would totally go for Mandy Patinkin if I were gay.

Two: Money Saving tip: The next time you go out to your favorite restaurant, bring along a small amount of tinfoil. Then, at the beginning of the meal, ask for an additional serving of the pre-meal bread, and then sneak that bread into your pocket or purse or knapsack or what-have-you, wrapping it in the tinfoil first. If waiters question you, simply whisper "recession," regardless of the shape of the economy. Adopting an attitude of haughtiness will shame onlookers.

Three: In Chicago, and I believe throughout the Midwest, *wafer cones* are called *safety cones.* We all know it's better that way. Let's spread the word.

Thank you.

The worst that could be said about Denton Brown was that he was fine, as soon as he was born, with being Denton Brown. He thrived on self-satisfaction. His body language, an I-got-nothing-to-prove slouch—that *insouciance*—fairly represented what he had done with his life, which (other than breaking sound barriers in my mom's Pontiac and dry humping the Janet Reno poster in the Social Studies classroom) was nothing to date. An implosive entrepreneurial phase didn't really count because, child that he is, financial loss didn't bother him (*Well, my ultimate career goal is to be a failed businessman,* he'd say. *I'd say it's going pretty well so far*). Employment for him was about as stable or promising as his relationships with women. It's not because he was inept. Not at all. He was just simple. He had one goal, even before the cancer:

"How's the world treating you?" I asked whenever I had a chance to chat with him.

"Pretty good."

"You still traveling it? Diving its many seas?"

"That I am."

Even if his proudest accomplishments, as far as I could tell, involved sending out half-comprehensible travel tips now and then ("Research has picked up but beer's like 8 bucks here because they have to ship it from Brisbane or something."), he is still my closest friend. He has been my closest friend for years, knows everything about me—my favorite gateway drug, my puberty difficulties, the embarrassingly low number of hookups since my puberty difficulties (a source of constant amusement for him: *...And then there was Shel.[1] And Shel was the pussiest of pussies.[2] And none would lay with him.[3]*) my secret desire to someday host a concert consisting entirely of audience participation call-and-response songs—he knows all these things. And still he's a listener to me, a forgiver of me, even when he's fielding strange questions from Joel and me—

"Dent? Dent? Dee-eent?"

"Yeah? What!"

"Do you . . . .do you ever . . . "

"What?"

"Well, when you're in the shower and you're bored . . . do you ever, you know . . . ever tuck one of your balls into your anus?"

"WHAT? NO! That's sick, man!"

"Oh, uh, I know. Me neither, me neither. That's messed up. Just making sure you're not messed up or anything."

—and I keep up with his emails, learning about the mysterious trumpetfish he encounters, and sometimes I run into his lesbian mother when I go home to the Northbrook Dominick's and tell her how wonderful it is that he is living the dream. That, even at his lowest point, he never had that stark look on his face, that dejected look of a sick person. He never had that look, at least not that I've seen. The calm of an escape artist, as if magic surrounded him. Denton Brown, warlock.

Dent could have handled these guys, these Meth Head brothers. He had, as Joel called them, monster balls.

"You got monster balls, man," Joel liked to say.

Imagine if he were here now. He'd use the .22, hold the Meth Heads at gunpoint, *tell* those motherfuckers. He'd feign some kind of familiarity with hand-to-hand. Or mixed martial arts. Or the opposite: He'd gain their trust with soft, pacifying whispers, invisibly drawing close to them, instructing them on how to roll a richer, fatter joint, how to supplement their methamphetamine recipe with herbal additives, and then jimmied the door and bolted.

Dent knows how to handle these things.

Dent has *experience*.

Somewhere in the South Pacific: Possibly New Guinea, Probably French Polynesia.

MacAlby ran back to the lab one last time.

No one believed that Dent wasn't going out tonight. He never missed harvest nights. The blackness of the water, the fluorescence of the anchor coral, your breath, isolated in the night air—Dent loved it. Just to be certain, MacAlby returned to the wet lab—an oversized surf shack that had been cleaned up and wired up—to check just once more. He found Dent on a stool on the far side of the lab, given over to his computer. MacAlby shook his head.

Man, still working, MacAlby thought. The only distraction was an old Toshiba 10-inch, where the Worldwide Pants logo was currently onscreen.

Even when they went out, dancing around a beach bonfire somewhere, Dent seemed incapable of peeling himself away from the ocean, the tests. He would half-participate in the revelry, jotting things in a small notebook held ever-tightly in his clutches. It felt strange to MacAlby, seeing a full-shouldered man so caught up with details. A man whose feet were black, whose legs were scarred. It was if there was a war going on somewhere that was missing him.

He's too intense sometimes.

"Dent?"

Dent looks up as if remembering something, his head nearly hitting the staghorn coral they had last week mounted in the lab.

"You sure you're not coming with us? Boat's almost loaded."

Dent glances at the clock. Eleven PM. They're late. He saves his spreadsheet and turns from the computer. No shoes again, MacAlby notices. Dent was notoriously barefooted. Dent knew the sand and earth and water of this island so well that most research assistants assumed he had been born there. His eyes reflected the ocean. His hair took after the sand. That was their poetry about him.

MacAlby was too young to be a research assistant, yet he knew Dent better than any of the others. He knew Dent had a preternatural way with people. He also knew Dent had secrets. He knew, he thought he knew, that Dent wasn't as at peace as some of the others assumed.

"The boat's already loaded?" Dent asks. "You have everything?"

"Yeah, you coming?"

Trumpetfish? They were uncomplicated, dull. Cardinalfish were what he was after, what Dent was after. But there was too much to be done in the lab tonight, apparently.

"Sorry, not this time. Trying to finish this up, then getting up early tomorrow to meet with EPA people about findings."

"Oh yeah, I forgot about the meeting. Good luck."

"Thanks. You have the tanks? Don't forget extra batteries. We don't want any dead lights this time."

The cardinalfish were captured at night. They hid during the day, nearly impossible to find during the day, so the team waited until dark. They used hand nets and lights, usually along a coral wall, harvesting fish about eleven centimeters in diameter. They were kept in pre-numbered Ziploc bags to be transported back to the lab, along with samples of their corresponding home corals. "We're all loaded. Batteries, tanks, nets. We'll debrief you on everything tomorrow."

"Great. Be safe, Mac. Remember your safety stop. Don't let Jill ascend too fast. She's always so excited about getting to the surface. It's dangerous."

"I know. I'll remind her."

It was one of the rare times he couldn't accompany them. Too much to do here, plus the meeting. The meeting that he hadn't marked on the desktop calendar, furtively checking off the days to it in the corner of his notebook, wanting more than anything to avoid hampering his team with undue worry. The meeting he stopped pretending didn't matter as soon as he came to grips with the fact that he couldn't be on the boat tonight. Still, he hated missing out. He had spent so much time working up to this moment—the actual running of the tests—that he hated missing any of it. Plus, it worried him when he wasn't on the boats.

Dent gives a look. "You're really going to remind her?"

"I'll remind her."

He turns back to the computer, reasoning out why it was okay to miss this one night. It would be good for the cold he was certain he was developing. It would be a test of his research assistants' independence. It would allow him to work in solitude and without challenge from Brian, a brilliantly petulant research assistant. The bubbling menagerie of tanks and samples and algae surrounding him were as good a haven as any. No distractions. Zen.

Dent pops open a Modelo Negro and continues logging the results of previous runs.

GEOFF GRAY

```
Log-Linear Model
Term tested           The model without the term    Removal of term from model
ln(MLE)    Chi-Sq    df   p-value    Chi-Sq  df   p-value
-----------------    ---------- ---- --------    -------- ---- --------
TREATMENT$ . .        -20.827    21.69   2   0.0000    21.68   -1      .
NIGHT. . . . .         -9.986     0.00   3   0.9999     0.00    0      .
NIGHT
* TREATMENT$ .        -11.048     2.13   5   0.8311     2.12    2   0.3456

Term tested           The model without the term    Removal of term from model
hierarchically   ln(MLE)   Chi-Sq  df  p-value    Chi-Sq  df   p-value
-----------------    ---------- ---- --------    -------- ---- --------
TREATMENT$ . .        -23.047    26.13   6   0.0002    26.12    3   0.0000
NIGHT. . . . .        -11.723     3.48   7   0.8375     3.47    4   0.4818
```

He labels the chart, Table 2: Log-linear model of displacement experiment. Treatment effect is due to term down-current being different from the combined terms up-current and control.

This particular run was not done in the lab. These data were from the field runs, the displacement experiment, a labor-intensive process involving the tagging (near the dorsal side, just aft of the *caudal peduncle*, a term Dent loved repeating and re-repeating) and releasing of fish, the emptying and refilling of holding tanks after each go. Fish were kept in ventilated buckets, i.e., buckets with holes, over the side of the boat until they arrived at the release sites, which varied in current and traversed terrain. Again, everything had to be done at night, to minimize predation and correlate with nocturnal behavior.

Dent steps back. *This is good. P-values are low, below 0.01, statistically significant.* There was something to their tests.

"Nice," he says out loud, nodding to himself.

"You sure that's right?"

What? Shouldn't everyone be on the boat by now?

"Mac?"

Dent turns around to find an overweight, chalk-faced man in the doorway.

"Paulson?"

"Hi, Dent."

"Aren't you supposed to be—?"

"Yeah, I was. It was canceled. So O'Neil wanted me over here. Caught a flight this morning."

"What? Why? We're still in the middle of experiments."

"I know—he just wants to make sure they're running smoothly. He wants to make sure you're getting results."

Dent makes a face. *This is not good.*

"Of course I'm getting results. It's the whole purpose of—"

"Yeah, but O'Neil wanted me to be here to make sure."

"You're usurping me."

"What?"

"You're here to usurp me. That's why O'Neil sent you."

Dent hated O'Neil. O'Neil was a dick.

"I'm not usurping you."

"Then what is this? How am I supposed to read this?"

"I'm just another level of scrutiny," Paulson says. "Think of me as a safeguard."

"For what?"

"To ensure we're getting the right results."

The right results?

"I won't get in the way."

"Won't get in the way? You're already getting in the way. You stink."

"I was on the plane all—"

"God, I mean really reek. Did someone pee on you? I'm not kidding."

He did reek. Gas mask reek. Call-in-the-HAZMAT-team reek. Seeing Paulson again was nothing he was all that excited about. Conversation with the guy could be difficult. It wasn't just that his English wasn't good. He also had the strange quality of being attractive from one angle—but from the other, inexplicably hideous.

Dent always did his best never to navigate far from his more pleasant side. He takes a sip from an orphaned WORLD'S GREATEST DAD mug he found on the beach last week.

"Like I said, I've been traveling all day. I'm sure you don't smell all that great when you fly from—where are you from again?"

"Illinois."

"Oh."

"Birthplace of Whitey Herzog."

"Who?"

"Never mind. Michael Jordan? Bulls?"

"Ohhh! And Al Capone, right? Home to Al Capone?"

He should have expected this from Paulson. He couldn't believe O'Neil put him in this situation. O'Neil really was a dick. A dickish dick. He hated O'Neil.

"Yes, home to Big Al. But in one of the suburbs. Parts of *Ferris Bueller's Day Off* were filmed near there. And some parts of *The Breakfast Club*, too, filmed in that high school. Don't know if you've heard of it."

"Not sure. Don't think so. Listen, I'm going to shower soon. O'Neil just wants me to tag along with your team—"

Tag along? Christ, O'Neil.

"—for the next couple of weeks."

My nutsack you're joining my team, Dent wants to say. *You're lucky I don't throw you out right now.* Dent and his team had spent nearly the last two years with the cardinalfish. They spent thousands of hours to understand its peculiar homing mechanism, how the cardinalfish invariably found its way back to its home reef from nearly two kilometers away. Even downcurrent, without any other cues like terrain, light or sound, it found its way back. Dent had worked hard. He was territorial. He had a right to be territorial.

But he doesn't raise his voice. Instead, he closes his computer. In an even, almost friendly voice, as if welcoming someone to a board meeting, he says,"Great. I'm glad you're here."

I Seriously Doubt Stockholm Syndrome Is Going to Kick in Any Time Soon, South Boston.

I do not have long to live. Snaggletooth has left with my ATM card. The Latino, Babyface, is sitting in the next room, talking on his cell phone. They still do not know I am awake, and I have a gun. An unloaded one, but still. It might work. I catch another glimpse of the Marx Industries Box. *Joel.* I still have my cell phone. I can call Joel. I can ask him for help. He's sure to help me.

I sneak my cell phone out of my pocket and dial. It rings. Please pick up. Please.

"Hey, Shel?"

Thank God, but he continues:

"Hey, getting murdered at work right now. Can't talk. I'll call you later."

He hangs up.

Why didn't I call 911? I had a choice between 911 and Joel. I called *Joel*.

Joel is worse off than me. Joel is secretly stressed, even if he doesn't have that much work to do, even if he spends his days looking at boobsbuttandsometimesbrains.com. He can change his situation simply by quitting his job. But not me. Right now, I am captive. At this point, I have no say when it comes to career matters.

Still his uncle rides him, uses him for his company. Joel is on course to have a nervous breakdown. He will crack, as those high profile attorneys so often do, wandering the streets, demanding forgiveness, then asking for it. He will walk around criticizing pigeons, giving the finger to cats. He will board a bus and defecate on the handicap seat. He will assault a fire hydrant, leg-dropping it. He will develop a complicated relationship with his anus.

He will do all this because he has run out of reasonableness, because he has been drinking, face flush with Olde English 800 or Colt 45, because his uncle has been a slavedriver, overworking him, stressing him. He has lost hair, years off his life. Sitting there, next to the hydrant (noting helpfully to any willing listeners that it is a dry barrel hydrant—useful in cold areas, as opposed to the wet barrel style, found in warmer climates), he will have an epiphany of sorts. He will get shirts made featuring this hydrant, become a worshiper of it, leaving votive offerings of Sour Patch Kids beside it.

He will bottle his urine.

(They all do that, bottle their urine.)

Then he will arrive at a low point. One week I will find him on the couch, listening to Hanson and switching between Cinemax and reruns of *Reno 911!*; the next, he will be identified in a halfway house in Albuquerque, New Mexico (this is after a stint in Bellevue) with his head shaved bald, knowing that it is 6 o'clock, not knowing if that is AM or PM. He will be wearing a shirt that says WALK FOR THE CURE, *never having walked for anything*.

No, it will be much less overt, Joel's insanity. It will take the form of small actions and be nearly unnoticed. It will start with a broken promise. He will tell Dent that I passed on the opportunity to visit him. That, despite the nagging, I stayed at work. Or stayed home, like every other loser high school friend we've ever had, Velcroed to the sofa, watching old episodes of *Harry and the Hendersons*, making Cup-a-Soup for dinner.

When Dent hears this, he's going to be angry, livid. He, vindictive being that he is, will take action. He will die. Just to make me feel bad, just out of spite, he'll die—right there, in Joel's apartment, in Seattle. They'll inter his body right there, in the shadow of the Space Needle, or perhaps tie it atop that 500-foot-high SkyCity restaurant, the world's largest and rotating-est bier. All of this, just so I regret not buying that ticket, so I regret not uprooting my life for a week to see his tan, smell his Coppertone residue, hear his (apocryphal?) stories about firewalking or cockfighting, or tribal rituals, or ritual slaughters, or group masturbation, or whatever happens over there.

If he has any brains, he will leave a note, blaming me, bemoaning the state of our friendship, our bond. He will write that he came to the States for reconciliation, to smooth things over between the three of us; but when he discovered I was a no-show, that I snubbed him, it was only natural for him to feel insulted. Slighted by a good friend. *May this rotting corpse*, the note will end, *be a reminder to all that Sheldon Wirth did not visit Seattle.*

I can't think of this. I am not thinking of this. And I am not . . .

"You trying to call someone, asshole?" Babyface is standing over me.

. . . and I am not thinking about Dent's rotting corpse.

"Tsk, Tsk, White Boy. This won't do. No, no."

Shit. Oh *Shit*.

"No, no. I was just grabbing my phone, you see, because I had dropped it, and . . ."

Babyface grabs my collar.

"Don't lie to me, White Boy. And don't you dare use the pluperfect with me, asshole."

He kicks me in the stomach. A flash of white breaks across my eyes. I curl up.

"Whatcha doing, White Boy?"

He wants to know if I was calling the po-lice. Not the police. The po-lice. The Po. Lice.

He toes my head like a soccer ball.

"You try anything like that again, you die."

He leans over and grabs my phone. I should pull my gun, when there's only one of them here, I should pull it and threaten him. That's what Dent would do. He would pull it, cock it, aim it, and say something badass, something like, *Naptime, motherfucker* (*Ooh*, this is good, this line. It is something Pacino or Willis might say—trite, yes, but all the more ominous in its triteness), and then smash his nose in with the handle. I lift myself off the ground in a push-up position, but I wobble. I fall.

I can do it. If I do it right now, just pull it right now, I can escape.

"Could only get three hundred," a voice behind me says. It's Snaggletooth, back from his ATM trip. An issue of *Skank Weekly* is under his arm. Or is it *The Weekly Standard*? It's hard to tell. Something with *Weekly*. He looks down at me.

"What's wrong with White Boy?"

"He tried to make a call. I thought you checked him for a phone."

"I thought you did."

"Shit, man."

Snaggletooth comes close, his breath hot on my cheek.

"Any other surprises for us today?"

Should I give up my gun? If they find my gun, who knows what they'll do? No, I can't give up my gun.

"No, man, no. I swear."

"Well, I got good news for you, then. Since there's a *per diem* limit on your ATM, we're going to keep you around another day, just in case. How's that sound, Rich Boy? That sound fun?"

I'm Rich Boy now. I liked White Boy better. How does he know what *per diem* means?

"Uhh, okay, okay, man. Is there anything to eat?"

Is there anything to eat? I am a stupid, stupid person.

"Oh, you hungry?"

God, why don't I just ask for a goddamn Slush Puppy?

"You *hungry*?" he repeats. "Let me go get the *foie gras*—oh wait, looks like we're all out."

Damn. I would have loved *foie gras*. I would have lunged for the *foie gras*.

"And *shit*," he continues, "I forgot my Zagat's," pronouncing *Zagat's* incorrectly. I decide not to correct him.

"But how about my dick? You want to munch on my *dick*?"

Yes, that would be nice, I would like to say, simply to make it uncomfortable. I keep quiet.

"Faggot," he says, as if reading my mind. His next sentence is filled with too many grammatical mistakes to understand.

I will listen to the kidnappers.

I will talk with them, Babyface and Snaggletooth, those inscrutable Meth Heads, and make them feel wanted, make it seem that I understand them, understand their needs (which I assume are Meth-related). I will plumb their *minds*, figure out what is wrong, exactly. I will administer a Myers-Briggs test. To really hone in on their psychological type, because *I know*. I know they are actually good people, god-fearing people.

I know this because they have just thrown me a sandwich, knowing how hungry I must be. It is a tuna sandwich—my favorite. (Did they cut it on the diagonal? No, they didn't. This is disappointing. I like mine cut on the diagonal.) But they are wonderful people, these two.

"How do you—how do you *feel*?" I will say. I will offer them a shoulder massage. Or a good Reiki treatment.

"Super," they will say.

"Super?"

"Super duper," they will say, avoiding meaningful discussion.

But in the hours to come, they will open up, will give themselves over to me—two flawed but deeply misunderstood hoodlums. The kidnappers will delve into their childhoods, exposing miseries and broken dreams that they haven't until now discussed with even their own families. They will get dark at times, their stories, but will find in me a good listener, a *resource*, if you will.

Together, we will acknowledge that change does not happen overnight, that it could take years, but that now is as good a time as any to begin a frank discussion about their options. We will set targets for improvement, outline strategies meant to maximize favorable results, engage in team-building exercises aimed at strengthening our core motivators (Storming, Norming and Performing), perhaps engage in an impromptu egg-and-spoon race to break the ice. We may use flow charts to visually reinforce our goals, and create *mood journals* to track our progress, and to reestablish ownership of our selves, our lives.

There will come a point at which we put on John Tesh.

It won't be long before my kidnappers notice marked improvements in their attitude and confidence, before they start to regain faith in their own abilities. My kidnappers will feel renewed, and feel as though, if but for an afternoon, they were treated like real humans, on par with contributing members of society.

If this doesn't work, if these therapy sessions misfire and they don't come around, if they don't open up and work toward self-improvement by being vulnerable for a few hours, I'll simply pull my gun and calmly inform them that I am going to paint the walls with their motherfucking brains.

Silly me.

Silly, silly me.

I thought I could talk to the kidnappers.

I thought I could convince them that letting me go would be in their best interests. I thought perhaps they would appreciate my offering them a shoulder massage—work out the violent urges. See that towel over there? Do you know what I am going to do with that cream-white Eco-Knit towel? That's right. I am going to moisten that towel by running it under warm water and then apply it to your face. Really steam out that stress.

Silly me. Talking, coaxing, does not work. I have just tried to inform my kidnappers that they have no further use for me, that our relationship is at an end. I look up, and Babyface, now holding his own sidearm, is standing above me. He does not look happy with me. I do not know why this is. I almost say *Wait*, informing that I understand him, that those studies showing that sexual frustration is closely tied to both creative *and* violent behavior—I have *read* those studies. But before anything comes out, he leans down and places the barrel of the gun farther into my eye socket than consciousness will allow.

VII.
Not South Boston

Dent hops across the hot sand and finds his way into a small tribe of cabanas at a beachside motel. He enters the one appearing most like an office and asks how much for the internet. Four francs an hour.

"Can I get you later?"

"Course."

The man does not look up. He is watching NASCAR.

Dent has an email from Shel, strangely one of the few people who, even after that last supper of White Castle sliders, after his blow-up, continued to email with any regularity. The specific woman-with-a-penis episode was never again mentioned, and Dent assumed their easy reconnection was due to common interests: both of them sharing an admiration for truckers; and skepticism of their mothers; and a very pure kind of disdain for government workers. And they both really liked Dafna.

Dent moseys to the bar, flashes an expired AAA card—good enough for this bartender. He orders a fresh drink—the beers aboard The Sea Note IV were flat, with an aftertaste of brine—and something greasy to eat.

"Heading back to the states today," he tells the bartender, a scrawny man with a large mole on the back of his neck.

"Oh?"

"Yeah..." he pauses, distracted by the mole. It is the size of a box turtle.

"My friend just started a business. He just sent me an email all about it. It's really blowing up."

Dent liked to lie to waiters when he talked to them. He liked to tell them things that could be true, that would be nice to be true. It made sense, Shel starting a business: Someone who had so much trouble with authority would likely be exceptionally good at exercising it himself.

"Good money?" the bartender asks. His shirt says **Pelé**.

"Seems like it."

That mole is really bad. He should have it checked.

"Hope he has good luck with that."

But really, Shel worried him. Shel had been mired in some soporific state of being, replying to emails with semi-complete messages, sounding detached on the phone. Kids might call this la-la land. Adults would likely classify it as a state of depression. He seemed to have difficulty completing his thoughts, which Dent attributed to a psychology of victimhood; Joel, to general asshole-ishness.

"Yeah," Dent said as the waiter returned. "And I'm not surprised. This guy was always the one getting in all kinds of trouble. There were certain nights where he'd call me up and ask if I was in the mood to squander my potential."

"Is that right?"

"Yeah, 'Ready to squander our potential?' he'd ask, which was the signal for us to mess with the neighbors' garbage, or harass the poor Blockbuster guy."

"Another drink?"

"Sure. Same thing. But I have a feeling that he's onto something with this idea. He knows what he's doing when he pays attention."

Srry for shrt mssg. Bsy at wrk, Shel had said in the postscript to his latest email—a strange thing for an email, Dent thought, given the editable nature of it. It was something Shel the Blusterer would say.

Shel the Blusterer would send emails about his grandmother's imprisonment on crack charges; about the escaped silverback from San Diego Zoo; about the midget albino he bought on EBay. Shel, by blending realities—of how it was and how he would like it to be—could often (and through sheer will, it seemed) make what he wanted to be true to be true, just by acting like it was. This, Dent thought, is how he had fooled Dafna into dating him. He pined after her so much that she finally gave in. He wore her down.

The waiter returns with his second beer. Dent asks for a phone. The waiter directs him to a corner booth, where Dent dials a memorized phone card.

"Hey, Joel?"

"Yeah?"

"It's Dent. I'm international. Can't talk long."

"Okay. Everything okay?"

Everything was not okay. *Paulson* was not okay. Any other Research Director would have taken Paulson's presence as an intrusion, a sign of mistrust. He was an affront, a threat—to his power, to the integrity of his research, to the cohesiveness of his team. To knowledge in general.

"Lunar?" Paulson said when Dent told him about that night's eclipse. "Who cares about a lunar eclipse? For me it's solar or nothing."

Any other research director would have thrown a tantrum, a fit, if they had a Paulson to deal with, a *Lead Research Consultant*. What a meaningless fucking honorific, *Lead Research Consultant*.

"Yeah. I'm just in the middle of research. I'm diving most days."

"You're doing research? I didn't know you were up to anything over there."

"That's because I never told you."

"Oh."

"So."

"So."

"So how's it going? The research?"

"Fine."

"Huh."

"So . . . why?"

"What do you mean *why*?"

"Just seems strange you're suddenly into this."

"It's not strange."

"It's strange, dude."

"No it's not. Remember how I always talked about working for NASA? I know this is different, but same concept—exploration, research, discovery. This is stupid, but I always envisioned myself flying to different planets, like an intergalactic hero. And I took those grad classes, remember? At Miami. I removed invasive algae as part of a restoration effort. The whole thing's pretty much a continuation of my Bio 154 final project."

"I know about the classes. But why now?"

"Don't know. Guess I was inspired by my doctors. When I was in the hospital, I saw how some of them were really into their jobs. Yeah, they were overworked, overeducated, poor, but the research and the science really got them off. They liked to be challenged; they liked working with other smart people. It reminded me of the college field studies, of my grad classes. Remember the summer I spent studying and tagging those Hawaiian monchong fish? Thought I'd give that thing another shot, only in a slightly different way. I wasn't changing the world or anything—I was just doing something that was very, very important to a very, very small number of people. And it made me feel good."

"That Revlimid's really screwing with your brain."

"Yeah. Must be the Revlimid."

"Do you have any of that stuff on you, by the way? What does the FDA list as the side effec—?"

"No, Joel. Just . . . no."

Oh, and the money. Paulson aside, the money was another issue. Dent's research assistants, already straining under their grad-student budgets, were taking pay cuts, and some of his *benefactors* had expressed skepticism about how funds were being used. Dent allowed Paulson's presence only because Paulson was closely tied to O'Neil, who was closely tied to funding. Who, essentially, *was* their funding. There were other, smaller donors, but everything was dependent on O'Neil, on his money. The last installment wouldn't come until he submitted his all-but-finalized study, *An Examination of Potential Homing Mechanisms in O. Savayensis*, to O'Neil. It was nearly complete. He assumes that is why Paulson is there—to ensure O'Neil was getting what he was paying for.

Until he did, Dent would have to live shoestring. Dent—only because the floor in the wet lab was, well, wet (and hard, and uneven)—would have to sleep outside.

"But I called about Shel. Have you noticed how he's been acting lately?"

"Well, I haven't seen him in a while."

"I mean his emails."

"What? He's sending emails again?"

"Yeah, that was like a week ago," Dent says. "Where've you been?"

"I stay away from computers as much as possible."

"Well, the email he sent, it was weird."

"You sure you're not reading into this too much?"

"Could be, but it's strange. We both know he needs help. He acts like he doesn't want our help."

"That's just Shel. He'd never admit to needing help."

"You sure?"

"Would you?"

"Would I what?" Dent says.

"Admit to needing help." Joel is irritated.

"Yes, if I needed help. But there has never been a situation in which this is the case. Except for now. I just need a—I need a small loan."

Dent knew Joel wasn't from New York, but if he were, he assumed he would be in the same echelon of society as Dafna, whose childhood he always imagined to be not unlike the one Eloise had, growing up in the Plaza. Joel squints.

"What's it for?"

"For Shel."

"For what for Shel?"

"For an intervention. Shel needs to get out of Boston."

"He is. He's coming to Seattle, when you visit. We can talk to him then."

"I don't think he's coming to Seattle."

"He'll come."

"I'm not so sure. And even if he does—"

"What are you talking about?" Joel says. "He seemed fine to me."

"He's not fine. I promise."

"Yeah, guess you'd know. So what are we going to do?"

"We're going to save Shel's life."

"A little melodramatic?"

"Do you have anything more specific?"

"Not at the moment."

"Then we'll have to go with my saving-Shel's-life plan."

"So what is it?"

"First, I need—I need—sorry, could you hold on a second? Paulson, PAULSON!"

Paulson is in the other room, listening to FM radio, lip-synching the lyrics:

> THERE'S NO SEX IN YOUR VIO-LENCE! / THERE'S
> NO SEX IN YOUR VIO-LENCE!!

On SEX, he rubs his nipples. On VIOLENCE, he sticks out his tongue. This is Paulson's routine.

> THERE'S NO SEX IN YOUR VIO-LENCE! THERE'S
> NO <u>SEX</u> IN YOUR <u>VIOLENCE</u>!!

What was the name of this band? PUSH or BUSH or BUSHED? Either way, it clearly deserved some kind of formal recognition, a Grammy or something.

"Jesus, Paulson. I'm on the phone."

Paulson gives a look that might be roughly translated as *Chill Out, Bro*.

"So, back to what I was saying. What was I saying? Oh. Yes. I need money from you."

"So you can . . . ?"

"For me to fly back to the States."

"I thought you already had a ticket."

"Well, I don't."

"What happened to it?"

"I don't have a ticket and need money for one. Can we leave it at that?"

"So what's the next step?"

"I need to talk to Dafna. She's part of the plan."

"I don't know if that's a good idea."

"Why? She knows Shel better than anyone."

"Just trust me. It's not a good idea. I'll tell you when you visit. Why can't you talk to her over the phone?"

"I can't."

"Why not?"

"Lots of reasons. I can't get into it now."

"You can't pay for this ticket yourself?"

"I'm broke."

"Ask your parents."

"I'm broke, Joel."

. . .

"Joel?"

. . .

"Joel. Jo-elll. Come ooooon. Seriouuuuusly. Seriouuuuuuusssssly!"

There is a breeze and no rain when Dent falls asleep on the beach that night. He books a flight online the next morning, and as a courtesy to Joel, chooses flexible departure dates and times to keep the cost low.

He arrives in Sea-Tac Airport the next week. He picks up a disposable phone from the airport and texts Joel with one more request.

DentB
Ok if i crash at your place later this week?

JJJones

Yeah. When are you getting in?

DentB
I'm here now. Maybe not need to crash til Wednesday, though.

JJJones
Won't be home most of that night, but come in anyway. i'll tell the neighbors to let you in.

DentB
Thanks. Buy beer accordingly. Corona and bud ice.

JJJones
K

DentB
I'd buy you dinner, but I'm broke.

JJJones
I got you. it's ok.

DentB
I'll pay you back with a sandy hj.

JJJones
Not funny man

DentB
Youre right. I feel small.

DentB
also, we need to talk about Shel at some point.

DentB
We really need to talk about Shel

That evening, Dent arrives at Joel's apartment and finds a note:

Dear Mr. D. Brown:

I have talked to Hairypuss (my cat), and you are more than welcome to stay at our apartment. There are two conditions:

1. Don't touch anything. If you need assistance, ask my neighbor, Bill Bill. Yes, that's his name. He can be reached by going up one flight of stairs and knocking on the door. Knock loudly. He's old.

2. Make me food. I like chicken. I like chickpeas. I like anything "chick"-related. I do not like kidney beans.

3. The oven's tricky, so if you use it, refer to the instructions above the Oxford English Dictionary (impressed?) in the kitchen.

4. Don't be worried if I call at odd times and immediately hang up.

5. Yes, there are more than two conditions. I got carried away.

This is Shel's sense of humor, Dent notices, not Joel's. It's too clever for Joel. Unless Joel was somehow harnessing his Shel-ness, trying to imitate, capture, that dry sense of humor. Which itself corroborated Dent's theory that Joel was somehow envious of Shel; that, if he had a chance, Joel would switch his life, looks, personality with Shel's without a second thought. He could never understand this quirk, wanting to be someone else, wanting a life different from the one you had. He never understood this apotheosizing of someone else. It was a kind of voyeurism, which itself, presumably, was a product of self-loathing. Not to overthink it or anything.

Dent unlocks Joel's apartment and goes inside. Joel returns after an hour.

"I took a waffle," Dent says as he enters.

Joel looks at his shirt.

"Still the Bears hoodie? We're not too old for the Bears hoodie?"

"I said I took a waffle."

"No problem."

"Wrong line."

"What?" It sounded like *Whut*. Joel still had some South in him.

"When I take a waffle, you're supposed to say, 'Leggo my Eggo.'"

"Why would I do that?"

"How many times do people actually steal waffles?"

"I don't know."

"Guess."

"I don't think these are the Eggo brand."

"Guess."

"Just spit-balling here, but can't say I know many waffle thieves around here."

"So how often is Leggo my Eggo actually applicable to real life?"

"Not very, I guess."

"That's a missed opportunity." Dent picks up his fork.

. . .

"Yeah. Guess so."

Dent cuts the waffle. His knife squeaks against the plate.

"It's good to have you back," Joel says.

"Lots to talk about."

"Yeah."

"Guess Shel didn't come after all."

"I know, man. I know."

"I knew we couldn't count on him. I knew something was different about—"

"Let's leave Shel for the morning. I can't think too hard tonight."

"Sure, sure. You're right."

. . .

"Beer?"

"Shit yeah."

Dent takes another bite. It is too big.

"Hairypuss. Is that really your cat's name? Do you even own a cat?"

"Heh."

After a few cartons of a microwavable atrocity—

"I can't help it, I like them. I'm not going to apologize for it."

—Dent and Joel are on the sofa, clicking through the channels, until a sci-fi series about inter-dimensional money laundering comes on.

"Lazy dialog," Joel says after a few minutes.

"What?"

"*You just don't get it, do you?*—no one says that. But all these TV writers use it. They love it. Whenever characters arrive at one of the emotional linchpins of the show, they say, You just don't get it, do you? That's lazy dialog. And the name of the guy, it's Josè Valiant. Really bad. It sounds like a porn name."

"It's just an outer space show."

"That's no excuse."

"Whatever you say."

"And don't say *outer space*. It makes you sound like you're in fourth grade. Man, did you hear that? The name of that guy is Jimmy Daytona. Awful."

"I know. It's no Mamet."

Pause.

"I said it's no Mamet. The playwright? David Mam—?"

"I know who Mamet is."

"You didn't respond."

"Jesus, everyone knows Mamet. I'm not as much of an idiot as you think."

"I just thought—"

"Let's just watch the show."

. . .

"Great, they're about to *hack into the mainframe*. That's how you know the writers have really phoned it in. And they just used the word *parsecs*. Honestly, that does it for me."

They switch to the comedy channel. It's featuring Thursday night stand-up all evening. They watch it.

"You look skinnier," Joel says during a commercial.

"I am. A little bit."

Joel thinks too skinny, particularly because Dent used to be the healthiest person he knew.

"You ok?"

"Yeah."

"How's the - the P cancer?" Joel asks, knowing it is a risky move, thinking that making his past mistake of calling it pussy cancer into a joke might somehow absolve him of it.

"Fine. I guess."

It wasn't just his thinness. Dent was hairier, too. Already the hairiest person Joel had ever seen, Dent had managed the seemingly impossibly: to grow hair between his chin and chest, on that tender part of the neck. The hair on his head had overtaken his eyebrows. It wasn't noticeable to most people because his hair was all blond—Shel always made comments about brush fires—so this alarmed him.

On the television, a fat, balding male comic makes light of the fact that he is fat and bald. Then a female comic makes light of the fact she menstruates. There is talent up there that night.

"These female comics have no shame, do they?"

"Anything for a laugh."

"But she is hot."

"That she is."

"I therefore rescind my statement. I am glad she's on TV."

"I as well."

For the first few weeks after Dent arrived in Northbrook, he dressed and acted strangely. Aloof. A loner. He was clearly not Northbrookian, at least not any kind that Joel had ever encountered. Everyone at school thought he acted too East Coast (in that he talked like an idiot) and looked too West Coast (in that he dressed like a homo). This made very few people openly associate with him. Joel and Shel therefore treated him like a kid whose parents were divorced (*Dent: That Broken Home Kid*), because they assumed they (his parents) were.

It wasn't until he, Dent, wore a sporty but very West Coast-looking Walter "Sweetness" Payton cutoff to homeroom that it was revealed he *was* from Chicago—not one of the boring North Shore suburbs, where apocryphal stories about microwaving cats and handjobs in youth group and liver bandits harvesting organs of these sexually active teens (oh, this happens—*don't think this doesn't happen*) make seasonal rounds at the public schools—but the city proper. Home of the **1908 World Series Cubs,** he liked to brag.

Dent never fit into any particular clique in high school. He was an athlete, a god at sports, but couldn't really be classified as a jock. He spent one month mingling with the skater crowd and learned how to look like he was on drugs without spending any money on them. He also went through a cult-classics phase, toting around DVDs like *Attack of the 50-Foot Woman* and *Pink Flamingos*.

He would sometimes show up at the parties of Beau Crach, the guy who had a kegerator in his basement, the guy whose parents were out of town a lot, whose parents were so cool, the way they never cared about what he did. They, his parents, seemed to spend all their time in—Naperville, or at least some place in the vicinity of Naperville. At the time, no one worried that the absence of Mr. and Mrs. Crach might suggest something awry with Beau's at-home support system—people simply assumed that there must be something about Naperville not to be missed. Maybe Beau's parents liked touring its libraries. Maybe orgies were held there (not the libraries).

Dent would walk around Beau's parties, smiling, drinking only socially. He wouldn't ever binge—he saved that for Bears games—but he would laugh with the drunkest of the drunk kids, encouraging people like Joel to jump in the pool, volunteering to blow up swimmies as an incentive. Of course, two hours later, Joel would be floating in his pool, wearing the swimmies, calling for Dent to throw him another Amstel, but by that time Dent would have been elsewhere.

No one was ever certain when he left.

"Hey, put any more thought into those last words, by the way?" Joel asks from the other room, where he has gone to change shirts, having spilled beer on the one he was wearing.

"My what?"

"Your last words, when you, you know, expire. Weren't you working on some final thoughts? And you ran them past me and Shel?"

"Oh, yeah. Those. I—haven't really done much else with those."

In fact, Dent had done a lot more with his last words, though he hadn't discussed them with anyone for a long time. He particularly liked COURAGE as a topic and had gone about unpacking the word, investigating possible senses of it—physical courage, moral courage, intellectual, political, emotional courage—and considering the various applications of it. But he simultaneously felt that such an examination of the word was as good as an autopsy at taking the romance out of death. Shouldn't his words be unrehearsed? Inspired? Fleeing from his body in last breaths like a ghost? He couldn't help but notice how this premeditation on COURAGE, the word, made his last moments seem as much a matter of dull procedure as algebra.

Will they be significant? was his other worry. Will anyone—

"How about, *I didn't let the bastards get -* "
"Vetoed."
—hear them, and if so, will they repeat them, and if so, will others care enough to look for significance in them and if so, will they *find significance* in them, and if so, will it impact their lives in a meaningful way, and if so . . .

"Want to go out tonight?" Joel says, now sifting through the three or four collared shirts in his closet, pushing aside his old Blackhawks jersey. "Let's go out."
"Not tonight. I'm going to watch the tube."
"Come on. Come ooon."
"No. I haven't even showered."
"You don't need to shower," Joel says, his back to him. "Looking sharp."
They pause to watch a Fisher Price ad on TV.
"I need to shower."
"Fine. Shower."
"It'll take too long."
"Why don't you just shower and see how you feel?"
"I'm not sure I should go out tonight."
"Well, we don't have to," Joel says, pulling a spread-collar shirt out of the closet. It says Brooks Brothers. "Just shower and see how things go."
"Maybe later."
. . .
"Dent?"
"Yeah?"
"Step under some fucking water and let's hit the town."
They do not hit the town. Instead, the two collaborate on the first paragraph of what might very well become The Seminal Work of Photojournalism, which reads: *The 345 miles that stretch from end to end of the San Fernando Valley can be traversed nearly any way imaginable: you can bike it, which might take a week; run it – just short of a month, depending on fitness; or drive it. Or, you could* **race** *it. This is what Denton Montgomery Brown chose to do.*

Then they turned on the TV. Then they turned off the TV. Then they discussed Calvin and Hobbes. Then they discussed The Viability of Sleight-of-Hand as a Way to Impress Women and Gain Favor in Social Situations. Then they turned on the TV again.

It was nice to see Joel, Dent thought. It felt comfortable. They had already gotten over the initial haven't-seen-you-in-a-year awkwardness.

Then, just when Dent felt his old friend was back, same as ever, just when he thought he was safe, Denton Brown made the mistake of engaging Joseph J. Jones in a conversation about Dafna Schwartzers.

Two hours later, they are on the same couch and the same channel, but the comedians have turned into law clerks. They use the word 'brief' too much, Joel notes, and suggests that a more original use of their time might involve moving away from the TV. Dent didn't like playing the guilt card, but when Joel persists, he finally comes out with an *Oh, I'm sorry. Please don't allow my deadly disease to interfere with your night out.*

"Hey," Joel says, "I didn't mean - You know, if you ever need any needles, for drugs or something, for the treatment, I can just put in a call to my uncle, and—"

"It's not that kind of treatment, but thanks."

"Seriously, just keep it in mind."

They look at the TV again. "Dude, the Trace Technician," Dent says, "she looks like a bustier version of Daf."

"What?"

"Like Dafna. The woman on the show who plays the Trace Technician looks like Dafna. With more stuffing."

It was a new show, about three law clerks who find themselves in a much more highly sexualized workplace than seemed realistic for people in their profession.

"Dafna looks nothing like that. Her hair is different."

"I guess. I guess it's because this woman's a little bit of a bitch, so she reminds me of her."

"What are you talking about? Dafna's sweet. She's not a bitch."

"Yeah, 'sweet.'"

"You don't think so?"

"Not after that whole thing with Shel. I can't look at her the same way again."

"It wasn't that weird. I mean, just because she wanted to experiment a little doesn't make her into some kind of adult film star."

"I wouldn't call that an experiment. She's one of those weird dominant-in-the-bedroom types. The ones who, outside, are like, *oooh, my pages are wet* if they drop a book in a puddle, but who, when you get them in the bedroom, are like, *gnaw on my nipples, you sexy, sweaty, boozebag!*"

"Don't talk about her like that."

Dent gives an asymmetrical look. "What? That's funny, right?"

"Sure."

"You have a thing for her? Oh shit, you really do have a thing for her."

"You really don't know?"

"No."

"I'm not supposed to tell."

"Don't do that. Don't you do that."

"Man, I can't believe you haven't heard."

"How would I have heard? Stop being an idiot."

"It's messed." Joel became Alabaman for a moment, his accent on display.

"So tell me."

"It's so messed."

"So fucking tell me."

"So, you know who took Dafna to the clinic, right?" He pauses, reluctant. A man testing the waters with a toe.

"Shel did."

"Right."

Pause.

"And?"

Another pause.

"And you know who comforted her *after* the abor—The *thing?*"

Dent pales. "Are you saying—did you *hook up with her?*"

"We didn't just hook up."

"You dated?"

"Yeah. It was legitimate."

"How long was this?"

"Well, we're still . . ."

"You're still what . . . ?" Dent stares. "Oh my God. You're fucking Dafna."

"Dating," Joel says. "When you like the person, the word is *dating*. You're really crass."

"Jesus. What's it like? Dating her?"

"Magical."

"This is insane. Do you take her to Ron of Japan for dinner?"

"Ha."

"Not an ROJ fan? And I assume Shel doesn't know."

"No, Shel's unaware."

"What'd you think he'd say if he knew?"
"He can't know."
He tilts his head, as though uncertain how this should be construed.
"It's going to come out."
"He can't know."
"Honestly, I don't see how that's possible."
. . .
"Joseph J. Jones and Dafna Schwartzers. I can't believe it. I bet she's doing this as a revenge thing. Because Shel never took her to Ron of Japan."
"You. You're a nut."
. . .
"He's going to flip."
"Who?"
"Shel. Shel's going to flip."
"He's not going to know."
"Right."
"He's not. Unless you tell him."
Pause.
"You're not going to tell him, so he won't know."

If there was one thing they both were certain of, it was that Shel would know. It was inevitable—like daybreak, or gravity. Joel always wondered what would happen when he found out. Shel likely wouldn't do anything, which was as bad a punishment as anyone could ask for. Instead, he would consider Joel a bad friend, or worse, a turncoat. Someone whom he had trusted to be loyal and supportive but most of all frank with him, someone who broken a contract, had squandered all of the emotional capital he had invested in their friendship by taking advantage of his ex.

"Man, I always knew you wanted to be like him, but taking his woman right after she had—that's all kinds of messed up. Like psycho-stalker messed up. I guess I don't have to tell you this."

Joel agreed. He didn't.

"I don't know how Shel's going to handle everything. No way we can keep this thing under lock and key."

"What do you think he's up to right now?"

"Shel? I bet he's sitting in his office, stamping papers or something. These days, he's bored out of his mind."

VIII.
Escape.

I have pissed off Snaggletooth.

He had been discussing his diet with Babyface, explaining how he likes bran for breakfast, a muffin or Cracklin' Oat Bran. He described how it strengthens and solidifies his stool, making for an easy pass and clean wipe when he BMs, but I interrupted. I tried to reason with him. I tried to tell him that they have noticed my absence at work by now, called the cops. I tell them it would behoove them (why did I use the word *behoove?* I am an idiot for using that word.) to let me go, that I work for a security firm, a place that deals with this kind of situation, and I can broker a deal with them, one that lets them off, consequence-free, because—and this isn't a threat, it's just a *heads-up*—it's only a matter of time before they sniff us out.

"Sniff us out? Can't let that happen, White Boy. Here, I'll cover your scent."

Now he is dribbling a can of Coke on me.

I would like to be in Seattle right now.

Despite my hesitation to get a ticket. When Joel told me about it, I flipped through Frommer's and read all about Seattle (pop. 582,000), where I had a chance to learn more about the 1919 General Strike, or the World's Fair, or the The Goodwill Games of 1990; or the founding of Starbucks or Nordstrom or Eddie Bauer or Washington Mutual, or any of the other business in this sometime boomtown; perhaps I would have run across Greg Nickels (D), mayor. I would have taken an architectural trolley tour, bought and stamped and sent postcards, visited the botanical gardens. There would be sickeningly touristy instances—getting lost, wrinkles in travel plans, unexpected local color. I would be hanging out in *chez Joel* (a cramped but charming studio in Capitol Hill, with a Pottery

Barn wine cart and Egyptian cotton linens, and a single bottle of Two Buck Chuck) with my old friends, my *good* friends, longing for a bygone era, defeated by nostalgia, overcome by richly perceptual schoolyard-related reminisces—Dent's penchant for laundry exhaust; Joel's penchant for being a lazyass—to the point of bursting.

Oh, and I almost forgot—how could I forget? The *Space Needle*. How nice would it have been to ride up the Space Needle's recently computerized elevators? It is said that these elevators, normally set at 10 mph, are, on windy days, slowed to 5, as a safety measure. This Greg Nickels (D) guy, he must have signed off on that. He seems like a responsible mayor.

I bet there is little to no crime in Seattle. Seattle is a crimeless city. It must be.

I am wet with Coke—all the more infuriating in light of my currently low blood-sugar levels—and out of a job by now, having been absent from work for the second day in a row. But I don't move. I don't complain. I sit and I wait and I say nothing.

I don't know how many hours I have been asleep. It is dark inside, possibly outside, too. The Samsung is tuned to CNN, despite the apparent nonexistence of any kind of cable line. Snaggletooth is lying on the couch. He seems distracted by whatever's onscreen—alternating shots of Anderson Cooper and rebelling Afghanis, it seems. He flips to a channel on which Georgina, a large, excitable Nebraskan whose breasts mimic the elasticity of bungee, is relating her problems to a very concerned-looking Maury Pauvich. Before we are allowed the privilege of Georgina's occupation, Snaggletooth flips back to CNN, where the camera is now circumnavigating Anderson Cooper. I have a cramp in my side, from a severe electrolyte imbalance. I need to adjust, and try to do so without disturbing Snaggletooth, but as I swing my leg around, a shoe slides against the floor with an audible squeak. He gets up, blocking the Afghanis. He grabs one of Joel's syringes. He fills it with a clear substance, and—

"Hold steady, White Boy."

—sticks it into my arm.

"Hope you ain't Anti-Drug."

Snaggletooth is the funny one, I decide. (This is later confirmed when he refuses to talk when his mother called, saying that he'd *rather exchange ideas with Ben Affleck over coffee* than talk to her).

I focus on the TV as the drugs begin to take over. I start to black out again, watching as Anderson Cooper informs the world that OJ Simpson has been convicted of various kidnapping and armed robbery-related charges and knowing with dread certainty that my life could not possibly get any worse.

It is well into day three now, and my flatulence is out of control. I have been farting uncontrollably for the part hour, so much so that I am interrupting Sally Struthers (who, on the TV, has been making clear efforts to impress us with her thighs and tell us as much as she can about the benefits of good taste), in a way that makes it appear like everything that comes out of her mouth is a bodily gas. The Meth Heads have been feeding me pizza (probable cause of said gassiness), talking at me, spitting on me, smoking something—Meth, would be my guess—and walking around shirtless. This is hazy, but at one point, they *use*, because they begin spinning around in circles ("I'm tripping balls, man! I'm *tripping balls!*"). I am pretty sure they are doing at least three or four other illegal things. At one point, I think I catch Snaggletooth in a chemise. They remind me of Joel, which is frustrating.

They still have my ATM card. I am stunned that I still have so much cash in there. Usually I am a paycheck away from overdrawing, but this week is different. I must be amazing these Meth-heads with my liquidity. I am immensely wealthy this week.

This is why they are keeping me alive. This must impress them.

Next I will impress them with my huge, hairy balls. Because I have had a gun for three days.

And now I am going to pull it.

Day Four.

I have not pulled the gun. I have fantasized about it, run through a number of gun-pulling scenarios. But I have actually not gotten around to doing it. Right now, I am not focused on pulling the gun, because my attentions are focused on the most recent news on E!, where I have just learned that Dixie Carter has died. This is too bad. I liked her. I wonder how she died.

No, I need to pull the gun. I need to be like Dent. I reach for my gun.

"What are you doing, White Boy?"

Babyface has pressed the barrel of his gun against my skull, in the scoop of my neck. *What's this?* he asks. *What the fuck is this?*

He sees my .22 sticking out of my pants. He grabs it and pokes me in the eye, still sore from the last time.

"Ooooh-hooh. Now you are going to die. Now I am going to fuck you up the ass with this," he says, handling the gun like some sort of sex toy.

He knees me in the groin. I buckle under my weight.

Snaggletooth is now at his side.

"No more games. Give me the gun."

I feel the steel of the .22 against my ear. I close my eyes but hear only an empty click.

"Fuck, you didn't even have bullets, White Boy?"

He throws the .22 across the room.

"Guess I'll have to use mine."

Again, a barrel against my cheek.

I hear the shattering of glass, and someone screaming: *Please! Please!*

My head hits the floor, and I hear more commotion, looking up briefly to see Snaggletooth crumpled near me, unconscious.

I hear a voice behind me: "Man, this is a sweet apartment. How'd a screwup like you afford a room with a fireplace? If I had a fireplace, I'd never leave."

That voice—it can't be. I turn over to see Dent. He is holding Babyface at gunpoint. I look at him quizzically.

"Tae kwon do," he explains. "Four years at Little Lee's Kick Shack in Old Hills."

I am in love with this man.

"Just call me Master Brown of the Secret Redneck Trucker Clan."

He always surprises me, Dent does.

"Let's go."

I grab the gun out of Snaggletooth's hand. I briefly consider pistol-whipping him. Now if ever is the time to pistol whip him, and I partially attempt it, but end up resting the barrel under his nose, as if preventing a sneeze.

"On the floor," Dent says. "Hands on your heads. Count to one hundred, loudly. You stop, you're dead."

I grab my cell phone from the counter, back out the door—"Keep counting, Assholes!" Dent yells—and pause to consider whether I should alter my usual workout routine to include spider stretching instead of the usual static stretching I do, increasing blood flow to my muscles and joints, thereby warming up rather than simply extending (and possibly hyperextending) my ligaments and muscles. Then I run.

Babyface counts, sounding worn, nasal, like a beaten child.

I almost feel bad for him.

Now I am in the middle of Dorchester Ave, waving a gun, frothing, sweating through my knockoff Tommy Hilfiger shirt, desperately looking for a cab, nearly running into a mailbox, feeling very much like some kind of mad extraterrestrial, or a demon, unfamiliar with the light of day, gnashing at the air, when,

Shel! Shel!

Dent is a block behind. I slow down. He catches up.

"What are you doing here?"

"Looking for you."

"How'd you know I was missing?"

"Dafna told me you were missing. Then we talked to your coworker. He said you'd been waving a gun around, and that's when we knew we had to come find you. And Joel, well, Joel apparently –"

"Does Joel buy drugs from those guys?"

"Well . . ."

"Does Joel buy drugs in exchange for needles?" I say, remembering the boxes in the apartment.

"Listen, I don't know how Joel found out where you were. But he found out where you were," Dent says, then looks at my gun. "What the hell is this?"

"My gat."

"Give me that," he says, taking my gat.

He throws it in a green barrel with the word **RECYCLE** stenciled on it. He hails a cab. We slide in.

"We're going to your apartment."

"How'd you guys get my keys?"

"Because I'm *Denton Motherfucking Brown*."

"Seriously, how'd you get . . ."

"Because I'm Denton Motherf—"

"Okay, I get it."

Dent is thin and his face is a shadow.

I need sunlight and air. The cab lets us off at Newbury. We walk toward my apartment. Sunlight. Air. I have been without these things for at least three days, and I need them more than food or water. It is an unusually temperate today, an Indian Summer, and I admire my surroundings. As we walk, I notice things I had missed before—the spirit of mercantilism of this place, the diversity of goods; passing American Apparel and Condomworld and Trident Booksellers & Cafe, with its brochure-length menus, herbal recipes and I-think-I-can spirit; now approaching Hereford, from which we can just barely see the city's South End, where there is now apparently a thriving gay community, then to Mass Ave, where—

"Man, I love Boston," Dent says. "It's so *historical*. I mean, *very* historical. You can taste it. You can taste the history."

—a Chevy has apparently failed to understand the science of green lights, and there is an accident, a small one, a mere fender bender, between it and a dairy truck. A man gets out of the truck, yelling something in Spanish, and (I prepare for a magnificent clash of civilizations here) the cabdriver starts shouting something at him in English, and from the looks of it, it's something personal, something near and dear, likely about his mother. A man in a hat who has nothing to do with the collision approaches and starts shouting at both of them.

"God, I love Boston," Dent says again.

We enter my apartment, but something is different. There, where an empty spot on the couch for me to throw my coat is supposed to be, is Joel. He insists that no one let him in. He also insists that if someone did, hypothetically, let him in—an absurd notion, of course—the identity of that very anonymous person would forever remain very undisclosed; but I know instantly who let him in. Linda Wirth, my mom, let him in. To whom, earlier this year, I foolishly relinquished possession of an emergency key. And she, apparently, mailed it to him.

I inform him that he is in violation of my privacy.

"Sit down," Joel says, and I do.

I am a man in an electric chair, upright, neck rigid. A swan is beside me. It wasn't there before. It is shiny on the table.

"What's this?"

I pick up the swan, turn it over in my hands. They say it's a 'room brightener' from my mom, who roped them into an hour-long expedition to Swarovski's en absentia.

"Swarovski's? What's that?"

The last room brightener from my mom, a show pillow with *Life's Sweet* embroidered on it, still lay on the floor next to my bed.

"A store that sells crystal," Joel says.

"Crystal what?"

"Crystal everything. Necklaces, watches, glasses, collectables, meth. Not that last one."

Is it okay to joke already? I have told them everything, about the Southie expedition, about the detainment. Yes, he saved my life, but I accuse Joel of supplying drug paraphernalia to hoodlums—

"Dent says you won't say how you knew where I was."

"I'm mad connected."

"Do you deal, Joel? I'm serious. They had *boxes* of your needles."

"Already told you, bitches," he says, using *bitches* because he thinks he's *street*. "I'm mad connected."

—and now they are joking about it. They don't believe I was dealing with Meth Heads, with dangerous, drug-fueled psychopaths. They think I create my own little dramas, that my story played well with my own image of myself—Messenger No. 2 in the *Dramatis Personae* of some tragi-comedy. Joel accuses me of making up the Meth Head part. So they joke with me, which some people might consider French for laughing at me, but this is okay. It's good to laugh.

"You know you're impressed. Everyone's a little bit gangsta," I say, struck with the thought that this would be a great title for a single by an up-and-coming or currently popular hip-hop artist.

"Ugh," Dent says.

"But really," Joel urges. "You should go sometime. To Swarovski's. It wasn't that bad."

"Okay, I won't be doing that."

"Seriously."

"I'll set aside an afternoon."

I fly the swan back to its place beside me. Joel's shirt says BUBBA HO-TEP. Dent's says CASE WESTERN.

"Your mom also wanted us to remind you to go to church. She said church will quote-unquote help."

I should have expected this from Linda Wirth, my mom. She was a churchgoer, but only in the technical sense, in that she went to church. She wasn't ever discernibly religious. All we knew was that she switched between the Episcopal and Methodist faiths so often that it eventually got to a point where she left the house on Sundays without a word about where she was headed.

"So are you?" Joel asked. "Are you going to church? Your mom wants an answer. She'll be pissed at me if I don't have an answer for her."

I wave the question away. "Don't worry about it. She doesn't really care. She just thinks it's one of those things that's her motherly duty."

Ultimately, hers was the religion of food processing. The blender was for Linda Wirth a small idol she doted on with the care of a true believer. Usually gazpacho; sometimes a Bloody Mary. The bloodiest of Marys. She waged a war against household evils, things like breakage or slippage, nearly fainting—

"Hey, wasn't that girl from *Full House* a Meth addict?" Joel suddenly says. "Wasn't Stephanie Tanner caught up in something like that? Man, contact with Bob Saget would do that to you. Those kid actors, they're always so sad."

—when FreddyChops, our Labrador, relieved himself on the floor. When the holiday poinsettias fell from the mantle, some kind of cardiac episode was imminent, I was certain. Linda Wirth would not have approved of those Meth Heads, not necessarily because they robbed, kidnapped and abused me—I'm a grown man and responsible for myself—but because they had no respect for order.

"Stop grinding your teeth like that," she'd tell me. "You'll ruin the enamel."

But I'd grind. She couldn't stop me from grinding.

Idiosyncrasies like these—noncommittal church-going, concern over spillage and enamel—made our neighbors' assessment of her simple. Linda Wirth: Fine Woman and Dear.

"Haven't I told you to walk on the outside?" she'd yell when I walked on the inside of the sidewalk. "The outside!"

How her son started hanging out with that terror of a Brown kid was beyond her.

Right now, *that terror of a Brown kid* is on his feet, jumping around. He is hyper. I don't know how it started, but Dent is yelling. *I'm naughty! I'm naughty!* he yells, springing around and spanking himself in a *giddy-up* motion, as if riding one of those hobbyhorses. *I'm naughty!*, turning his free hand into a mini-megaphone. Joel is cracking up, just losing it right now, red in the face and nearly dying. I don't laugh, I try not to laugh. I succeed in this until Dent places his butt exactly half an inch in front of my face. He cocks his head to the side like dog, the inquisitive now replacing his formerly rah-rah tone: *I'm naughty?*

And this is when I laugh.

He moves to the couch and sits on Joel, hands folded across his lap like an adolescent hiding an erection.

Christ, Dent.

You don't change. You are fucking immortal.

An hour later, Dent is calm, or appearing calm. He is on the couch with Joel, facing me. I must not have looked when I placed the swan back on the table, because it has turned its back to me.

"So," Dent says. "How's Javier?"

Javier? Who's Javier? Oh, yes. Javier. Dent's imaginary child. Javier lives on.

I give a weak smile.

"Oh, he's fine. I'm raising Javier like you would have."

"Don't let Javier forget his roots. His Mexican roots."

"Oh, I won't. I am teaching Javier important things. Like how to rush past people in a crowded bar only to be found snoozing in the back minutes later."

How would I describe my feelings about resuscitating Javier? Mixed.

"That's good," Dent says.

"But he's rebellious, too. He refuses to speak anything but his native tongue."

"Oh my. You'll need to discipline him. Force Javier into a contact sport Javier would otherwise have no interest in. Like rugby, or arena football. Let Javier fall victim to coaches with tempers and strongly held beliefs about The Olive Garden."

"Good thinking."

"Or bribe him. Get him a wiener dog, as a bribe. A Mexican is not a Mexican without a wiener dog."

I don't know where Dent gets this. It sounds true-ish.

"Good. I'm glad you're there for him."

Then, silence.

Have we exhausted it? Are we done with Javier?

"And remember that Javier needs to build character."

No. We are not.

"Yeah," Joel says. "He should take him to PF Chang's and force him to eat everything on his plate. Then call him fat. That should test Javier's mettle."

"Of course."

"Oh, and if Javier resists, make fun of him. Call him a loser. Or pay his friends to do it."

"Ah, yes. Gotta get at that self esteem."

"Mmmm. Really needle him."

"Gotta, gotta."

Okay. It is dead now. Javier is dead now.

Again, silence. Then:

"Seriously, we shouldn't joke about that," Dent says finally. "What if one of us did have a kid?"

My smile ferments into something less recognizable. *Is Dent really bringing this up? I'll kill him.*

"It's nothing to joke about really. We should . . ." but his words come to a crawl as if sensing the dense rage building within my jaw. "Anyway, we should really be more thoughtful when talking about . . . things. Having kids is a huge responsibility."

I let out air.

"Shel..." Joel says, apparently determined to pick up where Dent left off.

"Yeah?"

I can see them thinking, ready to unpack my language, gauge my tone, scouring for traces of insincerity or worse, sociopathy.

"When was the last time you spent a night with a girl? Talked to a girl?"

The last girl I slept with was a buyer for some big department store.

"Not sure. Can't remember."

It was Bloomingdale's. She, the girl, Karen, alternately inveighed against her incompetent boss and begged me to "unlock" her, as if she were a safe, or a puzzle. I honestly don't know why I bother with retail girls.

"Well, Joel and I both agree."

"On what?"

Dent ignores the question.

"We've been talking. About you."

On *you*, they both look at me. Not a look of concern, exactly. More of matter-of-factness, as if they had read sobering financial news about a breakdown in U.S.-China trade negotiations.

"We need to intervene."

"In what?"

"Never mind. Just listen. I'm going to teach you something." Dent's tone of voice sounds like something usually reserved for the handicapped.

"Oh?"

You're the one who's dying, Dent. You're the one who needs help. And Joel; don't even let me get started on you, Joel, you are beyond messed up

"Do you know what an atoll is? Never mind, of course you don't. It's a coral island forming a ring that encloses a small body of water, like a lagoon."

"Okay?"

"And we are going to take you to an atoll." Dent is wearing trendy Diesel jeans with zippered pockets. I have no idea how he can afford these.

And Joel is looking older. He could use some Propecia. I do not think he is too young for Propecia. Should I tell him this?

"And we are going to make you swim in that atoll."

"That's it?"

"It's more than that. The atoll is just a symbol."

"Ooh."

"It's a symbol of redemption. And renewal."

"Right. So what are you getting at?"

"We're making you take a vacation," Joel says.

"But weren't you guys just in Seattle?"

"Yes, but we were thinking some place more like Australia. Great tourism department there, we hear."

"Really? Australia?"

"Nah," Dent says. "I assume we'll just go to Mexico."

"But you never told me about Seattle. How was Joel's place? Nice? In a good part of town?"

"Modest. It's the type of place that can only be described with qualified abstractions, like 'barely liveable,' or 'almost indoors.' You know what kind of preparation he went through for my arrival? *He emptied a little bag of Skittles into a bowl.* I mean, talk about that extra mile. I don't think even Best Western could compete with this guy."

. . .

"That was a joke."
"I know."
"You didn't laugh."
"It wasn't funny."
. . .
"It would have been polite to laugh."
. . .
"Did you know those things are really nice in Europe," Joel says, bringing us out of our conversational funk. "I heard that Best Westerns are like luxury hotels in the EU. Top tier, like the Waldorf."

We tell him no. We did not know that.

Dent changes subject. "But back to the point, which is that you need a vacation, that we all need a vacation, something, as I said, redemptive, refreshing, *purging*. Something that will force us to reprioritize."

"So you're saying Seattle wasn't enough for you guys?"
"Shut up about fucking Seattle, ok?"
"Yeah, enough about Seattle."

This is unexpected. I didn't think I was overplaying the Seattle thing. I am being bombarded.

"Is Dafna coming?" I ask.

They look at each other.

"Yes. She's coming."
"What was that about?"
"What?"
"The look."
"It's nothing. We just knew this would be a problem."
"Never mind. It's not a problem. I'm serious."
"She also needs one. A vacation, I mean. And we have to realize that we can all be friends without weirdness, okay? We have to come to understand this."

I swing an invisible baseball bat. "I'm not going."
"Grow up."

Dent and Joel cross their legs. Both now sit across from me with the folded hands of parents who are giving their child *a good talking to*.

My voice deepens.

"Sounds pricey. Who's bankrolling this joyride?"
"My uncle," Joel says.
"But who's paying for *us*?"
"My uncle. He says he'll finance the whole trip."

"I'm not so sure. Your uncle's a little—"

"Okay, just stop," Joel says. "I don't like the way you talk about my uncle. He's a part of my family, and I'm tired of you badmouthing him."

"You're right. Sorry."

"That's not enough. So I want you to list three positives about him. Okay? Can you do that? Can you say three good things about my uncle?"

"This is stupid."

"I don't care. He offered to help us out, and you're badmouthing him. Three things.

"Okay, okay. He's . . . he is sure of foot."

"What?"

"No, really. He has really good balance. It's amazing. I've never met anybody who never trips. But he—I've never seen him trip. Not even close. Everybody trips. But not him."

"You're not taking this—"

"Don't tell him I said he was sure of foot. I'm afraid he'll get a big head about it."

"Forget it, Shel. You're a dick." Joel continues:

"I don't think you understand what he's doing for us here. He has convinced the company to send the three of us on a factory tour. They have a bunch of facilities in Mexico and he can write it off as a fact-finding mission. You two are my interpreter/chauffer team. And he has arranged to give us free transportation."

"Wow. That's pretty nice of him."

"Yeah. It is."

I was right about Joel's uncle. He is an asshole—the kindest, savviest asshole of all time. This man, who finds joy in mispronouncing people's names, who has an *elevator* in his house, who seems like someone who tampers with airline smoke detectors, who doesn't appreciate the beauty of the book *Tuck Everlasting*, who ruins family dinners, who—

"I've always wanted to Study Abroad. Get it? A *broad*? Like a woman?"

Yes, I know what he means.

—makes really insightful jokes, he is an angel. Mother Theresa. A very well balanced Saint.

"And what if I want to mack some fine young ladies when I'm there?" I ask. "What will I do then?"

"Please don't talk about macking," Dent says. "That's what urban youths do. And don't worry. Dafna says she has no interest in partying. She'll be in a different hotel room."

"Yeah, we'll have a guys night. And Oh! Oh! We can do one of those dollar nights at the titty bar!"

Why must he use that language? "There's a way of saying that without the caca mouth."

"Saying what? Titty bar? Tit-tit-titty bar full of titmice? Titty tit!"

Joel is crass as crass can be.

Dent admits that they had planned on telling me about Mexico, but they knew I'd resist. They had the whole thing plotted out, mapped, an intricate schema designed to trick me into braving MassPort security, forsaking my time zone, bopping around the world, country to country. Step 1, Dent explains, was to tell me that Joel was sick and dying (because Dent's sickness was old news and had therefore lost its aura of urgency), and that this would be a last-hurrah type of thing; Step 2, well, they hadn't planned Step 2 yet.

"So what was Joel going to be sick and dying from?"

"Not sure. Something stupid. Like a python attack or something."

"That's good. The Pacific Northwest Python, we'd say. Prognosis: Vacation or Die."

They wisely scuttled the plan—

"God, that's stupid."

"Whatever, you would have bought it."

"Yeah, I probably would've."

—as soon as they rehearsed it in their heads, realizing it was best to display their dedication physically, bodily, by saving my life, then intervening in it. I turn to Dent.

"You've gotten too much sun," I tell him.

"I know. So you're in?"

"What's an atoll again?"

"You'll learn during SCUBA lessons."

"No way."

"You have to do everything I do, Shel. It's part of the operation."

"It's now an *operation*?"

"Yes."

"When did that happen?"

"Just now."

This is a circus. *Ringling Brothers*.

"God, you've gained weight," he says to me.

"I know. Why do I need—?"

"God you really are fat. You need to because you're fat."

Is this a safe space? I thought this was a safe space where we could share our thoughts. I guess it is not. I retaliate:

"You're a - you're a buttwad."

Dent seems unaffected. He takes a bottle of Vitamin Water out of his bag. He swigs it, as if needing to rub it, my fatness, in.

Look at that. Dent thinks I'm weak. The way he talks about my fatness—it's clear he's talking about me and about Dafna. It's impossible to talk about me without talking about Dafna. Dent almost never saw the two of us apart. He thinks Dafna made me weak. I should signal to him that I know. That I know they know. But I can't actually say anything. I need a pen. Or a computer, for a PowerPoint presentation. Or, better, Play Doh. Teachers always told me how great I always was at expressing myself with Play-Doh.

"Your parents think you're stupid," I say to him. "They just told me that, behind your back. They called me before we came here. They have my number."

I assume his discussion of my fatness—which is overblown, of course—is a way to convince me that everything's all right, that his thinness is a consequence of a healthy lifestyle rather than anything more ominous. Or, and this is much more likely, he and Joel plan to team up on me. I need a quick retort, something superficial but hurtful, something hurtful *because* it's superficial. I settle on his hair, which is much blonder than it used to be, possibly bleached. Although I do not think this fairness of hair is a point of insecurity for him, I will nonetheless do everything in my power to make it into one.

"Thanks, Norway." I pat my stomach. "Some of us aren't able to swim four hours a day."

"True. Least I'm not fat. Just do 30 minutes of cardio, minimum, three times a week. Hit the elliptical or something. Gives your body a chance to change on the molecular level."

"It's called a job. Ever consider getting one?"

"Assman."

"Dickweed."

"And you're serious? You've been away for all this time, learning new languages, experiencing exciting, intoxicating ways of living, and this is what you come back with?"

. . .

"Butthead," Dent says. "Buttlicker."

"Buttlicker? I should wash your mouth out with soap."

We're arguing. It is good when we argue. It keeps conversation light. This is how it usually goes with us. We gut each other, rip each other apart, showing our affection by describing each others' attributes with the most dysphemistic language available, couching every compliment in insulting terminology, every insult in falsely complimentary terms. We do this knowing that we are all competitive—about who is working the hardest, about who is drinking the most, sleeping with the most women, breaking the most wind, but also who is most disinterested in all of these things. Who has these things just come to them, effortlessly. Who has the superior jokes, the sharpest insults, which are always the most obvious ones, the most puerile—

"You're a dicfor."

"A dicfor? What's a – oooh, almost got me! You're good. You. Are. Good!"

—the ones that avoid any flirtation with nuance, taking no brainpower whatsoever. We are Don Rickles.

"Quick—Joel: Male or female?"

It is an election year, and these are the things we force ourselves to consider. We talk about New Trier, former classmates.

"Did you hear about Beau Crach?"

"THE Beau Crach, from New Trier? Little Beau Crach?"

Other people are much more interesting.

"That one. He married Susan Shifflet, you know. The girl with the KISS obsession."

There is hardly anything *al fresco* about our time here. We stay boxed up, shuttered, sitting on the couch, gazing at the TV, *talking* to the TV, afraid of weather. "Was it Kiss? I thought it was Iron Maiden or something."

"Either way, she's off the market. Sorry, Shel."

I wring my hands, rend my garments. I curse the heavens.

"Wasn't her dad that slip-and-fall lawyer? No, wait—he was a bedsore lawyer! That's right. He sued homes that didn't turn the old people enough, so they got bedsores. They were called pressure *somethings*."

They were called *pressure ulcers*. That was the technical language. The term was explicit, sickening. It stuck in the head like a nesting beetle, entering through the ear.

"Weird. Need to turn those old people, I guess."

"Yeah. The oldies need to be turned. Weird. Anyway, Beau was the one with the kegerator, who threw the great parties, right?"

"Yeah."

"I never really got to know him. There was always weirdness between us at school. What's Beau up to these days?"

"He's dead."

God.

"Yeah. Leukemia."

. . .

"Hey, that's just like you, Dent."

I shouldn't have put it that way. I rescind, redirect to Joel:

"I mean no. Not really. But that's so sad. Which type?"

"Of Leukemia?"

"Yeah."

Joel stares.

"There are types?"

"Why not?"

We look to Dent. He nods.

"All I know is he went bald and everything from treatment."

"Oh. I thought that was just a movie thing. You know, slather on the pathos."

I need to escape this. I need to get out of here.

I go to the other room for . . . for *something*, I tell them. My computer is sitting on the club chair in the corner, and I open Word and play a game wherein I close my eyes and hold down the Z key until I am positive I have reached exactly forty-seven Zs. Why 47? Why not? I can't peek because peeking would be cheating.

ZZZZZZZZZZ. zzzzzzzZZZZZZZZZzzzzzzzzzzzzzzzzzz zzzz. Zzzzzzzz zzzzzzzzzzzzzzzzzzz.

But I still hear them. "Anyway, when he heard the news, he started to down-spiral (and believe me, down-spiraling isn't pretty), so his parents had to send him to rehab, but for depression. And they reneged on payments or something and got into this whole mess. All I know is that it wasn't pretty. It was one of those clinics you read about in the news . . ."

zzzzzzzzzzzzzzzzzzzzzzzzzzzzzzz

"Didn't his dad work for that Caterpillar plant out in Peoria? I know he at least had some kind of business relationship with them. He always went down there for – *Shel?*"

zzzzzzzzzzzzzzZZZZZZZZZzzzzzzzz

"Shel? You in there?"
ZZZZZZZZZZZZZZZZZZZZZZZZZZZZZ
What are you doing? Dent's doing his hermaphrodite impression. You're missing Dent's impression."
zzzzzzzzzZzzzzzzzzzzzzzzzzzzzzzzzzzzzzzzzzzzz
Close. Very close.

We used to be brothers in arms, brothers mercenary, brothers revolutionary—we were going to change the world, together. That was our high school plan. It was formed in the back car of the El, on our way to the Greyhound station. We would transfer at The 95th/Dan Ryan stop and take the bus all the way out to Decatur, IL. Why Decatur? We had never been to Decatur. What else was there to do on Saturday after soccer practice? So we went, still in our cleats and shin guards, tracking mud into the 7-Eleven for Big League Chew. (Big League Chew is like chewing tobacco. Only it's not chewing tobacco. It's gum. But scandalous gum, banned in the Evanston and New Trier Township school districts.) We brought this scandalous gum out in public, sitting atop an Archer Daniels Midland Corp. dumpster and chewing it like cud, then smuggling it across the Decatur border—and then across the Carleton W. Washburne School border—and selling it to the middle school kids. (The consequences of smuggling in real tobacco were much too severe in a District that valued future stability too greatly to tolerate less-than-exemplary behavior from their young).

Sometimes we bought and distributed Kings cigarette gum, discussing how we were going to change the world. How could we *not* change the world—we were born in a revolutionary era, a decade that began with the legendary passage of the Staggers Act and subsequent deregulation of the railroad industry. Opportunities abound, they told us.

Things have not gone as planned. There have been unforeseen obstacles. We have panicked, turned on one another—Out of necessity? Desperation?—showing pity only for ourselves. There is no all-togetherness, no gung-ho-ness, no there's-no-I-in-team-ness. We, shit-soaked and reeking, brandish our fangs, let at each others' necks, blood running down our throats. (If you didn't know better, you'd think we hated each other. We do hate each other, don't we? I can feel it, for a second, this hatred of my closest friends.) And when we're done, when we have cleaned the bones and tossed them like salt over our shoulder, who will assume custodial duties? Who will scoop our poop? Mop up our fetid, fly-infested shit?

I still hear them.

—If you had the choice between sharing personal space with Dent or making nice with a shoeshine boy, what would it be?

—Let's focus on what's really important here: Sheldon Wirth, and how much of a milkmaid he is for getting himself kidnapped.

And they do, they talk about it, about how I am a complete milkmaid for thinking that scoring drugs and buying weaponry will somehow prove me otherwise; how I waited three days before doing anything, how—

ZZZZZZZZZzzzzZZZZ

—I must have looked ridiculous the whole time; how ridiculous I look now, with my pale skin, my purplish eyes. They talk, at length.

Good is the thought that ambushes me.

This is how we bond. This is normal for us. I desert my computer, overrun with Zs, and grab a pair of shorts from my bag. I join Dent and Joel again in the other room.

"Outside, ten minutes," I say.

"It's too cold."

"Ten minutes."

"But it's . . . okay. Fine."

We are sucking. Hard. Just really losing. It's Joel and me versus Dent and a Taiwanese kid from the neighborhood who seems to have no awareness of the three second rule. We can't inform him of this, of course. We would look like poor sports. And racist, maybe. If Joel would box him out, it might not matter. But that's too much to ask. He refuses to box out.

God, we are sucking. I can't believe we are only eight points behind, given the hard-core shit we are eating on the court.

The three-second kid is fast. And good. He does an annoying leg thing when he dribbles, like faking us out, but it doesn't work. We are making him look better than he is. His name is Wei.

"Next point wins," Dent calls to us, showing mercy.

Fine. Let's do this, Joel.

Dent and Wei win.

Rematch?

No. God, we were atrocious. This is demoralizing.

Should we go in?

Yeah, yeah.

We fist bump Wei and head in.

Nothing has changed. We are in the same room as before. The swan room, I now call it. Joel has positioned himself on an ottoman, five feet from the TV, where he is watching the music video of a band with a heavy Motley Crue influence.

"Okay, now I'm only going to look at The Far Left Back Up Singer," Joel says. "Don't let me look at anyone except The Far Left Back Up Singer this time."

This is hour two of Joel's experiment, Dent explains, which began a couple of days ago. So far, Joel has replayed the video at least fifteen times.

"See? He has different colored shoes. God, you learn so much when you look closely at things."

Joel has thus far looked at: The Lead Singer, The Far Right Back Up Singer, The Middle Back Up Singer, The Singer Between The Far Right Back up Singer and The Middle Back Up Singer, The Bassist, The Backup Guitarist, The Drummer, The Synthesizer Guy, and The Second Row of the Audience. Joel is convinced that his enjoyment and understanding of the video is enhanced by this exercise, and he is still—

"Now I'm going to just look at his legs while pretending I'm in Camelot. You'd be surprised how much you learn when you bring Camelot into the equation."

—somehow able to participate in a conversation with Dent, who has not finished outlining the benefits of my taking a vacation, the advantages of my losing a few pounds.

They continue for ten or so minutes, it's hard to tell. I chuckle helplessly. Because they're right. I do need a vacation. I signal a consensus by standing:

"The atoll it is, then," I announce. I head toward the kitchen.

We have tequila, a celebratory thing. They tell me, just as I am making my lemon face, as I am sucking air between my teeth as if it will cool the fire that burns within, that they are glad that I have agreed to this vacation. I nearly say, *Did I have a choice?* But I don't say this. I redirect:

"Let's hear about Dent's adventures!"

I sound parental, treating Dent's travels like a field trip, a visit to the zoo. It works. Dent leans back, sets a Reef sandal on the edge of the table. He tells us that he really wanted to find cannibals (notwithstanding their scarcity) in New Guinea, that he had heard about them, read stories, and he wanted to see if they existed, satisfy his fascination with them, an urge not unlike my desire to befriend a real, live Siamese twin someday. We assume he's lying.

"That's stupid," Joel says. "They don't do that any more. That stopped happening in the '60s or something."

Dent ignores this and pulls out a package of photos. He pats the cushion beside him on the sofa. It does not look big enough for two.

"Cooome on, don't be bashful," he says in a voice sounding much like Regis Philbin's. "You won't see anything all the way over there."

I move next to him, barely fitting.

"They gave me an underwater camera, for research purposes."

I have to sit on my hands as he flips through some coral shots. I have only one question, a single thing that has been sitting with me this whole time:

"Is that a trumpetfish?" I point to a blur of color on the photo's periphery.

"No."

He continues flipping.

"How about that?"

"Nope. That's Brian, our research assistant."

I don't ask again. I sit like a child sent to a corner.

"See there, in the background? That's a trumpetfish."

I squint.

"It's tiny."

"Yeah."

"Is it poisonous?"

"Deadly poisonous."

"Really?"

"No. You can see a bunch of them at the Shedd Aquarium."

Joel shoots us a glance from the sofa.

"Will you guys shut up? This is my favorite commercial. Great. I missed the best part. You made me miss the best part of my favorite commercial."

We ignore him.

"What's it like? The trumpetfish?"

"Shy, mostly. It hunts by blending in with the sponges. Then it attacks."

On *attacks*, Dent makes a claw with his hand. This is meant to startle us. It does not. He then flips to a picture of him with three beautiful women in assorted states of *dishabille*, as he puts it. They are all over him.

He cradles it in his palms like a wafer.

"Oops," he smiles. "How did that get in there?"

"Liar," Joel says, still fascinated with the TV. "You paid them. I know places like that. You pay them huge sums of money for pictures with you. It's one big tourist industry racket."

"Jealous mmmuch?" He says, dwelling on the word.

We pause.

"See? See their boobs?"

We pause.

Yep. Those are boobs.

I shift uneasily.

We move to the couch, an old davenport. There is only room for two of us on it. Joel sits across from us, next to the TV We give him a funny look. It is strange, the way he has seated himself, until we learn that he wants to show and tell. He takes out his iPhone and shows us the massive collection of independent films he has stored on it, putting his English degree to good use —

"So this film, set against the backdrop of the Spanish Civil War, has all five elements of the Aristotelian drama, plus close-up nookie. It's ingenious, really."

"Is that guy with the handlebar supposed to be Franco?"

—and we, idiotically, humor him. Not humor, exactly, because I'd be lying if I said I wasn't fascinated by this particular movie. *GuerniCoitus*, I believe it's called. Joel props his iPhone on the sofa and joins us on the couch. Yes, it's awkward, but I watch on, proud of myself for recognizing a key switch to the subjunctive, hoping for at least a little bit of English. I am soon assuaged. Soon after the two principals are fully engaged, the male protagonist raises a hand, and, in his most guttural baritone, declares (and I quote):

"Fuck my cock."

We cheer, elated. This is a major plot development. Our hero has shown leadership, dominance. It is a milestone, this fucking of cock. He has . . . he has grown.

It seems like a good stopping point. Joel flicks off his iPhone and starts rambling, chatting away about the international implications of what we have just watched, his mind almost turning over on itself until Dent, innovator that he is, transforms his hand into a CB, holding a fist up to his mouth.

Ssshhht Forty-Seven, is how he begins. *This is twenty-two on the beast. Stand on it, One Four Zero. We got a clean shot up ahead. Ssshhht*

Ssshhht This is One Four Zero, on the handle. Just hit the big road and starting to backslide. On the hammer all the way. Ssshhht.

Ssshhht. Ten-Four. Ssshhht.

This is good. Joel starts laughing, a big, deep laugh, clutching his girth, almost choking to death on his own delight. He starts talking again, but not about religion. He starts talking Redneck Trucker lingo. We have saved ourselves.

"Man," Joel says, finishing his thought, "*Man.*"

We grab another round of Dos Equis from the fridge.

"Those were some nights, weren't they?"

We flip through my CD collection and listen to *REO Speedwagon*. Then we listen to *Linkin Park*. Then we watch the beginning of *Weekend at Bernie*'s but flip it off after ten minutes. Then Joel tells a drawn-out joke about Jew-sus, the Jewish Jesus, which does not go over well at all.

I realize my shoelace is untied. I tie it up.

Slam Dunking, Herman, The G-String.

We have spent the last three hours playing NBA Jam on an old SNES system, acting as though the announcer were God, or at least a very influential public figure. It's his way with words. Especially when we dunk. It is the best when we dunk. When we dunk, the announcer announces:

Boom! Shaka Laka!

And he does it so well. Some of our dunks are fancy, and when they are fancy—

Boom Shaka Laka.

—his enthusiasm is most apparent. Yes, when we dunk—it is the best when we dunk.

Boom! Shaka Laka.

And we mean it. We mean every word of it.

After Mr. Hakeem Olajuwon and I have publicly humiliated Joseph Jones' Utah Jazz in a 89-91 buzzer beater, Dent suggests that someone (not him)—

"I'm feeling a little peckish," he says, clearly regretting his choice of both the words feeling and peckish.

—order food. I agree. Someone (not me), should get food for us. Joel volunteers to run out for guacamole. Brilliant. Guacamole. I would like beaten avocado right now. Dent and I continue to play, enraptured by the announcer.

Boom! Shaka Laka he cries.

Boom! Shaka Laka we repeat.

"That would be good, for your last words. *Boom shaka laka.*"

"You think?"

"Why not? They're pithy, meaningful. They're also recognizable. It'll get people talking."

"True."

"Have any better ideas?"

"Honestly, no. So far the best I have is, 'The Hyena Also Dies,' and the hyena symbolizes Greed. I'd also considered *I'm Not Finished*, but for that to be funny, someone would have to interrupt me. The timing on that is tricky. I also think it's too Oscar Wilde, you know?"

"Planning on putting some more work into them?"

"Yeah. Probably."

"Okay. Let me know if you need any help."

"Will do."

"Seriously," I say. "I'm more than willing to help."

"Sure. Sure I . . ."

He trails off.

We switch from NBA Jam to another game that is both more and less realistic, in that the scenarios presented looked more real even if they were less likely to occur in everyday life.

"I could stab him in the stomach."

These games usually involved engaging in important, life-altering decision-making, which would no doubt benefit us in our future professions.

"Do you think I should stab him? In the stomach?"

They imbued in us the wisdom and prudence that, should any one of us ever decide to become President, would serve us well.

"I don't know," Dent says. "It seems . . . unoriginal."

"How about suffocate him?"

"Or disembowel? Disemboweling's always a good one."

The rules say he has to die. We are not above the rules. It would be foolish of us to think such things. I suggest an alternative:

"Disembowel with an option to behead?"

"Not bad."

To disembowel this man but not behead him, I should be careful to press X Y X instead of Y Y X. If I press Y Y X, I'll gouge out his eyes.

"Scimitar or ax?"

"Oooh, toughie. Go with the scimitar."

I go with the scimitar. The blade enters from behind, a clean cut. His neck becomes a geyser. Lovely.

The man, geyser man, drops to his knees. I get 200 points and 3 life. I should kill a hooker. I get a bonus if I kill a hooker.

Dent is mesmerized.

"That's a lot of blood."

Does he deserve to die? Does this man, this claims auditor from Aberdeen, SD or automotive technician from Waco, TX—this innocent—does he deserve this?

"Yeah. It doesn't seem realistic. For someone to have that much blood in them."

Yes, this man was a bad person. This man did bad things with his life. He was a white supremacist, a Klansman.

"Good graphics, though."

This man was a Nazi. He was Hitler.

We have made much progress in the past three hours. We are now watching the opening sequence of *Martin*, held in thrall by its lyrics. *Mah-iiiin*, we say, pronouncing it like *often*, dropping the *t*. We all agree that *The Fresh Prince of Bel-Air* is more intelligently scripted, but we have not memorized its theme song. *Mah-iiiin!*

Mah-iiiiin!

I search for the remote and prepare to throw it to Dent, when:

"Dent?" I suddenly ask.

"Yeah?"

"Both of you guys know about Dafna, don't you?"

"About the—?"

"Don't say it. So you do know."

"Yeah. I know about it," Dent says. "And we both know about it."

"Just curious."

I toss the remote over. He flips to a show about crocodiles.

"Wow," he says.

"What?"

"A rape *and* a kidnapping. Wow. You are *cursed*, man. Cursed."

He flips to *South Park*. I love *South Park*, but he flips away.

"Can I ask you something?" Dent says.

"No."

"Did she hurt you?"

I snort.

"That's a yes. You realize how ridiculous that makes you look?"
Fuck off, I nearly say.
"Shut up. I wasn't totally against the whole thing. We were dating. It's not like I didn't sorta like it."
"Didn't Joel joke about it at the time? Say something like she should throw herself down the stairs?"
Yes. Joel joked.
"Or off the roof when cleaning the gutters? That's what Joel was joking about. Anyway, it was pretty funny."
"No. It wasn't."
It wasn't funny.
"Yeah it was."
"What would you have done if she kept it? And it was a girl?"
"It wouldn't have been a girl."
"Why not?"
"It wouldn't have been."
"You know what else?" he continues.
Why is he continuing? I should bloody Dent's nose. I should blow him away.
"What else?"
He pauses. He senses the venom in my voice.
"You should look . . . at . . . my . . . Geeeeeee-."
"Absolutely not."
"Oh my Geeeeeeeeeeee-string!"
"Great."
"I know you need to see it. I know you want to see my Geeee-string."
Dent hoists up the legs of his shorts and tucks them around his crotch, prancing around as if he were stepping on coals.
"Do you see my Gee-string? Do you see how easy I wear it? How *easily* I wear it? How *sexily* I wear it?"
I should bloody Dent's nose again for talking about Dafna (talking about Dafna gives me bunions; it makes my eyes pop; it makes my ears bleed), but Dent and his G-string—and his hairless legs—make me smile. I do everything in my power not to.
Because—ah, ah—this is an old routine we used to do, the G-string routine, and it is difficult not to laugh. It began at Dent's house, and the process was simple. I would stick my head into the second floor laundry chute and call, "Dent. Dent. Deeeeent. Deeeeenton Brown." He, playing air-hockey in his basement, would stick his head up (Yuuuuesss?), cuing me to,

through the chute, pummel him with something disgusting. Sometimes it was Elmer's Glue; other times, cat food. He always knew something was coming, but never *what*; but he stuck his head up every time, as a sacrificial thing.

One day I found his sister's G-string in a hamper and knew there was only one thing to do:

"Deeeeeeent?" I called down.

"Yuuuuueeeeees?" He looked up.

"Delivery!"

Right on the face.

The next day, he wore it to school, outside of his Levi's. He attached a Hello! Kitty bauble to the partition, just for fun. "Do you like my Geeee-string?" he'd ask everyone in sight, even the teachers. He was the only one who could get away with speaking that way to them (giving them the *yessir*, *yesma'am* in as glib a way as possible), who could keep it going the whole day, and into after-school athletics.

Right now he is on the G-string routine, parading—no, *peacocking*—about the room:

"G-string?" he says.

"Yes! G-string!" he repeats. He shimmies over, modeling his sartorial innovation.

"My Geeeeeeeeeee—" he insists, his face close to me now, so close that it is vibrating my cheek. "—eeeeeeeeee string." I push him away, because he has made me laugh. I want anything right now but to laugh.

"You're laughing. You're crying and then you're laughing."

God. The G-string routine is legendary.

The G-string routine killed.

Before I can retaliate. We are distracted by an ITT Technical Institute ad targeting unemployed or underemployed individuals who are looking to make a change in their lives; this spurs an informal debate about the kind of life we would choose to lead if we were born under less genetically favorable circumstances, which is midway through interrupted by laughter brought on by Dent's hilarious misinterpretation of the word *probity*. Then we turn to *Washington Journal* on CSPAN and decide that the smokeshow on *Washington Journal* is not only hot but also tastefully dressed, making her that much more desirable as a potential mate. When former Chairman of the Halifax Bank of Scotland Lord Stevenson of Coddenham appears onscreen, we hoot and holler and act generally uncouth but eventually agree that the way he handles himself under pressure is impressive, to say the least.

Then the phone rings and it is a woman asking for a man named Herman, so we quiet down and demand to know why this woman is looking for Herman, what business she has with Herman, and how she came to know Herman in the first place; we then request Herman's height, weight, middle and last names, and a detailed description of Herman's physical attributes simply to see how long we can hold her there, which ends up being nine minutes.

We are interrupted by a shave-and-a-haircut knock on the door. *Guaaaac!*, Joel yells. He dumps the guacamole in a bowl, muttering, "I am going to eat you, guacamole. I am going to *consume* you. You are Jonah, I am Whale. I am—"

"Joel? No."

He puckers, as if considering something. He dabs his finger in the guacamole.

I look away.

"Does anyone here," I ask, speaking only to Joel, "find it depressing that we haven't really done anything today?"

"I find a lot of things depressing," he says.

"No need to be picky?"

"Right." He puts a hand down his pants.

A commercial for breath mints appears onscreen. The TV is muted, but we stare, enraptured.

"So what's the secret?" Joel says after a few minutes.

"What?"

"Didn't you say in your email you had a *top* secret?"

"Oh," Dent says, still staring at the screen. "Right. I did."

. . .

"Well?"

"Well what?"

The TV has somehow been tuned to *People's Court*. I can't believe that show still airs.

"What is it? You can't say you have a *top* secret and then not tell us what it is."

"Oh, it's that I'm fine."

"Fine?"

Dent nods impatiently.

"I mean I'm not fucking dying."

. . .

"You're—?"

"It was all bullshit. I'm fine and I've always been that way."

"But," I say. "This whole time, you –"

"Not dying, never was."

I flip to a Harvey Keitel movie, starring go-fast boats and breasts; co-starring a woman who looks like a man.

Interlude: New Year's Eve.

It is New Year's Eve, and I am celebrating with strangers in an unknown Beacon Hill apartment, off Charles Street. My coworker somehow convinced me that coming to this party would be a good idea. I believed him. I have one of those Blow Out party favors in my mouth, the kind that sounds like a kazoo and pops out when you blow into it. I blow into it. It pokes me in the eye. I did not expect this.

I join a group of people gathered around a collection of airbrushed Coors Light art. There are eight pieces of varying sizes, all framed.

"How delightfully white trash!" someone says.

I leave.

I head for the bathroom, down a corridor that's new to me. Jesus, this apartment is huge. I take a wrong turn into a bedroom to find my coworker. He is alone in his underwear, dancing.

"Roll-er Coaster!" he sings, gyrating, twirling his genitals like a pinwheel.

"Ro-ller Coasterrrr!"

Do you ever get the feeling of being surrounded by people who don't understand you? That, no matter how hard you try, you just don't fit in? I bet my coworker gets that feeling a lot.

I don't think he sees me.

I back out of the room.

It is almost midnight. There is energy in this room. There is a shared sense that everything will be better. There will be hope and opportunity next year. Next year we will make changes and do things we ought to have done before. We should look forward to this.

It nears midnight. Yes, we will look forward to next year! We will be ebullient and free and new next year! Yes! Yes! We will be new next year!

I meet a girl, Katy. We drink. Before long we are flirting. We take shots. I don't remember what happens next.

INTERLUDE: The Letters.

Below is a sample letter read to Sheldon Wirth by Linda Wirth on 11 January 2008. If she couldn't find anything interesting in the papers, Linda Wirth (formerly Linda Mercer) would regale her son with Mercer family history, reading verbatim from old letters that had been pulled from a meticulously organized and cross-indexed file, then transcribed to email. (NB: the below is not meant to be read in its entirety; rather to illustrate the kind of history we are dealing with here):

Now John Drayton Gunn, your great-great-great grandfather, came to Texas in 1842 and he moved his large family, mostly daughters and some spouses to Stringtown between 1850-56 where he owned 3000 acres. Before that he lived in Georgia and owned lots of land so that he was among the 2 or 3 wealthiest men in the state. Then came the panic of 1837 and he lost his land and a warrant was issued to throw him in debtor's prison. The historical marker at the Gunn cemetery says he was elected to the Georgia state legislature, but he was not, he was appointed to that position by the governor of Georgia. It was a smart move because while a legislator he could not be arrested. His business partner was Samual Koon, whose forebears were from the Netherlands and who moved to Dutch Point, South Carolina, and later to Georgia. An arrest warrant was also issued for Samuel so that he moved to Texas with John Gunn and changed his name from Koon to Kone. I had never before heard that story. Our speaker was Shannon Fitzpatrick, who knows the Gunn/Kone/Malone/Rylander history very well. However, she did not know that Ed Kone, your great-grandfather, in 1908 was appointed and accepted the position of president of Texas A&M, but it is confusing as to how long he served because about that time he was named as the first ever Commissioner of Agriculture for Texas.

Now, Re Stringtown, I will give you a copy next time you come to Dallas. I gave a copy to Linda but she can't locate it. It's a hard book to find as it was published in a very small number by Corpus Christi Press, and that was the only book ever published by CCP.

Re Louis Mercer genealogy, his death certificate says he was born in "S.C.", I assume to be the state of South Carolina on September 5, 1867 and he died on April 8, 1945 in Austin, so that he lived 77 years, 7 months, and 3 days. His parents were Jacob S. Mercer and Susan Olenick, both of whom were born in Poland. His sister lived in Austin and George Shelley, still in the same house on West Avenue, knew her and her family. Some of these Mercer children may still be in Austin, but apparently our side of the family never socialized with them. I know of no photos of papa Mercer parents or sibling(s), and why the two families did not get together is sort of a mystery. George Shelley may know how to contact papa Mercer's living relatives. If they can be found they probably have lots of information, including the delicate question as to why the brother and sister did get together from time to time. The fact that papa Mercer was a Jew does not really answer the question for me.

Anna has a family chart, Linda has the same one, and it shows that the Malones enter our family tree so that Jan and I may be distant cousins. As you know, one of her first cousins is named Malone Hill. Re the Rylanders, they married into the family through R.B. Rylander who married Jan's aunt and Billie's sister, Frances Morelock Hill, so that there is no blood relationship with the Rylanders although R.B. Rylander is related to the Stringtown Rylanders. To make it more confusing, Hill Rylander was married to Carol Keeton, the fighting grandma who ran for governor against Rick Perry, and the Hills and Rylanders are related, so that Jan is related to the Rylanders through Frances, her aunt. What a mess, I quit. Don't get me started on the Tracys, our great-great grandparents on mother's side of the family.

Part II

I
Have
Been
Made
To
Look
Like
An
Asshole

IX.

@ggray: So how are we today? Feeling okay? Better than last time?
@shelgames: Awesome. Just great. Really great. Going to Mexico soon, leave March 12th. Two weeks, and I'm in Mexico. Pronounced Me-**hee**-co. Can't wait.
@ggray: Sounds like an improvement.
@shelgames: Oh yeah. Mexico has saved me. Everything—my life, my work—has improved since I booked a flight to Mexico. It has given me a goal, an endpoint—no, a midpoint—and I don't worry about day-to-day trivialities any more. I worry about making friends, meeting women. Spring has come, and I will be working on a tan. Possibly a new wardrobe, too. I'm ridding my bureau of all miscellaneously stained items. I'll invest in a pair of those Rainbow flip-flops everyone is so crazy about. Because is it so bad to treat myself? To indulge? You do not have to answer that. Because I already know the answer: No, it is not. Not at all. Linda tells me I sound happier, that the voicemails I have left are more noticeably upbeat. I recently resolved to get outdoors more, mix it up with the community. There are new flowers growing near my stoop—daisies? Or begonias? Not sure. Need to brush up on my horticulture. Anyway, they're a good sign. Harbingers of good things to come.
@ggray: Wow, that's good news. Why so upbeat?
@shelgames: Because I am a new man. This kidnapping, it was good for me, a lemons-to-lemonade type of thing. I proved to myself that Dafna was wrong. That I am as tough as or tougher than—

@ggray: We discussed this. You don't have anything to prove. Remember?

@shelgames:—than any guy she knows. That I am as tough as Dent. As tough as the man who says he made up his is-it-cancer? disease, staged the whole hospital visit, paid off a doctor, (Why? *To escape his parents' control, dodge their absurd expectations,* according to him) though I'm not sure if he's telling the truth. I mean, telling the truth about lying. About the disease. In fact, I'm quite sure *he's not* telling the truth. I'm almost certain he's trying to spare us our worry for him, our impending grief—logic that, even if he is telling the truth, I don't quite understand. Anyway, whatever he is or isn't supposed to have, this MDS 5Q deletion—which, as I understand it, is the absence of the long arm of chromosome 5—seems like something difficult to fake, or stage, or do whatever he did. Also, I saw his meds, his Revlimid. I have no idea why he would do that, or why he would pretend to do that. There are guesses as to his motives, none of them all that good: 1) He's into the black market stuff. 2) Or working for his dad. 3) Or on drugs. 4) Or selling drugs. 5) Or working as a mule, ingesting the drugs and then pooping them out for general consumption. That last one's Joel's,

@ggray: Which is the most likely?

@shelgames: Not sure. All I know is that he had run into trouble with the law back in Illinois. The occasional night in the holding cell. No jail time, though. The worst was a civil suit brought against him by a dentist. The Humorless Armenian, we called him. (Because he was Armenian, you see.) The attorney moved for summary judgment, and it was never brought to trial, or at least that's how it appeared. The whole thing seemed to disappear before anything showed up in the Northbrook bulletin. Same with those other rumors about him, of petty larceny, theft—nothing in the police blotter. People think his dad had something to do with keeping it on the DL. Anyway, they seemed like your typical middle-class suburban predicaments—practically prerequisite for Midwestern youth at the time. But now we wonder if it wasn't something more serious. There must be something wrong with Dent. Dent might be as bad as my kidnappers.

FACT: There is something wrong with Dent.

@ggray: Why do you say FACT? I don't understand what this means.

@shelgames: Force of habit. As I was saying, it's time to focus on what's important. Mexico. It's time to focus on Mexico. Because in Mexico, Dafna will look at me differently. In Mexico, she will look at me, and she will say—wow, Shel, *you have changed*. And she will be right. I have come up with the perfect empowerment tool for this, to boost my confidence and to brag to Dafna about when I am in Mexico.

@ggray: Oh?

@shelgames: Yes, it's the perfect motivator.

@ggray: And?

@shelgames: Brace for it...

@ggray: Braced.

@shelgames: A Boy Scout.

@ggray: A Boy Scout?

@shelgames: Yes, I have gotten in touch with their leader. His name is Jason Chase.

@ggray: And this is supposed to help you? Empower you?

@shelgames: I know what you're thinking. It's no way to make friends. Or meet women.

@ggray: Something along those lines.

@shelgames: I don't blame you for being wary. I, too, tend to distrust chartered organizations. But these Boy Scouts—this is different. It's not cult-like. And there's nothing religious about it. No prayer circles or water rituals. Nothing weird like the Webelos. It's more like a hobby. Hobbies are what men do. I have of late become interested in what men do. I mean real men.

@ggray: Being one yourself, of course?

@shelgames: Yes. I've noticed that there are a number of things men do. One of which is: use periods. Men use periods. Not semicolons. Not commas. Another thing men do is hobbies. Men do hobbies. Like leatherwork. Or lapidary. And a common hobby for a man is training boys in how to become like them. How to become men. So, back to Jason Chase. Jason is a leader in one of these Boy Scout Troops. Troop 37. They operate mostly on weekends, out of the downtown Boys and Girls Club, where they conduct their meetings and merit badge work. The Massachusetts Junior Minutemen, they call themselves. He has even offered to make me a Co-Leader, and convinced me to go on their tri-annual camping trip. *This* is a brilliant idea. Tri-annual. These Scouts have their shit together. These kids are happy. They are enlightened. I bet they whistle a lot. Do you whistle? I never have time to whistle.

@ggray: *What do your friends think about this?*

@shelgames: Well, there's the typical Joel: "The Scouts? *The Boy Scouts: Where The Boys Are Men and The Men Like To Touch Them.*" He's such a bigot. And when he says it with that accent of his, oh, it's really bad. (Have I told you that I hate him? I might hate Joel.) I haven't told Dent about it yet.

@ggray: *What gave you this idea? To become involved with the Boy Scouts?*

@shelgames: My mom.

. . .

@shelgames: It was my mom's idea.

. . .

@shelgames: Are you listening? I said it was my mom's idea.

@ggray: *Oh, sorry. Was it?*

@shelgames: Yeah, there's no way I would have known about it if my mom hadn't told me. This Boy Scout idea is one of the few good ideas Linda—that's her name, Linda Wirth—has ever had. I was reluctant, though. Really reluctant, at first.

@ggray: *Interesting.*

@shelgames: My mom's an interesting woman.

@ggray: *Is she?*

@shelgames: Yeah . . .

. . .

@ggray: *Would you like to talk about your mother now?*

@shelgames: Yes. Yes, I would.

The Mother Invective.

I am sitting at my desk behind a stack of magazines. I have spent the last two hours flipping through each these magazines and tearing out every ACLU advertisement I come across, when—

"Why haven't you called, Sheldon?"
—Linda Wirth calls.
"Why haven't you **CALLED**?"
I look at the stack of extracted ACLU ads. Should I burn them? Would burning them be appropriate?
"I'm sorry, I've been tied up with - "
"You should have **CALLED**!"
I should change subjects. She beats me to it.
"Remember the local Junior Minuteman Troop in Illinois, Shel? Remember how I always wanted you to join that troop?"

She, Linda, had the habit of scanning *Boston* magazine for all the opportunities I was missing. When this became old, she would track down stories in her own local paper, the *Northbrook Star*, about childhood friends of mine who had made better life decisions than me.

"I was busy with Word Jumble when I saw this item on the *Massachusetts* Boy Scouts. You would have done so well in that troop, don't you think?"
"I guess."
"You would have."
"I don't think I would have liked it very much."
"You would have liked it."

Even when I was younger, Linda always worried about other people's opinions of me, as if every disapproving impression was somehow channeled onto her bedside armoire in the form of hate mail. This expressed itself in the inordinate interest she took in my performance at things like recess kickball games. She asked for details no sane parent would ever want.

> *How was kickball today, hon?*
> *Fine.*
> *Did you get any runs?*
> *No.*
> *Any good plays?*
> *One good out. At first base.*
> *Did people see it? You have to make sure people are watching when you do things like that.*
> *People saw it.*
> *Who?*

> *Dunno. Some teachers. I also hit a guy in the face with the ball. It was by accident.*
> *Oh, dear! Who was it?*
> *Rich.*
> *Richard Riley?*
> *Yeah.*
> *Good. That boy's trouble.*
> *How can you tell?*
> *I can tell.*
> *. . .*
>
> *How hard did you hit him?*
> *Dunno.*
> *Did you make him cry?*
> *No.*
> *Did anyone cry today?*
> *Mom.*
> *How many runs did you get again?*

It didn't dawn on her that mothers worldwide may not pay as much attention to me and my peers as she did; why that kickball game may not be the topic of discussion at those neighborhood parties she went to— evenings of over-hyped wine and abject etiquette, attended by people who liked getting competitive about how happy they were as a couple, a family, at their job with Deloitte. (The wives would be especially happy. Extremely happy. The most unhinged kind of happy you were likely to encounter.) It didn't occur to Linda that each of my missteps or imperfections might not immediately be picked up and scrutinized by all major media, newspaper and TV included.

Ignoring the Advice of His Dear Mother, Shel Wirth Continues to Sit at His Desk and Rarely Leave the Office, to the Detriment of Everyone Who Has Ever Cared For Him.
By Paul Krugman.

This was the headline she feared she would see in the paper one day. Or worse, on the TV, from a strong-chinned newscaster:

**Up Next:
Sheldon Wirth is not retarded.
Or is he?
You decide.**

I always suspected that my mother, under the spell of her new cable TV shows, might have welcomed this kind of news, the me-being-retarded-or-gay-kind. It would have been something surprising for the neighbors, something fun—fresh and novel—to bring to the Northbrook Woman's Coalition. Something to titillate them. Perhaps I could just settle for partial retardation. Wheelchair-bound. Or not entirely in my right mind. That didn't seem like such a bad negotiation.

"But you decided to let your hair grow long. I urged you to join that troop, but you wanted to let people make assumptions about you and your long hair."

"Is that what I did?"

I had bangs. No one but my mother would classify that as "long hair."

"Well, you didn't care nearly enough about your appearance."

False. I placed a high premium on my appearance, which is why I had bangs. Kurt Cobain had bangs.

"Anyway, that was a while ago. We've been over it. There's a picture in here of this rather unattractive Junior Minuteman. Looks like he's just as stubborn as you were. Why don't people smile for pictures anymore, Shel?"

"Dunno. That's it?"

"There's also a caption with the picture."

"Then that's it?"

"Then that's it."

"It's short."

"I don't know if there's all that much to say about it. I suppose they put him in there to show there are people who still do good in this world."

Is that our son on the phone? I hear my dad say in the background. *Is that Shel?*

"It would take a long time, I don't doubt, counting all those things. He may need a hand. Why don't you sign up for the Scouts, Shel? Become—"

That's Shel, isn't it? my dad persists.

"—a leader? Grant, please. I'm in the middle of a conversation."

But he persists: *Remind him that if he wants to come out of the closet, he shouldn't be ashamed. Remind him that there are support groups for something* like that. Not that you need them, as open-minded as everyone is these days. Tell him I want him to take full advantage of everything, if need be. We didn't have such a luxury when we were kids.

"Grant!"

What? We didn't. Opprobrium from all sides if anyone wanted to come out.

"Tell him yourself."

She hands him the phone.

"How you doing, Shelshock? Doing ok? Good. Opprobrium from all sides, if anyone wanted to come out when I was a kid. That's all I wanted to say. Don't tell Hinder. And don't tell her I called her *Hinder*. We won't tell Mommy that we called her Hinder, will we, FreddyChops?"

Joel always joked that my dad's excessive affection for FreddyChops was a sublimation of a more sinister relationship with the dog. His way of joking about bestiality without offending me by mentioning it outright.

"Thanks, Dad."

"Ok, here's your mother."

"Hi, dear."

"Mom, is dad gay?"

"I don't know, dear."

You don't know what? comes his voice from the background again. *What don't you know?*

Welcome to Middle America. We are loud. Tactless. We are the Griswolds.

"Nothing, honey. Anyway, Shel, I wanted to let you know that I'm concerned because you are underestimating how important it is to have people not just respect you but actually *like you*, honey. It's not wrong to have people like you."

I'm going out back. Dad says from the background. *Gotta take care of those damn beetles.* Grant was in a continual state of war against Japanese beetles in our yard. This was fine with Linda. It kept him out of the house.

" . . . and you have to understand," she continues, "that there are certain inefficiencies with having opinions like yours."

"I like to think of them as beliefs."

"Call them whatever you want, I don't give a sh—" but she stops, sticking as always to the behests of Middle America modesty.

"There are certain inefficiencies that come with those beliefs of yours. It can hurt your career, your social life, your marriage prospects. You are going to come to a point in your life when these beliefs will make you do something immoral *on purpose*."

I sense what Linda is thinking. She is thinking I am intentionally antagonistic to people, that I am *lashing out*. There was rarely a time she didn't think I was lashing out, a blanket term the Northbrook Woman's Coalition used to describe bad grades, drug use, sexual activity, or interest in music and movies. Now that I am older, she associates lashing out with not calling her, or failing to display a sustainable interest in the letters/articles she reads over the phone.

"So that's why the Scouts will be good for you. You should look into it."

"I already told you, I don't have the time."

Interlude: Why I Have No Time.

I spent this morning the following ways, often paired with Joel or my coworker. We: Did every *Don't* in the SpectraCop handbook's *Dos and Don'ts* section. Stole chairs, one per hour, walking it to the Dumpster and disposing of it. Discussed how long we could own a poodle named Sweetpea before giving in to the urge to puncture one or both of its lungs. Shopped online for a poodle named Sweetpea. Purchased the poodle named Sweetpea. Saved Sweatpea from death. Sweatpea is so baller it hurts. Discussed having sex with objects that weren't meant for sex. Conducted informal presentations about the nature and degree of our bowel movements. Made up a great name for a vending company, *Vending Over Backwards*. Became saddened to see that our name for a vending machine company was already taken. Made up lies—

"Did you know that the people of Milwaukee are required by law to own at least one Moo-cow?"

"That's not true at all."

"Doesn't it sound true, though? Those things are legal tender out there."

—but never really stuck to the lies. Collected things like pigeon shit, small bits of newsprint, or pubic hair. Napped. Messed with each other napping by putting things like pigeon shit, small bits of newsprint, or pubic hair into each other's mouths. Enjoyed an in-office cocktail. People watched. (See that man with the pinky ring? That's a very nice pinky ring. That's one of the nicest pinky rings I've ever seen.) Played the bend over/breathe heavy/pass out game. Passed out playing the bend over/breath heavy/pass out game. Died laughing. We did all this on company time, using company resources, without fear of backlash, all the while reminiscing about our best years, our high school years, because they were fun, weren't they?

"Why don't people elope anymore?"

"What?"

"I heard that Beau and Susan got married, and it made me think. Didn't people always used to elope?"

"Did they?"

"Yeah. It must have been a baby boomer thing, to elope."

"Not sure. People still elope, don't they?"

. . . .

"Anyway."

"Fun to think about, though."

"Yeah. Food for thought."

See? My days are full, chockablock.

Oh, I have the time. I have nothing but time.

"I would, but I really don't have the time," I repeat.

. . .

"Oh. Sheldon."

She sounds stricken.

"Are you ok, honey?"

"Never better. You know what? You're right. I'm going to take your advice. I'm going to contact the Massachusetts Junior Minutemen. What's that Junior Minuteman's name again?"

"Let's see here. Jason Chase. He's a student at Emerson."

"Great. Thanks."

. . .

"How's Dafna, honey?"

"She's fine."

"You still seeing her?"

"No."

Linda loved Dafna. Some commandment, celestial or hell-sent, consigned me to marriage with her, Linda was certain.

"That was over a long time ago."

"Okay, Shel. I love you."

"That's a cliché."

"Well. I don't care. I love—"

I hang up and walk to my desk with a flash of apprehension about punishing my mother like I do. Even now, I am unable to accept the *I l*ve you* line from her, or from anyone. I don't mind the sentiment behind it. I support it, in fact. I simply can't stand the words themselves. People all over the world use those words. They have stopped being rare.

I also note that the following words were used with my mother: Blind, Ignorant, Stupid, Cared, Nourished, Locked, Abandoned, Proud. There was no mention of my teenage years. I should remember to include that next time.

FACT: With fennel, garlic, leek and saffron, Linda Wirth's bouillabaisse sauce is unmatched—the best in Cook County.

FATHER FACT: Do you think my dad's gay? Dent says there's a 47 percent chance that he is.

@ggray: Wow. Your mother is an interesting woman.
@shelgames: As I said.
@ggray: So your dad - do you think he's—?
@shelgames: Yes.
@ggray: You didn't let me finish.
@shelgames: Whatever it is, yes.
@ggray: Would you like to discuss the MinuteMen now? Does that sound okay to you?
@shelgames: Oh yes, this will be good. I am going to be a MinuteMaster. This will be very good for me. This will teach me things I should have learned a long time ago. I will be making a difference. While others in my peer group are out celebrating evenings of unbridled charity, downing Hefeweizen and appletinis at Archdiocese of Boston events, making tepid pledges about the bottom-heartedness of their concern for a cause, a *very important* cause—
"So we're here for Breast Cancer, right?"
"No, no. I believe it's a microfinance effort in Rwanda."
"Does anyone know if there's going to be a silent auction? I refuse to give money unless it's via silent auction."
"Wait, are you sure it's not March of Dimes? Does that sound right?"
"Who fucking cares? We're rich!!"
"God, look at the rack on that tall drink of water."

—I will actually be *doing good*, not just supporting it. Because I am a new man, a man of consequence—

"Operation Smile! That's it! This is that Open Wide for Operation Smile gala!"

—a <u>doer</u>.

@ggray: *I also like how you do that thing with the dialogue. How you interweave it.*

@shelgames: I'm not done: A man who escapes life-threatening situations with only an unloaded gun and his own wiles. But also a man who needs no recognition. A man who is just as happy dining at Red Lobster or Arby's as any Madison Avenue brasserie. Who's after more than material rewards. Who seeks *spiritual* sustenance. Because even if he was denied certain rites of passage during his youth, he will *not stand by while it is—*

@ggray: *Bravo.*

@shelgames: I'm still not done: while it is denied others.

@ggray: *Bravo again.*

@shelgames: Oh yes, and you should have seen me when I called him up. I was in a great mood. I had it all mapped out, what I was going to say. And when I was on the phone, I really killed it. Authoritative but friendly. I was like:

"Yes, hello, Jason Chase, please. Yes, it's an emergency. Yes, this is his parent and/or guardian. No, I can't hold. It's an emergency. Listen, not all parents/guardians think it's responsible to give a college student a cell phone."

I was impatient with the operator. You know how old people get impatient when they're on the phone? That was me. I get the urge to cause him minor harm. Shine a very bright light directly into his eyes. I get testy:

"If you'd like to spend 70 bucks a month to provide my son with something that he will only use to 'booty call' or 'drunk dial' your undergraduate women, well, you are welcome to do that. I've heard all about those Emerson girls and their loosey-goosey ways, so – I was waitlisted at Brown, for your information - yes, please, if you would. Thank you."

@ggray: *Then?*

@shelgames: Then. Then I talk with him. With Jason Chase. I talk with this guy, boy, man-to-be who, unlike my own wage-

earning (and all too frequently underdressed) employees, *chooses* to wear a uniform. Who, on weekends, engages the community, makes an effort—perhaps out of a sense of duty, perhaps out of an appreciation for everything he was given in life, for the opportunity to make a difference *while* making a living. Perhaps—and I have heard about these people, my mother has told me about people, the kind of people who *never miss Jury Duty*—he enjoys it. I am right about this.

@ggray: *Are you?*

@shelgames: I *have* to be right about this. When I hear Jason's voice, I can tell. He has diligence in his voice. An understated strength. There is the sincerity of a committed history student, someone who knows better than to squander his potential with college drinking games like Flip Cup or Quarters or Caps or Circle of Death. Or Chandeliers, or Beer Pong, or Asshole. (Or Kings Cup. Or Beer Die. Edward 40-Hands, or Power Hour.) And he is not into the weird hazing rituals like fake branding and elephant walks. No, he is not into these things—like Never Have I Ever, or Boatraces, or Aces. Just from his voice, I can tell he is—

And there is Beat the Dealer. There is Drunk Driver. There is Across The Bridge. There is Up the River. There is Throw Down. There is Beer Checkers. There is Beer Snap. There is Dirty Hearts. There is Drag Race. There is Drunken Race. Oh, the variety! The variety of games! There is Fives. There is Golf. There is Hockey. There is Memory. There is The Name Game. There is Pass Out. There is Spoons. There is Trap. There is Trashed. There is Blink. There is Square. There is Three Man.

—not into puerile drinking games. I can tell by hearing his voice I know he is a serious scholar, one who shudders at the escapism of casual readers. A model student, something out of Norman Rockwell. He is aggressive about his reading, enthusiastic. Nay, ebullient! I can see him, digging through course materials—licking a thumb, turning pages—for something he's certain of. Sitting at a desk, scratching, books open beside him, a ballpoint moving deliberately on notebook paper, his breathing even. He pauses. *Patience*, he tells himself. *This is important.*

@ggray: *Sounds like a responsible student.*
@shelgames: Ah, but there's a twist: He is late handing in the

paper. But only sometimes. Only when he's busy with Junior Minuteman work, understand. I admire Jason Chase for this work. His dedication, his persistence. He will not use this work as an excuse for his late paper, because he has been taught not to use community service in such a way, as an *out*, so to speak. Community service is not a free pass. I know these things from hearing the voice of Jason Chase; from talking with him. I also know that I could be someone he looks up to. That I, after all my mistakes, can shuck off the trappings of my failed life and seem like a Man to these little Junior Minutemen, someone who shepherds them into adulthood, someone who *leads*.

@ggray: So, what happens?

@shelgames: A week later, I meet Jason Chase in person.

@ggray: Is Jason Chase what you expected?

@shelgames: Jason Chase is boring. He wears cargo pants, a tattered Jansport, and a Superman pajama shirt. I hope, pray, this is college-kid irony. His body type is "film school student"—lamppost thin, mop-headed—but he does not appear to be the kind of person who is late to lecture. He looks quiet, white, average. Boring. Jason Chase could be a serial killer.

@ggray: And you lose interest?

@shelgames: Not at all. He suggests we go camping. I nod. This is a great idea.

@ggray: Have you ever been camping?

@shelgames: I drove by Lake Winnipesaukee once.

@ggray: So the answer is no. You haven't.

@shelgames: No. But does that really matter? Because now, oh *now*, I am a figure of authority—responsible for people other than myself. I am, oh-so-selflessly, a Junior MinuteMaster, but the cool kind. The kind that doesn't teach knife safety without showing how to carve other knives out of twigs— the knifiest, most dangerous of other knives. The kind that not only shows them knots, how to use their bowlines, their half hitches, their sheet bends to secure a tent, but also how to lasso a neighbor's pet, or hogtie a kid brother or—but only when you're older—a woman. Essential stuff.

I sell myself to Jason, tell him I am the man. The *man*. I tell him I have experience with camping, experience with kids—both lies—and that I would be a great MinuteMaster. I pretend I'm not a *complete fucking pussy*. Another lie.

@ggray: How does that go? The lie?

@shelgames: Great. Less than two weeks later, I am in a Solar Yellow 1986 Dodge Caravan, responsible for the lives of more than a dozen Junior Minutemen, driving them to Vermont for the first camping trip of my life.

Somewhere in The South Pacific.

"So have you ever gotten a Finnish Massage here?"

There he goes again. Jesus Christ.

"Have you?," Paulson says, genuinely interested. "It's called a Finnish Massage because they finish you off when they're done. Did you know that? And I hear you can get those here."

Dent's work for the night was almost completed, in the process of being completed, but Paulson is on the local nightlife again. His results are almost in, and Paulson wants to know where the hookers are.

Does he really have to do that here? God. Great, now he's demonstrating. He's laying himself across the table, talking about a Finnish Massage. Something must be said.

"We're almost done. Al-most done!" Paulson screams. He is drinking a Zima.

"Want a sip of my Zima?" he asks, holding out his Zima.

Jesus, Paulson.

There had been few times in the past months that Paulson hadn't been a pain. As a member of the team, Paulson encouraged chaos, disorder. He would leave lab books open, tanks unfastened. Even when he wasn't in the room, Dent could hear his breathing, the whinny of a mare. Although Paulson had begun showering regularly since he first arrived, there was always an aroma to him. A stink of cod liver oil and Tic Tacs.

"No I haven't been to a—to a—would you move? You're crowding me."

Dent tried to avoid meals with him. Paulson ate without consequence. He had the habit of never looking at his plate, bringing his fork up to his mouth without knowing or caring how much food was on it, usually focused on his reflection in the mirror. Conversation during meals was affable, though it never strayed far from unsought details about Paulson's previous marriages, far-from-settled settlements, and sexual insecurities. Paulson blamed his ex-wives for everything, all of his woes—drinking and financial included. For Dent, the last straw occurred on the night Paulson started detailing his aunt's miscarriage.

"I'm done," Dent had said, clearing his plate.

From then on, if they did happen to eat together—usually by accident—Dent avoided eye contact at all costs. His fear was that he would be driven mad, looking Paulson in the eye.

"Or a Jack Shack?" Paulson says. "Did you know it's called a Jack Shack because—"

"Haven't been. And please don't touch me."

These frustrations, with Paulson, were turbulence—inconvenient, annoying, but petty. These things didn't incense Dent nearly as much as the fact that Paulson *didn't know how to swim.*

He could doggy paddle, keep afloat, this man, who was supposed to monitor marine research, sent there as an "underwater consultant,"—no, *Lead Research Consultant*, didn't know how to SCUBA dive, didn't display the level of underwater proficiency to be able to SCUBA dive, didn't have his PADI certification. Paulson didn't even know what a PADI certification was.

"It means you'd be certified by the Professional Association of Diving Instructors," Dent had explained.

"Is that a club?"

"You can't dive without being certified, so yes, sort of."

"Is it exclusive?"

Dent did not roll his eyes. It would be useless to roll his eyes. Instead, he messed with him.

"Very exclusive. It's a brotherhood of underwater adventurers. *Jacques Cousteau's son* is a member. PADI is also a member of the World Recreational Scuba Training Council (WRSTC), and therefore so are you, by association."

"So you're going to make me a part of two elite diving organizations?"

"That's the plan. Two *world-famous* organizations. You just have to work on your stroke."

Paulson looked intrigued. He said something, incomprehensible, in an excited voice, like *Word* or *Hell's Yeah*. Paulson was an idiot.

And now, in the lab, he, Paulson, continues to act like one, jumping around the lab.

"Seriously, stop. I can't concentrate. Go get a drink or something. I'll update you later. And I'll also teach you what a fish's *cloaca* is."

God damn it, O'Neil. Dent glanced at the TV in the corner. He had never hated anyone as much as he hated O'Neil just then. Paulson wasn't really to blame. He was just doing what O'Neil paid him to do. What that job entailed, exactly—other than giving useless pointers and vainly hitting on the youngest research assistant, a mahogany-eyed Miami grad student—hadn't become clear until that past week, when Paulson approached Dent with a request that had every characteristic of an order.

Sometimes you have to fudge some numbers Paulson told him, obviously parroting O'Neil. *For the greater good.*

"Fudge some numbers?"

"Yes. Just a few. For the greater—"

"I can't believe O'Neil is making you do this," Dent says.

"It's not O'Neil," he replied, clearly upset that Dent knew from the first that *it was* O'Neil. "We just need something to present to the commissioners."

Fudge the numbers.

"I know it's O'Neil. Don't lie to me. You're dumb and you're cheap." Paulson wasn't smart enough to blame for this. Compared to O'Neil, Paulson was Gentle Ben. "The only reason O'Neil sent you here was to make sure you had the results he wanted. God, fuck you. And Fuck O'Neil."

Fudge the numbers. This is not what happened.

It was strange, this euphemism *fudge*. *Fudge* suggested he made only minor changes in his findings, to better reflect reality, to adjust for error. It suggested respect for the research, and tenderness, as if he were simply giving the data a little bit of *encouragement*, a slight advantage. This is not what happened. *Fudging* was not what happened.

Dent had altered, fabricated—yes, fucked—the data. And he had fucked up months of research. He corrupted, perverted these numbers as Paulson looked on, monitoring, ensuring O'Neil would be content with the results.

"You know this is for the greater good. You *know* it. Remember, he needs the laptop next Monday. I'm taking the 5 PM shuttle to the airport on Sunday. Leaving from the Marriot, So I need it before then."

Dent had no choice but to fudge the data. He needed this last installment of funding. Not for himself. For his researchers. Most were UCSD or Delaware grad students, and they had worked hard. They deserved to be paid. So he agreed—he fudged, fucked, whatever. He fudged only under the condition that his name wouldn't be attached to the research, once submitted. He wanted no further association with it at this point.

"You can do that, right?" Paulson asked. "You're almost done? Right?"

"Jesus."

Even then, he wasn't sure O'Neil wouldn't use his name. Everyone on the commission knew how good Dent was. O'Neil would use it if he thought it might help him. There was nothing in writing. Just had his word. *O'Neil's word.*

"*Right?*"

"Right."

O'Neil, this man whose first name he didn't even know. Dent hated him. He would have killed O'Neil if he could have.

X.

"Oh. Hello there. My name is Sheldon Wirth, and all I think about is camping and fishing. Would you like to talk football? Too bad. Perhaps we can go on a tour of the city? Sorry. Not today. What's that? You'd like to visit a museum? You hear there's a great exhibit at the Museum of Science and Industry?

I ask you this: Will there be camping there? How about fishing? If I can set a tent up on the sidewalk, perhaps I'll consider it.

"Hello, that's an interesting article you have there. What's it about? The semicolon? An article about the semicolon? Oh. My competencies are more in the camping and fishing arenas. I'm sorry, but I tend to lose interest when it comes to matters of grammar or punctuation. If it doesn't concern camping or fishing, good day to you, sir.

>   *@ggray: You didn't actually use those words with them, I take it.*
>   *@shelgames:* No. They're just a manifestation of The Fear.
>   *@ggray: What's The Fear?*
>   *@shelgames:* "Oh. Hello there. Please take a moment to look below you. Do you see that there? What is that there, beneath your feet? Dirt, you say? No. Please do not call this dirt. This is soil. Soil is fertile, abundant. It is rich in nutrients and microbial matter. Dirt is something you sweep under the rug. There is opportunity in soil. See? Mother Nature's quite a gal, isn't she?"
>   *@ggray: I thought we were talking about The Fear.*
>   *@shelgames:* Oh yes. Sorry. I was just rehearsing.
>   *@ggray: So tell me about The Fear.*
>   *@shelgames:* The Fear is the fear I had before I left for the camping trip. The fear that Troop 37 had found me out.

@ggray: In what sense?

@shelgames: That they, Troop 37, had researched me, done military history checks, criminal background checks, employment verification. Went on an exhaustive fact-finding mission. And after all this, they came up with just one thing, one controverting tidbit. And it pollutes their very notion of me. It could be the fact that I didn't until recently know what NAFTA stood for. Or my troublesome FICO score. Anything. And from this tidbit, they extrapolated, made judgments about my motives and character. And realized I am a confidence man, an imposter who, this whole time, has been acting, and badly. So they treat my words as hollow, unavailing. My backstory, they know, is an amateurish caricature; my presence, a breach. Here stands Sheldon Wirth, a man with the trappings of a camping-and-fishing lover who is not truly a camping-and-fishing lover himself. They find out I am occupying an identity that is not mine. I am an imposter. A body snatcher.

@ggray: You didn't have to lie.

@shelgames: I did have to lie. I told them I have camped, having never ventured more than half a mile into any forested area without being stricken with a sudden urge for calamine lotion. And I told them I have fished—also untrue, given my natural aversion to murder. I build campfires, cook s'mores, erect tents. The stuff you read about in *Outside* magazine. I do these things. Because I told Jason Chase I did these things.

@ggray: Oh. So how did your meeting with him go, by the way?

@shelgames: Oh. Fine.

. . .

@shelgames: Would you like to hear about it?

@ggray: Sure. I guess. I mean, of *course*. *Gladly.*

I am in Jason Chase's barebones dorm room—a beanbag chair, a PC, a bunk bed and comforter—meeting him for the first time. I have shaken his hand, introduced myself. Still, he looks surprised.

"How'd you get into my dorm room?"

"The guards here, they know me."

"You work for SpectaCop?"

"I AM SpectaCop."

This impresses him. He does not look or sound impressed, but I am sure he must be. I remove a pack of gum from my pocket and fold a stick into my mouth.

"So what kind of work do you do there?"

"I—" The gum has lost flavor. I spit it out. "I'm not at liberty to discuss those matters."

He is less impressed.

"Do you have a badge?"

"Better. I have stationery."

I tell him I was a student at Emerson. He hesitates, unsure if he should believe me. I name the dean. A look of recognition flashes across his face.

"That's my dean," he says.

"Yeah, when I was here, all the kids called him Dean Ween, because we thought he was sort of a dick."

"We always call him Dean Spleen, because of his temper. Get it? Because he can be splenetic at times."

This is the nerdiest thing I have ever heard.

"You college kids with your words."

I sit in the beanbag chair because there is no other place to sit. This is not easy to do in work clothes. The chair resists. I slide off. Shit. When I am finally settled, after bobbling on it like a teeter-totter, it eats me up. Men do not sit in beanbag chairs. I stand up.

Jason crosses his legs. "So why did you want to see me?"

"Speak up, I can't hear you," I say, channeling my grandfather's don't-be-an-idiot attitude, "and look me in the eye when you shake hands. When we met, you didn't look me in the eye. Understand?"

"Yeah. Sorry."

This time he really is impressed.

"So why'd you become a Junior Minuteman? To develop leadership skills? Confidence?"

"Not really. I was forced into it."

"Really." He hands me a sheet of paper. It has Emerson University Dean's Office letterhead. "My credentials."

Dear Mr. Jason Frederick Chase. I skim it. It begins inauspiciously—"When a student begins to show signs of struggling with their academic obligations, we at the Dean's Office feel it necessary . . . "—and, skipping to the last paragraph—". . . our best efforts to make your remaining time here at Emerson University as enjoyable as . . . "—ends insincerely. The phrasing emphasizes *your remaining time here* in an ominous way, as if those at the Dean's office were nursing the hope it would be brief. I hand back the sheet.

"Looks like Dean Ween has you cornered," I say. "Did you tell your parents about this?"

"Nah. They wouldn't care even if I did."

> *Good. This kid needs someone. He needs a steady influence. I can be the understanding father-figure, the surrogate protector who steps in when the real one proves unfit; when he turns out to be a drunkard or a lout, someone who emotionally abandons his children, casting them into the proverbial wilderness.*

"So you skipped class?" I do my best to mimic disapproval.

"Yeah. And I turned in B.S. papers. I was lashing out."

He shuffles to his desk and fishes out a paper. He hands it to me. It is an amalgamation of footnotes, in-text citations and end matter, stapled to a one-page bibliography. He tells me to flip to the back page and points to the grade: F. Below it, in the comments section, he is reprimanded for bringing down the level of academic discourse. I nearly expect to find the word "dipshit" among the remarks. I sit in the beanbag chair again, this time successfully.

"They gave it directly to the professor," he says. "Apparently, the teaching assistant found it 'too upsetting' and refused to grade it herself. But I did manage to slip the word *disambiguation* into the essay. That upped my cred a notch or two. At least."

"At least," I say. Is this kid for real?

I rub the side of the beanbag chair, liking its feel.

"Seriously, what were you thinking?"

"'Let them flunk me. They won't get me on plagiarism.'"

"And they flunked you."

"They flunked me."

Awesome, I think. "That wasn't very responsible of you."

Jason's hands become two miniature tortoises, retracting into his sleeves.

"So, can you—" I begin, but my phone rings. It's Joel.

"Hold on, I have to take this," I say, knowing a call from Joel is the last thing I'd ever have to take.

A Call From Joel, Interrupter.

"Shel!" Joel says to me. "Hey Shel, so I need your opinion on something. What do you think of men with pierced ears? Do you think it's appropriate? Does it bother you? This is important stuff to consider."

Does it bother me? Until now, no.

"Hey, I'm with Jason, that Youth Leader I was going to meet, and I really can't—"

"You're with *Jason*? Right *now*?? Is he a huge lame-ass? A total milkmaid? Oh my god, what's he like? What kind of shit does he wear? Does he wear *Aeropostale*? I bet he wears Aeropostale a lot. Does he play Ultimate Frisbee? Is he on a Freshman team? Ask him about his record of scholastic achievement. If he doesn't have a record of scholastic achievement, you shouldn't bother with him. I can't believe you're actually doing this, man. I can't believe you're going to be that weird guy who joins the Scout troop. You're *that* guy. Holy, holy, holy."

"Yeah, I'm that g—"

"What does he look like? Will he be Marilyn Manson or something when he gets older? Seriously, what's he going to be like? I <u>needs</u> to know. Really. <u>Needs</u> to know. Where are you right now? Seriously, tell me where you are at. this. very. moment."

"I'm in his room."

"In a dorm? What does it look like? Does he have one of those *Study Hard* posters? Or beer-themed posters, with the subjects listed as brands of beer? Those things. Those things are great. Oh, oh, and what are you guys talking about? Have you touched on why you're there? *Have you touched him?*"

"We're just talking about homework. Listen, I really—"

"Homework? That's so lame. Who does homework?" he says, hopefully joking. "I'll tell you who does homework," he continues, answering his own question. "Two types of people: 1) Virgins and 2) The uncoordinated. Hey, wouldn't that be a great name for a horror movie, *The Uncoordinated*, with bloodthirsty zombie people throwing knives at their victims and missing? Or *The Uncircumcised*, with this 'skin-monster' chasing people around? By the way, I'm on this website, a great website, and there's this girl, this total smokeshow—"

This is when I hang up.

"What was that about?" Jason asks.

"Oh, nothing. Just business," I say, closing the phone.

"That's business? I think I heard someone use the word *smokeshow*."

"Yeah. Business. We deal with some . . . some complicated stuff."

The right side of the beanbag chair suddenly gives. I slide down.

"My problem is that I have trouble talking. I mean, I talk, but it doesn't make sense. I have trouble expressing my ideas. It's like I have these words coming out of my mouth in a linear way, even though the thoughts in my head aren't like that at all. Know what I mean?"

I know exactly what he means. I have known for years what he means, and this is what I would like to say to him. This is what I would like to tell Jason Chase:

> *I, too, have felt this way, Jason Chase. I have been there, in your situation, trying to express myself, struggling with a way to get more than a ticker-tape's worth of language out of my mouth, angry with my head's exasperated accountant, who is unable to represent my many, <u>very</u> insightful, <u>very</u> worthwhile thoughts, because these thoughts cannot be reproduced linearly. You see, in my head, there is a multiplex of expressions and images and emotions and multi-tiered messages, too complex (too mind-blowing) for an ordinary person to express or absorb through speech. So, yes, I do know what you mean, and—perhaps—if there were a way to link brains, to hook together our innermost wants and fears, we would discover that—is this going to far?—we are kin, brothers. We are one.*

This is what I say:

"Blows, man."

I fumble with a bottle of Flintstones Multivitamins on the bureau.

"Anyway."

"Anyway."

"Anyway, you in?" he asks.

"In?"

"Yeah, because we need you. Our next camping trip is in less then two weeks. And we need you to take us."

He slides a topographic guide to Vermont across my desk.

"In case you haven't made it to the Green Mountains," he says, "here's a map to get you started."

"Very interesting. Thanks."

I handle it like a tourist, looking flummoxed.

"Yes, we'll go camping. And fishing. I do these things, camping and fishing. All the time. I do and have in the past done both of these things."

@ggray: And I assume you went? On the camping trip?
@shelgames: Yeah. I went.
@ggray: How'd it go?
@shelgames: Great, but the Junior Minutemen acted . . . strange, standoffish at times.
@ggray: Standoffish?
@shelgames: Yeah. Standoffish. They stood off.
@ggray: Ah. Tell me about it.
@shelgames: See, beforehand, I had this genius idea, about paying these kids to do my chores. As long as I didn't go overboard, I thought I could take some liberties with the system. A couple bucks to the Junior Minuteman who makes my dinner. For the one who does my laundry a—I don't know, a fiver. Or I'd just award them with Merit Badges.
@ggray: I don't think that's how it works. That sounds like a debasement of the whole system.
@shelgames: But what is this system if not capitalistic? What is this Merit Badge system if not a labor pool, a system for the little achievers of this country? These kids are much less intelligent than I thought.
@ggray: Or perhaps their motivations are different from yours.
@shelgames: Yeah, that's what I thought. So I try a different approach. I ask Jason if there is a way to fire a Junior Minuteman.
@ggray: What?
@shelgames: Fire one of them. Can him, terminate him. Just one, to make an example out of him. Merely the *threat* of firing would do. What reason do kids have for performing if there are no consequences?
@ggray: I'm not sure that would be effective. I believe they have a different – what's the word? That French word?
@shelgames: Raison d'etre?
@ggray: Yes, that's it. They have a different raison d'etre from you.

@shelgames: It's a possibility. They do like going outdoors, camping. They like lanyards. Those Minutemen *obsess over their lanyards.* And First Aid, CPR certification. They really wet themselves over that, which I suppose is reasonable. But the camping. It's something I don't quite understand, frankly.
@ggray: *So I assume you're going to tell me about it? About the camping trip?*
@shelgames: That's the plan.
@ggray: *Good. I think it's good to talk these things through.*
@ggray: *You should have told the truth, you know.*
@shelgames: I'm not so sure.
@ggray: *I think you should have.*
@shelgames: Oh. It's too late now.

"Nature's canvas."

"The Lonely Mountains."

"See that tree there? That's a good tree."

This is their game. I am on I-95, driving seventeen scouts to Montpelier, Vermont, and this is the game they play. I have taught the scouts about Ruane Manning, and now they are making up titles to their own Ruane Manning paintings.

They are laughing. Almost crying. They are having a ball.

But they continue. Even when we park and hike uphill for miles, searching for a campsite, they continue. I should not have told them about Ruane Manning.

"Behold—*spotted beauty!*"

We search for a flat, open place to set up a tent. When this place is found, we fumble with shock-corded poles, then drench ourselves with DEET, lots of DEET, ungodly amounts of DEET, quantities of DEET that make it unsafe to approach an open flame, tying timber hitches to branches, dragging them near the fire pit, cracking them against our knees. I was told not to pack the following items on this trip:

1. Deodorant.

It will weigh me down, they say; it isn't "green." This frightens me, not being fresh. How will they take me seriously if I am not fresh? I surreptitiously slip in a tube of oil-free moisturizer, a certainly illegal substance, because I need it. (Yes, I moisturize. All over. Face, legs. Soft elbows. After showering. Or shaving. Particularly shaving. Have to. Razor burn). And the cold weather. Although all the snow has nearly melted, it's still chilly, and my skin tends to be sensitive to that type of thing.

We've got to rusticate you girls, I tell them as we unload the van. We have arrived at the campsite, organized the tarps and tents. I do not know how to set it up. I make a Junior Minuteman set it up for me. He does.

I stand back, watching with a finger on my lip, as though I were taking in art, a Duchampian readymade.

Camp is set up. Everyone is here. Everyone is safe.

What now?

What Now? A Blunder.

I am headed to my tent. I have spotted a path to my tent, a clear pathway with few leaves and even ground. Other than the upraised root of—an oak—there are very few obstacles in sight. I am almost halfway there when a Scout I have never seen before comes running up, and informs me that 1) He has a sister who he calls Sissy and she is eight years old and she thinks she has destructive Orc powers, and 2) Maine is the only state in which it is still legal to trap bears and 3) Alpaca farmers do not have to pay land ownership taxes. At least two of these things are incredibly interesting. I tell him this.

Oh. He seems surprised. *Thanks.*

He then informs me that trees are "sort of sucky."

I'm not quite sure what he means by this, but I give him a warm smile, trying to overlook the fact that the kid has one of those rattail haircuts.

"Where are you from?"

"Chicago."

I always say Chicago. No one has ever heard of my hometown, so I say *Chicago*. Sometimes I say Wrigleyville. It sounds more "in."

"Oh. Have you heard of the Fridge? His name is William Perry, but he's the Fridge because he's huge. He was a D lineman on the Bears. And he's actually caught a pass for a TD during his rookie season. Can you believe that? He's also really—"

Who has a rattail haircut anymore? I can't believe these things are still available.

"I don't really know much about that stuff," I say, approaching the upraised oak root, seeing it coming, bracing for it, but still tripping over it.

"I should," I offer. "I really should, but I don't follow them. I have a friend who does, though. He loves those guys."

He kicks a tree trunk. I'm not quite sure what to do. Should I say *Chin up* to him? No, there must be a better way.

"You're a good looking kid . . . kid. What's your name?"

"Willy Stone."

This name sounds fake, but I continue.

"Well, you're a really good looking kid, Willy, and I have faith you'll figure it out."

Then I add:

"You've got a really attractive face."

He gives me a strange look.

Oh no. Did I just cross a line?

"Thanks. So. Um . . ."

I should not have said that.

"What I meant to say . . ."

I should not have made the comment about the kid's face. It seemed harmless, the comment—his face has good symmetry, and I'm simply appreciating it. I'm doing him, this Scout with Disarmingly Pretty Features and Exceptional Facial Symmetry, a favor. I am overlooking his rattail, appreciating his strengths. Or is it more than appreciation? Am I a pervert? Am I some kind of criminal? What the hell am I doing out here with these adolescent boys anyway? I'm a deviant, aren't I? A Humbert Humbert, without the class?

I did cross a line. This is awful. I am going to be locked up, or relocated, forced to tell my neighbors that my name is Sheldon Wirth, and—

HELLO, I'm Sheldon Wirth, and I'm:
Required by law to tell you that I am a convicted sex offender.

—simply because, behind that rattail, is an objectively attractive face (*Excellent* facial symmetry. And a very dignified overbite. Not overly ambitious.) that I'm not afraid to admire.

Dafna was right. I do not deserve to be a father. I can hardly control myself.

Willy turns and heads in the opposite direction. He is halfway to his tent, skipping.

"Let me show you something," he says. He unzips the flap and climbs in.

Oh shit, is he inviting me in? Is he serious? Is he enjoying the wrong signals that I've sent him? Or does he *want me to seduce him*, luring me into an intimate, windowless setting.

Willy pokes his head out. He puts a hand underneath his arm and does an armpit-fart. This is hilarious.

He calms down and hands me something. It's Mac OS. A laptop. This spoiled, rattailed kid is more hooked up than me.

"Look, I get Wi-Fi, even way out here," he says.

This kid isn't so bad. This kid is smart. Perhaps rattails are culturally undervalued.

"Can you believe it?" he continues. "You can check the internet."

Another Scout pokes his head out of an adjacent tent and mentions that there is a town not a half mile away, information that I find not a small amount disappointing, considering I thought I was, at least for a weekend, really roughing it. But still, the fact that Wi-Fi is available way out here in Vermont still amazes me. I am compelled to tell the Scouts that the world is at their fingertips, because it really is, so I do.

The World At Our Fingertips.

I go online and do a number of things, one right after the other: I purchase a fertile sow and send it to a family in the country formerly known as Rhodesia. Then I sign up to meet and converse with and hopefully mate with thousands of hot Christian girls online.

Then I buy shares in Harley Davidson, and add its ticker (HOG) to my home page. Then I put a suffering chipmunk out of its misery by bludgeoning it to death with a tent stake. I go over my monthly finances, budgeting seventy dollars for sundries, thirty for et cetera. Then I do not cheat at solitaire when cheating is clearly the only way to win. Then I get fitted for a codpiece. When we were making breakfast this morning, the scrambled eggs and bacon took longer than it should, at which point I noticed that these Scouts aren't *efficient*. They really need to work on their *efficiency*. Perhaps they can follow my example.

Then I ride shotgun. Then I ride bitch.

Then I move to a shack in the wilderness and strip down to butt nakedness and frolic with all of the bright and beautiful and radiant beasts of the earth, sky and sea, only after making one hundred percent sure the ugly ones have been neutered, or put down altogether. Then I develop an unhealthy fetish for giggling Asian women's ring fingers. Then I read all 658 pages of a book detailing the tumultuous history of the Sri Lankan cinnamon trade over the years 1638-1641, underlining as I go. (I am not thinking about Dafna. I am not thinking about dying. There is a psychotic Scout out for my blood, but I am not thinking about that. I am simply computing. People compute all the time. It is a normal thing, to compute, which is what I am doing now). Then I give an informal presentation on the influence of Southwestern Culture in the popular *Where's Waldo* franchise, using words like *schema* and *juncture* to drive home my point, which happens to be a good one. I order a neck pillow from a catalogue promising the world of tomorrow today.

Then I find out I am half Jewish.

Then I find out I am also half WASP.

Then I composed a song with the refrain: I am half WASP/ And I am half Jew / So I disgust other people / But I disgust myself, too.

Then I call Dafna to tell her I am half Jewish but there is no service.

Then I walk to the butcher shop and demand their finest cut of steak, but the butcher says there is no steak, so I ask why is there no steak, and the butcher man replies because my knives have gone dry, at which point I tell the butcher what I think of his shop as a commercial institution and seller of meat products, making one hundred percent sure to utter something about the USDA, slamming the door behind me as I go.

I do all of this while listening to the soul-soothing sounds of vibraphonist Lionel Jones in his debut CD *Papa Jones*.

Does this campsite have ice?

> @ggray: *So you're still . . . afflicted? I mean, you still have to deal with your condition?*
> @shelgames: Yes. It's just as bad.
> @ggray: *Did you think the camping trip might somehow alleviate it?*
> @shelgames: No. Maybe.
> @ggray: *But it doesn't make it any worse, right?*

@shelgames: Yeah, no worse.
@ggray: These things that you do – do you really do all of them? Are you telling the truth?
@shelgames: No. I'm not doing all of them. But I am telling the truth.
@ggray: Um.
@shelgames: I know. I'm trying to figure it out myself. Sometimes I just go black.
@ggray: Hm.
@shelgames: Perhaps it's best if we just move on.
@ggray: Okay . . .
@shelgames: Ask me about the Junior Minuteman.
@ggray: Oh, right. So the incident with the Junior Minuteman—I assume that was forgotten?
@shelgames: Yes. For the most part. But there was another incident.
@ggray: Another one?
@shelgames: Yes. And it was worse.

There is hysteria back at camp.

I have just returned from going to the bathroom outside, from taking my *daily dook*, as the Scouts call it. I found the perfect place to go, a place with dandelions, ferns, elevation. A view of the river. A place where heat and insects contorted the sky, made it otherworldly. A place of splendor, where I could envision myself seeing—although I didn't see—a ruffed grouse or redheaded woodpecker. Some exotic specimen whose beauty humbles me, whose rarity brings me to my knees, to tears. My daily dook was the perfect daily dook. It required stretching: Arm rotations, torso circles, spine alignment. I used oak leaves to wipe.

But now, back at camp, there is chaos. Scouts shout, run. Before I left, I played a prank, leaving a note:

I've abandoned camp. You're on your own.
—MinuteMaster Wirth

Yes, this will establish my sense of humor, I thought, wandering off. But I am back now, and Jason is cross. He tells me it was a dangerous joke to pull, out here in the mountains. *Not funny. At all.* he says, but the hysterics are fake. The running, the single crying scout—neckerchief in hand, twisted into a tissue—is fake, and the wails of distress are fake. The tears, fake. And I in turn chide him, tell him *this* is a nothing. A game, if anything. Do they know what it was like to be in a *real* uniform? Not their little weekend uniforms, their costumes? A *military* uniform?"

"You were in the military?"

Yes. But they wouldn't have any interest in the real military.

Of course they have interest in the real military. They beg me for it. I tell them (and this is really the only true thing I say that evening) that it's not something I usually talk about.

Oh yes. Yes. There was action, don't worry about that. Every day we—me and my buddies—were gunned at.

Yeah?

I shouldn't be telling you this. You're too young.

Tell us!

I reiterate. Not something I talk about.

Talk about it!

Okay, but we need food first. We need to eat.

They listen to me now. They scatter to scrounge up their stainless steel bowls, their flatware. This is the first time they have listened to me, and they are back moments later, paragons of obedience. They have made a fire while I was gone, presumably through some kind of black magic. I tried making a fire before I left, but gave up after my third try, writing it off as impossible, Everest. But these Junior Minutemen, these practitioners of witchcraft have conjured fire, concocted a hearty carb-rich meal of Ramen Noodles and Creamy Stroganoff Hamburger Helper. We congregate around the fire, worship it. This rare thing, impossible thing. *Tell us about the military.*

What the hell do I have to say about the military? I make something up about Beirut. Oh yeah. I was in Beirut, under strict no-shoot orders, and—,

"Did you get shot?" a small scout asks.

"No. There were only—"

"Did you see someone get shot?'

"Shut up, I'm telling you."

And I tell them. I lie. Again. I tell them about the explosions, death, rain, and booze. I tell them I have scars but refuse to show them.

"MinuteMaster Wirth—"

"Shut *up*."

It is time to turn in, I say. One of them continues to ask questions, continues his chatter, mouth clicking like a typewriter, and I deal with it—

"Will you shut your *fucking* yap?"

—in a less than tender manner. The scout is unnerved, very visibly discomposed. I must show him that I do not really mean what I say. I must show him that I am sorry for giving him short shrift, so I do magic. Everyone likes magic, right? I do the only magic trick I know, the one in which I appear to remove his nose, when (and here's the trick) *I am not removing his nose at all.* I am rather tucking my thumb between my index and middle fingers, a convincing doppelganger, *giving the illusion of nose-removal.*

This trick does not amuse the Scout; what amuses the Scout is my expectation that it might. It is a stupid trick—elementary, patronizing. I can tell the scout tries not to laugh at me. I send everyone to bed before he has a chance to.

"Okay," I say, trying to lower my voice, reasoning that lowering of the voice is the best way to sound authoritative, "you know what time it is . . . "

"Aw, bedtime already?"

"Noooo . . . ."

"Okay, what time is it?" they say, mildly irritated.

"Hammertime!"

And this is when I dance.

It is the step and roll dance. I step . . . like this (*Huh!*), then roooolll . . . like this (*Yeah!*). Flawless execution.

My movements hurry the Scouts tent-ward. The symmetrical Scout moves the most quickly, I notice—not a good sign. They crawl in and peel off their socks, mist rising from their toes, wriggling into bedrolls. As I get up for my own Eureka! experience, I knock my head on the water bladder the scouts had hung on a low branch. There is something erotic about the trickle of water that releases onto my hand.

There is light rain that night. Droplets on the tent flaps, backlit by pointless flashlights. It's peaceful, this rain. There is a taste to the air when it rains.

@ggray: That doesn't sound so bad. There was some rashness, harsh words on your part.
@shelgames: Yeah, some blue language. But that wasn't the incident.
@ggray: It wasn't?
@shelgames: I haven't gotten to the incident.
@ggray: Oh.
. . .
@shelgames: Can I call you Charlie Rose?
@ggray: What?
@shelgames: Just for fun. I'll pretend you're Charlie Rose.
@ggray: I'd rather you not. Let's just talk about the incident.
. . .
@shelgames: Okay. It's pretty bad. The Incident.
@ggray: That's okay. I don't judge.

Jason Chase is either break-dancing or dying. No—he's sleeping. It is a frantic sleep. It is a sleep that has him kicking the tent flap, balling his fists together as if hatching a plan. Is it strange that I am watching him sleep? I should wake him up.

"Get up, muchacho."

He startles.

"*Man. Get off.*"

He crawls to the tent flap, brushing me aside. He pokes his head out. He whistles and gives a fairly convincing round-'em-up" signal, crawls out of the tent. I follow. Frost has appeared out of nowhere, like props in a department store display. I treat myself to a lungful of morning air.

The scouts break camp, dragging bags that look like giant tongues out of their tents, unzipping and hanging them on nylon clotheslines. They uproot pup stakes, fold tarpaulin, force the last resistant sock into their lumbar packs, cursing. They find a condom on the ground. They laugh at the condom on the ground. *"A condom! On the ground!"* they shout.

They load the trailer. I unlock the Dodge Caravan. I leave the engine running, to warm it up. I stay there for a while, acting busy. They prepare for breakfast. Oatmeal today. They get campfire ash and pine needles in the pot. *Flavor*, one calls it, scooping the Quaker Oats and what looks to be three pounds of sugar into his Yo Gabba Gabba thermos. I pass on the oatmeal. Instead, I stuff long cut and cured bacon into my mouth. I choke on it. Laughter from the scouts, shrieking. This gives me an idea.

Because the scouts don't *really* know me yet, I decide to be the kind of MinuteMaster that has quirks. I tell myself that any MinuteMaster who does not have quirks is unconvincing. I however do not know how to go about becoming quirky all of a sudden, until we're in the van, headed home. Should I use homespun phrases to describe getting angry at things, like *that really gets my dander up?* Or *don't you get my Irish up, y'hear now?* Oh, yes, this would be quirky, very quirky. But would it be quirky enough?

I should have them call me Cap'n. Not 'Captain.' Cap'n.

No, that's too quirky.

I know. I will suddenly love covered bridges. There were free postcards at the Hertz rental place depicting covered bridges, so I picked one up and threw it on the dashboard, thinking I might send Dafna a note, proving I am manly, proving I can be a caregiver, a leader and mentor. But now, the postcard inspires a fondness for covered bridges. I have an inexplicable obsession with them, a passion for them. My love for them is nearly as strong as that for Ruane Manning. (Have the Scouts already forgotten about Ruane Manning? This is important.) As we pull away, I advise the Scouts to *be like the distinguished Prentice.*

"Be like the distinguished Prentice," I tell them.

"The what?"

"The Prentice. It's a covered bridge in Southern Vermont. There's a subtle manliness to covered bridges. Something solemn about them. You Junior MinuteMen are the type of people who enjoy a good covered bridge, I can tell."

I also decide that, due to the nature, the ferocity, of my obsession, Jason should like them, too. I hand him my postcard.

"Here's one from Roanoke County. Beautiful. And know what?"

"What?"

"That's yours to keep."

I fold his hand over it, as if bequeathing an heirloom.

Jason doesn't want to keep it. I know this. But it is my duty as MinuteMaster to establish that I am not concerned with *what he wants*. I am concerned with what is best for him. I am concerned that about his character, his moral core. I am concerned with sending the right messages, with instilling a respect for hard work and old-fangled American ingenuity. Wonders of engineering, these Roanoke County bridges. Dafna would be proud of me.

"You'll understand when you're older," I say, a belch of laughter nearly escaping. This is fun, force-feeding Jason my likes and dislikes.

There is no response from the back seat.

@ggray: Are we getting to the incident any time soon?
@shelgames: No. I'm not telling you. There is no incident.
@ggray: Why? I said I'd understand.
@shelgames: No. Now it's built up. I can't tell you now.
@ggray: It's not built up.
@shelgames: Yes, I have built your expectations. Now it's too late.
@ggray: It's not too late. Tell me. I'll listen. I don't judge.
@shelgames: Okay. Whatever you say . . . Charlie Rose.
@ggray: What?
@shelgames: Nothing.

It is hour three of our return home, and this one Scout, who happens to be black, he is pissing me off. I tell him to settle down, and he tells me to (and I quote): *Shut Your (My) Pie hole*. I do not like this one black scout. I bet he does not belong in this troop. I bet they bus him in, from someplace dangerous, where there are cages on the playgrounds, to fulfill some quota, to satisfy some kind of affirmative action requirement. They pay him to be here, don't they.

This is wrong. Have I become hateful? These are the words of a hateful person, which I am not. I am open-minded, kind-hearted, even-tempered. I am a man who is a caretaker, someone who, had Dafna stuck it out, would have made an *excellent* father. I am not like Joel.

This is wrong. He continues to harass me. I summon the Dennis Kucinich-looking man and have him beat the shit out of that one annoying scout, the one who was rude to me. Because it's okay to have these fantasies. I don't really believe these things. And they're not hurting anyone.

It's not like I have done any inappropriate touching, like I'm stupid enough to hit a scout. It's not like—

The next thing I know, I hit him. I hit a scout.

He tells me to *Shut Your (My) Pie Hole* again, so I reach into the back seat and cuff him. It's not hard, just a back of the head slap, a "Hello, McFly?" But still, there is physical contact.

Have you hit a Scout? If so, I have bad news. You should not have hit that Scout.

It gets worse. The scout I hit, it's the black Scout. This is infinitely worse than hitting just a regular Junior Minuteman. People will judge me for this. I will be accused of things—untrue things, spurious allegations. Things that are the opposite of true.

This will end me. Yes, This is The End. This is Jericho. Hiroshima.

And what about the Scout? It could do emotional if not physical damage to him. What if there is bruising? Oh shit, the bruising. I am fucked if there is bruising. Fucked. And the legal consequences—can his parents sue? Could some vengeful jury see this as a hate-related offense? I didn't really hit the kid, when you think about it. It was a *Heeey, Buddy* punch, a love tap. I gauge how hard I hit him by hitting myself, but it's useless. I have no idea what harm I have caused him. I am worse than the worst of scum.

This is Armageddon. DEFCON 3.

I will compliment him on his maroon Keds. That will make him like me, show him I am not that bad. I am his buddy, a friend and advocate.

"Nice kicks. *Niiiice kicks*," I say, suddenly feeling filthy. He gives me a sideways look.

But he is laughing. He liked it. Maybe I didn't hit him that hard. Or the kid is messed up. This kid likes to be hit, yes, appreciates the attention, regardless of what form it takes. Come to think of it, the whole thing was affectionate, no big deal. But what if it's a vengeful laugh? An I-can't-wait-to-tell-my-mom-about-this laugh? What will I do then? I was so good during this trip, I had only a few hours left with these kids, and now, one of them is going to burn me bad. God, first I hit on a kid, then I hit a kid. I am such a fucker. I am done.

Should I noogie him? Muss his hair? Or call him *Buckaroo*? No. That's too creepy. I need to show it's all fun and games? No, there has already been too much physical contact with him, too many expressions of affection. I have crossed too many lines with these scouts. Willy and this kid—what's his name? Robert?—they are going to fry me.

"Listen, Robert, I'm really sorry about – I mean, what I did was completely out of line."

"It's Roberts. My name's Roberts, with an *S*," he says, and still there is laughter, and still I have no idea what it means.

@ggray: And that was the incident, right?
@shelgames: That was it. I told you it was built up.
@ggray: No, no. Not at all. It was really good. I was enthralled. Really.
@shelgames: I didn't tell it well. I should have included more description. And a funny voice. And not built it up.
@ggray: No, you did a great job. Really. I like how you were explicit with your fears, the potential consequences of your actions. I was entertained.
@shelgames: And when I mentioned DEFCON 3, did it – did it suggest urgency? Did it grab you?
@ggray: It did. I can honestly say that it did.
@shelgames: Really?
@ggray: Really.
@shelgames: Good.
. . .
@shelgames: I shouldn't have used the word *spurious*. Spurious makes it look like I'm trying too hard.
@ggray: No, no. It was fine. A little crass at points, and I thought the hitting and the language was a little—what's the word?—gratuitou, but . . .
@shelgames: . . . but it's not like this is the *Christian Science Monitor* or anything.
@ggray: Exactly.
@shelgames: Good.
. . .
@shelgames: Not that *The Christian Science Monitor* isn't a respected publication.
@ggray: Oh, of course.
@shelgames: The CSM's a fine publication.
@ggray: A worthy publication.
. . .
@shelgames: By the way, who names their kid Roberts-with-an-S? Roberts. That's not a first name. That's a bad first name.
@ggray: I hear you. Bad first name for a kid.
. . .
@ggray: Spank me. Call me a whore.

@shelgames: What?
@ggray: Nothing. Slip of the tongue.
...
@shelgames: Would you like to know how it ends up? The story, I mean.
@ggray: Of course I would.
@shelgames: Charlie Ro—?
@ggray: No.

We are still in the Dodge Caravan. I am driving with one hand, picking scum from my fingernails with the other, thirsting for silence. There are too many questions that I don't have answers for. *Do you know any travel songs?* (No.) *Any songs at all?* (Used to). *When was that?* (A while ago.) *Why not now?* (Because.) *Which songs did you used to know?* (Can't say.) *Why?* (Because.) *But why?* (I am here for your safety and am under no obligation to placate you.) I can't help but think that soon after I get home, I'll be placed under arrest. That scout is going to tell his mother, call the police. And my life will end there. But the questions keep coming.

I tell him to shut up. This was not the right thing to do.

I should have established that I have a *sincere, abiding interest in him, that any impatience I display is but an indication of my concern, and the last thing I would do is give him short shrift.* So I let this *junior* Junior MinuteMan, a half-a-MinuteMan, talk. He monologues, seized as if by some glossolalic fit:

"*So when you were in Beirut, was it just like 'Nam. Was it like 'Nam, and were you ops deep? I bet you were. I bet you were in the shit, too. It's so cool to be ops deep. The Shit! Wait, this is better: Did things ever get fubar? You do know what* fubar *means, right? I can't say the entire thing because there's the worst swear word in it, but – you were a devil dog, weren't you? That's what they're called, right? And fubar is a devil-dog thing and did things ever get fubar when you were ops deep in the shit?*"

This is when I nearly scream at him to *fucking shut the fuck up.* But I don't. I catch myself. I should not reprimand these kids. I should teach them.

"You can swear in front of me," I say. "I'm not your parents."

I take a breath.

"You can say shit in front of me. Or fuck. Or fuckity fuck fuck.

Fuckface. Fuck a dick. Fuck a duck. Fuck a butt. Fuck a fuckstick. Fuck a shitty penisvag. Vagin. Vaginnnnna. Vag. I. Na. Assfuck. Fuckass. Assfuckaduckfuckafuck. FUUUUCK. SHIIIIT. FUCKING ASS LICKER. SHIT SHIT SHIT. Assshit. Shitass. Motherassfucker. Fuckr. Fyker. FANNYFUCK. Fuckafifteenyearold. Shit. Jimmylick. Slapdick. Pussyfart. Fu. Tit Titty Teat TEEEEAT! Fucking vagpenislickerma me ma bo bop bop boo ba ba ba."

The scout, he says nothing. His mouth sags.

Awesome, someone whispers.

I am a god to these scouts. I am Hercules.

See, Dafna? I am doing better.

Chin up.

Troop 37 is silent as we drive back to Boston. I am the only noise, still on a high from my masterful oration, playing with Jason's name for a few minutes—

"Jason Chase. Jason Chason. Chasing Jason. Chas-ing Chase. Chasing Chase."

—but his head is turned. He may be asleep. Are those grey hairs? On a college student? I turn to the rear-view, focus on the Scouts. They sway with the van, dazzled by its engine, a low drone. Most of the boys are asleep. One has his index finger up his nose. The young Scout doesn't ask any more questions. We stop once, at one of those combination McDonald's/Dairy Queens, near a place that's still mostly forested. Sap still glistens on the maples. The branches quiver. The trees seem skittish. I see an abandoned nest in one of them, wonder when the chicks were pushed out of it. When that time came, I bet their mother did not waver. I bet she was merciless.

"I'm a bird!" Dafna always said when she danced. "I'm a bird!"

She was a strange woman, doing that.

I return to the Dodge, fitting my Dr. Pepper in the cup holder. We drive off. We arrive in Boston on schedule. I drop the Scouts off at a parking lot, where most of their parents are waiting. I promised to drive Jason home, but when we arrive at his dorm, he doesn't move. He remains in his seat, staring out the window, slouching.

"You know," he says. "I thought it was pretty impressive the way you started going on about you military service and all. You had some amazing stories. Do you recall what year that was?"

"Can't quite recall at the moment."

"'83. Beirut happened in 1983."

He knows. Fuck.

"Well, I'm older than I look, you know."

"Right."

Jason struggles with the handle as he steps down from the van. He turns to me.

"Shel? You're name *is* Shel, right?"

"Yeah, that part's true," I say, just as my phone begins to ring.

"I don't think you should come to any more meetings."

Then he gives me a look. I have seen this look before. But not on a human. Where have I seen this look? I know: When you are playing catch with a dog and fake out throwing the ball, pretending to throw it but not really throwing it, instead hiding it behind your back, causing the dog to run for it, then stopping, realizing something's fishy, then turning back and giving you that *Are-you-kidding-me-?* look. That is where I have seen this look. It is the look of a betrayed dog.

This is how Jason looks.

> @ggray: Wow. That's really something.
> @shelgames: You're not listening anymore, are you? You've stopped listening.
> @ggray: What? No, no. I'm listening.
> @shelgames: No. You've checked out. I can tell you've checked out. I don't blame you. I've spent too much time talking about a camping trip.
> @ggray: No, really. *You were telling me that Jason gave you a strange look. And it seems that this look really affected you. Did you respond?*
> @shelgames: Oh yeah. Yeah. I said something. Well, no. I didn't. I thought about it really hard, though. I should have said something, every corpuscle of my being told me to say something, but instead I watched him shut the door of the Dodge and walk to his house. I could have shouted something to him, something about autumn in Vermont, how the falling leaves and sky—oh the sky, on fire with color—made me see things differently, and how I couldn't have experienced those

things without him, but I am distracted by my still-ringing phone.

@ggray: Joel again?

@shelgames: No. Not Joel. It's Mrs. Lewis, the mother of the scout I hit, the black scout. She says I'm in trouble. She says Roberts came home and told her everything.

@ggray: Uh oh.

@shelgames: Yeah. "Do you know how hard it will be to put Roberts to bed these next few weeks?" She told me. "He won't stop talking about what a wonderful time he had this weekend."

. . .

@shelgames: Did you hear me? See? You've checked out.

@ggray: No, no. I wanted to pause for effect. Thought it would be more dramatic that way—you know, giving it some space . . .

@shelgames: Oh. Um.

@ggray: . . . to accentuate the disconnect between what Mrs. Lewis said and how you might interpret it. What sounded like a threat, you see, was actually a compliment. Because, as you told it, Roberts didn't say anything about the hitting.

@shelgames: Oh. Good. Yeah. No visible bruising, you know? Heh.

@ggray: Ha. So you're safe.

@shelgames: Yeah. I guess. Safe.

. . .

@shelgames: I used the following words this weekend: Good Probably Careful No Sorry Yes Understand Sure Penis Vag Fuckstick.

@ggray: Uh, okay. Good . . . good to know.

SOMEWHERE IN THE SOUTH PACIFIC.

It was nearly sunset when a newly showered Dent walked barefoot out of the Marriott Lobby with a Dell laptop and handed it to a man he was ready to forget, the man he only ever wanted to refer to as "Paulson."

"Everything there? All set?"

"It's all set."

"On this computer?"

"Yep. On the computer."

"Great. On the desktop?"

"Yes. On the desktop, on the computer."

He handed the laptop over, not exactly willingly. "I even typed some of the harder-to-grasp points in Size Eighteen Courier, dumbing them down for O'Neil. Do you have my cash?"

"Is it—?"

"Yeah, it is. Do you have my cash. My money?"

"Yes. Your money."

He hands him an envelope. Dent opens it. All there.

It had been hell, coping with Paulson. Dent had no choice but to get him SCUBA certified, to run him through the entire PADI dive certification course, both written and pool portions, before he could feel comfortable—

"What do I do with my arms? I don't know what to do with my arms here."

—diving with Paulson, or even having him on the boat.

"Just put them down. To your side. Okay, now. So what you're wearing now is a Buoyancy Control Device. Remember? We went over this in class. And this is your regulator. And this long thing here, this is your octopus. Your octopus is in case your partner needs to share your air, or if your primary device malfunctions."

"I'm going to put your respirator in your mouth. Like . . . that. Good. Okay, you got it now?"

"Yeah."

"It's hard to talk, right?"

"Yeah."

"Now put your face in the sink here, and practice breathing underwater. Remember to breathe in through your mouth only, not your nose."

"Breathe?"

"For air."

"What?"

"Air, air. Through your mouth."

"Okay."

"Now put your head down and—No, Jesus. Breathe through your mouth. Your whole face is underwater, so you can't breathe through your nose like that or you'll choke. It should be easier with your mask on."

"Okay. Shit, still can't—can't breathe?"

"No. You're breathing through your nose. I told you not to—shit, Paulson, stop using your nose."

It had been hell training him on the proper use and maintenance of underwater gear. It had been hell eating with him, and sleeping near him, and being near him. Simply knowing O'Neil sent him here—it bothered him. But today was Dent's last day with Paulson. Today, thank God, Paulson was leaving. Today, Dent walked like someone approaching a man at high noon to see Paulson off.

The shuttle pulls up. Paulson hands his bag to the driver.

"Are you sure you—"

"Yes, it's fine, perfect. It's right there, on the desktop. Most of the data is in Excel."

"Fine, fine."

. . .

"Sooooo, I guess you're glad never to see me again?"

Paulson laughs. Dent does not laugh.

"Will you do me one favor?" Dent asks.

"Sure. What?"

"Never contact me again."

"Okay?"

"And tell O'Neil never to contact me. It's my intention to forget about this, about what happened these past weeks. Go back and suck off O'Neil, or do whatever it is you do, and we'll forget this whole thing. Can you do me that favor?"

"I don't know—"

"*Can you do me that favor?*"

"I can do you that favor."

"Great."

Dent considers making a final joke, some farewell humor:

And tell him to ignore all the pornography on my computer. There is an ungodly amount of pornography on that thing. I couldn't live without my hours and hours of hard-core pornography.

But he holds back. Paulson didn't deserve off-color jokes from Dent. They weren't close enough. Only Joel and Shel deserved that kind of trash. Only Dent's real friends had the privilege of benefiting from his stupidity.

Paulson boards the hotel shuttle. He waves, the shuttle pulls away. Dent, fighting every urge to flick him off, or throw a rock, gives a *see-ya* gesture instead.

Sometimes you have to fudge some numbers. For the greater good.

This was not the greater good. *This* was one man's attempt to impress a Commission. O'Neil's attempt to trick Dent—and other people who love what they do, care about what they do—into doing research, not for the sake of research. For the sake of *appearing* to care about research. To give the Commission the results they wanted, to get the approval *he wanted*. The scientists—O'Neil didn't care what happened to them after that.

Which is why, on Monday night, after the Dell had been delivered to O'Neil, and after O'Neil had just finished off a larger meal of steamed asparagus and slow-cooked spare ribs—or a juicy, grilled swordfish steak—he, O'Neil, would excuse himself from dinner and retreat to his study, the computer in tow. He would settle behind a vast mahogany-finished desk and boot it up to find, there on his desktop, *The Study of Potential Homing Mechanisms in O. Savayensis*, just as Dent promised. He would open the file, already fantasizing about commendations from the commission, and find a single, mysterious, hyperlinked name: DENT.IS.RISEN. A click on the link would lead him—not to a report, but to a full screen photo: Dent, completely naked, save for a small, purple, thin-as-thread material between his buttocks, on which, in the bright blood-red ink of an eraser-board marker, is written:

DO YOU SEE MY G-STRING?

Part III
Dent
Is
Risen.

A MONTH LATER: AMERICAN AIRLINES FLIGHT 1088, BOSTON TO CANCUN, SEAT 6d, AISLE.

She is hot, the woman in 5b. I like small mouths, and she has one, and it glistens. I suspect she dabs her lips with Vaseline petroleum jelly, with her pinky finger, another turn-on for me. She is tasteful with her makeup, applying it sparingly, probably with a clean, dampened sponge—unlike those women, motley-faced, who, ashamed of their natural beauty, apply it over a weekend, in shifts. It is difficult to tell if she has used concealer, but if she does, she is careful about it, using an ivory-beige tone and dabbing it on the skin and gently blending with the fingertips. She buckles up.

It looks as though she does not need concealer. Her eyes are not baggy. There are no lines below them. They are flawless under-eyes.

Slow Motion Clip: She looks at me.

She looked at me. She was talking to the flight attendant, and there was a moment, fleeting, of contact. I overhear some of their conversation, a snippet, and learn that she is from Glasgow (of course: the accent), and that her first job was at Home Depot. This is the hottest thing I have ever heard. I am not all-too-familiar with *Home Depot*—other than that it delivers quality building supplies at sensible prices—but I am attracted to a woman who is. A woman who can install drywall while I'm nailing the rug to the floor—there is no sexier thing on this earth.

But the woman has become successful. She has fast-tracked. I can hear more of their conversation. I cannot concentrate. Because that S of hers, it is the S of a woman who is attractive. Who knows she's attractive. I don't catch all of the conversation but am able to outline on a napkin what I do hear, noting the Ss. The Ss kill me:

1) "Ye*s*. We pay a franchi*s*e fee."
2) "We already have a number of corporate *s*ponsor*s*."
3) "I began as a fundrai*s*er but am not *c*ertain what I should do after thi*s*. Po*ss*ibly *s*ecuritie*s* litigation."
4) "I think *s*ome time thi*s* week or the ne*x*t."
5) "My brea*s*t*s* are ready for your con*s*umption."

That last one is in my imagination.

I can sit next to her. If I ask to switch seats, I can sit next to her, explaining that I need the aisle, because I require unobstructed access to the bathroom, because—this is embarrassing, but—I tend toward airsickness on long flights. I can sit next to this clearly classy woman, remark how tastefully paired her Burberry bag and silk blouse are; looking suggestively into her shimmering eyes, asking what brings someone like her to Mexico.

Then, when we land, we'll plan to meet up again in Boston, and when we do, we'll go to The Lager Factory, have a Smuttynose or two; a glass of wine for her, presumably. Perhaps she'll express a desire sleep with me, but I'll refuse, because I care about her as a person. She is more than a sexual conquest. This will humble her, but I'll then say I had fun. We'll agree to see each other again. And we will. Again and again. By then we'll have started sleeping together. Not just sleeping, but becoming intimate. By that time, my tongue will have become familiar with at least three of her four main erogenous zones.

We'll get married, buy a house with blue trim, install ThermalPane windows with PolyFoam WeatherSeal lining (for the cold, New England winters); have marital spats, sexual dry spells, agree that some red hair dye on her would renew our procreative energies, remind us of our passion for each other and my passion for redheads (God, I love redheads). We'll raise a family with two buttoned-up angels and one Spawn of Satan. This kid, Erik we'll name him, will spend too much time in front of the computer, neglecting his chores, letting the grass get out-of-control long, the lawnmower rusty; and recycling only occasionally. The good kids will go to college; Erik, breaking out on his own, will become a Silicon Valley billionaire by 30. We will disapprove of his lavish lifestyle, his spending habits, but we will shrug, knowing—

"Beef Stroganoff or Chicken Cordon Bleu?"

Chicken cordon bleu?! Did I win the Lotto?

"Cordon Bleu, of *course*. Is there really any question?"

—knowing we can do nothing about it, taking comfort in the fact that he's safe, happy. I will occasionally become frustrated thinking about it, blowing off steam by covering our trees with Tangle Guard tree wrap (to prevent sun scald and rodent infestation), marking it on my calendar, reminding myself to do it winter after winter after winter. We will have at least one chaise longue in our house.

By then we will have reached our sixties, will be doing the stuff of old people, like taking morning constitutionals and drinking Metamucil, regularizing our BMs; grousing about aches, about places without senior citizen discounts, about our Social Security benefits, which do little good when it comes to shoring up a dwindling 401K savings, wishing our generation had been more directly involved in some kind of arms race. We will all of a sudden find ourselves in a Boca Raton retirement community, where our last days will be spent on the shuffleboard court (Oh, we will shuffleboard. You bet your sweet ass we will shuffleboard), realizing in retrospect how insightful and witty Bob Dole was, and asking ourselves where we went wrong with Erik, that no-good billionaire son of ours.

"He's a homosexual," she'll say.

"I'm afraid so," I'll agree.

I have not said a word to the woman in 5b. I have not asked to change seats. We land. We are in Mexico. Her mouth, her small mouth. That *S*. Her judicious use of makeup. Our children. That *S* was torture. Arms race. Metamucil. I don't see her again. I should have gotten her number. I should have complimented her. I should have tried to brush against her arm, or her breast. I should have engaged her *with my eyes*. It was a mistake not to have tried.

May I be honest with you? I would have sex with this woman.

Cancun, Mexico

There is no atoll. We arrive at Cancun International Airport, where *Total Eclipse of the Heart* is playing over the airport PA system. Dent has told me that we couldn't get a room within reasonable driving distance of an atoll (*"Wait, there's no atoll?" "There's no atoll."*). He has done one better: We have the ocean. Yes, that is better. We move to baggage claim.

"Can you believe Joel?"

These are his first words to me. I purse my lips.

"Why? What do you mean?"

"How he's changed. How he has suddenly started loving the Lord."

"What?"

"He's started going to church again. And he's trying to recruit people for his prayer group. He's becoming pretty intense about it."

"Really? Is that true?"

"Yeah."

"Shit. Pretty weird."

"Seems to be flipping out a bit."

The bag carousel groans, starts. Duffels pass us by.

"I mean he's suddenly found Jesus. How does that happen? How does someone go about changing like that so quickly? And Joel—sure, he's the right demographic for that kind of thing, but you never expect it to happen to someone so close."

"Yeah. Isn't that gay?"

"Just what the world needs," I say, "another racist evangelical."

Dent tilts his head back, laughs.

"Are you still on that?"

"On what?"

"You know."

I do.

What I Know.

It was always apparent to me that, starting from the very first day I met him, Joel was racist. Or at least in my imagination he was. All my life I acted as if it were true. I had never met a *real* racist—they were the Loch Ness Monsters of white suburbia, their existence rumored but never witnessed—unless you count the old women in Hubbard Woods who called the police on a Native American man. This man, as the story goes, was dressed in ceremonial garb and on his way to a history demonstration at one of the Maple Street homes when this lady, peering through her window, spotted him, speed dialed 911. The next day, it was the talk of the town. *That old harpy*, we all thought with some excitement. *Is there really a racist in the neighborhood? What do you suppose she looks like?* It was posited that she was one of those people who you expect to be really ugly (because racists are ugly, ugly people), but, at the end of the movie (this <u>always</u> happens in movies) you discover that – that she's *just* like you or me. *What do you think she said to the police?*

It became popular to hate her, to hate her stubborn, backward ways, but to do nothing about it, to hate and accept that she was an integral part of our the town, its backdrop—just think of all the people in our sheltered, racist-harboring community who were touched by her. Who may have lived beside her, or perhaps exchanged words with her, or accidentally jostled her in the supermarket one day—that old lady who called the cops on this peaceable man of *Chippewa* or *Iroquois* lineage. This woman who is so insulated from the rest of the world—who felt the best recourse was fear at the sight of this peaceable Algonquin man? At this harmless Navajo spirit walker? This woman. This woman should be lynched.

So no, I didn't really know any racists, and I had a right to experience it first-hand, to judge for myself how onerous their existence really is. I imagined—and this is after years of indoctrination by liberal-minded public school teachers—they:

> 1) Dressed in seersucker or bleached whites. Used some kind of walking stick. Owned large plots of land (or sauntered about as if owning large plots of land). Were, in general, genteel-acting. Were from the South.

Or,

> 2) Wore a wifebeater, stained. Spat. Were from the South.

I was excited when I first met Joel. He fit the profile so well—at least the one the TV taught me—in that he was from Alabama, and had a sincere fondness for the music of Johnny Rebel. There were also flashes of mildly intolerant language, becoming frustrated at a friend's *Irish Goodbye*, or annoyed with *those Guidos*, clogging up the line at Underbar. I also thought I overheard him tell a Civil War 10A classmate that the Confederacy "wasn't that bad," though it was wishful thinking on my part. *Does the government give you disability for being Irish?* he once asked my dad, who laughed it off, knowing of the Jones family's longstanding admiration for them, the Irish.

Then there were the generalizations.

"Black people love Looney Tunes," he whispered when a gangly African American in a leather Bugs Bunny varsity jacket passed us. "*Love* them."

I waited until the man was out of earshot to call Joel racist.

"It's not racist."

"Yes, it is. It doesn't matter whether it's true or not. It's that you're singling out African Americans. I never hear to talk like that about white people. I never hear you say 'White People like Frasier' or anything like that."

"That's because we're white. I'm already an expert on whites."

Another black man passes us, one who looks like he has no interest in Looney Tunes, or basketball, or rap. He is carrying a copy of *The Economist*. *Perfect*, I think. This man. This man is a perfect example.

"How about that guy?" I whisper. "Is he a Porky Pig fan?"

The man, this shatterer of stereotypes passes by. He says *hello*. I return his *hello*, but in as apologetic a tone as I can muster. We have had advantages, because we are white, which is bad. Very, very bad.

"See how he just went into that Walmart's?" Joel says. "You think he's buying that Vaseline Intensive Care lotion? Because his skin gets ashy. Many white people don't know that about black people—that they get ashy."

I don't respond.

The clincher was Joel's Nana. He (and he was in a large group when he brought this up, with people he didn't even *know that well*) talked openly about his black Nana, who raised and cared for him along with his parents. Who, when he was young, sang for him. Sang! This is vulgar, that the Jones family made her sing, that—

"She wanted to sing. She liked singing lullabies to me, even when I was too old for it. She let my sister brush her hair."

—they made her put on these minstrelsy shows, made her *work* for them. How savagely *unenlightened* of them, that they called her *Nana*, as if she was some kind of colonial wet nurse, running around in a smock, hands aloft, shouting 'Lawdy Lawdy Lawdy!'; even if they meant for the name to be grandmotherly, how patronizing. One wonders how they didn't—or did they?—refer to all people in the service industry as *the help?* One wonders how they never let slip some other n-word. One wonders how they. . .

Joel's Nana was named Gertrude.

Other aspects of Joel (mannerisms, dress, saliva expulsion) didn't jibe so well with my version, as he possessed neither stick nor seersucker. Nor did he have the collection of Confederate figurines I had expected. He also didn't *act* like he dismissed or disliked a certain people, but I knew better. He was from Alabama, and that kind of stuff is, you know, embedded. I'm sure his forebears exercised some kind of exploitation—commercial, perhaps agricultural. Joel did however enjoy the name of a good, traditional racist. His initials (JJJ, as alphabetically close to intolerance as three letters got) fit my perception of the Old South particularly well. When I first met him, I assumed he was dumb. Dent was convinced otherwise.

"Joel's really smart."

"Really."

"Yeah. Like super smart."

"You wouldn't know it from class. He just sits there."

"It's called paying attention. He keeps it to himself mostly. He's afraid it's not cool to act smart, you know?"

"That's lame."

"You're just jealous. You're pissed that he's smart and he doesn't even brag about it."

"That's right, I'm jealous." I pause. "What kind of smart?"

"Math smart. The good kind."

As I became closer to Joel and began to consider the possibility that he might be enlightened after all, I held onto this yes-I-am-friends-with-a-bigot fantasy, simply because it seemed like an inspired thing to do, being friends with a racist; looking beyond someone's beliefs, into their soul—flawed, yes, and reprehensible to some, but *real*—understanding that, even if their opinions were uninformed, their words untrue, they (and here is where it becomes tricky) led an otherwise unobjectionable life. *As long as your thoughts, deplorable as they may be, are expressed with civility and intelligence, yes, I will hear you out. Because even agents of intolerance are capable of change.*

I was reaching out, yes, to help; to usher this man into the fold of decent human thought and behavior. To prevent his contagion of hate from spreading to others. But I was doing this mostly for my friend, for Joel. Who was racist. Who made generalizations about the differences between black people and white people, and sometimes brown people.

Dent was always under the impression otherwise (Joel? Racist? Pfffffffpt!). He called me an idiot for having this fantasy, but ha!—I already knew I was an idiot for having it. I nonetheless persist, turning it into an inside joke between me and no one else, using it now, at the airport with Dent:

"Joel's thinking about going to a wine bar tonight," he tells me. "You in?"

"Single dudes at a wine bar?"

"Yeah. I'm sure we'll find some ladies."

"With Joel? Really?"

"Yeah."

"Does he know there might be black people there?"

"Shel."

"It's funny."

"Yeah, but that little old lady with the diaper just heard you. Yeah, I think she did."

"It's not like I'm saying it in front of Joel."

"Yeah, the diaper lady definitely heard you. She looks none too pleased."

I used to get away with things like this. But why is it that here, in front of this bag carousel—a vindictive, malicious bag carousel (look at it, snaking around, biting its own tail), refusing to deliver our luggage—Dent acts like he won't tolerate my shenanigans, my insult-your-friend games; whereas before, he was the instigator of it, reveled in our superlatively un-PC exchanges with superlatively un-PC language.

"Where is he, by the way? Joel?"

"He got held up, stuck on the Perillo account, whatever that means," Dent says, slipping into his best Joel impression: *"Someone's gotta pick the corn out of my uncle's shit.* Says he'll meet us at the hotel."

We walk toward bag claim in silence for a while, but Dent finally cracks, the inevitable coming sooner that I had expected:

"So I hear you joined the *Massachusetts Junior Minutemen.* I hear you're a *MinuteMaster.*"

"Yeah. So?"

"They do historical reenactments."

"Some troops do. So?"

"And community service."

"Dear God."

"I know."

"Wait, weren't you a Junior Minuteman?"

"Yeah. For a year."

"Well, what did your MinuteMasters do?"

"Some camping. But they spent most of their time farting around and setting bad examples. They were always the weirdos from the community."

"Well, I'm not so involved with it now. I just wanted to—to, uh—do something with myself."

We arrive at bag claim and grab our stuff from the carousel. Then, the bag-handlers come.

The bag-handlers make me uncomfortable, the way they kowtow, avert their eyes, looking as if they're about to scatter rose petals. I indicate that I can carry my own luggage, but they insist, nodding and smiling, beseeching us to trust them, visualizing what kind of tip they will get from me. *What choice do we have?*, and we relinquish the bags. They load the car, dwindle. I give them two bucks. Is this enough? Yes. It is enough. It is good, evidently. They cheer. I do not understand their cheering, and I do not like it. It makes me stiff, awkward.

Just as I am at the point of letting go of my worries about this whole thing, getting loosey-goosied up, ready for vacation, we arrive at this airport with these obsequious, wound-up men. I bet Joel would like it. I bet he would eat up their servility—no, expect it, *insist* upon it, wouldn't have it any other way—and do something patently disrespectful, like muss their hair encouragingly, or speak to them in slow, dumb-downed syllables, or press coins into their palms. Why aren't these bag guys bothering Dent?

We board the hotel shuttle, and—look! A *Fanta* sign! *Wanna Fanta, don't you wanta!* I march in mark-time, having a difficult time getting a hold of myself, here in the shuttle, so giddy to be here! In Mexico! This shuttle is slow. No, it's not. It's great. It's doing its job, smoothly, expeditiously. *Hooray for this shuttle!, Do the MBTA people know about this shuttle? Have the makers of the MBTA and this shuttle shared knowledge? Is there information exchange, idea pollination?* and after a short drive past palm trees and more, many more billboards for *Fanta*, we arrive at our hotel, *Casa Verano*. I suspect Casa Verano of being a Holiday Inn Express with a Spanish alias, if only because they share colors.

Our hotel is not nice.

It is far from nice.

Our hotel, a small white building with a lean frame, off-white paneling and gray, bare, window-boxes with one gasping flower each, doesn't even come close to nice.

Dent seems to think otherwise.

"Ooh, hospital corners! This place is niiice," he says as we enter the room. Joel looks up momentarily, semi-nods, then looks back down. He is sitting at the small table in front of the small window. He is writing something.

"And-Ooh! *Yale* locks. Ivy League locks! Classy."

He says he likes the *Feng Shui*.

There is a microsuede fold-out, a bare coat-hook, and low ceilings. A fridge and sink are the only distinctions between the living area and kitchen. I run the water and smell sulfur. There is a large closet that becomes a small bathroom when we open it to reveal a toilet. Dent touches the handle and it drains. There is no flushing sound. I am struck with an urge to watch *Telemundo*.

Joel needs the bathroom, so I vacate.

I hear everything. Joel has closed the door, but it doesn't matter. I have moved to the opposite end of the room, busied myself with unpacking, but it makes no difference. Everything. I hear . . . god, Joel.

Finally, after an hour-long wait, I return to the now-serviceable bathroom. On the bathroom mirror, Joel has scrawled the following word: "Weiner." I erase it with my palm. I say something to Joel but don't get an answer. He and Dent have left. I engage in an excavation of my face, attacking both black- and white heads, attempting to determine if my skin tone qualifies as anemic or simply pallid. I have angled the mirror toward the door, hoping to appear distracted by something—flossing?—when Dent or Joel return from wherever they've gone. I pour water over my head, gauging how wetness affects skin tone, paying only perfunctory attention to the mirror.

Then.

Enter Dafna. And her hair.

God, I love her hair. Just take it in, that hair. Take it in. I could spend all day in it, nesting, just fooling around with those curls, twiddling them on a finger, batting that teasing strand like a cat. That clean dirty-blond, sun-smelling hair. I could fall asleep in that hair, I could die in it.

"Hi, Shel."

She sees me. I didn't think she did, but she does. But she is coy. Was that a smile? Yes, it was. Or no. Can't tell. I should not be inside with her right now.

"Hi," I say. Shit, I can't believe I said *hi*. This is embarrassing. Might as well have said *Hiya!* But I continue. "Great to see you. Good flight? Good. Was just headed out. To the beach, that is." *That is? Who the hell talks like that?*

"Where's Jo-el? And Dent?"

"Don't know."

"I should—" but she stops. "Never mind. I'll see you at the beach."

"Great. See you there."

As she leaves, she gives me a look. Not a pitying look, not entirely. But something working its way toward pity, as if there were some intermediate emotion between it and sympathy. I will not let it discourage me. I am in good spirits. I walk to the beach barefoot, scat singing my way there.

I heard a rumor—from Joel, who heard it from Brandon Seidler, a cross country runner I knew from Evanston, now working in NYC for Bloomberg, who said he ran into the Schwartzers a while back—that Dafna is dating someone. A guy named Clark, he said, who went to Evanston High School with him. Although Clark's parents sent him to The Catholic School somewhere in Glencoe (birthplace, mind you, of actor/director/producer Fred Savage, of *The Wonder Years* fame), Clark always seemed to hang around Evanston HS, the public school Brandon attended before he moved away. It was presumed he played JV lacrosse there, if only because he always carried around a lacrosse stick but didn't have that varsity build.

Yeah. Clark. I know people like Clark.

Clark is one of those guys whose handshake is way too firm—

"He's one of those go-get-'em types," Brandon told me. "One of those guys who spends most his time on overcompensating and frisbee."

—for someone who ostensibly shouldn't have anything to prove. Clark is a tightass. Anal. Clark will spend a year at some buttoned-up egghead think tank. Clark is not interested in *making a difference*. He hasn't been brave enough to find out what he really wants from life. He gaffes off other students, the ones without obvious wealth, and kisses up to the people he thinks will make him popular.

This isn't his fault, entirely. I have it from very credible sources that he was an Army brat with no real stable home life, first living in New York, where his family knew Dafna's family at Buckley, before hopscotching around the country, ending up in Evanston, Illinois. No, we can't really blame Clark—with a father who was aloof, a mother who was clueless, a douche of an uncle—we can't take him to task for being such a—

"Aren't we being a little unfair to him? To Clark?" the Dennis Kucinich look-alike asks.

"Goway," I say. Yes. You, Dennis Kucinich, with your attractive wife. Your astoundingly hot wife. Go away.

Clark. Clark Clark Clark.

Clark is an asshole.

No, he's not. The animation is right.

Think positive. Chin up.

I arrive at the beach, sinking into the sand. I move to the edge of the water. I wade in and look at my feet. My toes squirm in the sand. I am excited about our dive. It is going to be a shallow dive.

We spend our first day at the beach. The sun is too hot. "It's oppressive," Dafna says. Otherwise, we're content. Joel has gone for margaritas. Dent, on a separate blanket a ways up the beach, feet splayed out in a V, is making small piles in the sand. A red PlaySkool bucket and scoop are beside him, a splurge at the hotel gift shop.

Dafna turns to me.

"Could you sun block my back?"

Hell no.

"Sure."

I am not careful enough with the bottle and squeeze too much onto my hand. I place my fingers on her back too gently, as if reading Braille.

"Harder. It won't rub in if you do it like that."

I leave a mess on her back, a slurry of sand and Coppertone. You'd think she'd be hesitant about physical closeness like this. You'd think her overburdened conscience would prevent her from letting me anywhere near the vicinity of her back, particularly because we have never really talked about the night of the victimization of *my* back. Sure, we had made halfhearted attempts to talk, but neither of us wanted it. We both treated it as something worse than onerous, a come-hell-or-high-water kind of thing, as though we were facing some elite ropes course, something out of *Celebrity Boot Camp*, but harder, until—

"Can we talk?" she says.

"Some other time."

"It *is* some other time. We have to talk."

—one of us got fed up. *Which* one of us it is lost among the psychological jetsam of my brain, but it doesn't matter. We didn't actually talk. Joel stopped by, to copy answers to a problem set. I still remember the answer to #4. It was $(85xy)/z$.

But look at her back.

It's right there. God look at her hair. And her skin. It's so soft. My proximity to it excites me. Not sexually. Aesthetically, if that's possible. She shouldn't tan her skin. It will ruin it. It's such soft skin, and nearly translucent, but not in that disgusting every-single-vein-in-her-forehead-is-easily-visible kind of way. She looks so soft, gentle from behind. She catches me out of the corner of her eye. She is mischievous.

The papers would get wind of it if I did anything to that back. THE COPPERTONE INCIDENT, they'd call it, and they'd profile me, knowing that their articles will be used for research when, years later, straight-to-DVD movies are made of the event. I should call for help, for someone to restrain me. I should call for Joel to come over and intercede. I rub in the rest of the sunblock and finish by play-punching her. I move over to Dent, pile-maker, who has now made four separate mounds in the sand.

"Yo."

"Sand igloos," he explains.

We look at Dafna in her swimsuit. Her two-piece, leaving very little to the imagination. Man.

"So," he says, "have you talked to your rapist yet?"

I glance at Dafna. She has busied herself with her hair, lacing it with dried seaweed and tiny pear whelks she has found along the shoreline.

"Kinda. Had brief a conversation with her. A *hello/goodbye* sort of thing. And please don't call her that."

I pick up an interesting-looking rock. Ah, sea glass. I pretend to skip it across the water but look at Dafna instead.

"God, look at her."

Dent laughs.

"The predator. There she is. How'd it end with you guys, by the way? I mean, look at her. Super personality, and hot. Jewish-hot, the best kind. God, I love Jewish chicks. She's like a Semitic Jacqueline Bisset."

When Dent first met Dafna, it was clear they'd become friends. This was not good.

"Who?"

"Jacqueline Bisset? *The Deep?*"

"That a movie?"

"Not just a movie. A classic. She was also in *The Thief Who Came to Dinner*. English actress."

"You watch the weirdest shit."

"I always thought Jacqueline Bisset was gay. Is Dafna gay? She could be. I mean that as a compliment—one of those hot lesbians. Lipstick. She's sexy."

"You think everyone's gay."

"Most everyone is, if only a tad."

"A tad" sounded gay. Now he's looking at me.

"What are you doing?"

"I'm looking at you."

"Why? Stop it. Stop looking at me."

"But you're beautiful. You're a beautiful man."

This guy has boundary issues.

"I am going to lay you out."

. . .

"You're still looking. Stop. Stop looking. Seriously, what was it?"

"What was what?"

"What it was you did as a kid that messed you up so bad."

"Lots of things, I'm sure."

This was not a question I expected him to consider seriously.

"Swear to God there's something wrong with you, Dent. Was it asbestos? Lead? Did you have a lead detector in your house? A CO detector?"

"It was the laundry exhaust. I loved to sniff that stuff.""

Ah yes, the exhaust. He has told me about the exhaust.

"You're talking about the shit that comes out of the vent, right?"

"Yeah. I didn't care. Sometimes I'd skip over to the house next door. Their laundry exhaust had a different smell. They used a higher quality detergent or fabric softener or whatever it was. It was a richer smell. Textured."

"This is a joke, right?" I think it has to be a joke.

"No."

"That can't be good for you."

"I was rather the connoisseur."

"You were getting high."

"Was I?" Then, "Yeah, I was. Shit. What were we talking about?"

"Dafna."

"Right. We should make Dafna an honorary trucker. She'd love it. We can set up an initiation *Schhhht* ceremony, here on the beach. We can have this cool ritual, this baptism-by-fire thing, bringing logs from outside and building a small campfire, and—"

"I don't think you realize how difficult that is."

"But we'd just dig a pit here in the sand, and we can surround it with rocks, and I'd be chieftain, and—"

"Dent?"

"Yeah?"

"Let's not."

We turn to look at Dafna. She shakes the sand off her blanket and lays it flat. She kneels and Army-crawls into position with a book.

"Hey, Joel—"

Joel has come outside. He trundles over, his stomach lopping over his shorts like the nose of a puppy.

"Yeah?"

"Up for some ice cream?" Dent says.

"Yeah," he says, and they look at me. I shake my head.

They canter off, and as soon as they do, I change my mind. A big scoop of Chocolate Praline sounds great right now. I follow them, jogging, and as I am about to catch up with them, as they are passing Dafna's blanket, I hear Dent whisper to Joel:

"How long would you give it before you head inside for an inappropriately rowdy and noisy hook-up with her?" He's nodding at Dafna.

What?

"What's the over/under?"

What?!?

"In minutes?" Joel says, "I'd say about 180."

"But she's in a two-piece. You gotta factor these things in."

What are they talking about? What the hell are they talking about?

"Then closer to 120."

"Why would Joel hook up with Dafna?" I say from behind, nearly yelling at them.

They stop walking and turn around, their faces those of people who had just been caught in bed together. In some way, they had.

"Um . . ."

"Um . . . *what?*"

"Ask Joel."

I turn to Joel.

"Why would you hook up with Dafna?"

The both look at me. There is silence.

"We were going to tell you. I mean, we were planning on telling you before we got here, but . . ."

Joel touches my arm.

"She needed someone. I was . . . this sounds so stupid . . . there. We became close."

I do not look at him.

"I'm . . . I'm going to get Margaritas. Want one?" He is sheepish.

I do not look at him. I say, "Jose Cuervo Gold. No salt."

I turn my back and sit down on the blanket next to Dafna. I look at her feet.

"What about Clark?" I say coolly.

"Clark? Who's Clark?"

Jesus.

I sit and I say nothing. I say nothing at all. But then, after a minute, I say a lot of things. I say things that I don't even realize I'm saying, that I have no business saying to a woman. To her, to anyone. I use the words *typical* and *ignorant*. I think *bitch* slips out. This goes on for at nearly five minutes, and I do not look at her, and I do not let her speak.

Then I hear her crying.

I hope she cries. She's . . . she's a floozie.

She deserves to cry.

She deserves this after what she did to me.

Wasn't Joel supposed to get margaritas? Where the hell is Joel with our margaritas? With Jose Cuervo Gold, no salt.

It's a good thing I was not in love with Dafna. It wasn't even close to love, whatever it was.

She always liked my back. Dafna loved caressing it, loved drawing invisible words on it, loved locating specific problem areas and massaging them out. I, of course could never see it myself, but she habitually told me it was broad and strong.

"Like He-Man," she cooed.

"Or Tar-Zan," she added.

She named a different superhero each time. Sometimes she made them up.

"Like Big–man."

"Or Mars-man."

It was nice of her to say that, to flatter me, when I know it looks funny, like that weird skin on those daredevil squirrels, the ones lunging airborne between trees. It was nice of her to make me feel like I am more of a specimen than I am—I would give myself a 6—to be charitable, albeit briefly, when I know there are too many freckles in a certain 3 cm^2 of space, which ruins the whole thing; and when I know that my neck was too "thorough." *NeckMan*, she called me once, and I freaked. *Sheldon Wirth. Sheldon P. Wirth*, she said me once. *I like that. I like how it sounds*, and I flipped again.

"She's sweet," Linda Wirth told me. "She's healthful. I mean, good for you."

My mother had no idea what the real Dafna was like.

Dafna Dafna wasn't always sweet. The real Dafna could be manipulative. Ambitious. *Dafna* Dafna could cajole me into fictionalizing a daughter (our first).

"Oh, this movie's not for us," she told the parents who were gawking at us in a squealing, hair-pulling showing of some G-rated insult/masterpiece like *Cool Runnings*.

"We're making sure the content is appropriate for our child," she said. "You never know with the PG rating these days, and our Esmeralda can be a sensitive one—yes, that's her name—*Esmeralda*," cupping her mouth and whispering almost pridefully, "she's *very unpopular* at school."

Dafna normally liked movies that only Goths and Vegans enjoyed, but this turned out to be much more fun.

"Our other daughter? Oh, we call her Third Avenue Lizzie."

We'd spread rumors about the director and stars, talking disparagingly about the plot—

"That's not what happens in the book. Have you read the book?"

"No. Is it good?"

"No. Awful book. You should read it, and be ashamed you haven't already. If you have time."

"If I have time."

—and put our knees into the back of their seats. We'd laugh at the movie only when no one else was laughing. When *they* laughed, we'd give them a let's-be-adults look. We'd crossly hush them.

Sometimes the real Dafna would grab my crotch and stick out her tongue. The real Dafna was not always nice. The real Dafna liked sex. The real Dafna hated watching TV.

"It's just a show."

"It doesn't make sense. This stuff isn't real."

"You *monster*."

"I'm serious. How can you sit and watch this stuff, knowing it's just the product of some underpaid writer's mind?"

What did Dafna know about reality? She was Jewish. She spent her days reading books by writers writing about writing. Or about Victorian sexual repression carrying over into mid 20th century war-torn Europe. I never judged her for it. I just thought it was unusual, and I always considered those people a strange type of exhibitionist, not unlike the ballet dancers, the ones who grace the stage in skin leotards, pudendum on display. I admired the people who went to those performances, in fact. They knew something I didn't.

"It's as good as anything else on," I would say.

"What about baseball? Most guys watch baseball. That's at least real."

"Is it?"

"Deep, Shel."

"Come sit."

"Not now."

"Please?"

I sulked. Sulking usually works.

"No."

"We can spoon."

"We'll have to watch something else."

"Hmmnnn. You can be big spoon?"

"I'll sit. Just for a minute."

"Good."

. . .

"This stuff—it's childish."

"Fine."

I then flicked to a reality show set in California. I checked the channel guide summary: *Rich, lugubrious teenagers complain (TV-MA)*.

"Better?"

"Almost."

"Jesus, Shel. Grow up."

"You smell like Christmas," I said.

I could spend most of the day smelling her hair. I could fall asleep in that hair of hers. Sometimes she smelled like Christmas.

I have left the blanket and am now walking along the water to a strip of beach bars. I enter the first one. In the corner, a tan man is under surrender to a video poker machine. He and a bartender wearing a TAKE ME DRUNK I'M HOME shirt are watching John Leguizamo wiggle into a lace brassiere. The bartender turns down the volume as I approach.

"Need anything?"

I shake my head and walk over to the pool table. I roll a few balls around under my palms. I am thinking what a relief it was that I was not in love with her. Not even close to it.

It used to be that I was convincing myself that I *was* in love, of course. That I was smitten with Dafna and that hair of hers. That's not the case now. Obviously it's not the case. There is no way I loved someone who is capable of dating Joel, of finding him attractive. Of finding him interesting. Joel is not interesting, not the way I am. She does not realize —*she doesn't have the objectivity to realize* . . . Dafna does not know what she is doing. She doesn't know Joel. I know Joel. Joel is Joel. And now that she is with him – it is worse than unforgivable. It is unexplainable.

I was not in love with Dafna.

I was in love with someone else, a man. I loved Dafna's father, Mr. Schwartzers, and he loved me in return—fully, unabashedly.

I pick up a cue and aim for number five, corner pocket. I hit five, miss the pocket.

I decide against remaining at this bar. Too empty. I leave just as John Leguizamo is starting to apply blush.

Mr. Schwartzers loved me in return, not just for dating her, but for something else—something that Dafna must have told him about me, something that I was never privy to but that made him very clearly infatuated with me as his daughter's lover. This adoration only increased my own love for him. It was a little love-fest, though I never admitted to actually loving Dafna, never made clear any intentions of being with her in her senility, sterility, dotage.

Dafna never had any way of knowing this, of course. I was never the romantic type, the Hugh Grant type; never one to buy candies, to tell her I fancied her (in a Hugh Grant accent); or to commit passionate musings to perfume-scented parchment (something I assume Hugh Grant would do). And although I often stood accused of being emotionally insolvent through much of our relationship, she still trusted that I was committed. Her love was never enthusiastic, never demanding. It asked nothing of me, which made it all the more troublesome. It was too close, too familiar.

I walk into the next bar, more crowded, but incongruously Disco, considering the current location and era. Techno, strobes, tube tops. I slide into a small booth. There are two young men in the booth beside me. One is wearing a wife beater: it says BANANA SLUGS. The other is wearing a jersey. MATTINGLY. They are having an intense discussion about the Coen Brothers. I observe.

"The Dude abides," they say in unison, clinking bottles.

If ever there were a time when the love shown by Mr. Schwartzers toward me ever wavered, I couldn't tell. Distance fortified it, in fact. He knew me strictly from our sporadic but somehow intimate encounters. As soon as he met me, he insulted me.

Goon.

So I insulted him.

Miserly asshole.

He laughed. He informed me I'd never be good enough, wealthy enough, for his daughter. I was not a proud graduate of Pace University, like himself. Or a proud graduate of CUNY, like his daughter. Nor was I Old Testament enough. Mr. Schwartzers loved playing up the Old Testament part. The first time I visited their Upper West Side apartment, Mr. Schwartzers planned an initiation of sorts, and for the first fifteen minutes of my visit, he remained only partly visible, hitching about the back room muttering, "Money, money, money," and rubbing his wrists.

Dafna waved him off. "He's not serious. He's just trying to scare you. That's just Dad."

But it didn't help. *Money, money, money,* I hear, standing in the foyer, looking at what appears to be a Lichtenstein. Authentic. He was what I aspired to be.

An asshole, and good at it. Or was it Jewish? Did I actually desire to be brought into the Jewish community, officially for once? Sometimes I thought it might have helped, times in the shower when I would look down at my floppy, intact member, wishing it weren't so. It was a strange kind of penis envy.

"Leave it to the Jews," he says, laughing fitfully, "to fail to understand the true meaning of Xmas."

I stop to listen while Mr. Mattingly Jersey insists that early work of the Coen brothers was inspired, and the only stuff of theirs worth watching; while the Banana Slugs guy, barely heard over the music, insists he's misled, that their career trajectory was in fact a curve upward (if you value aesthetic and experimental ingenuity over commercial success, and despite the creative lull they experienced with *Intolerable Cruelty*), becoming more sophisticated as they aged.

Best of all, Mr. Schwartzers reassured me. I laughed, loved it, passed his initial tests (by not hightailing it out of there), and became part of the family, Mr. Schwartzers introducing himself as the fat, old Jewish uncle he never had. I knew I could say anything to him after that.

"Have you done something with your hair?" I teased whenever I saw him, fully aware that he didn't have a lot of it.

"Money, money, money . . ." Mr. Schwartzers grinned, happy to concede that he had a lot of other things, not overly concerned that one of them wasn't hair. *Nothing can offend this old Jew*, is what his gaze told me, but that's not what he said.

"Yup," is what he said. Just *yup*.

This was a clear indication that Dafna had a trust fund, or at least some sort of escrow account.

It was a great feeling, to have a wealthy man want you to join his family (even if by way of loving his daughter). To have him give generously—of his time, his pocketbook, his self. Taking you out to dinners and interviewing you, not in a pushily interrogative way, but curiously. Asking how she challenges you, what about her attracts you, what about her bothers you. And listening with the intensity of a student:

Yes, yes! She is that way! You are so right! You have it exactly! Exactly! It's maddening! Isn't it maddening?

This is what he did for me. And he is all verve; he is all—here it is again—love.

And our discussions. We had hour-long discussions over three-hour long dinners. I was never so engaged as I was at those dinners. He made me feel more important than any human.

"You are a strong man, Sheldon. You have good physical genetics, the brow and the arms of a tree-dwelling creature, and the brains, too. If I ever were to cross you, I'm sure you would hurt me."

He would follow up by challenging me to an arm-wrestling competition, right there in the middle of Sardi's (a name, I always forgot, calling it

Talkies, for some reason, for which he'd always forgive me). He would go down without effort.

"But, my dear Sheldon," he added, smiling, "if you merely think about unbuckling yourself near sweet Dafna, I'd happily and without hesitation take an *izmel* to your tum-tum," reaching around the table and patting it, my *tum-tum*, lightly, "and feast on your entrails."

Later that evening, after taking us on a private tour of Madison Square Garden, then to an 8 PM showing of *RENT*, thinking people of our age would be more receptive to it than something by Sondheim, he'd ask, in all sincerity, when I planned on moving in with her after college. *Yup.*

Crazy bastard.

This is why I loved him. I was courted, wooed, by him, or as close to courting as that relationship between us could come. He trusted me. Even before the hell I went through for nothing—the gun, the drug use, the kidnapping (unintentional, but still significant), the Minutemen—he trusted me. Not because I was a protector. Because I was a good person. I was good to Dafna. At least that was the assumption.

"What am I?" he'd ask at random.

"A Jew."

"A *what?*"

"A Jew. A jü. A joo."

"Very good."

For this man to be my father-in-law one day—this would have made me the luckiest guy in the world. So I stayed with Dafna, even after her bedroom tooth-and-claw attack against me, *on* me. I stayed because I couldn't bring myself to abandon her wonderful, beautiful father.

The duo next to me continues their conversation. *Mattingly* persists; *Banana Slugs* counters. I listen, flabbergasted that this is happening now, with lights flashing, women in minis gyrating, music blue-baba-dee-baba-do-ing. And just as they are really getting into it, just as they are discussing intent vs. accident in *The Big Lebowski*, deconstructing Jeff Bridges' nudie trampoline hallucinations while I can't stop thinking about how it's all wasted now, on a woman who's now involved with Joel—Joel!—the least likely person in the world, someone less likely even than Dent, whom I could have come eventually to understand, he being the *man* she was looking for—and who will be dead in a matter of years or months or weeks—but with *Joel*, it's interminable, she could be in this thing forever; and the guys next to me continue yapping, investigating some sort of Steve-Buscemi-as-latter-day-Cassandra hypothesis, delving into the use of allegory in the Coen Bros script and how it relates to more complex social issues (the Maude character being emblematic of the underlying Anarcho-Capitalist sympathies of the film, specifically); and just as they begin to extrapolate, drawing on the movie to explore the relevance and efficacy of morality plays in modern media, and *art* in general, I interject:

"Know what I think?" I say, pulling up my shorts. "You're both fucking idiots."

I was not in love with Dafna. I am certain of it. But I stayed with her. I lied to her. I was not in love with her. Not a single word I have said to her since meeting her has been genuine.

A reef dive is scheduled for the afternoon. Because the whole point of the vacation was to go diving, I can't miss it; which means I will have to see Joel and Dafna; which means I will have to extend basic courtesies to them; which means I have to find some way to prevent myself from digging my fingers deep into their eyes when I see them.

Did I pack my green mask or blue mask? Green, it looks like. Good.

This need not be a burden. I can handle it, this news of their relationship. It could be both good and bad news; bad, because it is Joel; good, because being with Joel means she is still win-over-able. I have a chance to demonstrate that I have recovered, that I am not only capable of being everything she wants and needs, but that I am *more* capable than Dent could ever be. That, despite the completely fucked up thing she and Joel did to me (God, right after the whole operation—how long were we broken up before he moved in?), I will act adult about it. Because I *am* an adult, and have decided to enjoy the vacation, calmly, casting all thoughts of the betrayal (by my two best friends) from my mind. That afternoon, when we meet our dive instructor, I am calm, or at least give a fairly convincing impression (Are they *sleeping together?* Are they *fucking?* Please no, God.) of being so.

Our dive instructor's name is Francisco, with an *eesco*. Franc*ees*co. This man is big. Very big. He looks like a man who can tear the tusks off of a wild boar, whose smoking room (and of this I am sure, that he has a smoking room) is no doubt lined with dead pigs. When he talks, he growls. He has a tendency to project reproductive organs onto everything he sees. *Look at that shell. Would you like to know what I think that shell looks like?* But his words, though gruff, are melodic, poetic. They are assured. Francisco studied at the University of Hawaii. He majored in surfing. Was

I clear? *Surfing*. As in riding waves. Francisco is God. I would like to be Francisco. I would give anything for that man's life. Franc*ee*sco smells of coconut and resin. This man is *confident*. This looks like a man who breaks powerful wind. This man is wearing Capris.

Maybe he will let me towel him.

His plan, he says, is to take us out about a mile from shore. Because Dent has his Divemaster certification, he'll lead us in the dive while Francisco stays in the boat, watching our bubbles. There are only one or two rules.

If Dent raps on his tank—like this—you'll hear it. That means pay attention.

You can do almost anything you want, just don't touch the coral, and if you hear Dent rap on his tank, pay attention. Cool?

Yes. Cool.

He tells us, we should make our way to the beach—*go at your own pace, now,* he says—as soon as we're in the water, and he'll follow. *You'll probably be dehydrated, so I've stockpiled some ginger ale in this cooler for when we—*

Dafna can't wait. She jackknifes in. She floats on the surface, waiting. *Let's go.* Dent and Joel follow. I fasten the cummerbund on my BCD, then—because every diver should have something attached to their ankle while submerged, I bought a dive knife for this trip—make sure my Kn250 Fogcutter Delta, with easy push-button release, built-in scissors, and 420 stainless steel blade is attached. My stomach pooches out, along with a sad excuse for a happy trail.

Interlude:
I am fat.
Yes I am. So fat.
I am also poor.

I hold my mask and throw myself backward from the boat.

I have trouble with neutral buoyancy. I knew this would happen, because in pool training I had trouble with it. Neutral buoyancy is a state in which you are "floating" underwater, neither sinking nor rising. It is often difficult to attain, requiring you to inflate your BCD with an amount of air that allows you to hang in the water, parallel, without having to keep yourself steady by paddling.

"For beginners it can be tough," Dent said. "But it feels great when you get it. It's like a nice pat on the back. Or a minor acid trip."

I am not sure whether to believe him. At this rate, I'll never know. I am not good at Neutral Buoyancy. It requires even inhalation, but this, breathing steadily, seems like the least natural thing to me right now. I teeter-totter, draining air from my BCD and sinking, then inflating it and rising. Finally, I am parallel. I can catch up with Joel, lines hanging off of him like—*What is that motherfucker!? A fish! What kind? A shark? No. Possibly. No, definitely no. Nice. Just a fish. Right next to me. Thin, like a dollar.*

It's right there. I could touch it.

Dent is waving to me, vying for my attention. Is something wrong? Something seems to be wrong. I swim over. He pantomimes, pointing to me (YOU), then drawing a letter with his finger (R [ARE]), then, taking his respirator out, mouthing the rest (AN ASSHOLE). He shows some tooth and swims off.

Have I mentioned how glad I am that Dent's my friend?

I go deep. More than 40 feet. To me, this is deep. I let the current carry me, arms down at my sides and I close my eyes for a moment and I breathe in and I am weightless and I am eternal and the water has become my blood and it's warm.

It's over too quickly.

We get the signal to wrap it up and begin to head back. Dent and I are parallel, he beneath me, and as we near the shore, he starts moving in a strange way, as if he were trying to shake something off his head. He starts to writhe. He starts swimming faster, kicking frantically. We follow, standing up as we reach the beach, waddling up the sand in our flippers, but Dent doesn't get up. He floats. The surf pushes him onto the sand, and he is motionless. I rush to him. I turn him over. His nose is bloody. It is gushing blood. Oh fuck, oh shit. Oh my god shit. Medic. We need a medic. Medic! Not now. Please, Dent. Pleasedontdienow. Not when I can see you.

I can save you.

Please, I swear, I not right in front of me. I wouldn't be able to take it with you right there, in front of me. I can't watch. Wait, I've been trained for this. What are those emergency ABCs? *Always Be Closing?* No. Fuck! *Airways, Breathing, Circulation.* Yes, that's it—*Airways, Breathing, Circulation.* All I need to do is—

Francisco, he takes charge. He pulls me up by my tank, kneels before Dent, performs a manual auscultation, putting an ear to his chest. He's still. There's a hand on my shoulder. It's Joel. We wait. Under my breath, I tell Dent to live. I tell him that he'd better fucking live. He told us he was fine. He *promised* us there was nothing wrong with him, that he had faked the whole thing. He better fucking live.

Or else.

And this is how I know Dent will die. Because Dent won't listen. He won't live. At moments like these, when people are telling him what to do, what not to do; when all of his elders and betters are telling him that there was a way to live his life, or the rest of it, that there was some road less traveled set aside for people like him, whose lives were, um, *truncated* in such a way—and this is when he did the opposite, because *Roads? Where we're going, we don't need roads*; and sure, it may seem immature or, worse, uninspired, but coming from Dent, it seems *important*. Even if, technically, he is mistaken; he has every right to reject that dying-quietly-with-dignity horseshit; and *fuck you* for telling him what to do, how and when to die. Denton Brown might be the only person alive who, even if he *never did*, could say I love you as much as he wanted and make it sound meaningful every time. And this is how I knew I would always be more of a—not a sidekick now—a fan. Sure, we hung out together, we laughed together, we acted like white trash together, throwing garbage on the front lawn of Dr. Hunter's Kenilworth McMansion, or calling up all kinds of not-for-profits and donating millions of dollars under the pseudonym *Anonymous*, or slip fetish magazines, nipple clips and KY Jelly into the Trig teacher's desk at lunch break, but I was more often a non-participant, an observer of his work, an admirer of his stunts and of his offensiveness—cheering him on as he donned a pair of unnecessary ski goggles at a Sox game and pretended to be mentally slow; or admonished kids on Halloween, pointing and calling them candy-whores; or put a pair of discarded jumper cables to X-rated use; or used standard wire hangers as self-branding irons; or attached fireworks to the underside of his 21-speed and half-piped into Lake Michigan; or interrupted Act II, Scene III of the mid-summer production of *The Music Man* ("Gary, Indiana") by handing out flyers about the tumultuous history of *U.S. Steel* in Gary, IN, detailing how its 1986 layoffs gave rise to high crime and unemployment rates, as well as drug problems; or ran for school president on the HARDER TESTS, MORE HOMEWORK platform.

I stood and watched, envious of him but too afraid to be *like* him. This is absurd, when you think about it, to be envious of a dying man. But we all were, and Dent was the only person we knew able to do such a thing. Even when we found out something really strange about Dent—like he didn't object to the occasional foot sea-scrub treatment, or he had a longstanding interest in fabrics, or had spent a whole week experimenting with peeing in a sitting down position, noting how remarkably difficult it is to do, this female-urination trick—something totally, well, gay, he just became that much more intriguing, more heroic in a sense. (We should applaud. There should be a standing ovation. Being witness to his life). He was untouchable. He was super-powered. He was invisible, he was invincible. There was something infinite about him. A phantom limb of a human being—gone but still felt.

And this is why Dent has prepared for this moment—visiting Seattle Cancer Care Alliance for final advice, for counsel (not asking them when he was expected to die, but telling them when he was *going* to die), indulging in steak and lobster and bubbly and Cubans last night, getting up at dawn for a fifteen-miler, setting up this last dive with his three best friends, looking at peace with himself the whole time, calling me an *asshole* one last time—why he had planned for this to be a goodbye, a last-hurrah type of thing, and has chosen now as his time to die. Because he was, is, untouchable, and invincible. At least that's what I thought. Call it a *hope springs eternal* delusion. No one thought he could do it. And now, here we are, on this beach, with such white, warm sand, like an ocean beside the ocean, waiting for news of my best friend's death.

Dafna shrieks. Joel—I can hardly see Joel, who has made his way up the beach and is now sitting Indian-style just beyond the drift line. Franscisco, his back to me, is quivering. He is shaking his head. *Oh my god*, he says. He is laughing.

"They crying yet?"

Dent gets up, rivulets of blood running into his mouth, across his cheeks.

"Dent? Oh my God. Oh my God!"

"Assholes!' He yells, tearing off his flippers and jumping up. He is laughing. He boogaloos a little, shuffling in the sand.

"Dent Is Risen! Dent Will Come Again!" he yells.

"Your nose," Dafna says, her face waterlogged. "What happened?"

"It's just from the pressure. I didn't take a safety stop. Not great for you, but it happens all the time."

"That's fucked up. That's really fucked up."

Joel gets up. He walks away.

"God damn it, Dent."

"Yeah, great job. Really super. Thanks."

"Heh," Dent says, less enthusiastic, "I made you look like assholes."

We stare.

He turns toward the hotel. *I'm gonna get a brewski.*

He walks away. Dent, this man with privilege (the balls?) to live out our fantasies without us, the temerity to give us such a scare, force us to reveal how deeply we care about him, how readily emotional we become at the thought of losing him, is now walking away. He is showing us how selfishly we mourn him—or is all mourning selfish?—because, see? It's no big deal, Dent's death, so why are we treating it as one? It's not like we weren't expecting it.

Dafna hasn't spoken. She throws her goggles on the sand. Something, probably a compound of exhaustion and disgust, has her on all fours, and she retches. She turns around. She starts to crawl. She is coming toward me, crawling like a child within reach of something good, and when she is close she pushes me over and falls on me. I put my arms around her and I feel her back and I do not want to hurt it any more. I will protect it and it offers protection to me. She is here to protect me. She is still crying, so softly, and I hold her head back and put my mouth to hers and we lie there breathing.

Except I am not the one she crawls to and pushes down and lies on. It is Joel she wants, Joel she touches. And Dent does not get up. He does not play a joke. He lies there, motionless.

DINNER.

No one speaks that night.

Once Dent is resuscitated, he refuses treatment, displays the typical Dentian stubbornness—

"I'm fine. Totally fine. Just a small fuckup. What's for dinner? I'm hungry. Let's get Dominoes."

—but he is not fine. His pupils are different sizes. That is not fine.

Still, he insists it is time for dinner. So we plan dinner, no arguments. We plan it so dinner is had at small outdoor theater, where some kind of folksy history set to music seems to be happening onstage.

Is it a night of robust theatricality? No. It is not.

We listen politely, though it's difficult to hear, but at least we don't talk to one another or, worse, *look at one another*, although I steal a glance.

Joel is drowsing, his cheek and a dessert plate flirting dangerously close. His shirt says LIKE A STURGEON. Dafna, possibly drunk, giggles, cutely snorts. Dent—the seasoned traveler, in his liminal dying-but-not state, stage lights flashing across his face—has tied a napkin to his head and declared himself "Lord of Misrule," for the night. He snaps along to the music arhythmically, a hand hanging beside him like a tether. *No, he is not fine.*

Dent gets up, and, oh my. He has started to dance. It is not a good dance. There is too much hip. He starts playing the invisible castanets; his head swings like a gate. His movements—fraught, obscene—are frightening the women.

"You're no Balanchine, buddy," I say. I say it not knowing if I pronounced Balanchine correctly, not knowing if Balanchine is a person or a style of dance, or neither, or both, concluding it was wise to invoke the Balanchine name regardless. I look more intelligent because of it.

Dent does not notice. He is still dancing, sipping his Sam Adams in a way that looks more like an attempt at a first kiss than anything else. He spills. This gives him an idea. "We should pour beer on the other patrons," he says. I nurse my beer, ignoring him.

Dent has switched routines. He is now doing something with his right foot, now his left, and—is that the?—is that?—The *Hokey Pokey?* Lord above. This must be embarrassing. I am embarrassed for him. How would any woman, if there *were* any women around, stomach the sight of him nude if seeing him now, with him hokey-pokeying? But I will not intervene. It's not my place. I turn back to our table, but Dafna has left the table, her seat empty. She is doing her bird dance again.

I'm a bird! she sings. *I'm a bird!*

Crazy woman.

Dent is now done with the Hokey Pokey, doing something that, whatever it is, is not dancing. It is more like seizing. He looks like he is having a seizure. But now his leg is not his leg but some disembodied limb that *has no choice* but to move to the rhythm, that almost escapes him until he grabs it, reins it in. They are now playing the house-merengue hit *El Mueve Mueve* (Sandy y Papo MC, 1995), and I look at Joel, but he is passed out, limp, like an unmanned Muppet. When I look back at Dent, the music has changed again, and he has again switched dances.

"It's *electric!*" he shouts, wobbling as if climbing aboard a life raft, possibly on something.

He is not fine. There is nothing I can do about it.

I down my beer. I ask for the check. Joel wakes up and grabs the check from me, clicks the pen. He leaves for <u>Tip</u>: *Whatever* and as his <u>Signature</u>: *Guess, assho*—but does not seem to finish, losing steam on 'asshole.'

I do not like that Dent likes it. It is not okay that he is enjoying himself, or pretending to enjoy himself. He should feel guilty about this afternoon, or at least act it, that he is refusing to get looked at, refusing treatment, making me decode his behavior. I keep running through reasons for this afternoon in my head—this whole thing, yes, it was just a prank, was his way of getting us to appreciate him; or maybe it's worse than he has lead us to believe. He is simply playing it off, acting like a hardass—but none of this sounds right, because he is visibly disoriented.

Dent leans over.

"Know what?" he whispers. *What?* I mouth. "I'm not sure about that Francisco guy. I mean, when he was helping me put on my scuba gear, I think he molested me a little bit. Just a little. Anyway . . ."

I acknowledge the remark, raising my eyebrows, but say nothing. How productive would it be to be mad with someone who says things like that?

After dinner, I discover that our hotel has a hot tub. I turn on the bubbles and slide in. I stick my face in. This is nice. I do this for a while, the dead man's float. People will not find me here.

The worst part is, even if it was a stupid prank, even if he put his life and our feelings at risk, I will forgive Dent, because I always do.

I admire and respect him. He is one of those few people who refused the atomical view of life. He always saw it from a historical perspective—not any recorded or eternally-remembered history, but one which, if you consider the tide of men, is different. One which, although entertaining, may not be well understood until after the fact, why his decisions were somehow the right ones. Because when everyone gathers for his last rites—hopefully not on a random beach somewhere, but perhaps—no one dares speak politically. The last thing he would want was for someone to speak politically at his funeral. He wanted weeping, emotion, mourning colors. The beating of breasts. *Sprach Zarathustra* played without irony over loudspeakers. And dark. Not a shred of light. Not the bullshit let's-celebrate-his-life-not-mourn-his-death bullshit. He wanted people to know that someone important was gone, and that your lives—yes, you, in the eighteenth pew—would be deprived of something without him. He wanted tears, real tears. Drama. What's the point of a funeral if it's going to bore everyone?

That's ego. Or idiocy. Either way, it's what Dent wanted.

I return to the room. I know I should not, but I slip into bed with Dafna—*fuck Joel*—curling my arm around her soft . . . but she's not there. Her suitcase is gone.

The next morning, Dent is gone, too. Has everyone abandoned me? The phone rings, a nurse. Dent is in the hospital and dying for the third and final time.

Interlude: A Past Incident
11 June, 1998.
Wirth Family Two-Story, Beige, Cement-Fiber Siding.

Today Dafna thought I died.

It was just a trick. I do it all the time, having fun with Dafna, pranking her. Like the time I planted a pink "rabbit" vibrator in her underwear drawer, opening her underwear drawer, pretending to discover the pink vibrator, being surprised by it, mystified as to what this pink vibrator was, what function it performed, what end it served.

I began intentionally fumbling with the pink vibrator, accidentally flipping it on and off, nearly dropping it on the floor.

The joke, you see, is that she should be ashamed of having this device, and doubly ashamed for keeping it in a place so easily discoverable by another human.

Dafna laughed, got a little upset, pulled the invasion-of-privacy line.

But she will forgive me. She has to.

And it was worth it. Sure, there was the embarrassment of buying the pink, aptly named rabbit device from the sex shop, SWEET 'N EASY, I believe it was called, but still. Totally worth it. I told her she could keep it, the rabbit.

Today's trick is more involved, more creative. Some might call it genius. Dafna is visiting for the summer, and today, I trick her. I return from swimming in Lake Michigan, tell her I am going to clean out the gutters. She yells *okay*. She is upstairs, reading *Heart of Darkness*. Or *The Tell-Tale Heart*. I do not know. Something with Heart.

Five minutes later, she hears a yell. Then she hears a loud *Whump*. Then, silence.

Yes, Dafna. I am dead.

She runs downstairs, into the kitchen. She searches for me. She is frantic.

She looks out the window to see me on the ground, blood running from my mouth.

She rushes out, crying, yelling, and just as she is about to run for help, I laugh.

That is not blood, Dafna. That is ketchup. The *Whump?* It was me, slamming a pool noodle on the garage door. See the pool noodle, over there? It did not go very far. It makes a big sound for such a small thing, doesn't it?

I smile and laugh. See, Dafna? I am fine. I am not dead.

She overreacts.

Part IV

Finally!!
Finally!!
I
Am
at
Peace
with
Myself!!

XII.
Boston.

Border security at LAX is a bitch, and we have trouble at customs for reasons unspecified, though for a moment I suspect Joel of neglecting to declare certain organic items. At Logan, it is too late for the Subway, so I catch a cab. I slouch as we wind around Storrow, eyes out the window.

Life has not changed since Mexico. I thought something big was going to happen. I was expecting a cataclysm. Upheaval. I thought I was going to *feel something*.

Nothing happened. I don't mind.

One of those crazy cabbies is at the wheel of this cab, one of those kamikaze drivers who hangs strange charms in the windshield, weird burgundy and electric-blue baubles (which I am sure he fetishizes, prays to, chants to, makes small animal sacrifices to) and he made an illegal turn on red and nearly killed me. Sure, I saw it coming, could have said something, told him that he should drive with more caution, but is it my job to make sure cabbies obey no-turn-on-red laws? There must be a Sox game. Traffic is heavy. There's no room to park. There's hardly room to double park.

It's hell today in Boston.

I get back to my apartment at The Cheapskate—a nickname that Joel, in one of his rare moments of cleverness, gave my building, an apartment-complex called *The Chesapeake* (italicized to make it seem ever-luxurious)—to discover my Volvo encased in frost, icicles hanging from the side panels like mummified chrysalises. I kick them off. I check mail: A ValuPack coupon bundle, a Land's End catalogue, a claim from Intexel subrogation services, a Discover card offer. *Ooh, I'm Pre-Qualified!*

I open the door, expecting to filet a salmon I picked up next door (perhaps rubbing it with garlic and brown sugar, or marinating it in soy sauce.

Or lemon. I'll add lemon). But I'm too tired now. I skip the store. I don't unpack before I go to bed.

Wednesday, The Next Big Thing.
    They next morning is a Wednesday, and I wake up late, very late. Although I am now unemployed, I head to the office, because I have business there. I had planned on slashing the tires of my former Spanish teacher's car but instead drain them of air until they're at 2.0 PSI instead of their standard 4.4 PSI. Then I return to my apartment.

    Then I screw myself out of the current week's rent by giving it to a shoeless man who may not really work for the United Way, despite his claims to the contrary. Then I figure out a way to cheat on my taxes. Then I cheat on my taxes. Then I write short speech for next year's tech convention in Omaha titled THE NEXT BIG THING, about how the Internet is the wave of the future, and I consider changing the title to THE WAVE OF THE FUTURE but stick with THE NEXT BIG THING because it strikes me as concise and original.

    Inspired by my own eloquence, I go online and pose as Victoria, driving a forty-seven year-old bond trader named William to orgasm. Then I drive an MIT Applied Math major named Nicholas to suicide. Then I e-chat with a man whom I believe is LL Cool J because he tells me he is LL Cool J and his screen name is LLCoolJ10198, and I see no reason why he should lie to me. I saw this "Barack Obama" fellow speak the other night, and although he made some questionable assertions about change, there may be something to him and sincerely believe that he'll always act in the best interests of the U.S and world as a whole. Then:

    I blow the cover of a Peruvian masquerading as a Mexican at the local delicatessen.

    I catch wise to people taking more than one penny from the TAKE-PENNY-LEAVE-A-PENNY jar.

    I write a letter to a friend.

    I lead a girl on, then call her a name.

    I lick a part of my body not meant for licking.

    On the subway yesterday, a man with black hair and black shoes used the word *vivid* too many times in one sentence. I fought the urge to alert him of this.

    I step out for lunch.

    I binge.

    I purge.

Then I pick rock.

Then I poop a little.

I experiment with my sexuality, then my coworker experiments with it, then we both experiment with my sexuality together.

I get in touch with an emerging artist on the Lower East Side and commission an oil painting of my favorite hand, my left hand.

I bid one dollar on the Sealy California King size mattress (with memory foam and contour pillow) and box spring set, because the first guy obviously overbid, and because—well, because fuck him, that's my set.

I do all this while relieving a whole afternoon's worth of stress by softly but willfully passing gas, working up to a very satisfying crescendo at the end, providing myself a modicum of relief after an otherwise stressful, some might say trying, day.

I do all of these things, and still I have nothing to do. Until I check my calendar, realizing that I had forgotten to erase the Minuteman events. It is the 23rd today, which means the troop meeting will be held at the Swampscott Community House. Should I . . . yes, I really should, and I go.

It's a short drive. Jason is there. Another Scout says *hello*. I can't remember his name.

"Hey, *you*," I say. "I know *you*."

God, what's that guy's name? I recall the way it sounded, if not its specific syllables. I remember it was faintly evocative of VD. Before I embarrass myself, Jason interrupts with a *What do you want?* look. He is wearing a whistle this time. It's blue.

"Yooo, Jason. How's it going, Jason-banana-fana-fo-fason. . ."

He looks at me.

"What's up, asshole?"

"I came because . . . because I need to say something."

"Not stopping you."

"I mean to the troop. I need to say something to the troop."

"Gohead."

"Could you blow the whistle?"

"You blow it."

"It's around your neck."

"Won't get blown, I guess."

I deserve this.

"Fine."

I bend down toward Jason's chest, where, tied to a lanyard, hangs the blue whistle. I grab it and blow, an ear awkwardly folded against his collarbone. The Scouts turn around. I'm not sure if they know about me. If I were Jason, I wouldn't have told them. I hear a *Hey!* At least one of them is happy that I'm here. I stick my hands into my pockets and grab the bottoms.

"Listen," I say, "I'm not quite sure what to say to you guys. I guess, well, frankly, I screwed up."

I scan for reactions. None.

"To be honest, I don't know the first thing about this nerdy Boy Scout crap you do. But there must be something to it, because you guys are, or seem, happy, and I haven't been or even *seemed* happy in a very long time, so I'm going to volunteer, and I'm going to teach you about something I recently learned about, and that's SCUBA diving. I'm going to take you to an atoll. Do you know what an atoll is? Never mind, of course you don –"

A hand goes up. "It's a ring-shaped coral island that encloses a body of water, like a lagoon."

"Uh, yes. And I'm going to take you to one. We don't have the money, you say? That's what fundraisers are for, my Junior Minutemen. In return, you are going to teach me how to camp and fish—that's right, I don't know how to do either, which I've clearly already demonstrated—and whistle. That's the most important thing. Getting me to whistle. And I'm going to swear at you and call you "little fucking pissants," because let's face it, that's what you are. I mean you're goddamns kids, you're not real soldiers, out there defending the great US of A or anything, like I was.

"Okay, that was also a lie. I was never in the service. And I was never in Beirut. God, I can't believe you bought that shit. I mean, how old do I look? I was like three years old when Beirut happened. Do the math, guys. I always thought you kids were smart. The most dangerous places I've been are a KFC bathroom off I-95 and certain bars in New Orleans, toying with my blood-alcohol content. So I am going to learn—no, we are going to learn *together*—about discipline, and what it means, what respect for the community *means*.

"You're also going to teach me about knife safety. And fire safety. And all the other multifarious kinds of safeties in this big blue orb we call *Mother Earth*."

On *Mother Earth*, I give the "quote fingers." The kids do not respond. I should not have given the "quote fingers."

"And you're going to teach me why ancient cultures tended to anthropomorphize and feminize nature, because I never had a very good grasp of anthropology or whatever it is. Also, I read something about a safety circle in the Scout Handbook, and you're going to teach me about this safety circle. You are also going to tell me how to light a fire, which I believe is in fact an impossible thing—"

"The secret is kerosene," one scout says. "Boy Scout water, we call it."

"Yes, see?, that's exactly the type of thing I need to know. Kerosene! Ingenious! Yes, for the lanterns—the lanterns! I need to know all about lanterns. About how to pump them properly, how to light the mantle, adjust the brightness. Lanterns are so important in this process. Lanterns are key.

"So fucking A. Let's do this. I'm ready. To be instructed in the ways of Boy-Scoutery, to learn how to live outside, how to commune with, I don't know, *things*. Whatever you guys do, that's what I am going to do.

And in the process, if we run across a woman, some uber-hottie—a 'major smokeshow,' as my friend likes to call them—you're going to be on your best behavior. You're going to charm her, because it has been too long since this guy has, let's say, cavorted. In return, you'll get an all-access pass to me, Sheldon Wirth—arbiter of taste, maker of trends, eater of foods, reader of magazines, picker of noses—"

Are they finding this at all funny?

"—breather of air, passer of gas."

No. Shit. I switch tacks.

"Also, in return, I'll give you some invaluable hints about dealing with the ladies, particularly the aggressive ones."

They chuckle. *Good kids, these.*

I recall for a moment the weekend in the mountains with them, how silly I looked at times with them, but how happy I was. Sure, I had a tough job, but those mountains and that view made me forget it for a while. That view, in those mountains. I felt wealthy when we were in those mountains.

Jason follows me outside when I leave the troop. He wants to know why I'm doing this.

"What do you mean *this?*"

"Why aren't you partying and getting a girlfriend and going out, to bars?"

"I'm not all that sure. It must be because of this friend of mine, he's made me think about a few things."

And then I tell him about Dent—the dying, the not dying, the traveling, the shaving-the-head-like-a-cancer-patient-but-looking-more-like-a-healthy-Billy Corgin, the whole story, everything. Jason looks dissatisfied.

"Your friend sounds like a hypocrite."

"A *what?*"

"He acts all tough, but it seems like he's afraid, you know. Like he ignores certain facts. I don't know, I'd get really tired of someone like that. I mean, didn't he go to New Trier? I mean, that's a very good public school. Nationally ranked, right?"

"I guess, if you overlook that *Newsweek* story."

"What?"

"That cover story? 'High Times at New Trier High,' it was called? About the drug culture there."

"Must have missed it."

"Anyway, some egregious misreporting. Well-written but the fact-checker was really asleep at the wheel with that one. Still, an embarrassment for the superintendent. And the community."

"Whatever. My point is that it's a nationally-ranked school. Like always on that *U.S. News and World* report of top schools."

"Yeah, it's really good school. A great school."

"Well, it sounds like he's some privileged kid who just wants to run away from home. Seems sort of pathetic to me."

"No, it's not like that. He's different. He's . . ."

"He's *what?*"

"You . . . you wouldn't understand."

. . .

"Guess not."

I get into my Volvo and turn the ignition. "That's My Story (And I'm Sticking To It)" is on the radio.

"See you next week?" I ask, rolling down the window.

"Next week."

He mounts his bicycle, a Schwinn 21-speed, and knocks the kickstand up. He rides off. I drive back with a resolve to use the following words more often in the coming months: Yes Future Hopefulness Yes Good Certain Goals More Sure Can Yes. I can do this.

Yes, I can do this.

The next morning, I get up at dawn, which is really 7 AM but seems like dawn to me. It is strangely warm, nearly balmy out. I throw on an Olympia tee and running shorts, not the kind of running shorts that are usually associated with marathoners and 70s basketball stars—the really short shorts, which show more thigh than calf—but a standard mesh pair. I bring an old water bottle with me, an unwise decision since it miraculously retains the smell of whatever was in it last. In this case, chocolate milk. I don't have a watch, so I grab my phone as I run out the door. I run to the river. I am about midway there when it begins to rain. I take off my shirt, tucking it into the back of my shorts. The drops are cold on my back. I close my eyes as I run. I can hear my feet on gravel, and the rain is energy, and I am a determined Olympic hopeful. I can run forever. I will never die if I run like this. I will be like Dent.

I get to the river and drop my shirt and phone and slosh in. It is cold, excruciating. This will not deter me, this cold. I dive down and hold my breath and go deep, until there is no light and it is so so cold and my lungs start to burn.

I will run a marathon. The Boston Marathon. Or a triathalon. I will compete.

The burning has turned into pain. Fuck, this feels good. I will stay down here longer. Thirty seconds more.

A minute.

I come up like a missile and let air into my body and I stay in the water for two or three minutes more in the dead-man's float position, still in pain, but a *good* pain, knowing it is the kind of pain that *Denton Brown, Hero* endorses, swears by, until I remember something. I climb out and begin to run back.

There is music when I run back. A woman on an old Yamaha is playing what sounds like "In The Mood." I stop to listen, water dripping from my hair, and close my eyes and nod yes yes yes to the music. Yes yes yes. I am so cold, but: Yes.

"Play it, sista," I say.

She seems confused, but also appreciative. There is still rain, but she is still playing and it's not cold anymore. I nod yes yes yes and look along the river, and can hardly see another person. No one's around. No one's looking.

And this is when I dance.

I am nearly home again when I pass a park. Two kids are kicking each other on monkey bars. They are not differently skinned, but one of them is dark and one of them is light, and there is a sign on the street. CHIL-DREN AT PLAY it says. I have a good feeling about these kids. I have a good feeling about this playground, these kids. I have a really good—

I pick up the phone to call Dafna. But I shouldn't. I pause. I can't get in the habit of calling Dafna, because we are no longer—but it would be so much fun to call Dafna because I would have the opportunity to inadvertently insult her; then to flinch and mouth *sorry* when no, I'm not sorry but haven't the energy to suffer the Wrath of Dafna (which is surely as bad as Khan's wrath; though I admittedly don't know the extent of Khan's wrath—I assume it must be pretty bad, because why else would the phrase be so prevalent, other than its association with a popular science-fiction franchise, with Picard and Riker, and *Wesley*, who, by the way, seems like *such a bitch*—how he ever graduated from Starfleet Academy defies me—kid looks like he could hardly do a pushup—especially alongside Picard and Riker on the USS Enterprise.)

But then another thought comes to me, an image. A vivid, sickening image, one that has never come to me before, one that involves the mundane tasks of winterizing a house, of closing the chimney flues, removing the birdfeeders from the garden, putting up storm windows, but not doing it alone, in fact *showing someone else* how to do it, someone who is now strong enough to lift them himself; who, in a couple of years will be able to beat me at HORSE; then at an actual game of one-on-one, until he is taller and stronger than me, until he—

—Am I in love with her?

I will call her and talk to her and make her realize—show her that she has no choice but to realize—that she is still in love with me. Because Joel is not an option, and Dent will be dead soon, and we need each other. I will make her realize this.

Because, Dafna, you love me. And it is not how funny or strong or able I am. Yes, you. You love me. I know you love me. And this is why I need to call you now and convince you of this. Because I am done with cynicism for now. I know I can do it. It's just a matter of positive thinking.

I will call her now, but first, I stop in to say hello to the cheerful immigrant storekeeper who makes my day happier by being happy himself.

Then I place a prank call to Sam Zell.

Then I find joy in the strangest of places.

Last night, I slept pretty well. I didn't get up for ice. I let ice go for the moment. The Dennis Kucinich animation has stopped his private sessions with me. I wish him well. I really do.

Then I use the adverb "swimmingly" in a sentence.

Then I commit the last stanza of *The Battle of Blenheim* to memory.

Then I buy a lap dance for Bill Clinton.

Then I struggle a little. What is life without a little struggle? Life without struggle is not life.

Then I—

Then I—

Then I open my phone.

Then what will happen is I will call Dafna.

Then Dafna will answer.

Then she will not say no to me. I will not let her.

Chin up.

Epilogue
Fear Not!
Take Heart!

"I would like to talk to you today about Cowardice.

"I'm sure many of you might think it a strange thing to talk about at a funeral, but it really is the only topic that is pertinent to us today. There has been for too long this question—this large, lumbering elephant in the room, in this congregation, in our <u>community</u>—that we have not addressed. We all know why we have not addressed it. Each one of us knows why he or she has not addressed it. I can't say I blame anyone. It is a tough question, an unreasonable question to ask, having as it does many—or no—answers: Was Denton Brown a Coward? This is why many of us are here today. We are hoping someone—me? His mother? His third grade Art teacher?—will have an answer for us. We hope that by looking down into that casket, the answer will come to us. If by some divine act that does happen, I'm hoping to be the first to know."

11 December.

We are late for the funeral. I rush to Room 349, Joel's room, where the door is already cracked. I push it open.

"You ready?" I ask, catching Joel in the middle of experimenting how far down his throat he can stick his finger before the gag reflex takes over.

"Yeghh," he coughs. "I mean *yeah*. Ready."

"Your tie's not even on."

On his bed is a copy of *The Scarlet Letter*. Or *The Purloined Letter*. I don't know. Something with—

"I don't need a tie. You don't have to wear a tie to these things anymore."

"You need a tie."

He has a new haircut. It looks like he just removed a football helmet, but I kind of like it.

"Okay."

"And not that orange one."

"Fine, fine. I'll take care of it in the car."

I glance at Joel's computer, open on the bed.

"Jesus. Your desktop's a mess."

Joel always loved those games, those SimCity and Spore games. He went so far as to attend a tech conference in Palo Alto during semi-formal weekend to hear Will Wright speak. He spends hours playing them, sitting at his computer, alternating between fantasy role-playing and sexual role-playing, polluting his desktop with anime videos and spreadsheets of different levels and codes and cheats. There's a SOUTH BY SOUTHWEST background image. There's manga. Joel had some creative nicknames for that desktop of his:

"It's not messy. It's a marketplace of ideas."

"How do you find anything on that thing?"

"You don't understand. It's a laboratory of dreams, a cafeteria of viewpoints, a latticework of yearnings, a melting pot of—"

Enough. I head for the door.

"Do you have a lint roller?" he asks, catching me before I leave.

"You're fine."

"Yeah, but do you have one?"

"Sure. I don't know where it is. We don't have time."

"I'd feel much better with a lint roller."

"We're late," I say.

. . .

"Let's go."

"Little known fact: New York is also known as 'The Big *Apple*.'"

We are in Joel's Audi, playing a game we used to play with Dent, called Little Known Fact. The game originated one spring break during a road trip the three of us took all the way out to Haverford, PA, over four hours in the car. We visited Philadelphia's Independence Hall, where our tour guide, a Revolutionary-era character actor, loved the phrase "Little Known Fact." He used it approximately every two-to-five minutes, especially when such little known facts were anything but.

"Little Known Fact: Istanbul was at one point in time not known as Istanbul at all. Oh no, back then it was called *Constantinople*."

He also liked the phrase "at one point in time," our tour guide did.

"Little Known Fact: It is exclusively within the Champagne region in France that the eponymously-named beverage *Champagne* is produced."

We are loving it, laughing, having a ball, but, as with everything—

"Little Known Fact: International electronics behemoth *Siemens AG* was never in fact spelled without the *i*, as is commonly believed."

—Joel takes it to the next level.

Dent, he loved this game. He could go on for hours, couldn't he?

Yeah. He could.

I flip on the radio. We listen to a drink commercial that is doing its best to make our generation seem cool. *X GAMES! GEN X!* They use an X to make us feel cool. *XTREME! X FACTOR!* X denotes the variable, the unknown (as in a + b = x), but also—to be edgy—pornography (as in X-rated) and misspelled power-words (Xcellent!).

REMEMBER FOLKS, ALWAYS HYDRATE—TO THE XTREME!!!

We feel cool.

REDBULL! GINSING! ECHINACEA! ECHIN-AAAAAACEA!

So cool.

POWER! ENERGY! ECHIN-FUCKING-AAAACEA!

Joel turns it off. He pops in a CD.

"Tom Lehrer?"

I eject it.

"Absolutely not."

The funeral is being held in Lincoln Park, at the Church of Our Savior. Dafna is there, alone. She broke up with Joel; or he with her. I'm not sure which. She tells me that she could never date anyone she's envious of, and she's always been envious of Joel, of his confidence.

"I mean, I'm joking, of course," she says.

I listen closely, not fully believing everything she says—she seemed pretty attached to him in Mexico—and use these words: Interesting Okay Nice Yes Funny Great Great.

Joel and I are pallbearers. We meet in the church library, waiting for the hefty, turnip-faced pastor. Rows of out-of-print books line one of the walls. I run a finger across the spines. They are cracked, like dry orange rinds. The pastor sweeps in and gives a few brief instructions about handling the casket—line up by height, don't feel rushed.

"And don't drop the bastard!" Joel adds.

The pastor puts me in charge of the pallbearers.

I am surprised how traditional a service it is. There is no outrageousness, no hang-gliding or video montages or loudspeakers. There is no grand apology—in the Socratic sense of the word (and, come to think of it, the other sense, as well)—of Dent's life, as certain people in attendance might have expected. There is nothing like this. Men are in black; women, some women, wear veils. Soberness, somberness. There is one strange outburst, by a Merchant Marine guy Dent met overseas, who shouted, "We're gonna miss you, Dent-head! You are the *stars*." This was met with a few confused laughs, mostly disapproving looks. I don't think the guy was serious. There is no way he could have been serious.

The pastor also goes slightly crazy during his eulogy. He starts in an interesting way, posing an unpopular question about cowardice, and Dent's motives, but as he begins to sense the congregation's uneasiness, his talk takes a weirdly Christmassy turn. He discusses how a deficit in Holiday cheer this year could cause a North Pole recession. (He uses the term 'Joyeous.' Not 'Joyous.' 'Joyeous.' Joy.e.ous. Joy.E.Ous). He ties everything back to Dent of course, about the great happiness he brought everyone, but it's unconvincing. Is the pastor trying to be funny? It's not clear. He ends by relating Dent's love of fish to the fish as a symbol of the Christian faith—and although I'm not so sure how tenable a connection exists there, the ending's not bad.

Fear not! he says. *Take heart!*

I like that. *Take heart.*

Dent's mom speaks next. Her eulogy is better than I expected. She discusses what Dent taught her, and how he often assumed the role of a family leader, how he was an unconventional inspiration. There's a funny aside about how Dent always wanted to die owing money to someone. *I'm pretty certain everyone here knows if he was able to accomplish that,* she says. She is charming. She is clearly acting.

"Did you know you can order those things online?" Joel whispers to me.

"You can order eulogies online. They advertise it as *proven* and *100% Risk Free*—*"all the words you will need at a time of bereavement."* Can you believe that? Hey, do you think Dent's mom did that shit? Wouldn't put it past her."

There is a hymn and closing prayer given by a very young kid who seems conflicted about being up at the lectern. I fail to pay attention, realizing that the other pallbearers are in position already, waiting for me. Our team doesn't see the pastor motion for us initially, but we recoup. We pull it off well.

It is most clear at the burial that Joel is shaken, still. He made every effort to seem stoic, strong, indifferent—

"Hey, want to go to the Pancake House after this?" he says during the service. "I'm craving the Dutch Baby. Remember how big that thing is? Big as your *head*. Those Walker Brothers sure know their pancakes."

—during this process, but now, his face flushed, his posture bent, as if something were growing out of his back, you can see the lines below his eyes. This is the first time I have seen him since Mexico—we still talk on the phone, but less frequently, and with a sincerity of tone that feels new to me. We, Joel and I, hardly talk to Dafna. Even at the reception, we don't say much to Dent's mom, who, judging from the smugness of her responses during condolences, is feeling *pre-tty* good about the eulogy she just gave, which, other than the hetero-phobic (not to mention irrelevant) remarks about the pitfalls of traditional marriage, was pretty good. She mentioned Dent's research, how he was fascinated with the "homing" mechanism in *O. savayensis*, or the cardinalfish, how he spent nearly two years—

"*Oh my god*," Joel says, again interrupting. "I just had an epiphany. So Dent was studying how the cardinalfish finds its way home, just like *he* was having trouble finding his way home him*self*. So Dent is like the cardinalfish!"

—trying to determine if it is some kind of chemical or navigational cue responsible for the fish's incredible ability.

"This just changed my world," Joel continues. "This just blew my fucking mind."

And even though Dent's mom was usually an icy lesbian bitch, I see something. Yes, I swear I can see it, her love, that emotion. The loss of her son. We wait in line to shake her hand, or hug her. I am comfortable here, in my black gloves and long black coat. I am, disturbingly, professional. Not downtrodden, sad, whatever. I am here for business. That's why we're all here.

It's why we're here, right?

Fuck You You Dumb Fuckers.

You people in your black suits and dresses and your somber fucking hats and faces, pretending you knew Denton Brown. You didn't knew him. You dumb fuckers didn't—

You didn't—

You didn't—

Then I plant a tree.

Then I save the children.

Then I release a dove.

Ugly fucking dove.

Then I marry.

Then I cheat.

Then I divorce.

Then I root for the Bears.

Go Bears.

Then I learn Cantonese. Have you ever used Rosetta Stone? It's pretty wonderful. It's really quite wonderful.

Then I inadvertently enter a neighborhood wet T-shirt competition and win second place in the "Most Sloppy" category. Then I stand uncomfortably close to a young woman. Then I whisper in that young woman's ear. *I like your smell,* I say to the young woman. The young woman flees. I pause to ponder the nature of daintiness, wondering if, in some alternate universe, it could ever be considered a manly virtue. Then I stand uncomfortably close to an old man. *You are a strong one,* I say to the old man. Then I purchase and wear a shirt with the word WONDERBREAD on it and am immediately approached by a woman offering to sleep with me.

Then I place a dirty phone call to Dr. Jean McNulty of Thousand Oaks, CA, who has trouble with hot flashes.

Then I concoct an elaborate plan to, come winter, steal at least $30.57 in small change from Santa's Salvation Army bucket and spend it on over-the-counter drugs.

Then I walk into a bookstore and look at the books in the bookstore. I look at books like Wild Swans. Or the Ugly Duckling. Or The Pride of the Peacock. The Nightingale and the Rose. The Conference of Birds. Ravens in Winter. There is To Kill a Mockingbird. There is One Flew Over the Cuckoo's Nest. There is The Pelican Brief. The

Maltese Falcon. The Owl and the Pussycat. Blackhawk Down. Lonesome Dove. The Thorn Birds. The Raven. The Seagull. I Know Why The Caged Bird Sings. Make Way For Ducklings. There is Flaubert's Parrot. There is The Trumpet of the Swan. There is Mr. Popper's Penguins. Six Days of the Condor. Chicken Little. Convergence of Birds. The Swan Thieves. Harry Potter and The Order of The Phoenix. I Heard the Owl Call My Name. Oh the books! Oh the birds!

Then I knock on a door of a random apartment, and when a white female around age 47 answers, I recite recalled or invented nicknames for a woman's period, including Scarlet Fever, redeye, jelly honut, the ladybug, aunt flow, great aunt flood, cousin violet, The Stepchild, the butt spot, the stop sign, preteen surprise, Elmo, birth control, ring around the rosy; and just as I am about to list at least five or six more of these spectacularly illustrative nicknames, the woman slams the door in my face and shutters the windows for no reason I can think of.

Then I look out the window. When I look out the window I see an absurdly tall man high-fiving a preposterously short man. The juxtaposition of the tall man and short man is tremendously comical, because, you see, the short man is so short, and the tall man is so tall. I wonder if they did that on purpose. You know what? I bet they did.

Then I drop to my knees.

Then I sin and beg forgiveness for my sins.

You know what? I'm glad he's dead.

Fuck him. I'm glad.

Then I am alone.

Then I suffer.

I am cold.

Ice.

I do all of this while listening to soft rock on Magic 106.7, Boston's continuous soft rock.

Shamu, Tiki Torches, The Hulk.

In an alarmingly predictable move, my parents relocate to Sarasota, FL where Grant Wirth is on the board of his condo and Linda has become involved with local needlepointing efforts.

I ingratiate myself with Troop 37 again and help arrange a trip to Sea

World, to see Shamu, the one and only. When we get there, Jason tells me that the original Shamu is dead.

You mean this isn't Shamu?

No, it is Shamu, but it's not the only one. There have been many Shamus over the years. It's a marketing thing.

More than one Shamu?

I am aghast.

I win some clout with this expedition and start attending Scouting events again. I remember to tell the kids that they are lucky to be who they are, have the talents they have, and I tell them to do well in school. I repeat, *Do well in school*, at which point they call me a dirty word, something like 'pagina.' Not 'vagina.' Pa-jina. Pa. Jina.

No, but seriously. Keep those grades up, I say.

We have a time, we do.

"They say his last words were *Thanks, guys,*" Joel says, pulling out of the church lot, onto Fullerton. "That's what the guys at Evanston hospital told us, at least. I think they were adjusting his bed, something he'd been having trouble with the whole time there. So it was a real relief when they finally took care of it. That's not bad. An expression of gratitude as your last words."

He turns onto Lake Shore Drive. Lake Michigan shimmers, but there are very few beachgoers today.

"Yeah, not bad," he repeats, his face a totem of resolve.

Dafna calls, asking for directions to the reception.

"You do have a middle name," Joel says out of nowhere. "Dent told me, when we were in Mexico. Percy. Your middle name is Percy."

"Yeah. Sorry I lied. Not the best name for a guy."

"No, not the best. I believed you before because those things really happen. I know you think I'm stupid and gullible and—"

"I never thought you were stupid, Joel. Retarded, yes. Shameless? Definitely. Never stupid. To overcome the things you've had to—"

"Anyway, I believed you before, about your middle name, because things like that happen. Remember Doug Brennan—you know the guy from one of those Oak Park families, dad worked at the Board of Trade downtown?"

I do not remember.

"Yeah. Why?"

"He was actually Douglas *D.* Brennan. But the *D.* didn't stand for anything. The parents just liked the middle initial. So I believed you. Things like that happen. It's just a middle initial."

He pauses.

"And I am gullible. Fuck you for saying I'm not gullible."

"So am I."

We turn north onto Sheridan, toward the Northwestern campus. We pass the Baha'i temple on Linden. It looks like a white, ornately designed egg. Or a flower bulb.

"I hear there's only one of those on each continent," I say. "Strange that the leaders of the Baha'i faith chose to put the North American one in white suburbia."

We turn off Sheridan, making our way west to Green Bay.

"You know," Joel says, "the problem with Dent is that he always thought he was something special. Like he had some sort of destiny. And when someone relies on something like that—you know, on fate—they don't really care who they run over, do they? I mean, they don't care who they hurt?"

"I don't know what you're talking about. Do you think Dent hurt us?"

"Of course he hurt us. Every friend hurts you in some way. It's inevitable. But that's how we toughen up. *What doesn't kill you*, you know? Dent just hurt us a little more than a regular friend would have. That's why I'm surprised his funeral was so—I don't know—*funeral-y*. I expected something else from Dent."

We both had thought Dent was going to play some prank, like request that we take off an article of clothing and throw it in the burial plot. Or that all funeral guests do the Lindy Hop at the reception. We were certain he was going to leave a goodbye video—shirtless, bedraggled, bespectacled—like the ones we made together, with the 5 Cs. CUTTING, CLOSE-UPS, CAMERA ANGLES, COMPOSITION, CONTINUITY. There was nothing like this. There was no Denton Brown: Producer, Director, Thespian *nonpareil*. Nor were there stories, legends about Dent—embattled hero, misunderstood prophet, martyr, sufferer, leader of men, leader of—

"What a fucker," Joel says. "That guy was such a *fucker*."

We turn into the Indian Hill Country Club for a short reception. I order an orange juice from the bar and catch the eye of Lucas Brown, Dent's little brother. I never understood how he, Lucas, fit into the Brown household. He never really stood out in school. Whenever we came over, he stayed in his room. When we talked, he sounded—not depressed, at least in any clinical sense of the word—but downcast. As if he knew he would have to make some hard choices that might, over time, work out for him. But he sounds better now. He asks if I could use a ride back to the hotel afterwards. I already have a ride from Joel, but I tell him yes, I'd love one. Leaving in thirty, he says.

I search the reception area for Dafna, but don't see her. Has she left already?

A server sees me scanning the room.

"Sheldon Wirth?" he says.

I nod.

"A young lady wanted me to give this to you."

He hands me something. A note, folded in two. There is a strange doodle on the back: **We Are All Birds!**

"Is she still here?"

I must come off as overeager. He laughs and shakes his head.

I tuck the note into my pocket.

I meet Lucas in the parking lot. He introduces the brunette next to him as his wife Ariella. *What a name*, I tell her. She blushes.

"Did you hear about Dent's paper?" she says. She is plainly dying to tell someone about it. "It's being published in *Science*. Posthumously, of course." she laughs nervously, but continues. "That's a really prestigious journal—right, honey? It's really well-respected in the field. It's really rare for someone so young to get anything in there."

Yes, I had heard about this. The article, *Point of Origin: An Exploration of Glandular Cues as Potential Homing Mechanisms for Ostorhinchus Savayensis*, got a mention in *Playboy*, of all places. Ariella continues:

"I myself don't know much about these things—Dent was so much smarter than the both of us—but we do of course understand how big a deal it is. We're so excited."

Lucas nods. There had been a period when Lucas made it clear to his family that he was against Dent's decision to go off like he did. That it was unwise, foolhardy, unsafe. And although he stands firm in this position, even now maintaining and defending it, using words like *all along damned knowing blame stop fuck for god good always and know*, we catch him suppressing a smile.

We bunch in Lucas' Prius and head south. Discussion mainly concerns podiatry school—Lucas is finishing up his last year—and the disappointment the Bears must feel in losing their biggest fan, and who the hell that *you are the stars!* guy was at the funeral. They also mention they have a dog. His name is T-Bone Rex. *What a shit name.* I don't say this. *Fantastic!* I say.

As Lucas and Ariella start talking at length about T-Bone Rex, or *The Bone* as Lucas calls him, I take Dafna's note out of my pocket and turn it in my hand. I agree with Lucas when he says how glad he is that the ceremony is over, and I sympathize with Ariella when she says how much the Brown family has been through recently, and although I can't help but intermittently interrupt, wondering out loud where on the eastern seaboard would be the best place to pick up a really good enchilada—experiencing a sensation I can only describe as something approaching seasickness as I tear Dafna's note in two and drop it out the window—they do take the opportunity to break some good news.

"We're pregnant," Lucas suddenly says, both of them smiling.

His wife is wonderful. His wife is stunning. She will have another little Dent. Denton Brown, founding member of the SECRET REDNECK TRUCKER CLAN.

Don't forget me, Shel. Please don't forget me.

"We don't have a name yet," Ariella says, "but it's nice that whatever-we-name-him will be in the same school as MacAlby before he graduates."

"MacAlby?" I say, as if asking after the weather. "Who's that? A neighbor?"

Lucas laughs nervously.

"You're kidding, right?"

"What? No. Why would I be kidding?"

Ariella turns around, looking through me as though I weren't there.

"You really don't know who MacAlby is?"

"No. I've never heard that name in my life. What's the big deal?"

"He's . . . he's our nephew."

"Your what?"

"Our nephew. Dent's son."

The car drops away. We hover above the road, hanging over dust.

"You did know Dent had a son, right? MacAlby was overseas when Dent was doing research. He read the closing prayer at the funeral, man. C'mon, you've got to be kidding me. Aren't you guys best friends?"

Lucas gives a bleak laugh. Ariella turns back around, shaking her head.

I will find a woman just like her, like Ariella, one of these days. And I will have a son with her. I will teach the son how to play baseball, build confidence. I will make him like the Red Sox but will be okay if he moves to New York and starts liking the Yankees. I won't stop him from liking the Cubs but will worry that he is setting himself up for a life of disappointment. In any case, I will set up Tiki torches in our yard for his sixteenth birthday, serving alcohol only to the adults, and ribbing my son about his love of baseball and *Incredible Hulk* comic books in a public roast. Because my son will be an all-star. My kid will be an all-star because he will have come from my wife's womb.

"Dent never told you about his son?"

My wife will have a good womb. Woo-oomb. I understand why Dafna didn't like that word. It's a funny word, womb. Womb! Womb-sounds-like-tomb. A pre-life tomb.

"I can't believe Dent didn't tell you about Mac."

I still laugh when I hear that word.

"Courage, Cycles, Futility, Manhood (as a correlative to Courage), Homecomings, Mortality, Overconsumption, The '85 Chicago Bears, The Chicago Bears (All Other Years), Living Freely and Without Inhibition, Being Honest (to Oneself, to Others), Why Small Things Matter, Urban Living, Suburban Living (and, as a sub-category, Weird Suburban Rituals [e.g. community theater, potluck dinners]) The Summer of '89, Why Fred Willard Is A Force For Good In This World, Hopefulness (And Why It Is Important To Distinguish It From Mere *Hope*), Money: The Hard Truth. And Youth, and Sadness, and Stubbornness (another correlative to Courage), and 'What Now?'"

Table of Contents, Drink Pairings, Soundtrack Suggestions.

Because the author by no means recommends that you enjoy this book sober, suggested drink pairings are below:

Chapter 1: Amontillado, lightly chilled
Chapter 2: Seasonal Lager
Chapter 3: *Milwaukee's Best*
Chapter 4: Left Bank Bordeaux, or something similarly spicy
Chapter 5: White Zinfandel
Chapter 6: Beaujolais Nouveau
Chapter 7: Chablis, or any Chardonnay that's low on oak.
Chapter 8: Patron Silver, shooters; or Grey Goose Vodka Martini.
Chapter 9: Imperial Russian Stout.
Chapter 10: Pineapple Daiquiri with Sea Wynde Rum
Chapter 11: Any variety of tawny port

To enhance your reading experience further, the author has included the following soundtrack for you to prepare at home:

Chapter 1: "Pinball Machine," Lonnie Irving
Chapter 2: "Money," Pink Floyd
Chapter 3: Theme from *Night Court.*
Chapter 4: "Until The Real Thing Comes Along," Billie Holiday
Chapter 5: "Why Don't You Get A Job?" Offspring
Chapter 6: "Bad," Michael Jackson
Chapter 7: "Turn On Me," The Shins
Chapter 8: "Sabotage," Beastie Boys
Chapter 9: "Going Home," Brian Wilson; and "Father and Son," Cat Stevens
Chapter 10: "Mexico," Jimmy Buffet
Chapter 11: "And Embers Rise," Killswitch Engage

**"The Popcorn Song" by Hot Butter should accompany all interludes.

The author also thinks Beck's *Loser* is worth a listen, if only for the ingenious use of the sitar, an underutilized instrument in Western music. *Black Hole Sun* (Soundgarden) is pretty good, too. It doesn't have any particular relevance to the story; it simply has some gorgeous riffs, which aren't to be missed.
Whatever happened to REO Speedwagon, by the way? Do they still play?

Glossary.

***Front present** (n):* An ostentatious, sometimes aggressive gesture used to display excessive pride or confidence, or to pose a challenge. Commonly practiced by those in the Hip Hop profession and accompanied by phrases such as *What's your deal?*, *Represent!*, or *Yeah!* Often verbed.

So, the title. We need to talk about the title. The bird thing? It's out. *To Kill A Mockingbird* was pretty much the last viable bird title. If you can, do religious, something Protestant-friendly, something . . . take a look at Deuteronomy, or Ecclesiastes. But I'd prefer you just stay clear of the bird thing. It's divisive. The public doesn't want their authors wearing such aggressive avian attitudes on their sleeves. Know what sells? Short titles. *The Firm. Twilight. The Shack.* These things sell. Or *Something* Nation. *Prozac Nation. Fast Food Nation.* _____ Nation. *Blank* Nation. (Same with Club—Fight, Metaphysical, Joy Luck. Huge sellers). Or we could target the baby boomers. The baby boomers are always wanting to know what the young are doing with their time, so something like Tuesdays with ___. But more, uh . . . organic. Okay, last thing: the main character's name. Needs work. People hear "Shel" and they think *withdrawn, closed*. They think *turtle*. And it doesn't sound like a white person's name. Shel's white, right? Short for Sheldon? You get me? Are you getting me? So what I'm essentially saying here is: You have a bad title.

It's a Revolution!

(There be pirates.)

About the Author

Geoff Gray is a 30-year-old writer and entrepreneur living in California. This is his first novel.